THE
FAITHFUL

THE FAITHFUL

A NOVEL

ARTHUR CAVANAUGH

William Morrow and Company, Inc.
New York

Library of Congress Cataloging-in-Publication Data

Cavanaugh, Arthur.
  The faithful.

  I. Title.
PS3505.A899F3 1986   813'.54   86-16448
ISBN 0-688-04449-2

Printed in the United States of America

First Edition

1 2 3 4 5 6 7 8 9 10

BOOK DESIGN BY PATRICE FODERO

For
The Nuns

the dwindled ranks,
who gave us lessons
in valor and faith
and who, like us,
were human

CONTENTS

BOOK ONE

I
THE CROSSING

ONE

Louise's first glimpse of the ship, as the boat train shuttled onto the quay at Cherbourg, set her already quickened pulse to beating faster. Even from a distance, anchored out in the harbor the *Kronprinz Wilhelm* looked immense, a sleek giant, ribbons of smoke pluming from the four tall stacks, alluring as a travel poster. Except that it wasn't a poster, Louise reminded herself on this blustery March afternoon in 1908. It wasn't another of her dreams. She was actually sailing for America at last.

The train jolted to a halt and a blue-smocked porter flung open the compartment door demanding luggage. Louise got up, her nun's veil flowing to her waist, and tugged at the black suitcases on the rack above the seats. Mère Blanchard had not moved, indeed, had shut her eyes against the dreaded scene.

"*Dites-moi,*" said the old nun, her voice steeped in doom. She cocked an eye at the passengers who were pushing from the compartment to board the tender that would ferry them out to the liner. "We are ready"—her eyes clamped shut—"for the embarkation?"

"Yes, *chère* Solange, so we are." Louise handed the porter the suitcases and felt an enormous pang of guilt as the person responsible for the rash, improvident venture that was taking them not only to a new country but into the very depths of its wilderness. Louise was subject to a dramatic turn of mind: She thought of wilderness in terms of its depths, and when she experienced guilt, it was in large doses.

Ah, well, she thought as the two stepped from the train compartment, at least she understood the suffering it entailed for Solange to leave her native France. Although it was ten years since Louise had left Ireland, the memory of that last, terrible good-bye was a wound that had not healed. Memory was something she guarded against but was prey to.

The nuns, each with a black drawstring bag looped over her arm and carrying a bulging fishnet *sac* of the type French housewives bore to market, proceeded across the quay. Mère Blanchard maintained a dignified pace and detached expression, while her companion attempted the same with questionable success. Twelve years in a convent remote from any town, and now so much to see and take in—the fishing boats tied up at the wharves, the waterfront clutter of shops and cafés, the bustling quay and throngs of passengers chattering in a variety of languages as they queued up to board the tender. Of the two gangplanks, fore and aft, the one marked 1ST CLASS received a fashionable procession of well-dressed men and women in lavish furs, some with jewel cases and accompanied by maids. It surprised Louise to observe a young priest among them, American by the rugged look and energetic stride though he wore the long black cassock and wide-brimmed hat of a Roman seminarian. He was conversing with an older man and woman who were obviously flattered by his attentions. Solicitously, the young cleric went ahead into the cabin reserved for first class and staked claim to some window chairs.

Louise followed Mère Blanchard down the gangplank marked 2ND CLASS. The open foredeck, buffeted by the winds, was consigned to these passengers, who were vying for the row of benches that backed against the cabin. The hustling porters stacked the mound of luggage in the prow and lashed it secure with ropes. As Louise searched for the black suitcases, a gust of wind sent her veil flying, and laughing, the tang of the sea sharp in her nostrils, she caught at the errant, dancing veil. *It was happening at last, and was not another of her dreams . . .*

A glance from Mère Blanchard disposed of the laughter, then a whistle blew and the porters scrambled up the gangplanks and hauled them onto the quay. With another whistle toot the tender chugged out into the harbor. The presence of the nuns had prompted some passengers to offer them seats, but these Mère Blanchard declined with a gesture of dismissal. Clasping her skirts and with a faint rattle of rosary beads she took up a position at the rail, suitably removed, where she was joined by her associate—two figureheads, white-coifed, black-robed and cloaked, carved against the gray afternoon sky.

By no means were they identical figureheads.

Louise was unaware—it would have given her added reason for dismay—that she resembled her companion only in mode of dress. Solange Blanchard was seventy-one years old, small and round, shaped like a brioche. She was unmistakably French in bearing and attitude, but apart from a manifest dislike of all things non-French—God was not an exception, since she tended to regard Him as French—she displayed almost no emotion. Solange's grief at the receding shoreline was apparent only in the line of her mouth, set tighter than usual. The panic she felt at the impending voyage was expressed by her urgent telling of rosary beads, but that was hidden by the cloak.

By contrast, almost everything about Louise Anne Margaret Mary Maguire—what she was thinking, feeling, her hopes and fears of the moment—was apparent to even the casual observer. Tall and willow-slender, Louise presented a striking appearance not readily overlooked in a crowd. Indeed, she was already an object of scrutiny to at least one of her fellow passengers, a fact that would not have pleased her. Nuns, according to the discipline in which she had been trained, were to render themselves molelike and invisible in public, an art that so far had eluded Louise.

Her face, round, full-mouthed, winged black brows was as unredeemably Irish as Mère Blanchard's was French. It was a handsome face, brimming with curiosity, vibrant and glowing, seeming to rush at life full tilt, unrestrained by the stiff-pleated coif that symbolized the confinement she had embraced as a girl of eighteen. Her eyes, wide and lustrous, blue as a Killarney lake, were bright truants from detachment. If fear was to be glimpsed in them, sometimes overwhelmingly, it concerned her religious vocation. Louise counted herself a failure as a nun and looked upon this voyage, each chug of the tender carrying her out to the liner, as her final chance to prove worthy of her calling. She was en route to the frontier town of Cheyenne, Wyoming, to organize a mission school for Indian children under the sponsorship of the Bishop of Cheyenne. Louise had grown up in a land where the denial of human rights was common practice, centuries old. It had instilled in her a fierce sympathy for the oppressed and the persecuted, and to serve them was her reason for becoming a nun. She was prepared to devote her life to the Indian children of Wyoming, and rejoiced that such an opportunity had finally been granted her.

Oh, she must not fail at it! She held on to the rail, her gaze fixed on the ship that loomed ahead. The *Kronprinz Wilhelm* was another of Germany's contenders for supremacy over the million-dollar North Atlantic shipping lanes. Eight-hundred feet long, the liner was a magical sight, with its tiers of lighted decks glittering over the waters while orchestra music drifted from an upper deck. For Louise, the ship represented America, the new land she would behold in six days' time. New York, Bishop McAuliffe waiting at the pier, then the train to Wyoming and . . .

"How's it going, Sisters?"

Louise whirled around, startled by the man's voice that addressed her, which belonged to the young priest she had noticed earlier.

"Father Sean Regan." He introduced himself with a grin for Mère Blanchard. "Late of the North American College in Rome, returning to assume my priestly duties"—he gave the phrase a playful emphasis—"in New York." Rugged was indeed the description for Sean Regan—the powerful six-foot-two physique strained the seams of the black cassock, and the square-planed face, freckled at the bridge of the nose, was set with darkish brows and eyes as blue and penetrating as they were mocking and impudent. The reference to the North American College suggested that he was of unusual merit, having been chosen for study in Rome.

"You are Sisters of . . . ?" He trained brash, amused eyes at Louise.

"I—we—" She stammered and was vexed that she did. For twelve years her contact with men had been limited to elderly curés separated by the confessional and altar rail. "We are nuns of the Society of the Holy Virgin Mary," she managed to get out. "Of Montpellier, France, en route to an Indian mission in Wyoming."

"Well, listen to that, a French nun with a brogue to equal my Grandma Regan's."

Louise blushed and, worse, had to struggle against a sharp retort. "It is less astounding in that I was born in Ireland and entered the Society from there."

"Did I ruffle your feathers? It seems not to be any great trick." Father Regan had won the joust, if it was that. "But let me get to my purpose. My friends, the Tobins"—he nodded at the cabin—"are anxious to invite you both inside, where you'll be more comfortable."

Louise was spared the need to reply by her doughty companion. Delving into her repertoire of sign language, Mère Blanchard selected a gesture that simultaneously thanked the priest and declined his invitation. Then, with a bow of dismissal, she turned to the rail.

"I take it you object to comfort," Father Regan went on, with a teasing glint. "Myself, I'm all for it, but what'll you do aboard ship? Spiritual exercises, I daresay?"

"If you imagine that—" Exasperated, Louise turned to the rail, and Regan headed back to the cabin, though, in fact, his teasing had hit its mark.

By then the *Kronprinz Wilhelm* was a cliff, rising sheer above the tender that nosed up to it, and Louise was stung into questioning how the six days of the crossing would actually be spent. Surely with so many passengers to attend to some use could be made of two nuns, after all, why not? With Mère Blanchard she went to board the ship from the tender, unmindful of the impulsive "Why nots" that had made a trial of her life in the convent.

The question of the six days was disposed of by Mère Blanchard as soon as they reached the cabin on C deck in the stern of the ship.

The cabin was shaped like a shoe box and not much bigger, with two narrow berths, one above the other, a wardrobe, and a washbasin and mirror. Taking from her satchel a bottle of Lourdes water, Solange liberally sprinkled it over the cabin, thus sanctifying it. Louise's attention was drawn to the cablegram propped on the washstand.

"It is from Bishop McAuliffe; how thoughtful of him to welcome us on board. He wires that he is to arrive in New York the day before we dock—the Hotel Woodstock—and to expect him at the pier."

The cabin shuddered from an ear-piercing blast of the *Kronprinz*'s whistle, the engines churned, and the ship began to move. Solange, choking a groan as the French coastline dropped away from the porthole, rang for the stewardess, at whom she barked Gallic commands. Meals were to be served in the cabin, it being unthinkable for nuns to appear in a public dining hall. *Alors,* except for certain

unmentionable physical functions, and to attend daily Mass ...
what, only Sunday Mass was available? One might have expected it
of *les Boches,* tsked Solange, and she instructed the stewardess to
come back with dinner trays at six, fish or poultry, no red meat, and
perhaps some fruit. *"Et deux cafés,"* she added in a temporary lapse of
austerity. As if to atone for it, she took a towel the moment the stewardess left and draped it over the washbasin mirror to guard against
vanity.

"You know, it does seem to me," Louise remarked, "that with six
days at our disposal . . ." The towel over the mirror served to rebuke
her, and when a steward brought the suitcases she unpacked hers in
silence.

At six o'clock the stewardess delivered the dinner trays, and the
meal was eaten in silence. The ship had acquired a steady roll, and
Louise, a nagging headache.

The two nuns paced the swaying cabin, telling their beads and
reciting evening prayers. Louise tried to blot out the strains of orchestra music that floated down the corridor and the footsteps,
voices, and a baby's cry that sounded outside the door. She sat in a
chair that was wedged under a steampipe, attempting to listen as
Solange read aloud from a volume of spiritual meditations. The
headache was worse, and Louise had to grip the chair for support.

The stewardess was summoned at nine o'clock to chaperone the
passage down the corridor to the *Damen.* Nine was the convent hour
for retirement, and Louise's hands shook as she pulled the coarse
white nightgown over her head in the dark. She tied the fluted
nightcap under her chin and fingered the cropped hair shorn by the
scissors on the day of first vows. *A mistake, all a mistake* . . .

Louise climbed the swaying ladder past the inert form, stiff as if in
a coffin, in the lower berth. She slid between the cold sheets of her
bunk, under the rough wool blanket. *Why had she become a nun?* All
that she had fought to put behind her—Vincent and Honora, the
white stucco house, the village tucked in the rolling green hills, the
past—all of it flooded back.

TWO

Ballymar, situated in County Longford in the center of Ireland, was a picture-postcard village of thatched cottages, rambler roses tumbling over gates and doorways, and peat smoke curling from chimneys into a blue-crayon sky. It was also a village of poverty, disease, and ignorance, whose citizens were deprived of any means of bettering themselves other than by emigration to America.

Almost from the dawn of its history, Ireland had been an occupied country, and by the British since Cromwell's invading armies in 1649. The British had appropriated the land and rented scraps of it back to the Irish as tenant sharecroppers. By a series of laws—notoriously, the Penal Laws of 1691, enforced for nearly two hundred years—the Irish had been kept poor and uneducated, denied the right to vote, hold government office, serve as anything but foot soldiers in the army, and acquire property of any substantial value. For as long as there had been invaders, there had been uprisings against them. Rebellion and defiance were bred into the Irish character, together with a stubborn, contrary pride and the Catholic faith they had battled for centuries to uphold.

But for Louise Anne Margaret Mary Maguire, born into fortunate circumstances, Ireland was from the beginning a blessed land, exempt from criticism, and she could not conceive of a reason that would take her from it.

Her father, Vincent Maguire, was the son of the village greengro-

cer. As a boy in the 1840s, he had witnessed the ravages of the Great
Famine, the potato blight that had devastated the land and sent
tens of thousands from their homes to perish or to stagger along the
roads to Cobh and the ships to America that were the one chance for
life. The sight of so much helpless suffering and death had set Vin-
ent's mind on becoming a doctor. However, medical training was
not available to him in Ireland, which had no schooling beyond the
grade level. He spent nine years in Scotland, working in the Glasgow
shipyards to finance his studies at a teaching hospital. Vincent was
twenty-nine when he returned to Ballymar and hung up his doctor's
shingle above the family shop. He was thirty-seven before he married Honora Cassidy, raven-haired, rose-cheeked, who was from a
farm in Connemara and was employed as second parlormaid on the
estate of Lord Harleigh, Ballymar's leading squire. The delay was
partly due to Vincent's character. The only doctor in a fifty-mile ra-
dius, he refused his services to no one. Most of his patients were tenant farmers who paid what they could, a few shillings each month
till the amount was settled, or paid in the coinage of livestock and
grain—and if a debt was left unpaid, Vincent was not the man to
hound anyone for it.

The delay was caused by Honora's character as well. She was forever rounding up stray waifs and destitute old crones and vagrants
for Vincent to doctor, which did not contribute to his savings. Moreover, Nora would not wed until she had fashioned for herself the
bridal gown, creamy satin, frothed with Kenmare lace, and sprinkled with seed pearls, of her dreams. An extra year it cost her, in ex-
penditures and midnight sewing, before she walked in bridal glory
down the aisle of St. Columkill's Church to join her life to Vincent's.

Louise was born seven years later in 1880, the fourth child, the
only one of six not to be carried in infancy to the parish graveyard.
Thus, an unusual intimacy and closeness bound the Maguire family
from Louise's first breath. By then, Vincent had prospered enough
to acquire a house of whitewashed stucco that boasted six rooms and
the only upper floor in the village. The downstairs, except for the
large kitchen at the rear with its hearth and copper-gleaming pots
and pans, was given over to Vincent's practice. Upstairs were three
bedrooms. Louise had her own room, with a big goose-feather bed
and a window that looked down on the road that wound past the
house. An extension of Ballymar's main street—except for some

straggling lanes, the only street—it continued beyond the Maguires, dipping into the valley below.

The road had a special meaning for Louise. It meant going away, leave-taking, saying good-bye to Ballymar. She had witnessed the farewell parties that were a regular occurrence of village life. A younger brother or sister, an aged parent, a young mother with child, would be sent money and steamship tickets from America, and on the night before the departure, a roisterous party was held, attended by the whole village and countryside. A party merry with a fiddler's jigs and Tommy Laughlin, the piper, playing the old aires to the stamp and whirl of feet . . . playing till the dreaded moment of dawn, when the cart outside piled with belongings claimed its passenger. Then Tommy's pipes turned to a mournful lament, and the cart jogged off down the road . . . *good-bye forever to Ballymar. No, she could never do it.*

To Louise, her life was eminently satisfying. She loved the white stucco house and the yard out back, the apple trees and the flower and vegetable gardens; she loved the chickens and hens, and Tillie the cow, and Bridie the placid chestnut mare who, hitched to the trap, drove Vincent on his rounds and the family on Sunday excursions. "Really, we're quite rich, aren't we?" Louise remarked to her father one afternoon. She was six, home from her first day at the village district school where she had favorably compared her smocked challis dress and shiny new shoes to the makeshift hand-me-downs and worn clogs of her classmates. "Isn't it grand, how rich we are?" she crowed, then blushed under Vincent's reproachful gaze.

"It's God's bounty we enjoy, not our own," he said in gentle reprimand. "Rather than boast of it, we must share it with the less fortunate."

The blush of shame crimsoned as Louise thought of the beggars at the kitchen door whom her mother never sent away unfed, many of whom, to Nora's occasional grumblings—"They come from miles around, got up in rags to take advantage of you"—her father treated without charge. The next afternoon Louise returned barefoot from school, having presented her new shoes to Ella Rocket, who had none.

Jenny, Ella's older sister, was in the same class, and quickly became Louise's best friend. The Rockets were wretchedly poor, constantly on and off the dole, depending on whether Mr. Rocket was on or off the drink. As the eldest of a motherless brood of six, Jenny had been prevented from starting school until she was eleven and Mavis, the next oldest, could be trusted to look after the young ones. Jenny took seven-year-old Ella with her to school, for she regarded education as a prize beyond measure. A gangly bean sprout of a girl, plain as bread, Jenny cared for her rambunctious brood, cooking, mending, cuffing them around, keeping them together under one roof, and managed to shine at her studies as well. She was, in Louise's opinion, the cleverest, brainiest girl in all of Ireland. With a minute's study Jenny could memorize a page of geography or history, or an entire poem, and was a wizard at sums. She possessed a mind that went leaping and darting over a host of subjects and ideas, examining them, picking them clean. Louise frequently accompanied her friend home from school to lend a hand with the brood, and they talked and laughed together for hours. Jenny's favorite topic of conversation was the future. "Wait and see," she vowed as she stirred a pot of gruel, wiped Bernard Joseph's nose, or hauled Timsy down from a window ledge. "Someday, I'll get out of this prison here. Don't ask how, or where I'll take myself—America, if I can get there—but I'll win me a chance at life, just wait and see if I don't."

Such talks were oddly disturbing to Louise, and she would ponder them as she made her way home from Jenny's, aware that she had no thought or plan for the future. To regard Ballymar as a prison was beyond her imagining. It was a world where every person she encountered was quick with a friendly greeting, and to be rebuffed or treated rudely was unknown to her. The love that awaited Louise each day in the white stucco house was all that she wanted, or would ever want, and the mere thought of it sent her into a joyous gallop up the street.

She could never leave her mother, of that Louise was certain when she was twelve and came home one afternoon to find Honora in the attic seated at an old trunk, the bridal gown cradled in her arms. She had buried three infants since Louise's birth, but had not spoken of her grief until that day.

" 'Twas for all of you I sewed this gown," Honora said, and rocked back and forth, stroking the creamy satin that glimmered with seed pearls. " 'Twas for all of my girls to wear on their bridal day . . . sons too I hoped to raise, fine and good as Vincent."

"Never mind, Mother." Going over and kneeling at the trunk, Louise embraced the rocking figure. "There's me, you'll always have me. I'll stay here with you and Father . . . just the three of us, always."

Honora was shocked by the blind intensity of the declaration. *"Just the three of us, always."* It worried her, and later that night, lying awake in bed, she speculated what could be done to loosen the ties that were binding her daughter too closely.

Louise's association with St. Columkill, the parish church that stood on a windy, tree-twisted hill above the village, extended as far back as she could remember. As a small child she had picked flowers with Honora—the garden's choicest roses, begonias, rhododendrons—and brought them up the hill to Columkill's altar. She learned, under Nora's supervision, to sew the fine linen cloths that adorned the altar and to mend the priests' vestments. Vincent was an usher and warden of the church, and president of the mens' sodality. Father Grennan, the pastor, had baptized Louise, heard her First Confession, and administered her First Holy Communion. To climb the hill to the gray stone edifice was akin to approaching her own front door, and Louise felt guilty of betrayal when she started to experience emotions in church as intense as those she held for her parents.

Christianity in Ireland dated back to the fourth century. Great monasteries had flourished, centers of Christian learning. From them great saints—Boniface, Fiacre, Columbanus—had gone forth to preach the faith throughout Europe and Asia. A faith that came to be inextricably linked with Irish freedom, it, as well as the land, had to be defended against the invading Danes and Vikings. But the Penal Laws of England had dealt this Catholic faith a near-mortal blow.

Under the Penal Laws, all monasteries, convents, and churches in Ireland were shut down. Church lands were confiscated and redistributed. Monks, priests, and nuns who refused to renounce their vows were exiled. Mass and the conferring of sacraments were forbidden, and the scaffold awaited the fugitive priests who dared, as countless did, to return and minister to the people. One hundred fifty years of the Penal Laws, and in every part of Ireland the decayed ruins of monasteries and the hillocks crowned with crumbling moss-grown Celtic crosses gave mute testament of the outlawed faith. Nevertheless, the faith had prevailed. Lives were sacrificed, blood shed for it. In caves, cellars, wooded groves, mountain hideaways, Mass was celebrated by contraband priests. Marriages and baptisms were performed in secret. Denied religious education at home, generations of young Irish men and women smuggled themselves abroad to obtain it. Many had stayed on to enter monasteries and convents, religious exiles.

Then, in 1832, the Penal Laws were repealed, and once again the black-clad figures set out on the dawn roads on Sunday mornings. They were the faithful, clasping the worn Missals that were their badges of fidelity.

Faith, ancient and unyielding, was bred into the rough, impoverished, untutored men and women who crowded into St. Columkill each Sunday. It was bred into their flesh and marrow, it shone from every face ranged in the drafty pews, was defined by the sign of the cross traced on foreheads and breasts. And when the sanctuary bell rang and Father Grennan mounted the altar steps to say Mass, the voices that spoke the Latin responses, a touch defiantly in remembered combat, were a river of faith.

Dominus vobiscum.

Et cum spiritu tuo.

Louise, kneeling with Honora in a front pew—Vincent was stationed at the rear with the ushers—felt deep in herself this tremendous legacy of faith. At thirteen, she was growing into willowy slimness, black hair flowing down her back, ivory-cameo face upraised to the altar intent on following the Mass. The black pin-seal St. Joseph's Missal had been a First Communion gift, and Louise was adept at flipping the ribbon markers between the Ordinary and the Proper, outwardly composed while a torrent of conflicting emotions swept over her.

Liar, she accused herself in the very act of worship. Heaven was her promised destination, of that she was certain, and the principal task of life was to merit heaven, but one of God's commandments stood in her path, barring the route. She was commanded to love God above all else, but Louise knew that she placed her parents first. Childhood was fleeing fast behind her, and soon she must take a new role in life. She wanted to serve God as freely as she had given away her shoes to Ella Rocket, but she shrank from any commitment, caught by the other love that held her from it.

When Louise was fourteen and preparing to graduate from the village district school, tragedy struck the Rocket family. Ella died of tuberculosis, followed by Timsy to a pauper's grave. Their father, Anselm Rocket, had lurched off on a drinking bout, the last of him to be seen in Ballymar. Jenny left school to go into service as a scullery girl in Lord Harleigh's kitchen. She was required to live at the estate, which left her brood unattended, and the county magistrate took action to place the children into an orphanage.

Vincent and Honora had offered their home to the four destitute Rockets. Louise was always to remember with shame the gratification that surged through her when the court had ruled in favor of the orphanage. She graduated that June from the district school, relieved that she had not been compelled to share with anyone the white stucco house. She disregarded the suspicion that it was not her parents whom she loved best, but herself.

In September of that year, Louise was enrolled in a convent boarding school in the west of Ireland.

The decision was Honora's, against the initial opposition of her husband, who declared that it was natural for a child to be attached to her home and parents.

"*Child,* is it? A child grown old, never to venture beyond the doorstep if we're not careful. We must not allow it, Vincent."

The boarding school occupied an estate outside the town of Galway, and Louise's first year as a student passed without incident. The nuns were unacquainted with the lively girl of Ballymar and credited her subdued behavior to seriousness of character.

And Louise was not acquainted with nuns, which was understandable. Catholic teaching had been permitted again in Ireland only fifty years earlier. The convents and monasteries confiscated by the Penal Laws were an irredeemable loss; to build new ones would take years to accomplish. Nuns and priests were forbidden by law to teach in the state schools, and private Catholic academies such as Louise's were small in number . . . few families in Ireland could afford the tuition. Since native vocations had not yet proliferated, these private schools were conducted by foreign religious orders.

Louise did not know what to make of the French women in

starched pleated white coifs and flowing black veils and robes who whisked through the halls, aloof and detached, inhabitants of another world. They were nuns of the Société de Sainte Marie Viérge, an order founded in Paris in 1751 by a widowed countess whose estate in Montpellier in the south of France was the Society's Motherhouse. The nuns were rumored to be wellborn, having given up wealth and rank for the vows of chastity, poverty, and obedience, and lives of denial and sacrifice for love of God. They retained their family names and were addressed as "Mère" rather than "Sister." Formal in bearing and manner, the nuns at Galway maintained a distance from the students, living in a wing of the school reserved as a cloister, where they slept on straw pallets in bare cells stripped of mirrors and amenities and rose at five-thirty each morning for Mass and a liturgy of prayers in the chapel.

It intrigued Louise, this other, cloistered world of the nuns. At dawn one morning, stealing from her dormitory bed, Louise had crouched hidden on the stairs to watch the black veils file silently into the chapel. The flickering glow of candles and the soft chant of prayers had drawn Louise in her nightgown to the chapel entrance. The nuns knelt on prie-dieus, erect and motionless, absorbed in chant, transported, it seemed, to another world of peace and tranquillity. But then Louise shivered and hugged her arms, stricken by the thought of Vincent and Honora, the white stucco house and the goose-down bed, and overcome by longing, she fled back up the stairs.

The winter of 1895, Louise's second year at the convent school, was unusually severe for temperate Ireland. In February, the Mother Superior wrote to advise the Maguires that Louise was confined to the infirmary with a persistent fever. A telegram the following week expressed concern for the student's worsening condition. Vincent left immediately for Galway and was stunned by what he found—a semi-delirious girl, lips cracked and blistered, staring up with feverish eyes of dim recognition. Since she could not be moved, Vincent stayed at a nearby inn to be with his daughter. It was a week before he dared to risk the journey of taking her home to Ballymar. Louise's fever rose and fell, the weeks stretched into months, but none of Vincent's meticulous remedies cured his bedridden daughter of the malady that possessed her.

The cure was achieved by two events, following in rapid succession. One evening in April, Vincent came down the stairs with angry tread and shot a warning look at his wife. "A mistake, to have packed her off to school," he said, and brushed past Honora to the kitchen hearth. "I've given my solemn word that we'll not send her back. It had, I'm happy to report, a tonic effect."

"It would." Honora nodded and took up her sewing.

The fever had vanished and the April weather was mild enough for Louise to lie outdoors on sunny days, bundled in quilts. The rosiness had crept back into her cheeks, the sparkle into her eyes, but she was not able to manage the mile walk to Columkill for Sunday Mass. As a consequence, Father Grennan visited the Maguire house each Monday morning, bearing the Host in a silver glass case the size of a half crown.

Afterward, Honora served the priest tea and soda bread at the cherry-wood table in front of the hearth, but on this particular morning Father Grennan had little appetite for refreshment. He asked Louise, who reclined against pillows in a rocker by the hearth, "Was not Jenny Rocket in your class at school?"

"My best friend." For some reason, Louise hesitated before she inquired, "How is Jenny these days? She gets so little time off, I've not seen her since I've been home."

"I'm convinced 'twas an accident." The pastor shook his white-thatched head. "Lost her bearings in the storm last night and took the wrong turn."

Again, Louise hesitated. "Wrong turn?"

"Fished her out of the pond this morning at Lord Harleigh's." Father Grennan set his teacup heavily on the table. "Some puzzling aspects to it. What was Jenny doing out at night in the storm? They found a bundle of her belongings by the pond, as if she mighta been running away."

"Jenny, dead?" Louise sank against the pillows and shook her head. "The brightest in the class, and no one to give her a chance."

Honora crossed herself. "God rest her poor soul."

When Father Grennan had left, Louise rose unsteadily from the rocker and went to the stairs in the hall. Halfway up, she turned back, conscious of her mother's anxious gaze. "Yes, what is it?"

"Life is made of crooked lines, twists and turns goin' every wrong way," Honora said.

"And what is that to mean?"

"That you mustn't despair . . . because, y'see, God writes straight from crooked lines."

"I fail to see it, if it is true."

Louise spent the rest of the day in her room with the door closed. Her eyes were red and swollen when she came down for supper. She sat between her parents at the cherry-wood table and did not speak except to ask her mother, "Are you going to morning Mass tomorrow?"

"The six-thirty, as always."

"I'm more than able to go with you."

"But darlin'—"

"I'll wake and be ready."

Rain was a daily hazard in Ireland, and the next morning a sudden cloudburst chased the shawled women up the steep hill to the ugly stone church. It rained every morning that week, but Louise was not deterred by it. The overcast sky, the turbulent clouds, signaled the approach of a storm, and a few nights later it struck in a lash of thunder and lightning over the countryside. The crackling thunder shook Louise from sleep. After a moment's terror, she dressed in the dark, flung a shawl over her head, and went out into the yard where she stood at the far edge clutching the shawl to her breast. As the rain beat at her, she lifted her face to the black, flashing sky.

"I *will,*" Louise shouted up at the sky. "I'll give up those I love and come follow you, as the Gospel bids, and it will be my cross." She did not understand why life held crosses to bear, nor suffering of the depth that had killed Jenny Rocket, but she understood what she must do about it. "I *will,*" she shouted at the sky, wiping the sheets of rain from her face. "Make use of me, let me be of help!"

In September, Louise returned to the convent school in Galway to finish her education. She had spoken to Father Grennan of her aspirations, but not until senior year did she seek an interview with the Mother Superior, whose cool, unsparing response hinted at what was in store for the aspirant.

"We cannot accept into the convent young girls who languish in bed with mysterious ailments," the Mother Superior intoned. "However, it is God who sends vocations, so let us test your mettle."

Louise was required to attend daily Mass with the nuns and to take part in their prayers and devotions. To test her humility, she was given kitchen duties, which held the practical French advantage of labor for no wages. Before she was accepted for the novitiate at Montpellier, Vincent and Honora were summoned to the Mother Superior's office.

Louise waited outside in the corridor in an agony of doubt and faltering resolve. When her parents emerged from the office, Vincent's jaw was clenched tight and Honora bore something of the dazed look that had followed the small pine coffins to the graveyard, but then she smiled at her daughter. "Ah, y'see, it is as I told you—crooked lines made straight."

The summer after her graduation, one August evening in 1898, Louise Maguire was tended a farewell party in Columkill's parish hall. Young and old from miles around turned out for the affair. The guests feasted on Honora's baked hams, garden-fresh salads, and ginger cakes, and the men made frequent excursions out back for a swig of Vincent's whiskey. Young and old danced to the fiddler's jigs and stomped and swirled to Tommy Laughlin's pipes. Then, as dawn tinted the sky, Tommy skirled a sadder tune.

In the hush that followed, Louise knelt for Father Grennan's blessing. She embraced Vincent and Honora, and then went swiftly from the hall. The buggy would take her to the depot in the neighboring village for the train to Queenstown, where she would board the steamer to France. She climbed into the buggy alongside the driver and rode down Columkill's windy hill, through the village street, and past the white stucco house from which she averted her eyes. Louise sat erect and pinned her gaze on the valley beyond, but she was powerless to halt the piper's lament that followed behind and tore at her heart as though to break it.

THREE

Sleepless in the narrow, pitching berth, Louise heard the piper's lament and saw the road dipping into the valley. It brought a measure of solace to know that the wrenching good-bye would not be asked of her again in her life.

But what had she accomplished in her ten years in the convent? The period of noviceship at Montpellier was three years, but she had worn the white robes of a novice for a fourth year before she was permitted to take her vows. The week before the ceremony, the package that had arrived from Ballymar had nearly wrecked her resolve. The rules allowed for a monthly letter to her parents and one from them in reply, but visits were forbidden. The package was wrapped in brown paper and tied sturdily with twine, and in it, folded in tissue, was Honora's bridal gown, yellowed with age, to wear at the Clothing.

The ceremony was given that name because at the conclusion, after reciting her vows before the Bishop of Montpellier and submitting to the shearing of her hair, each novice in turn received the black veil and robes that henceforth would be her attire. The ritual had many of the aspects of a wedding, which, in effect, it was. Gowned in Honora's white satin, Louise bowed her head to the shears and pronounced her vows. Final vows were years away, but she had promised herself to Christ for life.

THE FAITHFUL

Useless! Useless!

Louise's difficulties as a nun stemmed from her inability to be anyone other than herself. The fields outside the convent were an invitation to run free with the wind, and time and again she was disciplined for heeding it. She could not, or would not, fit herself into the rigid and inflexible mold that was demanded of her. It was her voiced opinion that nuns were human beings and ought to be treated as such, and not as automatons. She subscribed to the virtues of chastity, poverty, and obedience, but not as they were practiced in the Society of the Holy Virgin Mary. Poverty was not served by having to request permission for a sheet of writing paper or a pen nib each time it was needed. The endless repetition turned the act into an empty, parroting gesture. To confess to a craving for a fruit tart did not indicate sensual abandonment, a breach of chastity. The denial of pleasure, if not checked, could in itself be pleasurable. Obedience verged on comedy when it instructed a nun to fall to her knees at every approach of the Mother General, who was constantly barging down corridors and in and out of rooms.

Perhaps if Louise had kept her opinions to herself she might have avoided trouble, but she was incapable of dissembling. As a result, it threw her into head-on conflict with her superiors. The Society conducted girls' schools in Biarritz, Toulouse, Lyons, Dijon and Marseilles. In the course of four years, posted to teach at Lyons and Toulouse, Louise was recalled from both schools at the request of the superiors. The pupils of Mère MaGear, it was reported, were inclined to rebellion and unsuitable ambitions. The school in Galway might have solved the problem, but by 1904 it had closed for lack of revenue. The decision was to assign Louise to the motherhouse, where, relegated to minor duties, she would create the least amount of dissension.

The years at the Motherhouse endowed Louise with a pallor that her restless, solitary walks in the fields did not relieve once the cloister door again closed behind her. She worked in the dispensary, the archives, the linen room—solitary duties that isolated her from the central function of the Motherhouse, which was to govern the Society by means of a constitution that, in Louise's view, promulgated injustice.

She disapproved of the rule that divided the Society into two classes. The Choir nuns, educated and wellborn, were the administrators, the teachers, and policy makers, and below them in rank were the Lay Sisters, ill educated, the daughters of farmers and tradesmen, who performed the domestic tasks and were denied a vote in the election of the Mother General and a seat on the council of eight nuns who formed the governing body. All were elected to five-year terms of office by a general vote of the nuns. Ideally, the procedure allowed for a healthy change of guard, but it imposed no limit on the relection of officeholders. As a consequence. Mère Générale de Brissac was enjoying, at age seventy-eight, her fifth term of office.

This autocratic woman, who sat on a throne chair in the chapel and at council meetings, aloof and imperious, had been made a despot by her long reign. She displayed a consuming interest in the vineyards the Society owned in the Médoc, which provided its largest source of income, and no interest in change or innovation. The Mother General controlled the Council by vigorous exercise of the veto given her by the constitution. Whatever she opposed was summarily dismissed, and that included any issue that did not preserve the Society intact, unchanged from the past.

And it was the Mother General against whom Louise pitted herself in the bold new cause she had found to champion.

Actually, the cause was not new, for she had come upon it as a novice, in a book from the convent library that described the adventures of a group of Ursuline nuns who had voyaged from France in 1727 to establish a school in the Louisiana Territory. The idea of the Society embarked to the New Land had thrilled Louise, but as a novice she was not in a position to espouse it, hammer at her though it did.

Why not the Society in America?

The idea would not let go of Louise, nor she of it. The convent's selection of books on the subject was meager, and she wrote to Vincent for them—books that told the story of America and the millions of immigrants who had crossed the ocean to settle in the cities and towns, farmlands and prairies, and found work in the mines and factories, the textile mills and logging camps, and on the ever-expanding railroads. Vincent had sent his daughter publications that reported the work of the Church in the westward migration. The majority of immigrants, Slavs, Germans, Irish, Italians, were Catholics in want of priests and nuns for their churches and schools. In response, nearly every major religious order in Europe had established foundations in America that had proliferated across the continent, from one coast to the other.

Why not the Society?

The years had not improved Louise's position, nor had they brought her a vote on the Society's agenda. The years had filled her with discourgement, and given her a pallor attributable less to the dim corridors of the cloister than to her sense of failure as a nun. The idea of America became a dream into which, thin and pale, she had retreated.

But then in 1906, after much delay, Louise was permitted to take the final vows that committed her to the Society until death. The simple ceremony had suddenly rekindled the flame of faith for which she had given up home and native land, and had restored her confidence that God would find some use for her, as she had asked.

America!

The dream had turned into Louise's battle cry. Here was the work, useful, needed, that she had envisioned for herself and set out to pursue. She discovered by chance one day a letter on a hall table addressed to the Mother General. It was postmarked "Cincinnati, Ohio," and was an appeal from the bishop of that diocese for nuns to staff the orphanage he planned to build. Since a reply was not attached to the letter, it was evidently to be ignored.

How many other appeals had been ignored, wondered Louise, and she presented herself and the letter at the next Council meeting. The formidable sight of Mère Générale de Brissac seated in her throne chair gave her pause, but she pressed on with her query of why the letter had not been answered.

"Let me direct you to article three of our constitution," said Mère Générale, who invariably spoke for the Council. "It states that we were founded in order to teach and educate in piety the young women of France."

"The world has changed in a hundred years," Louise parried. "In any case, article three did not prevent you from opening the school in Galway."

The Mother General pounced on the unwitting blunder. "Yes, a rash experiment, against my better judgment," she snapped. "We are still burdend with the wretched property, and unless you know of a buyer for it—"

"I—no, I—"

"Then kindly do not refer to it, but explain instead how you are in possession of a letter that was not addressed to you."

"It was lying . . . on the table in the front hall."

"May I have the letter, please?" Mère Générale thrust out a hand from the throne chair, and Louise knelt, as prescribed by the rule, and relinquished the letter. "As punishment, you will observe a week of silence, Mère MaGear. Go, you are dismissed."

Louise turned back at the door in a plea to the eight nuns of the Council. "America is the new frontier, and for us to ignore a chance to help in this great mission of the Church—"

"You are dismissed."

"It is not only wrong but damaging to our future, and I urge that . . ." Louise faltered, aware that of the eight, old Mère Blanchard alone was sympathetic, although she could not be counted on for support. "It is wrong and I am not a quitter," Louise said, and quickly left the room.

She was not, in fact, without advocates of her cause. The school in Galway, while a financial loss, had yielded the Society the dividend of vocations. The Irish nuns made up a small faction, but on hearing of Louise's plea, they eagerly lent their support. However, scattered as they were in the various schools, Louise was left to her own devices at the Motherhouse. Whether by design or accident, she had been effectively separated from her Irish sisters.

She was not a quitter, or so she kept telling herself while being deprived of any platform for her cause. At every opportunity, which was not often, she cast an eye on the morning mail, hurriedly scanning it for the postmarks. Over the following months she came upon letters from Mobile, Alabama, Portland, Oregon, and Cheyenne, Wyoming—appeals for nuns that she was certain would go unheeded.

In the spring of 1907, on a blossoming morning in May, something more than a letter from America arrived at the Motherhouse. Louise, at the parlor window, was startled to observe a man coming up the driveway, tall and angular with a look of the outdoors about him. He wore a Roman collar and sported, to her fascination, cowboy boots and a Stetson hat. He rang the pull at the grille, but the portress was nowhere to be seen and so Louise admitted the visitor.

"Since I didn't get an answer to my letter," he greeted her, doffing the Stetson, "I decided to show up in person."

John McAuliffe was the Bishop of the infant diocese of Cheyenne, which included all of Wyoming. Montpellier, he explained, was but one stop on his tour of convents in search of nuns willing to endure the frontier hardships of founding a mission school for Indian children. "I've lost track of the appeals I mailed out, but maybe I'll have better luck this way."

"You will—or a fair chance, at least," Louise assured him.

She escorted the bishop to the Mother General, striding into her office without permission to announce the visitor. Since McAuliffe did not speak French, Louise had served as his interpreter, taking care to emphasize the generous financial terms of his proposal for the Indian mission. When it was met with polite evasions, she had blithely suggested that the bishop stay over for the meeting of the Council, in two days' time.

"Our constitution requires the vote of the Council on any such proposal," she had explained, thinking that were she able to win one member of the Council to her side, the others might follow.

The upper berth creaked from the roll of the ship, and sleep was no closer. If she had won, thought Louise, it was because the Mother General had recognized in the Bishop's proposal a convenient means to rid the Motherhouse of a nuisance, at the expense of the Bishop. And yet, had it not been for that first hesitant vote of support . . .

Louise smiled at the bountiful snores from the lower berth that accompanied the throb of the engines and the slap of water against the hull. Somehow, despite her life of submission, Mère Blanchard had garnered the courage not only to speak out but to volunteer herself for the mission. Louise credited the cowboy boots and Stetson hat of Bishop McAuliffe with having beguiled the old nun, though she had expressed nothing but misgivings since her departure.

Misgivings seized Louise . . . *what if the mission were to fail? What then for her at the Motherhouse?* She peered in the dark at the wet-sprayed porthole above the berth. The ship by now must be off the coast of Ireland, how close or how far did not matter. She had survived the good-bye to her homeland, survived the captive years at

Montpellier from which she was set free, and God would help her not to fail in her new endeavor.

The rise and fall of the berth lulled her toward sleep. Mixed with the creak of the ship was an eerie sound, a moaning that Louise took to be the wind as she tumbled into dreams of the white stucco house and the road that dipped away into the valley.

FOUR

She awoke conscious of the stopped motion and idling engines. Light washed the porthole and she heard the flap of gulls outside. The ship's itinerary raced through her mind—Bremerhaven, Plymouth, Cherbourg, and then in six days, New York.

Or was she mistaken?

Louise knelt at the porthole and gasped at the bay of blue water and green finger of land that it showed. The *Kronprinz* was anchored off Queenstown, and chugging across the bay was a tender circled by gulls and crowed with emigrants. Grieving women in shawls clutched at children while the men were grouped stoically together and a piper in kilts on the foredeck skirled his mournful tune of farewell.

As if to flee the piper's lament, Louise climbed down from the berth. At the washbasin she splashed her face with cold water. The towel fell from the mirror and a wild face stared back at her. Two years ago Vincent Maguire had suffered a stroke, which had precluded any visits to Montpellier. She had thought herself resigned to it, but the face in the mirror bid her to hurry and dress. In Queenstown a train to Cork and then to Longford, hire a trap and . . .

The chug of the tender grew closer, and with it the skirl of the piper. She took her clothes from the wardrobe, pulled on the heavy bodice and skirts, and fumbled with the coif and veil. Unless she boarded the tender while it was moored to the ship, she would never again see her father alive. Shoes unlaced, coif askew, she hastened to the cabin door and slid back the bolt.

Mère Blanchard pushed up from her pillow. *"Ou sommes-nous, sur le mer?"*

"Ireland . . . to pick up emigrants."

"Ah, *c'est-ca?* In my sleep I fancied—"

"No, it is Ireland." She must wait for heaven to meet with Vincent, thought Louise, and slid the bolt over the door. She stood there, listening to the cattle tread of the emigrants boarding the liner. The tender gave a departing whistle and the piper commenced to play a final tune. With that Louise rushed to the porthole, but was restrained by a gentle hand.

"Courage, ma petite . . ." The dour countenance of Solange Blanchard was creased in sympathy. "To look upon one's *patrie* . . . a cruel trial, but you will win over it, as you have won before."

"My parents—it is so long since I've seen them." The piper's aire drifted across the water, and she clung to Solange who assisted her to the chair under the steampipe. "I must wait for heaven to see them, mustn't I?"

"Always, the courage." The old nun straightened the white coif and smoothed the black veil. "Opposed by Mère Générale, cast down by her, but never did you surrender your convictions." She dampened a cloth at the washbasin and applied it to Louise's aching temples. "But then, *enfin,* I ask myself if it is not we, so attached to the past, who are wrong."

The engines started up. "I was stunned when you volunteered for the mission."

"Ah, *pauvre* Solange was not always a mouse." A deafening blast of the *Kronprinz*'s whistle shook the shoe-box cabin. "When I was young, if you can believe it, I dreamed of adventure."

"The Bishop's cowboy boots spelled it for you."

"I confess they did, but why should it not be an adventure to be a nun?"

"Indeed, why not?"

Having declared herself in favor of adventure, Mère Blanchard was uncertain of what to do with it. She washed and robed, negotiated the passage to the ladies' room, rang for the stewardess, and ordered breakfast. The ship had acquired a lurching roll by the time breakfast was delivered to the cabin. The bowls of farina skidded across the trays, and cream sloshed over the milk jug. Solange was the color of the greenish pear that, uneaten, she returned with a groan to her plate. "We have not said *matins.*" She knelt at the berth with her prayer book to seek refuge in convent routine.

"Do you hear it?" asked Louise.

"Which psalms shall we choose for the day?"

"Solange, *listen.*" Louise strained to identify the windlike moan she had heard last night. "What is it, do you think?"

"It is the wind, and we are nuns vowed to prayer."

"Yes, of course." Louise fetched her prayer book and knelt at the chair for the morning psalms. The sound rose and fell with the ship, as mournful and haunting as the piper's lament. "Solange, it isn't the wind, can't you hear it's not?"

"My attention, as it happens—"

Louise stood up, her prayer book closed. "Prayer is action as well as words," she said, and reached for her cloak in the wardrobe. It fell in black folds from her shoulders as she unbolted the door. "Those are voices we hear, crying for help."

She went to the stairs midway down the corridor. The voices were coming from above, and she followed the haunting sound up the stairs and the landings to the second-class lounge and out to the promenade deck. The sea air rushed at her, and the rail showed an ocean mountainous with peaks and chasms. The gray tent of the sky stretched in flashes of sunlight to the far-off horizon. All had turned to stare at the nun, the passengers in the rows of deck chairs and the stewards who were serving them morning bouillon. Louise dropped her gaze and considered retreat, but the sound of the voices drew her forward along the deck, growing louder as she reached the observation rail that wrapped around the front of the liner.

Some passengers idled at the rail, among them the young American priest from the tender. Hatless, his dark russet hair whipped by the wind, he was sipping bouillon and watching, as were the others, the scene on the deck below.

The bow of the *Kronprinz Wilhelm* was seventy feet long, and penned into the deck space were a thousand or more men, women, and children. They were pressed five deep at the rails and were swarmed over the lifeboats and the canvas tarpaulin that covered the cargo hold. Of every age from swaddled infant to grizzled octogenarian, and of mixed nationality, Serbians, Croatians, Poles, Ukrainians, most had boarded the ship at Bremerhaven. The Irish group from Queenstown was huddled below a lifeboat, pale and woebegone, fearful of the swarthy foreigners who in turn were fearful of them. Families clung together guarding possessions—bedrolls, quilts, oil lamps, copper pots, and cooking utensils. The fierce-eyed men, bearded and moustached, were garbed in rough jackets and trousers stuffed into muddied boots. The women wore babushkas and aprons tied over many-layered skirts, several of which bulged in the advanced stages of pregnancy.

These were the steerage passengers of the *Kronprinz Wilhelm*. By sheer massed forced, they exuded an overwhelming vitality, but coupled with it was a terror no less compelling, a force in itself. The wild tundra of the sea upon which they were tossed and pitched spoke of shipwrecks and watery graves, and they cringed from it, lashed by the winds and spray. With each upward, downward plunge of the bow, they voiced their terror, as they did at night in the steerage hold. A collective moan went up each time the bow righted itself, then another at the downward plunge.

Suddenly, as Louise watched from the rail above, a scream rang out from the steerage deck. A woman in a babuska held a baby aloft, and the surrounding crowd pushed back, clearing a patch of deck for her. She lay the baby flat on the deck and crouched over it, slapping at the tiny bundle. It brought no response and the woman screamed and gestured at the crowd for help, but no one stepped forward to answer.

Louise turned from the rail of gawking passengers. For years afterward, she was to think of this moment as her indoctrination into the true life of a nun. She went to the gangway that led to the steerage deck only to find it barred by a chain and a sign that warned, VERBOTEN. Unfastening the chain, she struggled down the pitching steps. The wind tore at her veil and billowed her cloak and voluminous skirts as she battled across the slanting, pitching deck of the bow.

The steerage passengers parted to make a path for her. Hands lifted in the sign of the cross, and from the Irish contingent a voice piped, "Jesus, Mary, and Joseph, 'tis a holy nun of God."

Louise knelt by the side of the frantic mother, who had unlaced her bodice as a last resort and had exposed a milk-swollen breast. The choking baby, eyes rolled back, had turned a mottled blue. Helpless as to procedure, Louise glanced up at the observation rail and singled out the American priest.

"Bring a doctor!" The wind swooped at her voice and carried it aloft. "Hurry, in the name of Christ, and bring a doctor!"

The baby was choking to death. Louise lowered her lips to the baby's mouth and breathed into it, but to no effect. Just then a sparrow of a girl, clothed in rags, pushed forward from the crowd.

" 'Tis mucus or the like that's chokin' the bairn." Taking the baby, the girl tossed it over her shoulder and whacked vigorously at it. "Sure, ain't I looked after me sister at the orphanage since I was old enough to walk?" She kept up the whacking until congested phlegm spewed from the babe's mouth. A lusty wail followed, and to the gratified murmurs of the crowd, the infant was handed over to the sobbing, joyous mother.

Louise was startled by the bursts of applause that salvoed from the promenade deck, thronged by then with onlookers. She turned to thank the girl, who was plucking at her wispy braids. "I'm Mother Maguire, and you are a lifesaver. May I ask your name?"

"Bridget Mary O'Shea, from Cork, mum." The girl's thin, under-nourished face was animated by an elfin grin and lively agate eyes. "Fifteen, I am, crossin' the deep by meself, and scared out of me wits."

"All these children." Louise nodded at the boys and girls who peeped shyly from behind skirts and trouser legs. "We ought to organize games and activities for them."

"Furriners, the whole bloomin' pack, and us not speakin' their tongue."

"We'll manage, one way or the other," Louise said, committing herself to the task. "The conditions below, are they deplorable?"

"A pigsty, mum, ain't fit for humans."

Father Regan clambered down the gangway with the ship's doctor in tow, and shouldered through the crowd to Louise. "Well, where's the life-or-death emergency?" he demanded.

"It is over," she informed him and turned to the doctor. "You might at some point have a look at the women in steerage who are on the verge of delivery."

"Well, listen to the Mother General." Sean Regan slicked back his dark russet locks. "I'll call you M.G. for short."

"May I inquire if your priestly duties include Mass each morning?"

"Strictly the first-class lounge, to a select and appreciative few."

"Why not steerage one morning? I'm sure it can be arranged."

39

"By you, needless to ask?" The handsome, square-planed face was both amused and cautious. Nuns were not Regan's cup of tea, unless something was to be gained from it. "I get the sense that once you've started, little will stop you."

"Oh, it was a slow start," Louise confided, and spied Mère Blanchard who was gripping the rail of the gangway, poised on the brink of adventure. "But watch out for my companion and me, or we'll not give you a moment's peace."

The pattern was set for the rest of the crossing. Each morning after breakfast, Louise and Solange, descending the gangway, organized games for the children whom Bridget O'Shea had collected in a roped-off section of the steerage deck, while behind the rope several of their elders gathered to watch in rapt wonderment.

Language was no barrier to blindman's buff and London Bridge, nor to such songs as "Frère Jacques" and "Sur le Pont," which could be learned by rote. The songs were followed by a story hour, and the children, grouped at Louise's skirts, heard their first account of the land toward which the plunging ship in the mountainous sea was taking them. Louise read aloud from the books that Bishop McAuliffe had sent to Montpellier, histories and tales of America that were packed into the fishnet satchels. Her audience grasped the drama, if not the content, of what Louise read to them, and listened in breathless quiet. Solange, anxious to practice her English, attempted some chapters from *Uncle Tom's Cabin*. Whether it was Topsy's pranks or her Gallic rendition of them, Solange was rewarded with gales of laughter.

When the lunch gong sounded at noon on the promenade deck, Louise was reluctant to leave her charges. Every day among the crowd of spectators stood Sophie Wojciechowski, content to look on while she hugged the infant son whom Bridget O'Shea had saved. Bridget had become Louise's indispensable ally. From the age of four, she had been reared in an orphanage in Cork, where she had left behind a younger sister. Bridget's plight was of increasing concern to Louise.

"How is it you were allowed passage, when you are under age and unaccompanied?"

"Sure, 'twill turn out grand once I get to America and a payin' job, so I can send for Ag to come over."

"But won't you need a sponsor in order to land?"

"Ah, mum, sure. I'll worry about that when it's time for it."

On Sunday, the fourth day out, Father Regan celebrated Mass in the dismal cavern of the steerage mess hall to an overflow crowd bound together by the familiar liturgy. At the concluding prayers, a Czech woman doubled to the floor with labor pains, and Louise called for the ship's doctor. The woman was delivered of a seven-pound girl, not in the fetid, roach-infested dormitories but in the gleaming sanitation of the ship's hospital. Father Regan went along with Louise and baptized the newborn before he dashed off to join his friends, the Tobins.

"I'm persuaded that I can serve the Lord equally well in the amenities of first class, or don't you agree?"

"I just think . . . well, look at how you were needed in steerage. Mass wouldn't have been said, or a baby baptized, except for you."

"Yes, but that doesn't discount the Tobins of the world. I've told them all about you, by the way. Why don't you come meet them?"

"Thank you, but I'm late for the children's games."

The climax of the voyage in steerage was the farewell party that was given in the mess hall the last night out. Louise had not considered a party until that morning, when Father Regan had baited her into it. He had become a fixture, like Sophie Wojciechowski, in the crowd that watched the children's games on the foredeck.

"A memento for your scrapbook, M.G." he had said after the games that morning, and presented her with a photograph taken by the ship's photographer. "It illustrates the shameful difference between us."

The photograph showed Louise reading to the children while Regan was to be seen in the crowd of spectators. "Why shameful?"

"See, there you are, intent on your Christian duties, and there I am, lolling around in indolence."

"It must bother you, or you wouldn't joke about it."

"On the contrary, I had the time of my life at the captain's gala last night. Really, M.G., it behooves you to arrange a little festivity for your steerage pals."

"Very well, I shall. Come have a look at the mess hall tonight."

Lieber Gott, thought the purser later that morning at the approach of the bothersome nun with her outrageous demands. He agreed, for the simple expediency of getting rid of her, to donate the balloons and streamers and noisemakers left over from the gala, but drew the line at her next request. If the nun wished to beg food from the kitchens, it was the chef's affair, not his. As it happened, the head chef was a man whose religious sentiments had been fostered by his aunt, a nun in a Bavarian convent. A feast of pastries was contributed to steerage as well as platters of ham, turkey, and potato salad.

The party that night was a rousing success. Louise had assembled a soap-and-pail brigade to scrub and scour the mess hall, which was strung with balloons and crepe-paper streamers. The noisemakers were received by the children with shrill delight. The men in steerage had waxed their moustaches and polished their boots, and many of the women were costumed in the stiff headdresses and embroidered aprons of Slovakia, Romania and the Ukraine. Sophie Wojciechowski, who was en route to join her husband in Pittsburgh, made a fetching picture in the finery of her native Gdynia. She held her baby in one arm, and in the other a gift, wrapped in burlap, which she insisted in halting Polish that Louise must accept.

Enfolded in the burlap was a painted wooden carving of the Virgin, less than sixteen inches tall, crudely but reverently executed. The Virgin's blue mantle and girdle were emblazoned with stars, and in the carving of the face and the outstretched arms was captured a sweet tenderness.

Sophie was adamant that Louise not refuse her offering. *"Miraculi, miraculi."* She kept pointing at the Virgin and then at her son, as if to testify that Louise had helped to work a miracle.

"I will keep her always." Tears stung Louise as she clasped the Virgin. "In memory of our crossing."

The noise and the merriment grew with the night's progression. The ham and turkey and potato salad were washed down with jugs of wine dug from knapsacks. A bearded Hungarian in a scarlet tunic produced an accordion, and the tables were pushed back to clear the pitching floor for the thump of czardas and polkas. Every so often Louise glanced at the stairs for Father Regan to appear with his jests and mocking grin, but her expectations were not fulfilled. An Irish fiddle took over for the accordion, and Bridget O'Shea, who had been morose and distracted all evening, flung herself onto the floor in a twirling jig.

Dressed in the patched skirt and ragged shawl she had worn throughout the voyage, Bridget lifted a scrawny arm proudly above her head and beat a tattoo with her clogs, faster and faster, until with a strangled sob she pushed through the crowd and ran from the mess hall.

Louise found the girl huddled at the rail of the foredeck, shivering in the night cold and staring down mutely at the black water and the foamy white ruffles by the prow.

"Nothing's so bad that you can't tell me of it, Bridget. Are you a stowaway?"

"That I am, and I'd jump to me death in the sea if it wasn't for Ag."

"You ran away from the orphanage?"

"The ships were miles away, but I could glimpse 'em from the rooftop. 'Twas the only hope for Ag and me, so I sneaked onto the tender, but tomorrer the immigration will find me out."

"How is that?"

"I won't have a number." Bridget clutched at her shawl, her despairing face wet with spray from the bow. "You've got to have a number or they'll send you back."

"Listen to me, Bridget." Louise turned the distraught, trembling girl away from the rail. "If we can pay for your passage, half the problem is solved. Look for me tomorrow when they call out the numbers."

Mère Blanchard's ample snores filled the shoe-box cabin, undisturbed by the light that Louise switched on to investigate her drawstring purse. Of the money that Bishop McAuliffe had wired for travel expenses, sixty francs were left, less than the price of a steerage ticket. The bishop would be at the pier tomorrow, but that was too late for Bridget's needs.

Before she climbed to the upper berth, Louise unwrapped the wooden carving and propped it on the washstand, and the Virgin's air of calm quieted her anxiety.

Early the next morning, struggling up the stairs with suitcases and satchels, Louise and Solange encountered Father Regan. Relieving them of their baggage, he declared that they were the very persons he sought.

"Compliments of the Tobins," he grinned, and handed an envelope to Louise. "Dolly won the ship's pool yesterday and wants you to have it."

The envelope contained ten crisp, new twenty-dollar bills. "If you'll give me the Tobins' address"—Louise shifted the statue in her arms—"I will write and thank them."

"You and me both, M.G." Regan's big shoulders moved up the stairs and he swung the bags as if they were feathers. "Took the whole crossing, but Mike finally came through last night. Saint Pat's, our cathedral in New York, is five thousand bucks richer, in return for a stained-glass memorial window."

"How wonderful."

"Yes, especially when I present the check to Monsignor Hayes. He's the Chancellor of the Archdiocese, and it'll ease the fact that I spent a week in Monte Carlo with the Tobins."

Father Regan deposited the bags in the second-class lounge, where the passengers were lined up for the immigration procedure. "Y'see, I'm to be the chancellor's secretary and he won't be happy that I showed up late. Are you staying over in the city?"

"We're to leave for Cheyenne tonight. The Bishop who is sponsoring the mission will be at the pier."

"It's a pity to waste you on the Indians." The rugged face reflected genuine regret, but the mocking grin eased it and Regan thrust out his hand in good-bye. "Well, best of luck, M.G., and don't forget to paste me in your scrapbook."

"Thank you for your kindness and . . ."

"What?"

"And for your bark," Louise laughed, "which is a good deal worse than your bite."

With a bow to Mère Blanchard, Regan made off for the first-class lounge. "He is mad," exclaimed Solange in her role of adventuress. "Completely mad, but *très charmant.*"

"Come, we must hurry. I told Bridget to look for us."

The *Kronprinz,* having taken on the pilot and immigration officers at Ambrose Light, steamed through the morning haze that enveloped the harbor. Gulls flapped and swooped in the liner's wake, cawing hungrily, and the haze rang with buoys and the bleat of fog horns. Luggage was stacked along the deck, ready for transfer to the pier. In the bow of the ship the steerage immigrants were herded together once more, this time for the transfer to Ellis Island.

Louise stood with Solange at the observation rail searching for Bridget O'Shea in the weary ranks below, engulfed in their worst apprehensions of the voyage. The first- and second-class passengers would proceed through immigration in the lounges, but for steerage the process began on the fog-shrouded deck of the bow. Before the ordeal of Ellis Island or the sight of the lady in the harbor lifting her torch of liberty, the steerage immigrants first had to be certified as legitimate passengers.

But where among them was Bridget?

Louise saw what had frightened the shivering girl the night before. Pinned to every man, woman, and child on the foredeck was a numbered tag. Some of the ship's officers went from group to group calling out the numbers, while another officer checked the ship's manifest for the corresponding numbers that had been issued at the port of embarkation. Without this number, no one in steerage would be permitted to disembark.

"I can't find her." Louise scoured the misty deck. "Solange, do you see her anywhere?"

"Ah, *non!* So brave, the little one. Where can she be, I wonder?"

The officers were again combing through the mute-stricken groups, but not to call out the number tags. Evidently, some other discrepancy had been detected. The ship's officers then conferred with the immigration officers. Some crewmen were dispatched to fan out across the bow in a search party. They peered into the hatches and ventilators and coiled ropes, and under the canvas rigged over the lifeboats. From one of the boats they dragged out a girl who bolted away to climb the rail and crouch for the leap into the water.

"Bridget!"

In an instant Louise was at the gangway unfastening the chain, spurred by visions of Jenny Rocket drowned in the lake at Ballymar. Veil flying, Louise Anne Margaret Mary Maguire ran toward Bridget O'Shea, who had been seized from the rail and was released to the nun's arms.

"It is over. It is over." Louise sheltered the weeping girl against her, only to be confronted by the immigration officers. She studied their faces, which were veritable maps of Ireland, and inquired, "From which counties do you hail, gentlemen?"

Kerry, Sligo, and Antrim were mentioned in the smiling replies.

"Then surely you will not deny assistance to a greenhorn nun from Longford and a poor orphan girl from Cork? A slight irregularity exists, which I'm most anxious to straighten out."

An hour later, the *Kronprinz Wilhelm* steamed past the Statue of Liberty in the harbor to a cacophony of tugboat whistles and the greeting toot of ferries. The haze had lifted, revealing in the morning sunshine the city of New York, at which sight a hush fell over the passengers crowded at the liner's rails. Mère Blanchard was owl-eyed with wonder, and Bridget, whose passage was paid and immigration papers stamped, nestled against her guardian and sniffed the air of freedom.

"I'll send for Ag soon as I've got the money. Oh, mum—" She touched the folds of the black cloak. " 'Tis me life I owe to you, and give to you, if you have use for it."

"Saints above, have you ever seen such a sight? Look, Bridget, isn't it glorious?"

Louise clasped hold of Sophie's Virgin, spellbound by the spectacle that loomed beyond the rail of the deck. Tipped by the green fringe of Battery Park and extending north and east as far as the eye could see was a fortress of buildings and streets, spires and rooftops, pulsing with a vibrant hum that struck in Louise a responding chord, restless and seeking.

New York was a city reaching, as she was, for the sky, and for a moment she was gripped by frustration at having to depart that evening with the city unexplored.

But then, mindful of Bishop McAuliffe waiting at the pier, she went below with Mère Blanchard and Bridget to the deck where the gangplanks were to be raised.

FIVE

By ten-thirty, two hours after tugs had nudged the *Kronprinz* into the pier in Hoboken and the gangplanks were raised, the customs shed was almost as quiet as a tomb. The mad scramble of porters with handtrucks, the mountains of luggage, the queues of passengers vying for customs inspectors, the crowd waiting behind the visitors' barrier, had been disposed of and the steerage immigrants ferried to Ellis Island.

One of the few remaining passengers in the shed was Sean Francis Regan, newly ordained priest of the Archdiocese of New York. The Tobins had traipsed off to the Waldorf Hotel for a lunch of lobster salad, having delegated Sean to settle the dispute over the uncrated, gold-framed oil painting that Mike had acquired in Rome under the impression that it was an original Raphael.

"Listen, I don't shell out that kind of dough for a fake," Mike had argued with the customs officer. "As an original, it's duty free." Whereupon a fine had been levied against him for false claims.

Another half hour elapsed before the chief of inspectors, whose name was Flanagan, sauntered over for a look at the painting. "Sorry to keep you waiting, Father."

"Don't mention it, you're a busy man, and this dispute is really a—"

"Michael Tobin," mused Flanagan, eyeing the tag on the crate. "Ain't he the feller paved the entire streets of the Bronx?"

"Yes, the Cement King—it was my privilege to travel from Rome with the Tobins."

"Rome, is it? You must of got to know plenty of the higher-ups."

Sean Regan picked up the cue. "Anything I can help you with?"

"Mind you," said Flanagan, scratching his ear, "I'll not pretend that my son Brendan is a scholar or ain't had his troubles at school, but the lad is set on the priesthood, and if the right person was to speak up for him . . ."

"Tell you what, Inspector, give me the lad's name and parish, and when I meet with Archbishop Farley next week, I'll put in a good word for him."

Following that exchange, the question of the painting was speedily resolved. Authentic Raphaels, Inspector Flanagan pointed out, did not arrive a dime a dozen in the port of New York. "However, if Mr. Tobin was to declare it as a *religious* object, instead of a work of art . . . d'ya get my meanin'?"

"You mean, it would be duty free?"

"I ask you, are we to charge for the Blessed Mother like she was a crate of dishes? Here, let me stamp the papers for you."

"Thanks, and I won't forget about Brendan."

"The girls must weep at a handsome feller like you wearin' the collar. Watch your step, Father."

"Don't worry, I always do."

Sean Regan hustled down the city-block length of the pier, his shiny black shoes echoing sharply in the concrete vastness. No less shiny was the expensive cowhide suitcase, a London gift of the Tobins, that he swung in his muscular grip. If the girls had wept when he'd departed at age seventeen for the seminary in Yonkers, Sean had disregarded it. Sexual desire was a threat that ice-cold showers and workouts in the seminary gym kept under control.

From Yonkers, Sean had been sent to the North American College in Rome, the plum of all plums for a seminarian without family connections who had grown up in a cold-water railroad flat on the Lower East Side. He'd always wanted to be a priest, and his concept of it as a boy had been idealistic, a pure and noble calling that he yearned to answer. The idealism had lasted as far as the seminary in Yonkers. The magnificence of Rome, that is, of the Church in Rome, had effected a profound change in the boy from Forsythe

Street. Not until then had Sean associated his calling with the attainment of power and prestige.

In Rome, Sean had been chosen by his superiors for a prize assignment. The grand tour was a requisite for rich Americans, and for the rich Catholics among them the holy city was the grandest stop on the tour. They arrived with letters from their bishops at home, expecting and receiving preferential treatment. A young American seminarian such as Sean was the perfect choice to act as a Vatican guide for these wealthy countrymen. Affable and engaging, knowledgeable in art and history, Sean had scored such an immediate success that it was something of a status symbol to secure him as a guide. He in turn had used his position to his advantage. The more important of the visitors were invited to the receptions given by the foreign embassies attached to the Vatican, and Regan often accompanied them to these glittering international affairs. It wasn't long before his own name was included on the guest lists. Good looks, he'd learned by then, were a potent asset and he'd employed them with men and women alike. While appearing not to discourge sexual entanglements, he had at the same time managed to avoid them. Sean had remained celibate, less from scruples than from the conviction that to do otherwise was a threat to his ambition.

By his final year in Rome, Sean Regan had become a favorite with the ranking American prelates who came on matters of official business. As yet, no American priest had penetrated the highest echelons of Vatican power. Sean's ambition was to be that man, but to achieve it he first must climb the ecclesiastical ladder at home. Archbishop Farley of New York had attended the young seminarian's ordination at St. Peter's, accompanied by his Chancellor. Monsignor Patrick Hayes was regarded as Farley's successor to the throne of the Archdiocese, and from Hayes had come the invitation for Sean to serve as his secretary upon his return to New York.

The politic move was to report by the next boat for the enviable appointment, but Father Regan had dallied in Europe with the Tobins and sailed home with the them, first class. The tight rein of caution and ambition had developed in Sean the counter motion of defiance and recklessness. It was as if the idealistic boy that he had cast aside were exerting a form of protest, expressed by rash impulse and a mocking humor whose prime target was himself.

But as he headed past the customs barrier on the pier, Regan applied once more the brake of caution. Mike Tobin's five-thousand-dollar check would help to mollify the irritation that Monsignor Hayes might feel at the tardy arrival, but bolder action was required, something to take the initiative from Hayes.

Regan knew in an instant what course to adopt. Rather than wait for a summons, he would proceed at once to the Chancellor's office and confess that the delay was prompted by doubts of his worthiness for the appointment. He would offer to relinquish it, and then the onus would be on Hayes to persuade him out of it.

Significantly, as Sean entered the visitors' lounge at the street end of the pier, he was not greeted by any welcoming member of the Regan clan. For one thing, he had not advised his family of his arrival date, and for another, he did not intend to renew his intimacy with them. The halcyon years in Rome had created a distance that Sean had coldly accepted as permanent.

Still, the deserted lounge held a group that for Regan was as unwelcome as his family would have been. They were huddled together in fearful trepidation—the old nun, the steerage girl, and Mother Maguire, who was attempting a semblance of calm and spied Regan before he could manage a hasty retreat.

Louise held out the cablegram clutched in her hand.

"The Bishop wired that he'd meet us at the pier."

"He's not here yet? Did he give the hotel where to reach him?"

She glanced at the cablegram. "The Hotel Woodstock, but what could have delayed him?"

"Let's try to find out. What's his name?"

"McAuliffe, John McAuliffe."

"Wait here." Regan set down his suitcase, resigned to this extent of involvement. He made for the telephone booth across the lounge, and when he came back from it, the involvement had deepened.

"Bishop McAuliffe isn't registered at the Woodstock. He had a reservation for yesterday but never appeared to claim it."

Louise nodded, her thoughts skidding and sliding like the beads of a broken rosary. "For some reason, he's been delayed . . . ought we to telegraph Cheyenne?"

"It'd take the whole day for a reply." Regan was loathe to give up the strategy with Monsignor Hayes. "It looks as though you'll need a place to stay while we learn what happened to the Bishop."

"You mustn't think you are under any obligation to us."

"Well, I know of a convent where I can take you." Regan gestured at Bridget to help with the bags. He scooped up his suitcase and one of the fishnet satchels. "Besides, I've said it's a pity to waste you on the Indians." He grinned at Louise and conducted the wayfarers down to the street and into the bustle and clamor that seemed an extension of the city waiting across the river.

II
THE SCHOOL

SIX

New York was an explosion of sidewalks and people, noises and smells, electric signs and traffic lights, all of which combined to assault Louise as she stepped from the ferry shed at the foot of West Fourteenth Street.

"I'm taking you to the Sisters of Charity in Greenwich Village," Father Regan advised, gripping the bags. "They'll give you a bit of lunch at the convent while I get a line on the Bishop."

The curious procession moved across the cobblestones in the bedlam of activity that surrounded them. Trolley cars hurtled onto a circle of tracks, discharging passengers for the ferry and taking them on for the crosstown ride. The whistle blasts of the liners at the piers blended with the shrieks of barges and tugs. Horse-drawn wagons clopped up to the wholesale meat markets and were loaded with bloody carcasses, and sailors lurched in and out of the waterfront saloons.

" 'Tis holy nuns and a priest," trumpeted Bridget O'Shea as they approached the crowded trolley stop. "God bless all who make way for the nuns and priest."

The announcement was effective, for the conductor himself scrambled down from the trolley to escort the party on board and dust off the wooden-slat seats. Louise and Mère Blanchard shared the seat in front of Father Regan, and behind him sat Bridget with the pile of bags. The conductor would not hear of collecting fares.

"Dennis T. Cooney," he said with a tip of his cap. "Say a couple of Hail Marys for me."

It was the language of home for Louise and made her feel less of a stranger. With a clang the trolley screeched over the tracks and she turned her gaze to the window.

The trolley rattled past a block of tenements hung with fire escapes and then plunged under the Ninth Avenue El to the overhead thunder of trains. Interspersed with the tenements were tidy red-brick houses fronted by stoops. At Eighth Avenue, the mob getting off the trolley battled the mob that pushed up the aisle, people of every nationality redolent of garlic, cheap cologne, sauerkraut, and sweat. The same variety populated the sidewalks, every color of skin, black African, pale Nordic, coppery Asian, swarthy Greek. Strolling at leisure among the crowds were silk-hatted men and stylish women in long, sweeping coats and fantastic birds' nests of hats. The street was clotted with every form of traffic, wagons and buggies, hansom cabs, pushcarts, and the new-fangled automobiles that panicked the neighing horses. The hum of motors, clatter of hooves, and roar of El trains created a decible of noise that both unnerved and exhilarated Louise.

Father Regan leaned forward from the seat behind to act as tour guide. "When I was a boy, Fourteenth Street was the hub of uptown," he described. "The big shops, hotels, and theaters were all on this street, but the biggest of the stores, Macy's, moved to Herald Square, the Metropolitan Opera opened at Thirty-ninth Street, new theaters went up on Forty-second, and suddenly Fourteenth Street was downtown."

Regan's annoyance at having to look after the nuns had vanished. He'd fogotten the excitement his native city could generate, arousing in him the same hunger for conquest as had Rome. "Nothing like New York to spur you on," he said, and felt the pump of adrenaline fire his blood. "I can't wait to get started again."

Astounded by the roar and vigor of the street, Louise was shocked to observe the poverty, stark and unrelieved, that existed in the midst of the thriving commerce. Ragamuffin boys darted weasellike among the crowds, barefoot in the chill April weather. Beggars with tin cups were as common to street corners as were the newsstands. Derelicts rooted in garbage cans, and one old man was strapped front and back with sign boards that advertised, JOE'S LUNCH—25¢.

Louise watched from the trolley as a bedraggled old woman was ejected bodily from a doorway and her ragpicker's bag tossed after her. The crowd swallowed her up and Louise shivered with apprehension. Any number of reasons might have delayed Bishop McAuliffe, but why hadn't he wired her? She hugged the Virgin, the burlap wrapping rough on her cheek. Stranded in the city, and if what she feared was true . . .

They alighted from the trolley at Sixth Avenue and stood buffeted by the shoppers that swarmed in and out of Hearn's Department Store at the corner. "The convent's a short walk from here," Regan said, gathering up the luggage with Bridget. "If it's not too much for Mère Blanchard."

Solange was braced for exertion. "The difficulty, *mon curé*, is for a mouse to become a lion. *Allons-nous!*"

The El tracks overhead made a checkerboard of light and shade on the sidewalk as the party headed south on Sixth Avenue. The shouts of children playing hopscotch mingled with the hurdy-gurdy of an organ grinder, and on the tenement stoops women as dark-eyed as their children gossiped and fussed over baby carriages. "The Village is packed with Italians," Regan commented. "And just as many Irish too. They settled here because it's where the ships from Ireland docked. The men got work on the piers and construction gangs, the bottom of the ladder. Next, they graduated to policemen and firemen, and ran saloons that functioned as political clubs and put up candidates for city office. Politically, the Irish control the city, and they've done the same with the Church. Two out of three pastors in New York are Irish, and it goes straight up to Archbishop Farley at the top."

They crossed Eleventh Street and Sean Regan gestured at the rows of handsome brownstones that stretched to Fifth Avenue. "Today, the grandsons of dockworkers own some of those houses, doctors, lawyers, bankers, up from the tenements. They are the select few, but the number keeps increasing. To date, New York's had only one Cardinal, but I wouldn't object to a red hat in my future."

"You *are* ambitious," Louise said.

"You'll see, so are you."

The convent to which Father Regan brought the wayfarers occupied a brownstone on Waverly Place, a quiet tree-shaded street off Sixth Avenue. As a seminarian he had worked one summer at the parish church of St. Joseph's, whose school was staffed by the Sisters of Charity. He went up the stoop and rang the bell, which was answered by a stout, hearty Sister who wagged a scolding finger at him.

"Back from Rome, you scoundrel, and nary a postcard since you left." Informed of their plight, Sister Matilda ushered the weary travelers into the parlor. "Sometimes, a missing Bishop is the best kind to have," she remarked with a chuckle and nodded at the gawking Bridget. "Where does the colleen fit into the story? A stowaway? Well, it was certainly an eventful voyage."

Sister Matilda's black poke bonnet evoked images of pioneer women crossing the plains, and her dress was modeled after the widow's weeds of Elizabeth Seton, who after her husband's death had founded the Sisters of Charity in America. "Now, you mustn't worry," Matilda urged when Father Regan had departed for the parish rectory, which boasted a telephone, to check into the Bishop's whereabouts. "Have you had lunch? Let's take care of it before you perish from hunger. Is the colleen looking for work?"

"Oh, I've got to earn wages," Bridget avowed, following the group down the basement stairs. "Earn 'em, the minute I can."

"We'll send you to Tessie Fay, one of our parishioners. She runs a boardinghouse on Perry Street and is always short of help."

The basement refectory was furnished with an oilcloth-covered table and oak-varnished chairs. The pattern was worn from the linoleum floor, but Sister Matilda's cheerful dispatch compensated for the spartan frugality of the room. Despite her position as the superior of the convent, she prepared the cheese sandwiches and tea in the adjacent kitchen, although there was a practical reason for it.

"Sister Estelle, our cook, is in St. Vincent's to have a goiter removed, size of a grapefruit," she explained. "As a consequence we take turns at the stove, with mixed results. Of course, nobody goes into the convent for the quality of the meals."

It heartened Louise to see that each bite of sandwich and sip of tea helped to revive Solange, who was pale and drawn with fatigue. Louise was ravenous, having eaten nothing since a roll at dawn, but her eyes kept straying to the clock on the wall. An hour had elapsed since Father Regan had departed, and fear of what news he might learn of the bishop gnawed at her.

The remedy for her fear were the Sisters, who flocked down the basement stairs a short while later. It was three-thirty and school had let out. After pouring themselves steaming mugs of tea, the Sisters gathered at the table with the visitors.

The lively opinions that Louise heard expressed, the interchange of ideas, were the antithesis of the rigid conformity imposed at Montpellier. The talk ranged at liberty over a variety of subjects— home and families, theology, civics, neighborhood parish activities—but it centered on the Sisters' work as schoolteachers.

"We conduct two schools in the parish." Sister Matilda made the rounds of the table, replenishing the mugs of tea. "The income we derive from our girls' academy goes to support the free school for our poorer children."

Louise forgot her predicament in her admiration for the Sisters' endeavors. "What a splendid mission, to educate the poor."

"Without a free school, those boys and girls would be deprived of Catholic teaching. It is our vocation to minister to the poor of the city."

"You can't have chosen a worthier endeavor."

The Sisters, in turn, were fascinated by the Wyoming mission, and plied Louise with questions about it, which reawakened her fears.

"At the moment, of course, it seems to be up in the air . . . that is, until we find out what happened to Bishop McAuliffe."

Father Regan did not return to the convent until six o'clock. He waited in the front parlor while Sister Matilda went to fetch Louise from the chapel that had been improvised in the back parlor. Mère Blanchard was upstairs resting, and Bridget had been sent with a note to the boardinghouse on Perry Street.

"*Faith*," Matilda whispered to Louise, who knelt at the minuscule altar of the chapel. "God's holy will is not to be feared."

Sophie's Virgin lay in her burlap atop the luggage in the front hall, forlorn and neglected it seemed to Louise as she entered the parlor.

Regan stood at the mantel, his masculine presence at odds with the chaste and maidenly room. "Sorry it took so long with Cheyenne," he apologized. "The connection was terrible and the line kept fizzing out, which meant endless delays."

"Tell me, is Bishop McAuliffe dead?"

"Quick and to the point, I admire that."

"It's the only explanation. . . . Please tell me."

"Two days ago he was taken off the train in Chicago with a fatal heart attack." Regan was sparing of details in the belief that it was kindest. "I talked with his vicar, who's in charge for now."

"The plans for us—canceled?"

"The vicar wouldn't commit himself, but it's highly probable."

"Yes, I'd expect as much." Louise went over to the parlor window, her hands tightly clasped. "Bishop McAuliffe was a good man, so concerned for his diocese. May I ask you to offer Mass for him?"

"First thing tomorrow." Regan paused uncertainly. "What are you going to do?"

"I shall cable the Motherhouse." Louise parted the white curtains and looked out at the men and women who were hurrying home from work under the pools of lamplight. "The likelihood is that we'll be ordered home."

"You've got Dolly Tobin's money to tide you over for a while."

Louise turned from the window. "What are you saying?"

"Look here, do you want to go back?"

"I, no, I—" She moved across the carpet, propelled by an urgency she could not contain. "Today on the trolley I saw beggars at every corner and boys without shoes, barefoot on the pavements." She reached out a hand to plead her cause. "The first useful thing I did in my life was to give my shoes to a girl who hadn't any. Until the ship, I'd felt myself a useless nun, and I dread to go back to what I was."

"Then don't send the cable," Regan said. "Hold off and examine your options."

"Options? What options?"

"Do you know that we're alike, the two of us?" Sean Regan looked at her, slender and tall and erect, standing across the carpet from him. It was alleged that aristocrats were born, not made, but she possessed the stuff of one, proud and of instinctive command. "What an idiot I am," he exclaimed. "What a clod for not seeing it before."

"What?"

"The perfect choice, right in front of me, and I didn't even see it."

Louise was utterly perplexed. "The choice for what?"

"In Rome, you know, the Vatican often assigned me as a guide to visitors from the States." Regan paced the carpet, rifling at his hair in excitement. "Important visitors, some of them."

"Ah, the Tobins and First Class."

"The gentleman I've got in mind is in a class of his own. Last spring, the Pope made him a papal marquis for his benefactions to the Church in New York. I was his guide in Rome, and one day he spoke of . . ."

"Yes?"

Regan applied the brake of caution. "He spoke of a project that you might be suitable for. It's enough definite that he's already cleared it with Archbishop Farley."

"What sort of project?"

Regan took care with his reply. "Let's stick to procedure. It calls for an interview with Farley—I'll see if I can arrange it through Monsignor Hayes." He paused and checked his watch. "Listen, I'd better run before he puts out an alarm for me."

He was in the hall collecting his suitcase, and Louise was left in the parlor with her bewilderment. She went to the archway as Regan swung open the door.

"A goose of a nun scarcely off the boat—what could the Archbishop want of me?"

"You underestimate yourself." Father Regan lowered the suitcase for a moment, in less of a hurry to leave. He reflected on the advantage it gave a nun to be endowed with a Roman coin of a profile. Good looks had not hurt him, why should they not serve her as well? "I'll be in touch . . . and Sister Mattie says she'll be glad to provide you with a room at the convent."

"But what of—?"

The door had closed and Louise stood looking at it in bemusement, aware that she had no idea of what had transpired or where it would take her.

Two weeks later, Louise descended the stoop of the brownstone convent bound for the meeting with Archbishop Farley, which had finally been arranged.

She went briskly along the leaf-shaded sidewalk, accustomed by now to outings by herself. The project that Father Regan was promoting was still a mystery, but as he'd said, the Archbishop was the next step in the procedure.

"Top o' the mornin', Sister." The policeman at the corner of Sixth Avenue doffed his cap and halted the traffic for her to cross over. " 'Tis a fine spring mornin' to be out in the fresh air."

" 'Tis that, Officer Cody."

The crowd at the trolley stop pushed back to make space for
Louise at the curbstone. It continued to amaze her, the courtesy she
was extended wherever in the city she traveled. The Irish were especially demonstrative, and there seemed no limit to the vast numbers
of countrymen Louise had encountered at every turn. Each morning, when she and Mère Blanchard attended six-thirty Mass at St.
Joseph's with the Sisters from the convent, the largest percentage of
worshipers was Irish, housewives and dockworkers, office clerks, students, nurses and interns from St. Vincent's Hospital, who had
elected to begin their day with this act of fealty and devotion. Not
since the church at Ballymar had Louise so identified with those in
the pews around her, nor had she experienced more ardently the desire to serve God by serving His people.

She rode uptown in the clattering trolley, accustomed to the clang
of the bell and the overhead roar of the El. If she attracted stares, it
was because she was alone and nuns were inevitably to be seen in
pairs, but it was of little concern to her. Although the prospect of
meeting the Archbishop invoked awe and nervousness, Louise was
not worried about the outcome. She had conceived of a project of
her own and was fully prepared to recommend it to the prelate.

She thought of the ending she had feared, which had evolved into
a new direction to pursue. Contrary to Father Regan's advice, she
had cabled the Motherhouse of the Bishop's death, but had not yet
received a reply. The longer it took, the better was her chance to secure a future in the land she had already adopted as her own. None
of her apprehensions had been realized. Mère Blanchard, rather
than panicking at the setback, had disposed of her timidity and
plotted a crafty means of survival.

"If we are to stay in this convent, we must earn our keep," Solange had recommended.

"I've insisted that we pay board, but when the money runs
out ..."

"What is it the *Supérieur* remarked yesterday of the cook?"

"The cook is in the hospital for the removal of a goiter."

"*Oui*, the size of a grapefruit." Clucking her tongue, Solange had
delved into the fishnet satchel for a notebook of ancient lineage and
faded script. "Fortunate that I think to bring to America the recipes
of France, taught to me in the house of my father. Tonight, perhaps,
the Sisters would enjoy a cassoulet?"

"Why, Solange, how enterprising for you."

The cassoulet had been followed by a ragout of veal and on Friday by a fish chowder of superlative flavor. Mère Blanchard had taken charge of the basement kitchen in payment for her keep. Daily, she sallied forth to the Village markets, a basket over her arm, to haggle over prices and return triumphant with her cache of delectables.

"Is it not an adventure to be a nun? I will prepare for Easter a roast of lamb fit for a king."

"You are spoiling the Sisters for ordinary fare. They dread the return of the cook."

"*Bien,* I will instruct her."

Louise reflected, amid the stops and starts of the trolley, that Bridget O'Shea's future too was assured, as housemaid in the boarding establishment of Miss Tessie Fay . . . and then one morning, as she stood across from the parish school of St. Joseph's, Louise had found a project for herself to launch.

The street in front of the school was thronged with boys and girls racing noisily to and fro. They were shabbily clothed and some of the children looked undernourished, but not one lacked for shoes or wore the haunted face of starvation. Two of the Sisters were on sidewalk duty, each with a circle of pupils who were showing off a new cap or scarf or pencil box. At the ring of the bell the children formed lines and marched up the steps of the school building. The bell rang out in liberty for these American boys and girls, who were guaranteed by law the right to an education and the practice of their religion. As a free school St. Joseph's was supported by the Archdiocese and parish contributions and was open to every child in the parish boundaries.

Spurred by a vision of the contribution she herself might make, Louise had crossed the street and gone into the school. She had proceeded along the corridor, past the classrooms of children at rows of desks and Sisters at blackboards, to the principal's office.

"Good morning," said Sister Clarita at her desk, who knew Louise from the convent. "Come to tempt me with tonight's menu?"

"No, to learn, if you'll have me." Louise advanced from the doorway, fired by her vision. "Someday, God willing, I hope to establish a school like yours, a free school, but I need to learn your curriculum and teaching methods and which textbooks you use—everything connected with it. Solange and I can give the children French lessons, and I'm rather good, if biased, at Irish history. Will you have us, Sister?"

"Take off your cloak and we'll start by letting you observe the classwork."

From that morning on, Louise had reported to the school, listening, learning from the teachers and children . . .

The clang of the trolley roused Louise from her reverie. The green of the Reservoir park at Forty-second Street spun past the window, and she got up from her seat. The trolley deposited her a few blocks later in a tawdry district of saloons, pool halls, and walk-up lodgings shadowed by the El. She went along Forty-ninth Street, no longer free from nerves. She had not seen Father Regan since the night of her arrival. He'd sent word of today's appointment via the rectory, but not of what to expect from Archbishop Farley or the meeting.

The spires of St. Patrick's soared above the rooftops, and as Louise reached the corner at Fifth Avenue, the great cathedral itself rose in splendor. The site had been acquired by the archdiocese in 1852 in what then was the rural outskirts of the city, and construction, begun in 1859, had taken more than twenty years to complete. The cathedral stood now in the preserve of millionaires, the Fifth Avenue palaces of the Vanderbilts, Astors, Goulds, and Harrimans. It rose up, a bastion of faith for New York's million Catholics, vast and awesome.

All at once the confidence Louise had gained from her two weeks in the city melted away. The appointment wasn't for another ten minutes, and she hurried across the avenue and up the cathedral's wide steps.

SEVEN

The hushed cathedral enveloped her in the scent of incense, candlewax, and burning tapers. The touch of holy water from the font was cool and soothing to her brow. She went up the aisle and knelt in a pew below the main altar, and felt lost in the soaring, gothic-arched interior. High above, in the ceiling of the nave, hung a single red hat, the *bolera* of Cardinal McCloskey, who had died in 1885, the one Prince of the Church whom Rome had granted to America. It reminded Louise of Father Regan's allusions to a red hat, and it struck her that today marked her introduction to the worldly power of the Church.

She wanted no share in it, had not sought it, and would not seek it now. The project she had conceived of seemed altogether insignificant, unworthy of mention . . . and were she to speak of it, would the Archbishop listen? She doubted somehow that he'd listen beyond the requirements of courtesy. No, something else was wanted of her . . . and who was the benefactor that Regan had kept carefully anonymous?

Going from the pew, Louise lit a candle at the altar of St. Joseph, the patron saint of nuns. Simple acts, the lighting of a candle, the telling of rosary beads, had defined her faith, but today called for resources that were unknown to her.

She left the cathedral by the side door and followed the ivy-bordered walk that led past the Lady Chapel at the rear. A flight of steps brought her onto Madison Avenue and the Archbishop's residence at No. 452, which was built in the ornate French-Gothic style of the cathedral. Above the wrought-iron doors, the crested seal of the Archdiocese gazed down at Louise, symbolic of power. It was as much as she could do to mount the steps and press the bell.

The cold formality of Father Regan, who opened the door and conducted her across the marble foyer as if they were strangers, so unnerved her that her hands shook.

"Mother Maguire is here, Your Excellency."

The reception room, while of lofty dimensions, was as plainly furnished as the convent parlor on Waverly Place, a reassuring note, as was the portly, white-haired prelate who came toward Louise. Though robed in purple, with a silver pectoral cross at his breast and a jeweled ring on his outstretched hand, John Farley gave the impression, accurate to a degree, of a friendly neighborhood pastor. He waved Louise to her feet when she knelt to kiss his ring.

"Forgive the delay in meeting you," he apologized. "We are to celebrate the centennial of the archdiocese in a few weeks and the preparations for it are enormous."

"A proud event, Your Excellency." Louise had heard excited talk at the convent of the banquets and special events, climaxed by a mammoth parade up Fifth Avenue, that were to be held for the centennial. "It seems as if all New York will turn out for it."

"Not to mention the guests from around the world." Farley turned to the priest who stood below a portrait on the wall of Pius X, the reigning pontiff. "May I present Monsignor Hayes, our Chancellor?"

In contrast to Farley, the iron discipline that had molded Patrick Hayes and carried him to high office was evident in his demeanor. When he smiled as he did at Louise, it revealed the shyness, legacy of an orphaned childhood, that hid behind his austere reserve and kept others at a distance.

"Father Regan tells me you crossed on the same boat. He has nothing but praise for your work among the steerage passengers."

It flustered Louise to hear herself praised. "The conditions were deplorable ... and I did little to improve them."

"It is the effort that counts."

"Well, now, Mother Maguire." Archbishop Farley moved benignly to a grouping of chairs and indicated one for Louise. "Tell us about yourself and how you happened to come to America."

Louise sat in the designated chair, which was placed by itself, and Monsignor Hayes and Father Regan took the chairs that flanked the Archbishop's. The effect was to isolate her from them, like a witness in the box facing the jury. She glanced at Regan, but his aloofness offered no support. If anything, it contributed to her sense of inadequacy.

"You are the first of the Society of the Holy Virgin to reach our shores?"

"Yes, Your Excellency, with my companion." Louise folded her trembling hands in her sleeves and gave a halting account of the Society's history and the schools it maintained in France. "I must confess I was the chief advocate for coming here, and now with the Wyoming mission canceled . . ."

"Your superiors were opposed to America?" Archbishop Farley frowned at such a thought. "That can be countermanded by Rome, should the need arise."

"Countermanded?" It was Louise's first hint that plans for her were under consideration. "I—I'm not sure I understand."

"If we should require nuns from the Society, Rome will attend to it."

"But gentlemen . . ." She regarded the tribune of clerics seated before her and thought of the red hat in the cathedral nave and of the keys of the kingdom, passed down from Peter. "I have been told nothing, except of a project known to Father Regan."

"Are we correct to assume that you would be interested in it?"

The fact that the assumption was already made prodded Louise into speaking for herself. "As it happens, I have found a project of abiding interest to me."

"Oh?" There was a magisterial pause. "By all means, let us hear about it."

"For two weeks I've been teaching at St. Joseph's Free School in Greenwich Village." She had recovered her voice and with it the fervor of conviction. "Practice teaching, really, but it has shown me the needs of the children that are unfulfilled. Sixty boys and girls are to graduate from St. Joseph's in June, but only a mere handful can afford to go on to high school."

"The blight of poverty!"

"The girls are the worst victims. Exactly four will continue their education, and I asked myself . . . why not a Catholic high school, tuition free, for the girls of the archdiocese? The need for such a school is acute, and I would regard it a privilege to work in that behalf."

"Ah, the battle for our schools." The Archbishop rose pensively from his chair and went to the lace-curtained window that looked onto Madison Avenue. "Originally, and not that long ago, the public schools of the city were governed by a board of men, all of whom were Protestants. The result was that Protestant doctrine was incorporated into the school system. Understandably the city's Catholics balked at having to subject their children to these teachings, but the board resisted every attempt to change its policy. It left us with no alternative but to establish parochial schools for our children. The battle, however, extends much further than that perimeter."

"It is a ceaseless battle," contributed Monsignor Hayes with a grave nod of assent.

Archbishop Farley looked across Madison Avenue at the Villard mansions that were sequestered in a private court behind towering gates. For him the mansions symbolized a force as real and mighty as that represented by his purple robes and pectoral cross. He turned to Louise with a gesture that forgave her ignorance of a country to which she was so newly arrived.

"Religious freedom is guaranteed by our Constitution, but the reality is another story," Farley observed. "The men who colonized America came here in pursuit of that freedom, but strictly in terms of their own sects. The founding fathers of our nation were Protestants, and they went on to control the wealth as well as the government. The Constitution does not refer to it, but America is a Protestant nation and heir to the old prejudices and divisions that trace back to England's break with Rome. The bias against Catholics here is almost as virulent as that of the English for the Irish."

"The comparison would not have occurred to me," Louise said, caught up in the emotion that colored the Archbishop's words.

"So you see, Mother Maguire, you find yourself on a battleground," he went on. "The poor that you speak of—we are the Church of the poor and they are our loyal troops. Nothing fills me with deeper pride than the immigrant poor who helped to build our diocese. When I walk up Fifth Avenue past the mansions, block after block, I think of the maids and footmen in those mansions whose pennies and dimes went to buy the stones and mortar of St. Patrick's. It is for them, the poor, that we celebrate the centennial."

"Of course," said Father Regan, brushing lint from his coat sleeve, "that's not to ignore our great benefactors . . . men, say, of the caliber of Connolly Moore."

The name itself invoked a moment's silence, during which the Archbishop returned to his chair. "Quite so, a man of exceptional merit, but I daresay," he inquired of Louise, "you have not yet heard of him?"

The gears had shifted with an almost audible click. "I believe I heard Father Regan refer to him, but not by name."

"What honor invests the name of Connolly Moore!" Farley eulogized. "He is a trustee of the cathedral, which without him would be in ruinous debt. He has given us the Poor Boys Fund and other charities too numerous to list. Connolly sprang from poverty, but in his wealth he has not forgotten the poor. If the Irish of the city were to select the man who best exemplifies their hopes and strivings, it would be him."

Clearly a response was expected, but Louise was trying to fathom how in one leap the conversation had moved to its present subject. Or was that where it was headed all along? The answer was obvious and she chided herself for being a nincompoop.

"Forgive me, Your Excellency, but I'm somewhat confused. If we are discussing the project that I'm told Mr. Moore has in mind, then I'd welcome—"

"All in good time, Mother Maguire, all in good time." Farley rose from his chair and turned to consult Monsignor Hayes. "Are we in accord as to the next step?"

"It's my estimate that Father Regan hit it right on the mark."

"Mine too." The Archbishop proceeded to a desk at the other end of the room. "We expect tremendous crowds at the centennial parade," he said to Louise, "but these tickets will admit you to the reserved section."

There was no choice for her but to accept the tickets and restrain the questions on her lips. "Thank you, Your Excellency."

"The parade will serve as your introduction to Connolly Moore, who is to be the grand marshal. We'll let him tell you of his project at some later date."

She had that much to go on, along with Father Regan's congratulations as he escorted her back across the marble foyer. The pose of aloofness was dropped in his obvious pleasure at how well she had performed.

"Sorry to act the cold fish, but I had to let you sink or swim on your own."

"Swim? It was barely a paddle, and I'd appreciate some tiny kernel of—"

"It's big, M. G." Even as he smiled his pleasure, Regan was gesturing her out of the door. "Big doings are in store for you, I guarantee it."

She exited from the Archbishop's residence no better informed than when she had pressed the bell, and on the ride downtown the name of Connolly Moore rang in her mind as repeatedly as the trolley's clang.

The Sisters at the convent did not lack for information about the man. That afternoon, returning from school, they crowded around Louise in the parlor, eager to hear every detail of the appointment with Archbishop Farley. It was thrilling all by itself, but to learn that Connolly Moore was behind it elicited cries of wonder and incredulity.

"Bless us, you must have passed by a Shamrock dozens of times," Sister Matilda expostulated. "Go over to Hudson Street, or Bleeker or Christopher, or anywhere in the city, and you'll find the grocery stores that made Connolly Moore a millionaire. You can't mistake them, with the big shamrock painted on the sign and the green storefronts. I doubt there's an Irish family in the city that shops elsewhere for groceries."

"He started out penniless, off the boat," another Sister took up the account. "He built a chain of stores bigger than the A and P and his charities were on an equal scale."

"Not that his life is without tragedy," one doleful Sister vouched. "He married the most beautiful Irish girl in New York, a queen of beauty, but she died a few years ago and left him a broken man for a time."

"Connolly Moore," Sister Matilda summed it up, "is the pride of his people and the help of the poor, and a dashing romantic figure to boot."

"When are you to meet with him and for what purpose?"

"Not until after the centennial." Louise produced the parade tickets, which were as scarce as hen's teeth to obtain and brought a fresh wave of excitement. "The date is still to be set. As for the purpose ... I'm as much in the dark as anyone."

The Sisters went off in a chorus of speculations to the basement refectory for tea. Louise was going up the stairs to her room to sort out her thoughts when Sister Matilda called to her.

"Sakes alive, I forgot your cablegram. It came this morning just after you left."

Louise took the tissue-thin envelope and by pushing at the cellophane slot verified from where it had been sent. "At last a reply from the Motherhouse," she laughed. "I can hazard a guess as to the contents."

"Now, don't get in a stew about it." Matilda reached a hand to the banister. "It's right for you to stay here. I'll go pray in the chapel for that intention and we'll trust in the Lord."

A buzz saw of snores greeted Louise as she went into the back room on the second floor. The white curtains stirred in the breeze, and on one of the white beds Mère Blanchard was taking her afternoon rest prior to assuming her dinner chores. She looked old but peaceful, and content with her new life.

How to tell Solange that soon their new life was to be curtailed?

Louise stood at the dresser, tapping the cable against her palm. If she had not heeded Father Regan's advice to delay communication with the Motherhouse, it was out of a sense of loyalty, and this was the reward.

Whatever the cablegram's message, it would call upon her vow of obedience ... but not until she had opened and read the cable. Given the leeway of time, her situation might alter dramatically within a few weeks.

She left the cablegram unopened in a dresser drawer and went down the stairs, a name clanging again in her mind as if in rescue.

The approach of Holy Week was secondary to that of the centennial, at least in terms of excitement and anticipation. The holiday air that prevailed in St. Joseph's parish extended to every parish and Catholic home in the city.

Louise spent the days before spring recess at the Free School, rehearsing the students in the hymns for the Children's Masses that were to be held in the churches of the archdiocese. The Sisters exchanged the usual lessons in geography and arithmetic for lectures on the history of the Church in New York. By turn, each class was taken to visit St. Peter's on Barclay Street, the first city parish, and to Old St. Patrick's on Mott Street, where the early history of strife and prejudice had been enacted.

At the convent, the edition of the *Catholic News* devoted to the centennial was passed from Sister to Sister and discussed at length. The guest list for the week's celebration was distinguished, including as it did Cardinal Logue, the Primate of Ireland, Cardinal Gibbons of Philadelphia, the Apostolic Delegate from Washington, and the bishops of fifty dioceses across the nation. Miss Anne Leary, a papal countess, was to entertain the guests at dinner in her upper Fifth Avenue home. The two Cardinals were to be divided between Miss Leary and Mr. Herbert D. Robbins, who was to host a dinner the same evening at *his* Fifth Avenue residence.

The city newspapers gave columns of print to the event as the date for it drew nearer. A rally at Carnegie Hall, banquets at the Catholic Club and the Irish Historical Society, special Masses, and choir recitals were among the festivities that were to culminate in the Saturday parade up Fifth Avenue. Lists were printed of the prominent New Yorkers—Morgan O'Brien, Adrian Iselin, Maurice Bouvier, Clarence Mackay, Gerald Borden—who were to march in the parade. As Louise noted with nervous anticipation, the name that appeared most frequently in print was that of the parade's grand marshal.

In the years afterward, she was never to retain a clear memory of the parade, only intermittent pictures of it. She would recall leaving the convent with Solange that Saturday morning to go with the Sisters to watch the platoons of men from the Knights of Columbus, the Ancient Order of the Hibernians, the Friendly Sons of St. Patrick, and the parish Holy Name Sodalities assemble for the march in Washington Square Park. Because of the crowds, the Sisters had voted for the El as the swiftest means of transit uptown, and Louise would remember in alarm the mob-packed cars rocketing over the Sixth Avenue tracks while the crowds below fought onto the trolleys at every corner. It seemed as if for this one day all of New York had turned Catholic for the parade. The crowds were jolly and good-natured, but so dense that it was a struggle to walk the one block from the El to the parade site.

The reserved tickets admitted Louise and Solange to the roped-off block of sidewalk across from the cathedral. The Sisters had managed to obtain some tickets, not enough to go around, but the indulgent police officers waved them all past the ropes.

Vivid in Louise's memory would be the brilliant reds, purples, and lavenders of the Cardinals, Bishops, and Monsignori who were seated in the grandstand erected on the cathedral steps. The colors were dazzling in the bright noon sun, and Archbishop Farley looked supremely gratified at the record turnout for the climactic day of the centennial. Monsignor Hayes was at his side, and moving astutely among the grandstand elect was Father Regan. Louise had not heard from him since the meeting with the Archbishop. It puzzled her for she couldn't think of a reason for his sudden disinvolvement in her affairs.

As far as her eye could travel, the blocks up and down Fifth Avenue were crowded to the curb with spectators, pressed ten deep against the stoops and iron fences of the mansions. They were for Louise the steerage immigrants, the legions of Germans, Poles, Italians, Slavs, Czechs, and Irish who had safely arrived in port and were bound today by a common faith stronger and more powerful than allegiance to flag and state.

The attention of the massed crowds was focused on the distant blocks of lower Fifth Avenue, from which sounded the ruffle of drums and the blare of fifes and cornets. A deafening roar went up and Louise caught her breath as the line of marchers swung into view in the sunlight, an unforgettable spectacle.

Yet it was at this very juncture that Louise's memory of the parade in later years became blurred and indistinct.

The marching columns were led by three men on horseback, but out in front of them rode the grand marshal in solitary splendor. He was broad of shoulder, militarily erect, and dressed formally in a silk top hat and black riding coat and britches of superb cut. He rode the black charger with practiced aplomb and the sunlight flashed off his silver stirrups and the polished gleam of his riding boots. He reined in the prancing, snorting horse tightly, and rode the blocks to the cathedral grandstand amid the blare of music and the roar of the crowd.

The stunning figure on the prancing horse drew nearer in the thunder of cheers, and Sister Matilda turned to Louise at the curb. "I needn't tell you who *that* is," she declared. "You've nothing to fear, with the likes of Connolly Moore behind you. Any day now you'll be hearing from him."

The grand marshal, as he passed in front of the cathedral, lifted the silk top hat from the silvery hair and made a sweeping bow of homage to the grandstand. He rode past Louise and she stared after him, aware that her future was as much in the grip of his hands as were the reins of his horse, a future that left her without alternatives.

By then she had opened the cablegram and read the message, a thrifty composition that had instructed, *"RETURN AT ONCE."*

EIGHT

The morning had gotten off schedule, but Patrick Connolly Moore had set it right again.

He stood toweling himself in front of the pier glass in his dressing room at Faircrest, the country estate on the Hudson that afforded him considerable pride of ownership. Earlier, he'd been awakened at dawn by the groom from the stables with the news that Lady Erin, the Widener mare, was in foal. The treacherous breech birth, at which Connolly had assisted, had shorn two hours from the morning and had almost cost the lives of mare and colt.

Almost, but once delivered the frisky colt had lurched up on wobbly legs, hungry for the teat. Connolly had then repaired the morning schedule. He'd arranged for a nine instead of ten o'clock Sunday Mass to be said in the library. The hour's gain had permitted breakfast with his daughters, though at a quickened pace. Kinsella, who managed the farm at Faircrest, had asked to discuss a new irrigation system, but instead of visiting the farm, Connolly had summoned the manager to the manor house. By eleven o'clock the morning was back on track. Promptly at 11:30, Boylan, the chauffeur, had driven off to meet the 12:10 from the city at the Peekskill depot. It pleased Connolly that he still had time for a shower and change of clothes before his guests arrived for lunch.

He was not pleased with the reflection in the pier glass, as he discarded the towel. It showed the muscular body of a man several years younger than forty-eight, but with a definite thickening at the waist. The hairy legs were disproportionately short for the torso and Connolly couldn't change that, but he made a mental note to add an hour to his morning ride and calisthenics. Faircrest was limited to three-day weekends, and the balance of the week was spent in the city. He blamed the thickened waist on the enticements of New York, although these were not restricted to the pleasures of the table.

Connolly Moore was a firm believer in change, indeed, was a product of it, but as he padded naked into the bedroom, he sniffed at his talcum-powdered body to verify that the needle-spray shower had erased the stable smells. For most of his boyhood Connolly had bunked in the stables of Camden Court, the baronet's estate in Wicklow where he was born Paddy Moore, the gamekeeper's son. He'd chosen the stables in preference to his father's roof, despising his parent for the fawning servitude that concealed a mean and petty tyranny. The clashes between father and son were such that at fourteen young Paddy had run away. He'd taken with him a sack of stolen silver to compensate for the wages he felt the elder Paddy had cheated him of.

Jonah, the butler, had laid out a change of clothes on the colossal four-poster in the master bedroom, but Connolly's gaze went to the door that connected with the rooms his wife had occupied before her death. Twelve years ago, when he'd acquired Faircrest, Connolly had made over the north bedrooms into luxurious suites for Rose and himself. The resemblance of the Georgian manor house to Camden Court had gratified him, and he'd expected to enjoy the style of living to which success had entitled him, but, alas, Rose's notion of style was sadly . . .

Today was for her, Connolly vowed, dressing with alacrity to be ready to receive his guests. The proposed school would have made Rose happy, with the nuns to counsel her daughters and guide them to maturity, and he chose to ignore the aspect of it that had to do with the settling of old scores. In twelve years at Faircrest, he had yet to be invited to the estates of his neighbors, for reasons well known to him. How it would infuriate them, a Catholic school opened in their exclusive midst.

Connolly dressed himself in hacking jacket, tattersal shirt, and cord britches, relishing the feel of French silk and Scottish wool. The English-made clothes helped to dispel the image he carried of himself barefoot and in rags, straight off the Ellis Island ferry, groveling for the miserable job in McGreevey's grocery on Ninth Avenue. The pay was two dollars a week, out of which he'd paid back fifty cents for the privilege of sleeping in the back of the store, where, hidden under the floorboards, lay the silver goblets that were to set him on the road to riches.

The gold wafer-thin Boucheron watch read 12:25. Connolly slipped it into the pocket of his britches, calculating that his guests would arrive in exactly nine minutes. He stood for a moment at the balconied window admiring the scene below. The Hudson flowed in a wide expanse, dotted with islands, with Storm King Mountain to the north and the green hump of Bear Mountain on the opposite shore. Here, in the miles between Croton and Poughkeepsie, the Hudson Valley provided some of its most spectacular scenery. The gentry had for generations claimed the view for their own, but now Connolly owned a share of it, and so would the school for which, as a bargaining tool with the Archbishop, he'd already secured the property.

Connolly's boots struck the polished stairs that swept in a graceful curve to the great hall of Faircrest. As he descended he knotted a foulard scarf at his throat and whistled, incongruously, a few bars of "Danny Boy." The peaked black brows in the square-jawed face made a virile contrast to the silver hair, but the aggressive thrust of chin was refuted by a look in the steel-blue eyes, ever to seek and yet to find.

"Lunch at one o'clock sharp, Jonah. The nuns are to be served in the breakfast room—it's against their rule to eat with seculars."

"Yessuh." Jonah Reeves set a Waterford bowl of pink roses on the Chippendale sideboard in the hall. He was accustomed to priests at Faircrest, ranging from Cardinals to South Seas missionaries, but nuns were a new departure. "De breakfas' room, like you say."

"Did you tell Clarice to make plenty of beaten biscuits to go with the baked ham?"

The cook was Jonah's wife, as soft-voiced and light-skinned as he. "Yessuh, she fixin' to."

"No biscuits for me, I'm putting on weight, but our guests will enjoy them."

Between Connolly and his butler had grown a close but unspoken bond. Jonah and Clarice were from Kentucky, hired during one of

Connolly's annual jaunts to the Derby. It had set a precedent and the other servants, Ruby, Della, and Mamie, had all traveled north to work for Connolly, but it was Jonah's vigilance and supervision that had made Faircrest a house of flawless service and enviable comforts. More than that, Connolly was indebted to the butler for reasons that, while never alluded to, were known to them both.

"The table is to be set with the China Export?"

"Yessuh."

Connolly whacked at his middle, overtaken by a sense of well-being derived from the splendid rooms whose archways opened from the hall, a vista of high-ceilinged opulence. The furnishings were eighteenth century, French and English antiques from the best dealers in New York. If their authenticity gave the rooms somewhat the quality of a museum, the caliber of selection, whether Connolly's or the dealers', was impeccable. In the hall a portrait of Connolly was hung above the sideboard, depicting him in the court dress of a Papal Marquis. It represented the summit of the honors the Church had conferred on the ragged youth who had slept in the back of McGreevey's grocery store, the youth who had pawned the stolen silver, gnawed by ambition and a hunger for justice.

The portrait was not a match for another in the house, but Connolly was proud of it. He recalled, as he crossed the black-and-white marble squares of the hall, that Father Regan had located the artist for him in Rome. Clever fellow, Regan, for he'd also found a nun for the projected school. Of course, whether she was suitable was still to be judged, and not by Regan.

Connolly marched onto the east terrace of Faircrest, which overlooked the lawns that sloped down to the wrought-iron gates. He took up his position as host under the white columns of the portico and surveyed this portion of his domain. The cavorting Irish setters had erupted into joyous yelps and two of Connolly's daughters had paused in their lawn play to shout and wave at him. Flavin, the eldest, who was seated on an Adirondack bench, glanced up shyly from her music scores.

What a contrast between the sisters! Monica and Anastasia were engaged in a roughhouse game of tag, hair ribbons flying, white lace dresses from Paris rumpled and grass-stained, while Flavin was as fresh and pristine as when she'd knelt in the library at Mass. At seven, roly-poly Monica possessed a generous and affectionate nature, and little else in her father's estimate. Anastasia, with her temper tantrums, gave every indication at nine of stormy trouble ahead. The discipline of school was essential if the two girls were not to grow into hoydens. A succession of governesses had failed to instill in them any degree of refinement and gentility that were Flavin's possessions since birth.

Impatient for his guests to arrive, Connolly turned his gaze upon the oval, midway up from the gates, around which the graveled drive circled before it continued on to the house. The oval was planted with privet hedge, clipped in the shape of a gigantic shamrock, clearly visible from the road. It was a deliberate vulgarism in the elegant acreage of Faircrest, a defiant announcement to passersby of the owner's antecedents and the tradesman's source of his wealth. . . .

The silver goblets were his, payment for injustice and servitude, of that Paddy Moore hadn't a doubt. For two years he'd slept over the hidden cache in the back of the grocery store, digging it up every few nights to make sure that McGreevey hadn't appropriated it for his own. The man was cut from the same cloth as the elder Paddy, a petty tyrant who cheated his customers while he fawned over them and concealed a vicious streak that itched to wield the strap. McGreevey had worked Paddy from dawn to night and doled out the weekly two dollars pay minus the fifty cents for "lodging" and deductions for food. Even then, a nickel or dime would invariably be missing from the pay.

For two years Paddy had gone without supper to save up the price of a brown-checked suit and yellow shoes, which he bought from a peddler's cart, in order to attend Sunday Mass. The village church had been his mother's refuge from the beatings of life, which was to say her husband. Paddy had begged her to leave with him: The question, after all, was whom did she love? She had stayed behind, but the faith she had taught her son had crossed the ocean with him. Each Sunday at Mass he prayed for the day that his mother would come to make her home with him.

In one respect Paddy had profited from working for McGreevey. He'd learned the grocery business and had shown a talent for merchandising, the subtle differences that spelled success or failure. The extent of what he had learned was owed to McGreevey's weakness for the racetrack, which often left the hireling in charge of the store. At sixteen Paddy had grown into manhood and sported a black beard that he trimmed each morning, stripped naked, his body diligently scrubbed clean. He was popular with the customers, courteous and obliging, and held himself at a proud distance that intrigued the Irish housewives from the tenements, who made up the bulk of trade. The trick, he learned, was not to sell a woman what she wanted, but what she didn't want, and Paddy grew deft and accomplished at it. His most valuable lessons were taught at the wholesale markets, where McGreevey, off to the racetrack, sent him to buy supplies for the store. Volume was the secret of buying at the markets. A crate of eggs, wholesale, cost seventy cents, but ten crates cost six dollars. The discount increased with the number of crates and allowed for a lower retail price while still netting a profit. In the grocery business, profit was measured in pennies, but pennies were turned into dollars, hundreds, maybe thousands of dollars, by the volume of sales. It was the secret behind the success of the Atlantic & Pacific stores that were multiplying throughout the city.

Paddy hungered for a store of his own, where he could implement his ideas and methods for attracting customers. A store of his own, yet not a dollar, not even a dime, to finance it, nor had he the credentials for a bank loan. The hunger festered in him, fed by his hatred of McGreevey and the need to avenge the injustices committed against him. Still, it was months before Paddy was willing to part with the hidden cache as a means toward his goal.

The silver goblets were worth money, he knew that from having pawned one of them in Cork to pay for his steerage ticket—but how much would the remaining five goblets and matching tray fetch? Not enough to open a store, but money in the pocket was better than empty pockets. At least it would give him the push to look for a better job.

The year was 1877 and Paddy Moore was seventeen when he dug the sack from the floorboards one morning at dawn. McGreevey had refused to give him the day off, but that was incentive to go ahead with his scheme. Paddy had long since explored the city beyond the West Twenties neighborhood where the store was located. Sunday excursions had taken him south to the Battery and north to the outer environs of Central Park and Harlem. Dressed that morning in the brown-checked suit and yellow shoes, he headed for the Tenderloin strip in the West Thirties, a gaudy district of pool halls and honky-tonks, painted women on street corners, and pawnshops.

All that day, Paddy trudged from one pawnbroker to another, puzzled by the sums offered for his wares. The Jew in the first pawnshop had specified fifty dollars for the goblets and tray, and when Paddy hesitated, he upped the price to seventy-five. The other offers were much lower, and by the end of the day Paddy reasoned that either the first Jew had overestimated the value or he himself had underestimated it. The solution, he concluded, was to consult an expert on the value of silver.

Late that night, Paddy stole back into McGreevey's and performed the ritual washing of his body: Would he never be rid of the smell of the stables? Crouched over the silver, he polished it to a gleaming and perceived why he'd taken so long to part with it. It was beautiful, and he was starved for something of beauty in his life.

Again Paddy was gone from the store before dawn, suit brushed clean, shoes shined to a gloss. This time he was bound for the Metropolitan Museum of Art, which, until its new building uptown on Fifth Avenue was completed, occupied temporary quarters on West Fourteenth Street. Paddy was directed to the curator of silver, who checked his catalogs and appraised the value of the goblets and tray at one thousand dollars as rare examples of the work of Paul DeLamerie, a London silversmith of the early eighteenth century. Paddy responded with a tale of a widowed mother reduced to poverty and forced to sell the family heirlooms. The curator gave him the address of a dealer in antique silver on Broadway at Twenty-first Street, where Paddy repeated his tale and declined to accept a penny less than the appraised value, in cash. He walked from the dealer's with ten one-hundred-dollar bills in his pocket, but faint from hunger having eaten almost nothing in two days.

Paddy Moore eyed the fashionable area of shops and department stores and the ladies in plumed hats who were assisted by footmen from carriages. For lunch he selected the Fifth Avenue Hotel, which he'd admired from the sidewalk on his Sunday excursions. To enter the plush lobby took all of his daring, but when he compared his cheap suit with those of the gentlemen he observed in the lobby, Paddy made a hasty retreat. Vowing that someday he would frequent such a hotel the equal of any gentleman, Paddy settled for ribs of beef in a nearby chophouse. Hunger appeased, he covered the blocks across town to the grocery store on Ninth Avenue. Rage smoldered in him and his eyes flashed, as if he were about to confront his father in a reckoning for the years of cruelty.

"If yer lookin' to keep your job, forget it," McGreevey snarled from behind the counter.

"I'm lookin' to buy your store," Paddy hurled back at him, legs astride the doorway.

By 1887, when he was not yet thirty, Paddy Moore was the owner of eight grocery stores in New York City, which were identified by the green fronts and the signboards that had been a chance invention with the first store. Having spent his last dollar on the renovations and stock, he had painted the first sign himself, embellished with shamrocks for want of lettering. "Hurry, darlin', and run to the Shamrock for a quart a' milk," the Irish housewives were soon bidding their children, which gave the store both a name and a trademark. Later on, the canisters of tea that were a store favorite, the newspaper advertisements, and still later the gift coupons, all were embellished with the distinctive shamrock trademark, a lure to the particular customer Paddy wished to attract.

New York was a city of ethnic neighborhoods, and the stores were located wherever the Irish predominated. Immigration had reached a peak of two million in 1890, and the new arrivals flocked, as those before them, to what was familiar from the old country. Pasta in a shop window signaled home to the Italian, links of sausage to the German, and Paddy's shamrock was a beacon for the Irish. The stores were staffed by Irish clerks in white butcher aprons and green shirts whose brogues were as thick as those of the customers they served, and who were not adverse to a friendly chat while they scooped coffee beans from a shamrock canister or sliced into a wheel of cheese. Yet value was the trademark that accounted for the steady ring of the cash register.

Every item in stock was priced at a penny less than the competing stores. Friday was payday for the typical Shamrock customer and crowds stormed the doors for the famous Saturday half-price sales, unrivaled by the competition. The profits were in pennies, but with the volume of business generated by the number of stores and the corresponding discounts from the wholesalers, the weekly profits totaled in the thousands.

By 1892 the number of stores had increased by half, with

branches in each of the boroughs of the city. Shamrock Enterprises, incorporated as a private company, occupied a suite of offices in a prestigious new building on Twenty-third Street. Paddy had developed an interest in real estate, and was negotiating for the purchase of the building. He signed the payroll checks "P. Connolly Moore," though it was a curious fact that the employees did not refer to him by name. They regarded him as a hard taskmaster, but fair-minded and ready to reward excellence. Promotion was from within the company. The executive officers of Shamrock were all former store clerks and were genuine in their devotion and loyalty, but none claimed to know P. Connolly Moore to any personal degree, and so they called him "the Chief."

Connolly occupied modest bachelor rooms in a brownstone on West Twenty-fifth Street, a block away from St. Columba, the parish church where he had worshiped as a youth. It was not generally realized that he owned the brownstone as well as the livery stable around the corner, where he kept a horse for morning canters in Central Park. For a man as prominent and active in the neighborhood, P. Connolly Moore was a figure of remoteness and even of mystery. He'd clerked at McGreevey's not so long ago, but that youth was not discernible in the reserved and autocratic man of thirty-three, his black hair flecked with silver, who was difficult to approach on any but a business level.

When Connolly entertained, it was at hotels and restaurants, but two evenings a week he received a visitor in his rooms. Gordon Morris, an English instructor at Columbia College, came twice weekly to tutor Connolly in grammar and literature. One by one the books grew on Connolly's shelves—the plays of Shakespeare, novels by Dickens and Scott, and current works by Tolstoi and Galsworthy. Gordon Morris was an impecunious member of an old and distinguished New York family, and his background proved useful to his pupil. Morris introduced Connolly to Briggs, the English tailor on Fourth Avenue who thereafter made his clothes. Morris was Connolly's guide to the opera at the Academy of Music and to the theaters—Wallack's, Daly's, the Star—that clustered in a diadem of lights in the vicinity of Union Square. The two men would sup after the theater at Delmonico's, which provided lessons in dining and etiquette, until the evening that Gordon Morris blundered.

"You've heard me speak of Cousin Ethel, who has that divine

place at Newport? Well, you keep reminding me of someone, and I've finally realized who it is."

"Oh? Who?"

"You remind me of Ethel's coachman—Pat or Mike, one of those names, but a dead ringer for you."

Morris was at a loss to understand it when his services were terminated shortly afterward. He needed the money and it was a damnable nuisance to be cut off from it for no apparent reason.

Connolly's neighborhood activities were centered on two organizations, both of equal dominion in his life. He belonged to the local Tammany Club, which represented the Democratic party of New York City. The drama of torchlight parades and fiery orations at city elections appealed to Connolly. He felt a kinship with the men of Tammany, who shared his ancestry of deprivation and were redressing, as he was, a wanton fate. The fact that the men were largely crooks and grafters offended his sensibility, but it did not prevent him from buying the municipal favors that the men peddled. The deeds to city-owned lots were sold to Connolly in backroom deals, cash in a paper bag, rather than at public auction. If it troubled his conscience, that was the concern of his other neighborhood involvement, the parish church.

He was a trustee of St. Columba's and a generous and unstinting supporter of the church's needs. The poinsettias that banked the altar at Christmas, the lilies at Easter, the Thanksgiving turkeys for the poor, were gifts of Connolly's. He paid for the new church roof, and for the uniforms that had enabled the school band to march in the annual St. Patrick's Day parade. The ushers at Sunday Mass were outfitted with frock coats and gray-striped trousers from Briggs, thanks to Connolly Moore. He served as head usher at the ten o'clock Sunday Mass, and the women of the parish vied to have him escort them up the aisle. Mass was as close as they got to Connolly, since at other times he chose to visit the church when it was empty.

Annie Moore had not come to America to live with her son, and Connolly sought solace for her absence at church. He chose the hour before evening devotions for his visits, alone in the empty pews as he was alone in the world. He did not want to be alone, and yet he knew that he had shut himself off from the everyday intercourse that might have altered his circumstances. Money was Connolly's abiding pursuit, and he didn't apologize for it, but money was poor compensation for his growing loneliness. The Chief, they called him at Shamrock, when he wanted to be called friend and husband, lover and father as well. Connolly believed implicitly that God loved him, but in his lonely vigil in the empty church he feared that he risked the forfeit of God's love. There were secrets that he dared to confide only in the confessional.

It was as if under the floorboards, instead of the silver, Connolly had taken to hiding secrets.

He was a secret drinker, periodic bouts with the whiskey bottle conducted behind the locked door of his bachelor rooms. Connolly drank to blot out the memory of his father's abuse and the sting of the whip on his back, which he still could hear in his dreams. He drank to obliterate another of his secrets, which concerned the painted women of the Tenderloin and later the silk-and-satin brothel uptown that he patronized. At least the whores didn't pretend they were selling love. It was strictly a money transaction, but the thought did nothing to stem his disgust for the women or himself. Some nights, the drinking turned violent and resulted in smashed furniture, broken lamps, and shattered mirrors. Those were the worst nights, when Connolly was haunted by a fear that the whiskey could not eradicate.

The fear, Connolly's secret, haunting fear, was that despite the money, the gentleman's clothes and manner, the patina of cultivated taste, he was no different from the cruel and devious father that he despised. Connolly kept a revolver locked in a drawer, and on the drunken nights when the fear overwhelmed him, he would smash a chair or hurl a bottle against a mirror in order not to seize the revolver and press it to his temple.

The morning after these nights and the nights with the whores, Connolly traveled to distant churches in the city. He was too ashamed to confess his sins to someone other than a priest who was a stranger. Kneeling at the altar rail, he said his penance and asked for God's forgiveness. He prayed for help, for something to happen that would redeem his life and save him from ruin.

And in the spring of 1893 at Sunday Mass at St. Columba, when Connolly glimpsed the radiant girl poised in the church vestibule, he felt as if the heavens had opened and delivered an angel into his life. He stared at her like a country bumpkin, but somehow his feet propelled him forward. She was accompanied by an older couple, whom he ignored; he simply offered the girl his arm, as though to his bride at the altar.

Mary Rose Falvin was eighteen, and off the boat less than a week that Sunday. A knitted shawl, a calico dress, and a straw hat were her clothes, but with them she wore the raiment of beauty. Spun-gold hair flowed down her back, and her face, the arch of her nose, the curve of her cheekbones, the bud of her mouth, was perfectly formed. Rose Flavin blushed under Connolly's rude stare and drew back to the protection of her aunt and uncle, who were the older couple. Yet she had no choice except to take the proffered arm and go up the aisle.

After Mass, coming down the church steps, Rose encountered Connolly again, shouldering toward her through the crowd of worshipers. He greeted her aunt and uncle, whom evidently he knew from the parish. Rose sensed the effort it cost him to approach and smiled as they were introduced, but she thought little about it afterward.

The last thing on Rose Flavin's mind was matrimony. She had come from Tralee in County Meath to live with her Aunt Bea and Uncle Mike Nugent in a tenement flat on Tenth Avenue for the purpose of securing employment. This she did the day after meeting Connolly, as a waitress at Maillard's Confectionary and Tea Room on Fifth Avenue. The eldest of four, Rose was determined to bring over her three younger brothers, and for that she needed passage money. She paid no attention to Uncle Mike's talk of the richest man in the parish, who was the despair of every mother with a marriageable daughter. Rose was in no hurry to think of marriage, certainly not until she'd set up house for her brothers, and maybe not even then.

It took a year for Connolly to change the thinking of Rose Flavin, in a whirlwind courtship that left her without recourse to anything but his wishes.

The Saturday night following their meeting Connolly did not appear at the Nugents' flat, but he sent a barbershop quartet to serenade Rose, to her acute embarrassment, from the sidewalk below.

The pale moon was rising above the green mountain,
The sun was declining beneath the blue sea . . .

She was for Connolly the rose of the song, "The Rose of Tralee," *his* Rose, and never had he pursued a prize as ardently or relentlessly, armed with as many inducements. The following Saturday, having asked Uncle Mike's permission, Connolly called at the flat with a bouquet of red roses so big that Rose could scarcely see him behind it in the doorway.

"A tribute," he said, offering the bouquet, "to the loveliest rose in New York."

From the start of the courtship Rose Flavin had misgivings, but she was unable to express them in the shower of gifts and attentions that rained upon her. She had only to mention her love of music and a piano arrived, hoisted up by ropes over the fire escapes. Connolly arranged piano lessons for her and squired her to the Metropolitan Opera and to concerts at Carnegie Hall. For her birthday, Rose was feted with a private recital by the celebrated tenor Chauncey Olcott in the ballroom of the Astor Hotel. Later, she tried to explain to Connolly it was the music she cared for and that she'd as soon listen to it from the peanut gallery as from a box or in an audience of two.

"You see, Connolly . . . money isn't important to me, it simply isn't."

"Of course not, I've only begun to show you what it can buy."

"No, really, I—"

"Allow me the honor of showing you, Rose."

Allow it or not, Rose returned from work one afternoon to find her three brothers grinning at her from the tenement stoop. Aunt Bea and Uncle Mike, who had been conspirators in the plot, were on hand to take the party up to the flat on the second floor, rented and furnished in advance. To top it off, Connolly had jobs waiting for the brothers at Shamrock. At dinner that night he apologized to Rose for the secrecy that had cloaked his actions.

"Otherwise, I knew you wouldn't accept."

"I . . . Connolly, I've no way of thanking you."

"Oh, I beg to differ."

"Forgive me, but I feel as if I've fallen into debt, way over my head, and it frightens me."

"Marry me, Rose."

"I—I must look after my brothers."

"Your Aunt Bea's in the same building. She'll look after them."

"I've not really thought of marrying, except in terms of the future."

"The future, my Rose of Tralee, shines before us."

That spring, a year after they'd met, Connolly strolled with Rose Flavin in the greenery of Madison Square Park. She wore an afternoon dress of lavender georgette and a Gainsborough hat with a matching plume. Aunt Bea had insisted that she provide her niece with the clothes suitable to a man of Connolly's position. From the park the couple went to the Fifth Avenue Hotel, where Connolly had reserved a window table for luncheon. Later, a gilt elevator whisked the couple to a suite of rooms overlooking the park and Connolly presented Rose with the keys to the suite. She backed away when he produced a blue-leather jewelry box from Tiffany.

"No, wait, let me speak my mind for once. I'm not the sort to live in a hotel; it's far too grand for my taste. I want a simple home and a simple life."

"Hotels are a convenience, but what would you say to a country home up on the Hudson?"

"I'm content with a railroad flat."

"My dear Rose, you are the most beautiful woman in New York, and I shall make New York cognizant of it."

"Why can't you see that I'm the wrong choice for you, and not someone to show off in jewels and fancy gowns. I'd be no good at it and such a disappointment."

"Rose, I'm alone in the world, and lost, more lost than you know."

"Yes, I've sensed it about you, so alone and closed off . . ."

"Then love me, can't you?"

Rose faltered at the tears in Connolly's eyes. Her defenses crumbled before the loneliness in him that reached out to her.

"To our life together." He slipped the ten-carat ring on her finger. "We will be happy, always and forever, I promise you . . ."

NINE

The dogs were barking and running toward the gates. Glancing over the velvet lawn from the portico, Connolly saw that the Pierce-Arrow had turned in and was coming up the graveled drive.

Twelve-thirty, exactly on schedule.

As the open-top roadster drew closer, Connolly observed that it bore one rather than two nuns. He liked the fact that Mother Maguire looked unperturbed at being on her own. She sat opposite Father Regan in the facing seats of the emerald-green automobile and did not attempt to disguise her pleasure at the leaping, chasing dogs. Connolly approved of the sense of presence she conveyed without having yet uttered a word. She held on to a manila envelope, somewhat combatively he noticed, liking the spirit that it indicated. All these were qualities that the school would demand, and he credited Archbishop Farley with having sent a likely candidate for the difficult assignment.

The Pierce-Arrow swung under the columns of the portico, but Connolly waited until the chauffeur in his dark green livery had handed out the guests before he went to greet them.

"Mother Maguire, how good of you to give up your Sunday and travel to Faircrest."

"Mère Blanchard sends her regrets, Mr. Moore." Louise shook hands and held on to the envelope. "She volunteered to cook for the parish social today and was unable to come."

"We will miss her company. Sean, it's splendid to see you again." Connolly waved at his daughters, who raced up from the lawn. "Here are my poor little rich girls," he boomed, laying the ground-work for his strategy. "Ragamuffins, two of them, but that's the pity of motherless tykes, even with plenty of servants to look after them."

The giggling, dirt-smudged Anastasia and Monica curtsied to the guests. "Flavin, of course, was named for her mother," Connolly said as his quiet eldest daughter reached the steps. "It must be why she is the angel of the house."

The three girls stood awkwardly in a row, and Louise was imme-diately struck by the disparity between them. Flavin was clearly the beauty, with the delicacy of fine porcelain about her, but her sisters looked to be made of sturdier material. The rumpled dresses and dangling hair ribbons had not the slightest effect on Monica and Anastasia's carefree exuberance.

"Upstairs with you, and tell Mamie I want no ragamuffins at the luncheon table," Connolly ordered, and watched the girls file into the house. "They'll grow up wild hoydens at this rate, without de-cent schooling to curb them." He shook his head in distress and turned to his guests. "Well, now, shall we have a brief tour of the place before lunch?"

The tour extended to the Italian gardens at the south end of the manor house and the rose garden at the north end, and was hastily conducted. The stables and paddock were merely indicated from the vantage of the hill above. Connolly was a man of quick decisions that were seldom revoked. He'd made a decision about Louise and was impatient to get on with it. The tour was concluded on the west terrace of the house, with its panoramic view of the Hudson crowned by rolling green hills and the distant Catskills hazed in the golden sunshine.

Louise was awed by the magnificent vista. "It quite robs one of breath, Mr. Moore . . . and speech."

"It doesn't, when I think of what some of my neighbors command. The Astors own thousands of acres up in Rhinebeck. Compared to them or the Roosevelts in Hyde Park, or the Aspinwalls or Delanos or Rogerses, Faircrest is a modest few acres . . . but still it's mine."

Connolly planted his boots on the terrace steps and looked out over the sweep of river and mountain. "I was a stable boy on an es-tate in Wicklow and knew only the back door," he said, and went to open the screened door for his guests. "It didn't take long, I'm glad to report, to accustom myself to the front."

In the great hall he rang for Jonah, who appeared with a tray that held a mint julep in a frosted silver tumbler and two mint-sprigged glasses of iced tea. As instructed, Jonah served the julep to Father Regan.

"You and I are the abstainers," Connolly laughed, clinking glasses with Louise. "Tell us, Sean, how does an American drink go down, after the years in Rome?"

It seemed an effort for Regan to engage in the light banter at which he was so adept. "Well, let's see ... after Chianti, it's like a bolt of lightning."

Off kilter, thought Connolly, studying the young priest. Definitely off kilter and preoccupied by some other concern. He turned to the portrait on the wall. "What's your opinion of that Roman artist you dug up for me?"

Regan looked at Louise and flushed a brick red. "It shows Mr. Moore in his papal court dress—an excellent likeness, I think."

"Ah, but there's a far superior likeness for us to admire." Connolly conducted his guests across the black-and-white squares of the hall to the mahogany-paneled music room. "My beloved wife, as painted by John Singer Sargent."

The gold-framed life-sized portrait was of Rose Flavin Moore seated at the same Beckstein that stood across the music room. She was fabulously gowned in ice-blue satin, white kid opera gloves, and ropes of pearls, and exhibited the fragile, ash-blond beauty that her namesake had inherited. The portrait exemplified the lustrous sheen of opulence for which Sargent was famous, but it was the eyes that compelled Louise's notice from the archway.

"Devil of a time getting him to take the commission," Connolly recounted, standing behind her. "The fellow can pick and choose as he pleases, but a hefty bonus of Shamrock stock did the trick. The pose was my idea."

The eyes, the cornflower-blue eyes, Louise saw, were touched with a sadness that contradicted the portrait's lush aura of wealth and prestige.

"Rose adored music and my idea was to pose her at the piano where she played every day, sometimes for hours." Connolly paused, a gruffness in his voice. "It took a week for the sittings and months before Sargent finished the portrait . . . and within the year my wife was taken from me."

Gripped by emotion, he moved away from his guests. "The rich aren't always as fortunate as is generally imagined," he reflected. "Sorrow makes no distinction between rich and poor."

The remark drew Louise's compassion, as was intended. "Mr. Moore, allow me to express my sympathy at your loss."

"I daresay lunch is a happier subject. Has the country air sharpened your appetites?"

Jonah stood at the entrance to the dining room, the signal that lunch was ready to be served. Down the stairs marched Connolly's daughters, freshly dressed and stiff as dolls, but his mind was already focused on the strategy to follow the meal, which called for the absence of Father Regan.

"Our credo at Faircrest is simple food, well prepared," he went on in his capacity as host. "The fruits and vegetables, butter, eggs, and cream are fresh from our own farm. Mother Maguire, when I arranged for you to lunch in privacy, I did so thinking that you'd have a companion."

"It's no matter," Louise assured him, and then as bidden she proceeded after Jonah down the long corridor.

For all the perfection of the meal, the savory baked ham and scalloped potatoes, the broccoli with hollandaise and the feathery biscuits, Louise was unable to enjoy it. Father Regan's moody silence on the train ride from the city had confused her and his behavior since had seemed to indicate that he'd prefer to be anywhere but in her company. She had liked Connolly Moore at once though she found him overpowering at times, like a gale wind that swept away obstacles in its path, scattering them to left and right.

And what did he want of her? As yet no direct mention of it, but Louise estimated from the remarks about his daughters that he wanted a school for them. The teakwood table inlaid with ivory at which she sat had originally graced a maharajah's summer palace, and it suggested the type of school that would interest a man of Connolly Moore's extravagance.

The maid appeared with dessert, a crystal bowl of fresh strawberries, but Louise's glance was for the manila envelope she had brought with her to the table. It contained the prospectus she had worked out for a city high school for girls, free of tuition fees. The cablegram from Montpellier had spurred Louise into a last, desperate effort to determine her own future. If Connolly Moore intended to propose a school to her, she was no less intent on proposing one to him.

A short interval later, she looked up from her coffee to find her host in the doorway.

"I've packed Father Regan off to the stables with the girls," he announced. "Our prize mare gave birth to a colt this morning. It might cheer him out of the gloom that is so unlike him."

"Yes, I've noticed."

"Come along, I'm taking you for a buggy ride." Connolly handed her the manila envelope as she started from the table. "I expect you'll want this, given the importance you attach to it."

"I . . . yes, I will, thank you."

Waiting below the portico steps was an Irish trap of the kind that Louise had not ridden in since her girlhood, although this one was distinguished by solid silver fittings and a velvet-cushioned seat. The black charger of the centennial parade was hitched to the trap and a groom stood in attendance holding the reins. Connolly assisted Louise into the buggy and relieved the groom of the reins and whip.

"Thank you, Matt." He climbed into the trap and with a crack of the whip the horse cantered smartly down the graveled drive, hooves crunching into the white pebbles, chased by the yelping setters.

"Mr. Moore." Louise held on to her flying veil as the vehicle bounded out the gates onto the road. "May I inquire where we are going?"

"I'll answer your question by asking one. What in that envelope is so important to you?"

She smoothed a hand over the envelope. "It contains hope for the future and myself."

"Go on, I'm listening."

The country road, a green tunnel arched with trees and streamered with May sunlight, made the city streets seem remote and far off. "There is a need in the city for a high school for the girls who cannot afford to continue beyond the primary grades."

"No tuition, do you mean?"

"Free of cost, except for books, a school that would strive for the highest standards of education. I'd gladly devote my life to help foster it." Louise nodded at the envelope. "If the research I've done is accurate, the financing would be modest to start with. It presupposes, of course, that the archdiocese will provide the building and site."

The road turned and brought into view the rusted wrought-iron gates of the property adjacent to Faircrest. "You won't get a dime from Farley," Connolly said, pulling at the reins, "but I can suggest another means of financing."

The horse slowed to a clop and Connolly gestured at the rusted gates, which were padlocked and chained. "We are about to invade enemy territory," he declared. "The Prentices were for years my next-door neighbors, but in the course of that time they did not invite me to enter those gates." He pulled the horse to a stop and climbed from the trap. "Indeed, not until last month when I bought Hightower for the back taxes was I privileged to enter."

He took out a set of keys and applied one to the padlock. The chains fell in a rattle and he pushed back the creaking gates. Then he climbed into the buggy, flicked the whip, and the horse trotted through the gates. "It was, I assure you, a moment to savor."

The weed-choked drive upon which they entered wound steeply upward through firs and evergreens whose forested shade shut out the sunlight. Birds twittered in the pine-scented silence, squirrels and jackrabbits scurried across the rutted road under the prancing hooves of the charger. "Terrible, how the gentry can neglect the land and allow the taxes to pile up," Connolly observed. "Nobody's lived here for the past four years."

The woods dropped behind and sunlight broke through as the drive made its last turn, revealing a broad sweep of ground with the river spread below it. Louise glimpsed a giant oak silhouetted against the sky on a grassy knoll at the top of the drive. Across from the oak stood the house on the rise of a hill, a red-brick Victorian sprawl of turrets and cupolas and gingerbread porches, surmounted by the tower that gave the estate its name. The impression was of neglect and ruin, of weed-grown gardens and lawns, a wilderness reclaiming what had belonged to it.

"Here is my school," Connolly said without preamble, in a tone that invited challenge. He steered the trap around the horseshoe curve of the drive. "Surely you must have surmised my objective by now."

"Not really." Louise sat dumbly in the trap while he tethered the horse to a rusted jockey post below the porch steps of the house. "I am a slow-witted creature, Mr. Moore."

"It is my estimate"—he handed her from the buggy—"that you lack for nothing, except a slight adjustment of priorities."

"You flatter me, but I must tell you—"

"Let me first show you the house." Connolly barged up the porch steps, exerting the right of ownership. "Lots of repair work, but it's to be expected." He flicked the whip at the broken windows, the peeling white paint, and the vines that strangled the porch rail. Birds' nests roosted above in the bracketed eaves. "There'll not be a school in the country to equal it when we're finished. The view, Mother Maguire, just look at the view that is yours."

Hers? It wasn't hers, the breathtaking expanse of river, sky, and hills, Louise wanted to protest, but her host had unlocked the front door and she followed him inside.

Connolly stood in the entrance hall at the foot of the massive carved-oak stairs that turned at a landing and mounted into the shadows above. "Twenty-eight rooms, enough for a start, I think." A stained-glass dome in the roof cast a jeweled light on the whorls of dust that chased across the floor. Dust webbed the oak mantel, carved with a frieze of pine cones above the blackened grate. "Are you familiar with the Sacred Heart nuns, the Madames, as we call them?"

"A French congregation, with a school in New York, I believe."

"Madison and Fifty-fourth, very select and ladylike. The Sacred Heart nuns turned down my proposal, which makes it twice as gratifying to give them some competition."

"Mr. Moore—"

"The Sargent portrait will go up there." Connolly indicated the wall above the mantel. "The school is to be a memorial to my wife. It would have pleased Rose, a school for her daughters, the finest that money can create."

"Mr. Moore, before you proceed any further—"

Connolly opened a pair of sliding doors that led to the drawing room, bare of furnishings and hung with cobwebs but of stately proportions. French windows gave access to the porch that wrapped around the front and sides of the house, and a stone fireplace loomed at one end of the room. "Imagine the teas and receptions you'll give here," Connolly boomed, throwing open the doors to the connecting rooms. "Why, this dining room can easily seat sixty or more. Here's your library and music room, and we'll convert the billiard room into a chapel."

"Mr. Moore," Louise asserted herself. "My plan is for an entirely different school."

"A school for the poor?" Connolly took up an indignant stance at the cavernous fireplace. "Am I to infer that your compassion is reserved for the poor?"

"Not reserved, but—"

"The rich might find it as hard to enter heaven as for a camel to pass through a needle's eye, but would you presume to shut us out?"

The criticism stung Louise. "I'm sorry if I gave that impression."

"The Catholic rich are penalized for the faith they were born to and uphold." Connolly stalked the room, flicking the whip against his palm. "Flavin will be ready for school in September. Ostensibly, she has the pick of the crop—Miss Porter's, Rosemary Hall, Emma Willard—but she is not acceptable to those schools, and I refuse to apply to them. Damn it, I'll provide my daughters with a school of their own faith to match the very best in existence."

Louise was still apologetic. "When I met with Archbishop Farley ... he said that America is a Protestant nation, ruled by Protestants."

"Yes, and you'd be amazed at how many of them think we're in league with Rome and want to put the Pope in the White House, but I'll tell you something." Connolly strode the length and width of the room, beating at his palm with the whip. "I know a fellow up in Albany, name of Al Smith. He's a little guy in a brown derby, Irish as Paddy's pig, from the Lower East Side. When he was elected to the state assembly, Al was a nobody, but today he is the majority leader of the assembly. The talk in some quarters is to run him for governor, and from there, who knows?" Connolly fixed his piercing gaze upon his listener. "It's hogwash about the Pope, but someday by God we'll elect a Catholic to the White House ... and you, Mother Maguire, can be a part of it."

"I—I don't understand."

"What if the wife of the president were a graduate of your school, molded by your principles, formed by your values. Think of the influence she would exert for the good of the nation, and then dare to inform me that such a school is unworthy of your efforts."

Louise gestured in futility. "I seem to be left without a reply."

"The day is past when the want ads read, *'No Irish Need Apply.'*
Our time is coming, I've watched it come, men on the rise, proud to
be Irish and Catholic. Would you deny them a rightful place or the
right school for their daughters?"

"Mr. Moore, I ..." Louise crossed to one of the windows and
looked out at the ruined lawns that sloped below the porch. "The
school I told you of ... you said you could suggest a means to finance it."

"Yes, I said that."

"Then, if I might ask ... ?"

Connolly paused as he often did for dramatic effect. "By making a
success of this school, you will be able to finance the other."

"I doubt that either is possible." Louise turned to him from the
window. "I came to America against the wishes of my superiors.
They have ordered me to return to the Motherhouse."

"You disappoint me," Connolly laughed. "Are you so easily intimidated by your superiors? My friend Cardinal Gatti in Rome will
straighten them out. They'll listen to his request for additional
nuns."

"Nuns of the Society?"

"We'll ask for six; that's a reasonable number to start with, don't
you agree?"

"Oh, indeed." Louise was swept up again by the gale-force wind.
"A reasonable number."

"For my part, I will underwrite the entire cost." Connolly stood at
the fireplace, clasping the whip behind him. "Well, what's to be
your answer? If I've indulged in a certain amount of secrecy, it's because no is difficult for me to accept."

Louise looked out at the wild lawns and imagined them made
smooth and verdant. She imagined a procession of girls moving toward her across the lawns. "I must have time for prayer and reflection."

"Not if the school is to open in September."

She swung around to him with a gasp. "It's simply not possible."

"I like the impossible—one year I opened nine Shamrocks in as
many months."

"It can't be done—and what makes you think I'm the person
for it?"

"The answer is yes?"

Louise hedged, despite the alternative that faced her. "I've not said it is."

"Then say it," urged her benefactor. "We'll have you living here within the week and the other nuns by June. Carpenters, electricians, plumbers, engineers—we'll hire double crews if necessary, but the school will open in September, no question of it."

"The question, Mr. Moore, is whether I'm up to coping with you."

Connolly went toward her from the fireplace. "Trust me," he said, and held out the ring of keys. "Give me your trust and I promise you a long and rewarding partnership."

"But I ..."

Louise did not at once accept the keys, but when her hand closed around them, it was in response to the cablegram as much as to the offer she had received. . . . No, she couldn't go back, not when life had swept her up, so fresh and green with promise after the years of drought.

TEN

Louise awoke the next morning, her lingering doubts at odds with an escalating sense of good fortune and opportunity wrested from defeat.

Mère Blanchard was overtaken by joy as she dressed in the pink streaks of dawn from the window. "It is *la Vierge* who has arranged it," she affirmed with a nod at the wooden carving that reached out its arms from the night table. "Each day I have prayed to the Virgin to find us a home in America, and she has heard my prayers."

"The Motherhouse will be incensed at having to supply nuns for the school. Perhaps Mère Générale will defy the Cardinal when he contacts her."

"She has hoarded power for years and it will benefit her soul to yield it." Solange pinned her veil secure and collected her prayer book. "*Vite allons,* we must not keep the Sisters from Mass."

Louise was made aware that morning of the swift and radical change in her position. When the Sisters left the convent on Waverly Place to teach at the free school, she was obliged to remain behind. It was ended, her association with the school and the lively, inquisitive boys and girls she had grown fond of. The prospectus for the high school lay ignored in the manila envelope in her room. She had not given up on it, but was forced to acknowledge that it would take years before she could implement her plan.

The convent lacked a telephone, but Connolly had said to expect to hear from him and she passed the morning awaiting that prospect. Father Regan's behavior yesterday kept intruding on her thoughts. On being told of the school, he had congratulated her, genuinely pleased and without a trace of resentment at his exclusion from the buggy ride to Hightower. Once on the train to the city, however, Regan had settled into his former moroseness. Connolly had provided parlor-car seats at opposite ends of the coach, since nuns did not travel in the company of priests. Louise's view of Regan, for the two-hour ride to the city, was of his handsome, brooding face staring out the train window. At Grand Central, he'd been abrupt and in haste to depart from her.

"Mind if I just put you on the trolley? It's getting late and I'm tired, and tomorrow's a dreary round of conferences."

Regan had waited with her at the trolley stop, and when she'd turned to board the car, "It's wrong," he'd said in a rush. "Wrong ever to be certain of yourself." Then he'd swung off into the shadows, leaving her with the fading echo of his heels on the sidewalk.

The convent doorbell rang and Louise went to answer it.

The telegram the messenger handed her was from Connolly Moore. It reported at expensive length that he had cabled their needs to Cardinal Gatti in Rome last night and had received a cable in reply assuring him of prompt and effective action. The telegram instructed Louise to reserve her days for a series of appointments in connection with the school.

"GET BUSY AND THINK UP A SWELL NAME FOR US," the telegram exhorted her. *"NOT THE SAME OLD SAINT STUFF BUT SPECIAL AND EYE-CATCHING LIKE SHAMROCK. NO TELEPHONE AT CONVENT A BOTHER BUT WILL MANAGE TO OVERCOME IT."*

Western Union was not Connolly's only device for getting around the lack of a telephone. That afternoon, to the oohs and ahs of the Sisters at the window, the emerald-green Pierce-Arrow rolled up to the curb outside. Boylan, the chauffeur, made a show of bounding up the convent stoop in his dark green livery.

"Compliments of Mr. Moore," said Mick Boylan, infatuated with his importance as he gave Louise the shamrock-embossed letter. "He says to let him know will ya be wantin' the car, 'tis at yer disposal."

Louise was open-mouthed at the folly of herself wafted around the city in the luxury of the Pierce-Arrow. "Thank Mr. Moore, but I'm quite able to use the trolley."

The letter was as imprinted with Connolly's personality as had been the telegram. It listed appointments that would carry Louise through the week and introduce her to lawyers, accountants, textbook publishers, advertising agencies, school and church suppliers, stationers, and the uniform department of B. Altman and Company. The addresses were given and alongside some of the names Connolly had jotted his comments. *"Watch out—crafty,"* he'd warned of John Geoghegan, who was his attorney. *"Susceptible to charm,"* was noted of Edward Donohue, whose agency handled the Shamrock advertising and was to design the school's brochure. *"Come up with name yet?"* queried the bombastic postscript. *"At Plaza Hotel when in city or can reach me at office. Hightower ready for you by Saturday. Packed yet? With September deadline, not a minute to spare."*

The last was literal fact for Louise. The first appointment was scheduled for four-thirty, which allotted her fifteen minutes to make it on time. What did she know of textbooks? she wondered as she flew up the stairs for her cloak. Or law or advertising or money or anything else?

In the matter of law, she was taught a lesson the next morning in her meeting with Connolly's attorney. Legal documents, she was to learn, were not always as munificent as they were made to appear.

JOHN J. GEOGHEGAN, ATTORNEY AT LAW, read the directory listing in the lobby of the office building on East Forty-second Street. The elevator whisked Louise upward, pinned among the clerks and stenographers who plainly questioned what a nun was doing in a place of commerce. She didn't think she belonged there either, and when Geoghegan had ushered her into his office, his very solicitude contributed to her unease.

"A prince among men," Jack Geoghegan eulogized the man who was his principal client. "Everything I have, I owe to the Chief." The lawyer was pink-cheeked and fastidiously groomed, and looked as if he'd buffed himself to a glossy shine. He described for Louise a tenement boyhood in Hell's Kitchen and an after-school job in the neighborhood Shamrock. "The Chief came in every so often, as he does with all of his stores, and it absolutely changed my life. Who else would have loaned a punk kid the money for college? Shoot for the best, he said, so after Fordham I aimed for Harvard Law and got in, the only Catholic in my class. Well, the Chief was proud as punch. After graduation I went to work for him as a Shamrock lawyer, and then left eventually to look after his personal affairs. I worship the man—I'd cut off my arm for him." Geoghegan's arm shot up to illustrate the point, after which he lowered it and trained his watchful eyes on Louise.

"But, of course, as the latest recipient of his generosity, you know whereof I speak," he observed, and reached for a red morocco-leather folder on his shiny desk. "May I assume, Mother Maguire, that you've had little experience with the law?"

"Not a thimbleful," Louise replied, "but how does it concern me or the school?"

"The law is always concerned when property and money are involved." Geoghegan extracted some papers from the folder. "Now, let's go over the agreement I've drawn up between you and Mr. Moore. It defines the terms under which the school is to be established. If you have any questions, I'll be glad to answer them."

Louise followed the explanation from the copy handed to her, a review, clause by clause, of the terms of the agreement. The school was to be registered as a private, nonprofit corporation in papers filed with the state attorney's office, with Connolly named as president.

"Mr. Moore prefers to dispense with a board of trustees. He wants the agreement kept strictly between the two of you. As you will see, the financial provisions are entirely in your favor."

The agreement specified that the corporation, that is, Connolly, was to assume the cost of renovating Hightower and equipping it to function as a boarding school. An operating fund of ten thousand dollars was to be set up and the money was to be disbursed by the accounting firm of Joseph Slattery Associates.

"Joe is a Shamrock boy too," Geoghegan said with a regretful sigh. "He left the Chief to go out on his own and he's been having a tough time of it."

"I'm to meet today with Mr. Slattery," Louise volunteered.

"Don't get me wrong, Joe's a crackerjack accountant, but he's a diamond in the rough. The lawyer regarded his pink nails, buffed like the rest of him to a gloss. "Let's say Joe doesn't attract the carriage trade. It shows you the kind of man the Chief is for throwing him work when he can. He never forgets his Shamrock boys. Now, where were we?"

"Clause Six, I believe."

"Ah, yes." Geoghegan resumed his editorializing. "It states very generously that your Motherhouse is to be paid the annual sum of two thousand dollars for each nun assigned to the school."

That, if nothing else, reflected Louise, would sway the Mother General to part with nuns for America. She listened attentively, consulting her copy of the agreement, as the lawyer continued to spell out the terms. Another clause designated Louise as the head-mistress, empowered to appoint the faculty, determine the curriculum, and hire personnel as needed. It was the final clause that triggered a warning in her mind, but she did not speak until the lawyer had commented on it.

"This, you understand, is a temporary proviso, and you're not to worry about it."

"But it does worry me." She read over the clause, which specified that *"ownership of the property known as Hightower, and of all buildings on the property, existing or made to exist, shall be held by the Corporation. At such time as the School is judged to be in satisfactory fiscal condition, title to the aforesaid property and all buildings thereon will be transferred to the nuns."*

"It means that the school is not ours," she said in quiet protest. "It will be owned by the corporation . . . Mr. Moore, in effect."

"Temporarily." Geoghegan tilted back the leather swivel chair and massaged the bridge of his nose. "Surely you appreciate that Mr. Moore is owed some protection. If the school fails, is he to recoup none of his investment?"

Louise frowned and examined the clause again, as though the misunderstanding were hers. "I grant my ignorance of the law, but oughtn't it to protect both parties of the agreement?" she asked. "As it's worded here, the school might never be ours, without Mr. Moore's consent."

Jack Geoghegan smiled and straightened his gold-linked cuffs. "Is that likely, based on your knowledge of Mr. Moore? Really, now, is it likely?" He sprang up from the swivel chair and skirted around the desk. "In any case, as his attorney it is my duty to protect his interests."

"Was this clause at your behest—or his?"

"Here you are, Mother Maguire, on the threshold of a great undertaking, with every provision for success."

"Truly, I am grateful to Mr. Moore, but if we're to—"

"Why not look after your end of it and let us attend to the business details?" The lawyer slipped the agreement and Louise's copy into a manila envelope, which he presented to her. "I won't ask for your signature until you've had the chance to study it at your leisure."

"My signature?"

"Mr. Moore wants it settled before he leaves for the Derby this week."

The whoosh of the elevator cables reminded Louise of the gale wind that had swept her up at Hightower. The keys she had been given were merely a token gesture, she realized as she crossed the granite lobby of the office building. At the revolving doors, a bronze tablet identified the building's ownership. SHAMROCK REALTY, it read in Gothic lettering.

The appointment with Joseph Slattery was not for another half hour, and Louise surrendered to the pulsing crowd of pedestrians that conveyed her along Forty-second Street. Across the street, crews of workmen swarmed over the gigantic excavation site of the new Grand Central Station. The noise and din, the swing of pickax and shovel, were a forecast of what awaited her at Hightower. Yesterday's sense of good fortune had evaporated and left her with the bone chill of inadequacy and impending failure.

In contrast to the attorney's prestigious office, that of Joseph Slattery Associates was located one flight up over a luggage store, hard by the Third Avenue El. Louise could only speculate as to who were the associates, other than a cadaverous clerk bent over a ledger in the anteroom. The door of a frosted-glass cubicle opened and out came a bantam-sized individual who sported a handlebar moustache and a plaid suit that called to mind a horse blanket. The grin that he bestowed on Louise was the equivalent of a bear hug.

"Got an aunt in the nuns." Joe Slattery led her into the cubicle. "She's a Sparkhill Dominican, teaches up in the Bronx, crazy about baseball and prays every night for the Yankees to cop the pennant." He seated Louise at the ledger-piled desk. "Hey, what happened to you?"

"Beg pardon?"

"You look like you've been put through the wringer." Slattery appraised her, thumbs hooked in the plaid vest. "I've got it, you met with Jack Geoghegan this morning."

"I . . . it's all such a new experience."

"He'd ask for your teeth, if he could get 'em." Slattery went behind the desk and rooted through the ledgers. "Did he tell you how he'd cut off his arm for the Chief? I notice he's still got both arms. Listen, what d'you know about credits and debits?"

"Not a thing," Louise admitted with an upsurge of trust in the straight-talking accountant.

He hauled a brand-new cloth ledger from the pile and slammed it on the desk. "The Chief says that all disbursements for the school are to be paid from this office, but I don't always obey the Chief."

Louise was impressed. "You don't?"

"Me, I'm one of them independent-type guys. It's why I left Shamrock and became my own boss. Maybe I'm short of clients, but you won't find a better C.P.A. than me and it'll pay off one day. It's terrific of the Chief to give me this school account, but I'll handle it my way or he can fire me."

Joe Slattery opened the ledger and pressed the ruled pages flat. "Now, take the operating fund of ten thousand dollars. If I'm to control it, where's it leave you, except out in the cold?"

"How is that?"

"Well, suppose you're up there at Hightower and need a broom or a muffin pan. Why should you have to ask me for the money? No, sir, I'm giving you some scratch of your own to spend."

"You are?"

"Bet your sweet life I am." Joe dipped a pen in ink and inscribed the amount of two thousand dollars in the left-hand column of the first page. "As of tomorrow, that's what I'll deposit for you in the Peekskill branch of the Westchester National."

Louise drew her chair closer to the desk. "And is that what is called a credit?"

"No flies on you, for sure." He indicated the right-hand column, where she was to enter the amount of each expenditure. "Okay, total your debits at the bottom of the page, subtract it from the credits, carry over the balance—and presto, you're in business."

"Mr. Slattery, if I might ask your . . ." Louise eyed the manila envelope and took out the agreement. "I've been asked to sign this, but if you'll read the final clause . . ."

"*Don't*," was Slattery's advice after a quick perusal of the terms. "Let me tip you off about the Chief. He'll take advantage of you every chance he gets, but stand up to him and you'll earn his respect."

"A formidable stand."

"Look, maybe I'm a diamond in the rough and not polished smooth, like Geoghegan," Joe acknowledged with a shrug. "Yeah, I'm rough, but the Chief knows a diamond when he sees it. I'll bet it's why he picked you for his school, so don't take any guff from him."

"Without him, there'd be no school."

"What about without you?" Joseph Slattery presented Louise with the ledger and another bear hug of a grin. "Think it over, and if you need a friend to call on, listen, you've got one."

"You are very kind . . . and I thank you."

She found a church around the corner from Third Avenue and went up the worn steps of St. Agnes into the dim, candle-flickering interior. It was noon and hunger was prodding at her, but she welcomed it as an expression of her vow of poverty. Of what importance were keys, unless they were the keys of the kingdom? She prayed for the courage not to be influenced by the ways of the world, but to keep poor and humble of heart in the Lord's service. Father Regan slipped into her thoughts, and she suddenly interpreted his odd behavior as a sign that he was in trouble. The world was Regan's temptation and perhaps some crisis had brought him into conflict with his ambition . . . but why direct his antagonism at her?

Louise left the church for her next appointment, conscious of the pull of the world taking her in directions over which she had little say.

By Thursday afternoon, when she stepped from the trolley at Waverly Place, Louise felt weighed down by more than the armful of sample textbooks, folders, and catalogs that she carried. For three days she had gone from office to office and in the process had lost any real sense of who she was other than a person engaged in business, like everyone else in the teeming city.

As she turned the corner of the Village street to which she was shortly to bid farewell, a girl in servant's cap and apron skirled down the convent stoop. Bridget O'Shea was wringing her hands in such consternation that she almost failed to notice who was coming toward her.

"Mum, oh, mum," Bridget wailed, racing over the pavement. "I've pestered the Sisters all day, askin' was you back yet."

"What is it, child?" Louise had kept in touch with Bridget during the preceding weeks. The girl had visited her at the convent and turned up every morning at the six-thirty Mass, waiting outside for a minute's chat. "Is something wrong?"

"I . . ." Bridget's agate eyes grew wide and she plucked nervously at her apron. "It come to me like a dream while I was scrubbin' the kitchen floor," she blurted out. "I seen it clear as daylight, the house that's to be yer school. 'Tis on a hill above a river, with a tower risin' up from the roof."

"You *saw* it?" Irish tales had abounded in Ballymar of persons gifted with second sight, to Louise's fascination as a girl. "You've described the house quiet accurately."

"I seen it all, bits of the future too, you and the nuns and . . ."

Louise shifted the armful of books, intrigued. "And what?"

"I seen . . . meself with you," Bridget said, as though in the grip of an apparition. "At the school, by yer side, servin' the Lord with ya'."

"Is that what you want?"

Bridget looked crushed. "Are ya' forgettin' the boat and me wantin' to give you the life that you saved?"

"But you're working to bring over your sister from the orphanage."

"Sure, if I work for God, He'll get me the money to send for Ag."

Louise made a decision, the first of her own in behalf of the school. "Can you be ready to leave with us on Saturday?"

" 'Tis ready I've been since the boat."

"Very good, but you must allow us to pay you wages." Louise felt light-headed at the thought of her bank account. "Fortunately, we've the money for it."

"You'll take me, then?" Bridget seized the black-gloved hand and kissed it, then ran down the street, flinging the apron over her pigtails. "I'll go now and inform the Missus that I'm quittin'."

The light-headedness lasted as far as the climb of the brownstone stoop. In the front hall, Sister Matilda was shouting into the mouthpiece of the instrument affixed to the wall, a gift to the convent from Connolly Moore. Installed two days ago, the telephone was an enthralling novelty for the Sisters, an audience of whom listened raptly to Matilda's shouts.

"Can you hear me? Land's sake, you're clear as a bell, isn't it a marvel? I'd better ring off," she added, with a glance at Louise. "You-know-who might be trying to reach us."

As if in verification of it, the telephone rang the moment the receiver was hooked to the box. "It's himself," Matilda hissed, scattering the audience as she offered Louise the receiver.

She had to crane to speak into the mouthpiece, which was level with the top of her veil. "I'm fine, thank you, Mr. Moore," she said, and the wind swept her up.

"How'd it go with Ed Donohue? Did he have the sketches of the brochure to show you?"

"Yes, but since the school hasn't a name yet, or a curriculum—"

"Can't expect students unless we advertise. The point is to get moving on the brochure. Aren't you due at the chancery tomorrow to go over the curriculum?"

"Yes, with Monsignor Hughes, the superintendent of schools."

"Great, and listen, the feedback on you is unanimous—a thoroughbred, but I could've told 'em that." There was a pause and the wind softened a degree in its velocity. "I hope you know that I consider myself profoundly in your debt."

"And I in yours," Louise said, tensed for the next assault.

"Gatti's summoned your Mother General to Rome. No way for her to wriggle out of it. Did I mention that I'm off to Lexington tonight?"

"Tomorrow, I thought."

"Some yearlings I want a crack at. Hightower's all spruced up for your arrival on Saturday. Boylan will meet the train, the ten-forty, is it?"

"Yes, the ten-forty."

"Well, that seems to leave us with one remaining item on the agenda."

Louise's hand trembled as she grasped the receiver and a weariness overtook her, the week's accumulation of strain and effort. "I'm sorry, Mr. Moore, but I haven't signed the agreement."

"It can't mean you object to the terms?"

"No, but I . . ." Louise heard herself falter. "I must be certain they are equitable to both parties."

"My dear Mother Maguire, where is the trust I asked of you?" Connolly's tone was of joshing reproach, as with an unreasonable child. "I don't say it to influence you, but where would this school be without me? It's worth some reflection."

"Yes, Mr. Moore."

Louise hung up the telephone and collected her books from the hall table. Joe Slattery had raised the same question in reverse, and it spun like a pinwheel before her as she went up the stairs.

Without her, would there be a school?

She was too exhausted to wage battle over it, and in the morning she signed the agreement and notified Geoghegan of it, who dispatched a messenger to pick up the documents.

The fishnet satchels were packed, the suitcases clicked shut, and Sophie's Virgin lay wrapped in burlap for the journey to Hightower.

Below in the front hall, the Sisters were assembled to say goodbye, Saturday-free of desks and blackboards. Bridget O'Shea, whose worldly goods were tied up in a calico scarf, sat agog on the coatrack bench at the door. She leaped to help with the bags when the two nuns came down the stairs.

The good-byes were accompanied by gifts, an omelette pan for Mère Blanchard, in tribute to her culinary skills, which would be sorely missed, and for Louise a medal of Elizabeth Seton, the foundress of the Sisters of Charity in America.

"Let her be your model," Matilda said, embracing Louise. "May God give you the same courage to bear your crosses, for who is without them? No tears, we're none of us to shed a single tear."

Solange had nevertheless to wipe copiously at her eyes in the hansom cab that rocked and swayed uptown to Grand Central. Louise, carved in silence, listened to the rhythmic clop of the horse's hooves on the pavement. It was the rhythm of the past, she thought, and it was carrying her into the future.

The future was unlike any that she had envisioned, but she was not a quitter and would succeed at it. The wilderness of the West was not to challenge her, but was Hightower less of a wilderness?

Louise paid for the cab with the last dollar of Mrs. Tobin's shipboard winnings. It seemed to close that chapter of her life. Yesterday at the chancery, though Father Regan had passed her in the corridor, he had not stopped to greet her, and so the chapter had closed on him too.

The train shuttled out of the station and next was rolling through the Bronx countryside studded with houses and apartments. The tracks made a turn at Spuyten Duyvil and followed the silver band of the Hudson, which roused Mère Blanchard from her doldrums.

"*C'est le Ood-son?*" she inquired of Louise and pressed her nose to the window. "I would not have thought to behold the equal, if not the superior, of the Rhone."

"Solange, you sound like an American."

"*Zut alors*, have we not taken the citizen papers? Is it not what soon I become?"

"Glory be, a cow!" piped Bridget, guarding the bags in the seat behind. "Cows is balky creetchers, I've heard."

"Up the road from the school, Bridget, at Mr. Moore's farm, are chickens and cows and pigs galore."

"Pigs, God save us!"

The conductor shouted, "Dobbs Ferry," and the train slowed to a clacking halt. The rustic little stations, set every few miles at the foot of wooded hills, whisked past the train window, and Louise experienced a stir of anticipation that surmounted her fears and doubts. The onerous week, viewed in retrospect, paraded its accomplishments for her. The meeting at the chancery yesterday had yielded a tentative curriculum and faculty requirements. The design for the school brochure had advanced to the dummy stage and she had made a start on the text. In her suitcase were the sketches from B. Altman for the school uniform. She had chosen from the multiple swatches a royal blue for the pinafore that, paired with a white shirt of Egyptian cotton, made up the uniform. It had suggested to her the school colors, which would be blue and white.

And yesterday she had come up with a name for the school as special and meaningful as Connolly Moore had wished for.

"Peekskill," the conductor called out, and the train gave a whistle toot and rounded a bend in the tracks. The giant hump of Bear Mountain reared up from the opposite shore, crouched above the glinting width of the river. "Here we are," Louise cried, getting up, her excited glance switching from the station to the river and back again. She turned to lend Bridget a hand with the bags and saw that Mère Blanchard was clutching the armrest of the seat, gasping for breath.

"Solange, what is it?"

"Uhh . . . uhh." After a scarifying moment, the old nun's breath grew steadier. "It is nothing of consequence," she insisted, pushing up from the seat. "Did you not say we are here?"

The sun beat down on the dusty station platform onto which they stepped from the train. The town of Peekskill, a clutter of roofs and chimneys, hugged the hills in which it was nestled and across the tracks flowed the gleaming expanse of river. An excursion boat decked with flags was preparing to sail from one of the wharves. In the parking lot adjacent to the station, the emerald green of the Pierce-Arrow stood out among the buggies and farm wagons, and a goggled Boylan doffed his visored cap as he hastened to attend to the nuns. Anastasia and Monica Moore had turned out for the occasion and ran skipping and giggling behind the chauffeur.

"What a glorious day, sure, the angels must a' spun it out of gold," waxed Boylan, who fancied himself as greeter and host in his master's absence. "You'll not recognize Hightower; it's that fixed up and ready for your comin'." He gathered up the bags and admonished the girls, who were squabbling. "Now, is that the way to behave in front of the nuns? Dip 'em a curtsy, like 'tis proper."

The bags were stowed in the trunk, and with the girls in the seat facing the nuns and Bridget up front with Boylan, the Pierce-Arrow rolled majestically from the parking lot and up the steep-climbing streets of Peekskill. Louise sat holding the wrapped Virgin, uncertain of how to communicate with the unruly youngsters who were to be given into her care. The want of discipline was woefully apparent from their twistings and pokings and utter disregard of manners and civility.

"Where," she inquired for openers, "is your sister, Flavin?"

"Can't you guess?" snorted Anastasia, digging a bag of chocolates from her dress pocket. "Naturally, it's her that Father picks to go to the Derby with him."

"He likes to show her off to everybody, which he can't do with us," Monica explained.

"Oh, sure, you and me are lepers or something to hide out of sight."

Louise was dismayed by the exchange. "Is that what you think of yourselves—lepers?"

"We're not to Jonah and Clarice," Monica avowed. "They're our butler and cook and my two favorite persons in the world . . . them and Mama, but she's in heaven and don't count."

Anastasia bit into a chocolate cream that trickled down her lips. She was overweight and her face, square-jawed like her father's was blotchy from indulgence in sweets. "All she did was to leave us to the maids."

"She couldn't help it that she was sick."

"Wise up, why don't you? Except maybe for Flave, nobody's cared a hoot about us."

Louise stared at the two sisters, startled by what their talk revealed about them. Behind Anastasia's contemptuous remarks, she sensed, lay a residue of hurt and rejection. Monica was the innocent of the two, but it was a pathetic innocence, vulnerable and painfully exposed. The girls' expensive hand-smocked dresses, no doubt immaculate an hour ago, were wrinkled and dirt-smudged. Anastasia's fingernails were chewed to the quick and her mouth was a chocolate smear. These two of Connolly Moore's daughters were as he'd described them, poor little rich girls, left to fend for themselves as neglected as they were indulged.

High in the hills above the town, the Pierce-Arrow turned onto a road that ran north to the estate area and the neighboring villages of Garrison and Cold Spring. "Tell me," Louise asked, "are you looking forward to school in September?"

"Well, *I* am," Monica confided, hugging her scratched-up knees. "When I grow up I intend to have lots of babies so that I won't be lonesome, but in the meantime school will bring me friends."

Anastasia chewed a caramel and subjected Louise to a cool and insolent appraisal. "I'm not a pushover like Monnie," she warned.

"You don't look forward to school?"

"In my opinion, who needs a bunch of dopey girls for friends?"

Louise girded herself for a skirmish. "You will kindly not masticate while you speak."

"What's that mean?"

"Chew, masticate, and you will please address me as 'Mother Maguire.'"

"Since when?" The car trundled along the tree-arched road and Anastasia pointed toward the wrought-iron gates looming ahead. "That's where I live," she boasted, and waited for the vista of lawns and gardens and white columns to appear. "I live there and at the Plaza in New York and the Poinciana in Florida, and when I grow up, nuts to babies, I'll be rich, ask my father, with heaps of—"

Louise appropriated the bag of chocolates. "How did I ask you to address me?"

"Heaps of money to spend and I won't care if I'm fat and ugly."

"Anastasia, give me your hand."

"Don't touch me, I know about nuns, they smack you with rulers and lock you up."

Louise took the girl's hand and held firmly on to it. "I want you to repeat after me, *I will*," she instructed.

"Leggo of my hand."

"Say it for me, as I said it to God once and was heard."

Of a sudden, the blotchy face crumpled and with it the angry defiance. "To what? Say it to what?"

"To the good that's in you," Louise said, glancing up at the turn in the road and the gates thrusting up from the trees.

A beseeching hand tugged at her skirts, and Monica asked, "Don't I get to say it, too?"

"Of course, dear."

"Okay, here goes." Monica shut her eyes tight and screeched. "I will, I will, I will," in a rapturous chant.

"I rather think God heard you the first time."

The gates, opened wide, glistened with fresh black paint, and the driveway onto which the automobile swung was paved smooth of pits and ruts. Louise wasn't prepared for the emotions that assailed her as the car drove upward through the dense shadows of the firs and evergreens. She had left Ballymar ten years ago as though her heart would break of sorrow, and now her emotions were those of a traveler coming home after a long journey. The drive curved up from the woods, and the sweep of hills and sky, lawns and towered mansion, spread before her gaze.

The lawns were scythed of weeds and wild grass and the giant oak at the top of the drive bowed a welcome. Stacks of lumber, buckets of paint, spools of wire, and lengths of pipe thronged the driveway in front of the mansion, so that Boylan had to park some distance below the porch steps.

"You did not tell me," exclaimed Mère Blanchard, gesturing at the rolling expanse of grounds and the red-brick tower. "What a school we shall make of it!"

" 'Tis jist like I seen it," clucked Bridget, gawking from the front seat. "Everything, jist like it come to me."

The two girls clambered down from the car and went racing and squealing over the lawns. Boylan, who was hauling the bags from the trunk, kept up his role as official host.

"You'll find the house is well provided. We've stocked the larder and laid wood for the fire and made up yer bedrooms nice and cozy. Mr. Moore's cook—" he produced a wicker hamper—"has packed ya a fine lunch and I'll be bringin' over fresh eggs and butter and milk from the farm as yer need 'em."

"What of Mass tomorrow?" Louise asked as he assisted her from the car. "Is there a conveyance to get us into Peekskill for Mass?"

"Conveyance, is it?" Boylan laughed. "Sure, the monks are to say Mass right here, same as they do at Faircrest. Who else, I'd like to know, paid for the monastery at Crugers?"

The chauffeur carried the bags up the driveway. Louise held on to the Virgin and stepped over the lumber and cans of paint, followed by Mère Blanchard and Bridget. It was rare for solemnity to settle upon Louise, but it did so as she went up the porch steps. The tangled lair of wisteria vines had been trimmed from the railing, the rotted boards torn out and replaced with new flooring. The tall French windows shone with glass panes and in them she glimpsed the future, as real and palpable as if she could reach out and touch it. This was her future, her wilderness, her challenge, and she would not fail at it.

She turned and called to Monica and Anastasia, who were cavorting raucously on the lawn. If they were typical of the students who would be entrusted to her care, then her work was cut out for her. "Young ladies," she called to the girls. "Come, I've something to tell you."

Boylan stood back with the bags while Louise took the ring of keys from her drawstring purse and unlocked the door. After a moment of hushed silence she went in.

The cobwebs were swept from the carved-oak stairs and the whorls of dust from the parquet floor. The light from the stained-glass insert in the roof fell in soft hues upon Louise and the figures grouped in the doorway. She unwrapped the painted wooden carving and set it on the mantel. "The Blessed Mother will be the patroness of our school," she said, and knelt before the little statue in prayer, asking not for miracles but for strength and courage and perseverance.

The others knelt praying with her, and when she stood up Louise was all at once the headmistress, turning to address her fidgeting students.

"We are to have another mother to watch over us," she told Monica and Anastasia, and gestured at the wall above the mantel. "Your father wants her portrait to hang there, to look down on every student who enters this school, which is to be named in her memory."

"Our mama?" asked Monica, in an awed voice. "Named for her?"

Louise gazed at where the portrait would hang and wished for it a thousand blessings. "For her, the school is to be called Rosemoore," she said, taking off her cloak and rolling up her sleeves for the work that awaited her.

III
THE OPENING

ELEVEN

A week later Louise was on the porch, an apron tied over her skirts, pouring a pitcher of lemonade for a group of perspiring workmen taking their lunch break. For this brief period the air did not resound with the bang of hammers, the *zzzth* of saws and drills, the crack of axes, and the swing of shovels digging up the earth.

Every morning at eight-thirty the wagonloads of men clattered up the driveway to lay siege to the house and grounds. "Big Bill" Guinness, the contractor who had worked previously for Connolly Moore, was always first out of the wagons, waving his blueprints and supervising the crews of carpenters, plumbers, and electricians in the day's assault. The red-brick house, all three floors of it, appeared to be in a permanent state of chaos and wreckage. Everywhere, walls were stripped to the lathing and holes were drilled in floors and ceilings to accommodate the electrical wiring. Clouds of plaster dust enveloped the rooms and barrels of debris were carted out daily. The basement was dug up for the installation of a steam-heating system. The upper two floors were in the worst throes of alteration. Here were to be the classrooms, offices, and dormitories, and scarcely a wall was left intact. Some of the larger bedrooms were being divided up, with closets and bathrooms fitted into the reapportioned space. The back stairs winding up from the kitchen were to be reconstructed to conform with the state regulations for fire stairs. Out back the stables were in the process of being converted into a gymnasium. Still ahead were the plastering and painting, the furnishing of the house, and the landscaping.

Louise made the rounds on the porch with the pitcher of lemonade. Below on the driveway and lawns the workmen sat hunched over lunch boxes, and passing among them with refreshments were Mère Blanchard and Bridget. The unlikely partnership of nuns and laborers was based on age-old reciprocities. Each morning the men were greeted with fresh-baked doughnuts, compliments of Solange, and plentiful pots of coffee, and at noon by the pitchers of lemonade clinking with ice. Louise knew many of the men by name and one of them by design. Duffy, as he called himself, was a hop-and-skip of a fellow, a Jack-of-all-trades—plumber, carpenter, electrician, as needed. A faulty circuit or clogged drain worked when Duffy got finished tinkering with it, a briar pipe clamped always in his mouth.

"I take the jobs I want and then I move on," he'd told Louise during a lunch break. "Strictly my own boss."

"We're looking for a school janitor," she had replied.

"Oh, maybe one day I'll light down someplace, but for now—"

"He'll have his own quarters in the gym, at no cost, and I'd want him to be his own boss."

Duffy puffed on his pipe. "For a nun, you're a square dealer. I like that," he allowed. "Let me deal square with you—I'll think it over, okay?"

"Okay, Mr. Duffy."

As she started from the porch to replenish the empty pitcher, Louise heard the swift pounding of hooves on the driveway. The black charger was galloping up from the woods with Connolly Moore astride it in a pink hunting coat and shining boots, riding at a lightning clip. The men scattered at his headlong approach, and when a wheelbarrow reared up in his path, he jumped the horse straight over it.

Louise, who had not known that Connolly was back from Kentucky, went down the porch steps in a dither of nervous expectancy. It wasn't until he rode up closer that she saw the bunch of red roses slung in his arm. Dismounting, Connolly hitched the panting horse to the jockey post. The look on his ruddy face as he offered her the roses was compounded of emotions so powerful that for once speech did not spring to his lips but came faltering out.

"I—the girls couldn't wait to tell me," Connolly stammered. "Drove up from the city this morning and those two hooligans raced to the car with the news. It—I—the name for the school—"

"You approve of it?"

"Ever since the loss of my wife, I've—" He shook his head, unable to continue for a moment. "Rose died of pneumonia, forty-eight hours of delirium and she was gone, taken from me with such awful suddenness." The steel-blue eyes were rife with a pain the years had not diminished. "As I've said, this school is my tribute to her, and now to have it bear her name, well, I—"

Connolly drew himself up, not as tall as he had wished to be but compensating for it with a ramrod stiffness of carriage. "I deplore a grown man who weeps," he said, honking at his nose with a silk handkerchief. "You're a thoroughbred, Mother Maguire, and I intend to show my appreciation of it."

With that sentiment and a pat for the horse, Connolly barged up onto the porch and shouldered past the workmen, leaving Louise to follow in his wake, clutching the roses and the empty pitcher and relieved of the nervous anxiety that he'd always instilled in her.

"I've heard from Cardinal Gatti in Rome," Connolly boomed at her in the front hall. "The Mother General's sending us six nuns; not bad for a start, eh?"

Louise nodded, absorbing the information. "Six are better than I'd hoped for."

"Two are servant Sisters, if that's what you call them. They're all booked to sail July fifth from Cherbourg."

"The house ought to be in shape by then." She carried the roses into the cloakroom off the hall, which was furnished with a rickety table and chair salvaged from the attic. "If you'll excuse me while I get some water for your flowers—"

"What's this?" demanded Connolly, poking his head in the door.

"It's my office, temporary but quite adequate."

"Your *office*?" He picked up a ledger from the table and flipped the ruled pages. "Joe Slattery was right to give you a bank account—can't have you begging for every dollar you need."

"Well, it *did* seem—"

"You'll want to meet the nuns at the pier when they dock, but how will you transport them up here?"

"The train, I expect, and—"

"I've ordered a Pierce-Arrow for you, delivery in a month. Boylan can give you driving lessons in my old rattletrap."

"Be careful," Louise said, touched by the spirit in which the lavish gift was made. "Keep it up and I'll lose any sense of feeling intimidated by you."

Connolly took the roses from her and dumped them on the table. "As for your pathetic choice of an office, it calls for a lesson in showmanship." As he marched into the front hall a whistle blew, ending the lunch hour. He ignored the workmen trooping past him and stood at the foot of the carved-oak stairs, where he launched into a lecture on showmanship.

"That first store, the sleepless nights I spent figuring out the look it should have to bring the customers flocking. Trim and sparkling clean I opted for, white soapstone counters scrubbed clean, spotless tile floors, green shelves with every item neatly displayed, and a novelty to catch the eye—the shamrock tea caddies and later the penny sales and giveaways. It sure did the trick and I'm glad to report the customers are still flocking to us. You, on the other hand, are faced with a different breed of customer, and it's all important, the first impression you make."

The slam and bang of hammer and spike were not an interruption to Connolly, who pitched his voice above the racket. "Now, let's imagine that you're about to receive some parents interested in the school for their daughter. They ring the doorbell—we'll want chimes—and what next? Are you to pop out of your closet to greet them? No, indeed, a nice little servant Sister will answer the door. You, the headmistress, are nowhere in sight."

"Where, then?" asked Louise, her curiosity piqued.

"The Sister proceeds up the stairs to announce the visitors." Tarpaulins covered the stairs, but Connolly's extravagance of gesture rendered the staircase in full carved-oak glory. "The visitors must wait and what do they spy as they wait? A Sargent portrait, no less! It knocks them for a loop, whereupon the Sister comes to fetch them."

He bounded up the stairs, with Louise following behind as usual. "They can't believe it's a Catholic school, not this mansion, this aristocratic show of taste. Ah, but when they see the office of the headmistress, it's the clincher."

Connolly strode down the second-floor corridor to the foyer at the tower end, which led to the master-bedroom suite. He dismissed the workmen, who were stripping the walls of the largest room, and beckoned to Louise. The room was circular, since it was enclosed in the tower, and of lofty dimensions and elegant detail. A Victorian fireplace at one end was dressed with marble swags and tassels, and from a raised platform at the other end a bay of windows looked down at the driveway and lawns.

"Your desk will go here." Connolly strode the platform that had formerly supported a gilded swan-boat bed. "From here, you'll have command of the room and your visitors."

"Mr. Moore, I—"

"We're getting Ariakian to do all the furnishings. He's an estate dealer, top-quality stuff. Try to imagine this room when Ari's finished with it!"

"But I can't," Louise confessed. "At least not in relation to myself."

"Granted, it won't be the usual nun's office, but—"

"Really, Mr. Moore, I'm not suited to such grandeur."

Connolly looked at her for a moment and turned away. He gazed out the bay of windows at the chimneys that could be glimpsed in the distance over the hills. "Funny thing . . . my wife once said something very much like that to me," he reflected. "I doubt that Faircrest brought her much happiness. I found it inconceivable that anyone would miss life in a tenement, but Rose apparently did. She often sat on the terrace listening as a train whistle sounded over the valley. No, grandeur wasn't suited to Rose, either."

Louise groped for an appropriate comment. "Surely, her children were a great source of happiness."

Connolly swung around, his melancholy instantly dispelled. "You ought to have seen Flavin at the Derby," he enthused. "She's only twelve, but her poise was remarkable and the sweetness of her nature captivated all who met her. I sometimes think that in Flavin I've been given a second chance . . . that is, if I failed with her mother, I mean. The world on a silver platter isn't half good enough for my Flavin, but it's hers for the asking."

"And Monica and Anastasia too?"

"Those hooligans?" Connolly jumped down from the platform and brushed at his pink hunting coat. "Turning those two puppies into young ladies is the job you've taken on for yourself. By the way, would you like one?"

"Beg pardon?"

"A school mascot—one of the setter bitches is due to whelp. We leave for Spring Lake in a few weeks, but I'll tell the groom to save the pick of the litter for you."

Connolly trooped down the stairs, discoursing on the complexities of moving to his summer residence on the Jersey shore. "Somehow Jonah manages the whole process; we'd be lost without Jonah to look after us."

Mère Blanchard was in the front hall, having discovered the cache of roses which she was taking to the kitchen for water. It was her introduction to Connolly, who quickly disarmed her with courtly expressions of gratitude for her contributions to the school. He then pulled a wallet from the pink coat and, going from room to room, distributed ten-dollar bills to the workmen, exhorting them to keep up the good work.

"You won't let us down? We're to open in September and by golly we'll have it ready."

That done, Connolly hesitated, took some papers from the coat, and went to Louise at the door.

"I've approved the design for the brochure—terrific, the royal blue." He tapped the papers in his hand. "Are the monks coming to say Mass every morning?"

"Oh, yes—Father Anselm, usually."

"Nice fellow—good sense of humor." Connolly frowned at the papers as if to tear them up, but instead he handed them to Louise.

"Thanks for signing our little agreement—any regrets?"

She looked at her copy of the agreement, which bore his signature as well as hers. "You asked for my trust, Mr. Moore, and I've given it."

"That's right, so you have." He marched back onto the porch. "Now, you'll think over my recommendations for your office?"

"I'll think it over."

From the porch rail Louise watched her benefactor mount the black charger and gallop away. He plunged into the woods, obscured from her by more than the trees. She was not adept at probing or analyzing behavior, hers or anyone else's, but she estimated that something in Connolly had prodded him to tear up the agreement but he had reneged on it. He was akin to Father Regan, she thought, in that both were prey to inner conflicts difficult to fathom, at least for her.

Going back into the house, Louise did not think of her next action as a response to Connolly and his values, which it was. Solange had fetched a jug for the roses and was placing it on the mantel in the front hall, but Louise claimed the flowers for another purpose. Amid the hammering and sawing of the workmen and the clouds of plaster dust, she bore the jug of roses to the billiard room, where the monks said Mass each morning. A portable altar and some prie-dieus loaned by the monastery gave the room the semblance of a chapel. Permission to house the Blessed Sacrament on the altar had not yet been granted, but poised on a table at the side was Sophie's Virgin in her blue, star-spangled mantle. The rose was the Virgin's symbolic flower, and Louise endowed the school's name with a dual meaning, in behalf of the Mother of God, as she installed the jug of flowers at the statue's feet.

Next, she climbed the back stairs to the attic, and that too was a response to Connolly.

The attic was a rabbit warren of servants' rooms tucked under the eaves. The scratch of mice on the bare boards greeted Louise as she went along the passage that ran between the rooms. Some were piled with discarded furniture, but it was the tiny rooms by themselves that interested her. Each measured nine feet by eleven feet and each had a slit of a dormer window in the eave, opaque with grime. She counted fourteen rooms in all and estimated, half choked by the layers of dust, that each afforded space for a cot, a chest of drawers, a desk, and a chair. Tomorrow, she and Bridget, armed with mops and buckets of soap, would clean and scour the attic to prepare it for a coat of white paint to match the curtains she would sew for the windows. The bank account would provide the necessary furniture and the rooms would be ready for the arrival of the nuns in July. They and she would live in the attic exactly as had the servants, though in the hire of another master.

Why not today? thought Louise, and she hurried down the back stairs to fetch Bridget and the mops and buckets for the job.

By the second week of July, when the nuns were to arrive in New York, the major renovations of the house had been completed. The electricity, plumbing, and heating systems were installed and the walls and ceilings restored. A team of gardeners was deployed for landscaping the grounds. The lawns, spaded and spread with fertilizer, had sprouted a soft green fuzz and the driveway was lined with a blue-and-white border of anemones.

Louise, pupil of Boylan, drove the Pierce-Arrow to the city to meet the nuns at the Cunard pier. The automobile was the exact royal blue of the brochures that had just come off the presses with a text composed by Louise.

> *Rosemoore, a convent boarding school for girls, is situated on the former Prentice estate, overlooking the Hudson River in Peekskill, New York. The school is conducted by the nuns of the Society of the Holy Virgin Mary, of Montpellier, France, and offers a program of studies, religious observance, sports and social and cultural activities designed to educate and . . .*

The brochure and the Pierce-Arrow were both emblazoned with the school crest. Edward Donohue had adapted it from Louise's own script, a bold, slanting *R* transected by a cross, and with the stem of the *R* curled in a rosebud. It made a striking design, as individual and eye-catching as Connolly's trademark shamrock. The crest was to be engraved in royal blue on the stationery ordered from Tiffany and embroidered on the breast pocket of the school uniform. In time it would appear on every article associated with Rosemoore, a signature that was readily identified.

Louise handled the car skittishly in the traffic of the Post Road. Mère Blanchard basked in the seat alongside, enjoying the ride and assuring Louise that her worries were groundless.

"Did we not ourselves rejoice to arrive in the harbor of New York? Wait, it will be the same with *les nouveaux*. The eyes, how do you say it, will pop!"

"Yes, I know, but . . ." Louise was thinking of the letter she had received from the Mother General. It had, in the guise of offering congratulations, accused her of "willful insubordination." The Mother General had been sent a copy of the agreement and was indignant at the terms of ownership, which the letter made clear. She had castigated Louise for signing the document without permission and had threatened disciplinary action if "future directives" were not upheld. Any hope that relations with Montpellier were to improve had been canceled for Louise, and she worried that the hostility would be reflected in the new arrivals.

"Tell me, *ma chère*." Solange had grown wise in interpreting the thought processes of her companion. "Is it Mère Générale who arrives on the ship? Or is it six of her young eager to try their wings?"

"I want them to be happy at coming to us and not bitter and resentful."

"Ah, wait, they will be the first off the gangplank."

The four nuns and two Sisters who passed through the customs barrier on the pier looked overwhelmed and bewildered by the noise and crowds, but not for long. Apprehension gave way to jubilation when Louise hurried forward to welcome them in a round of embraces.

The Pierce-Arrow parked outside the pier, gleaming royal blue in the sunlight, was the subject of excited speculation as bags were stored in the trunk and Louise cranked up the motor. Was this the vehicle of transport, this astounding machine?

"I too shall learn to drive," Solange announced, snapping the trunk shut. "*À l'Amérique*, such things are not forbidden to nuns."

If the automobile suggested what to expect of the future, the six passengers in the rear facing seats showed no hostility to the idea. True, the flying veils were a problem, and it was somewhat embarrassing to be the focus of curiosity at every street corner, but the sensation, like the alarming speed of the vehicle, was enjoyable. As for the city, the tall buildings, the teeming sidewalks, the roar of the traffic, evoked several requests to explore the concrete canyons. By the time the metropolitan landscape had yielded to that of the Westchester hills, quietness prevailed in the rear seats. Some of it was the result of nostalgia for what was left behind, but in equal measure it denoted contentment with the new surroundings.

The contest for allegiance that Louise had expected to wage was not to be held. She steered the car through the school gates and up the winding, shadowed drive, waiting for the moment that had first captured her allegiance. The driveway curved out of the woods and the sweep of hills and lawns, river and mansion, came into view to a collective intake of breath from the rear seats. If further persuasion was needed, it took the form of the fiery streak of tumbling legs, floppy ears, and yelps of delight of the puppy racing to meet the car.

"Tyrone is a month old and already spoiled beyond redemption,"

Louise said, pulling up to the porch steps. "He will demand that each of you shake his paw at least twice or give you no rest."

Scaffolds were hanging from the mansion, where a crew of painters was at work on the gingerbread porches and red-brick exterior. Across the drive, tractors were leveling the ground for a hockey field and tennis courts, but it was useless to point out these features to the six new arrivals. They had formed an admiring circle of which Tyrone was the tail-wagging center, proffering a tufted paw to each nun and Sister in turn, not once but shamelessly twice.

The days accelerated for Louise, rushing past in an unending cycle of work and preparation. What had seemed the slim chance of the school opening in September was by now a certainty. The date was already set for the eighth of the month, a feast of the Virgin. Connolly's daughters had been fitted for uniforms at B. Altman, as had Edward Donohue's girl, Shelagh. The enrollment stood at four, but brochures had gone out to a select mailing list and inquiries had started to come in.

The attic rooms, freshly painted white and each furnished with a white iron cot, pine chest, desk and chair, and crucifix over the bed, quickly became home to the nine who occupied them. Each morning at six-thirty Louise passed along the corridor ringing the awakening bell. She was up and robed before the others, conscious of her new responsibilities as their superior. At seven o'clock the little community of nine was gathered in the improvised chapel in the billiard room for Mass. Father Anselm had been assigned this function by the monastery at Crugers, though occasionally another monk substituted for him. The Nazarenes, as they were called, were an Alsatian order of monks whose principal benefactor in America was Connolly Moore. They were listed in the brochure as chaplains to the school, and they received a yearly stipend that Joe Slattery had said was better than okay.

It was Mère Blanchard's delight to cook breakfast afterward for the monk and the nuns, served at separate tables in the kitchen. She cooked the day's meals and would not listen to Louise's plea that someone else help her at the stove. Solange was still afflicted with the shortness of breath that had first attacked her on the train to Peekskill, but she insisted on her full share of the work, however strenuous it proved.

"Do you not see?" she had remonstrated to Louise, a touch indignantly. "*Le bon Dieu* has sent me a renewal of life and I must not waste a minute of it."

Louise, who would have chosen the same course for herself, let up on her pleas that the old nun relinquish some of her work.

The house was in the final stage of transition, supervised by Mr. Takis Ariakian, dealer in estates, a dapper gentleman in an ice cream suit and waxed moustache who had taken over where the painters had left off. As inevitable as the red silk umbrella that Mr. Ariakian carried, protection against both sun and rain, were the lizard notebook and tape measure that he whipped out on his visits to Hightower. Darting from room to room he had measured wall space, floor space, the space between windows, the height of mantels, the length of corridors, and the angle of doorways while jotting the findings in his notebook. In his dome-shaped head, Ariakian carried a mental inventory of every bibelot, objet d'art, chandelier, silver and china service, sofa, armchair, table, lamp, carpet, and rug with which his warehouse was stuffed. The disposal of estates, either through death or bankruptcy, was the source of Ariakian's bounty, and his Saturday auctions at the warehouse were crowded with bidders. Everything that wasn't auctioned, or so it appeared to Louise, proceeded to be shipped to Hightower from the city. The wagons arrived every few days loaded with all manner of goods, a Gorham silver service for fifty, Spode china, a Meissen tea service, a Bisendorfer piano for the music room, sets of books for the library. Sister Léonie, Sister Colette, and Bridget would scarcely finish unpacking the crates and barrels before a new wagonload showed up. Ariakian's emissaries, drapers, upholsterers, picture hangers, and decorators then took over the premises under his darting supervision.

By the first week of August, the red-brick mansion was almost completely furnished and decorated. An enormous crystal chandelier glittered in the cream-colored drawing room, which was resplendent with brocade sofas and lounge chairs, silk-shaded porcelain lamps, burgundy carpeting, and a bronze and ormolu clock on the fireplace mantel. The Biedermeier table in the dining room sat twenty-four, and with the addition of leaves, forty. The carved-oak stairs were carpeted in royal blue and the antler-horn chandelier that hung above held a hundred tiny frosted tulip light bulbs. Upstairs the students' rooms were furnished with cherry-wood beds and dressers acquired from a defunct hotel and the infirmary boasted three regulation hospital beds.

Mr. Ariakian was proudest of the chapel, transformed by blue-velvet hangings, mahogany pews, chased-bronze stations of the cross, and a rose-marble altar, but when he brought Louise to admire it, she saw only what was missing.

"The little painted wooden statue—where is it?"

"So cheap, so crude, I take for myself the liberty—"

"You didn't throw it out?" She hastened to the trash barrel in the hall and dug out Sophie's Virgin, half buried in the debris.

"My dear Mr. Ariakian, you have your treasures and we have ours. This is one of them and must be given a place of honor on the altar."

"As you say, Madame—I will find a nice pedestal for her."

Except in one instance, Connolly Moore had left the furnishing to Ariakian's discretion. He stipulated that the tower suite, whatever Louise's aversion to grandeur, was to be her office. The outer room was equipped with file cabinets and a desk for her future secretary. The suite included a maid's room, which was furnished with a daybed and bookcase for her use as a study. She took to avoiding the tower suite while Ariakian and his team of decorators were at work on it. The sumptuousness of the downstairs rooms were of uneasy concern to her, but she dreaded what might be practiced on the office of the headmistress.

It turned out not to be as ornate as she had feared. The clever Ariakian had limited himself to the school colors of blue and white, which gave the office a simplicity and airiness that the other rooms lacked. Louise had no means to judge the cost of the Sheraton desk that stood on the raised platform at the bay of windows, but the clean lines appealed to her taste. A blue-and-white chintz sofa and chairs and a rosewood tea table were companionably grouped in front of the Victorian fireplace, whose mantel sparkled with a display of Bristol glass. The deep blue of the Syrian carpet was repeated in the blue window draperies, and across from the desk was a wing chair upholstered in white linen.

Louise did not think of it as capitulation when she moved into the tower office. If a price were to be paid in return for Connolly's prodigious generosity, and above that for his nonintervention in regard to curriculum and school policy, then she willingly paid it.

She met with the four nuns in the tower office each morning to devise the cirriculum. At least for the present, Rosemoore was to consist of an upper and lower school, the latter in order to accommodate the age range of Connolly's daughters. At seven, nine, and twelve, each would require a different level of teaching in the primary subjects of grammar, spelling, history, arithmetic, and geography, with French as an additional unit. It was decided to group the Moore sisters together in a reciprocal learning process, and to give Flavin supplementary teaching as her studies progressed. The curriculum for the upper school was based on the syllabus prescribed for diocesan high schools.

Louise considered herself fortunate that the four nuns had settled so amicably into their new lives. Two were French and two were Irish, and all were experienced teachers. Mère Delacroix had been the organist at Montpellier and was qualified to teach music as well as general studies. Louise was quick to envision for the gentle, self-effacing Mère Bonnefils a vocation away from the classroom. Nuns were the key to the future of Rosemoore. Someday it would be home to a thriving novitiate, and in the young nun's quiet sanctity Louise saw an ideal Mistress of Novices. Of the Irish pair, Mother Shearin held a *licence* in art and showed a talent for it that deserved to be encouraged. New York State law did not require college degrees for secondary-school teachers, but Louise was resolved to eventually provide every nun at Rosemoore with at least a baccalaureate. The youngest and gayest of the foursome was Mother Larkin, who combined sound common sense with wit and humor, qualities that singled her out to Louise as a potential headmistress. The future was very much in Louise's mind at the faculty meetings. Meanwhile, when not occupied with housework, the nuns were busy evaluating and choosing textbooks, preparing study outlines, and Mère Delacroix and Mère Bonnefils with honing their English.

The Pierce-Arrow, kept handily parked on the driveway, made Peekskill a breezy ten-minute ride away. Louise thought nothing of hopping behind the wheel for a trip into the bustling river town, and she was soon on chatty terms with the proprietors of the stores that she patronized. She paid for her purchases by check, and in line with this had presented herself to Mr. Bigelow, the manager of the Westchester National Bank. As Joe Slattery had pointed out, nuns were not exempt from overdrafts and it was useful to know a bank manager or two.

Other benefits accrued as a result of the excursions into town. At the pharmacy one day, Louise noted that the courteous young man who tipped his hat to her was carrying a black physician's bag.

"You're the nun at Hightower who whizzes around in that spiffy car," he said. "The whole town's talking about you and your school."

"And you," said Louise, liking him at once, "are the very person I'm looking for. May I ask if you practice here in town?"

Dr. Robert Gavin offered the information that before setting up practice in Peekskill he'd interned at St. Vincent's Hospital in New York. Before she left the pharmacy that day, Louise had acquired a school doctor and a lifelong friend.

Emerging from the stationer's on another trip to town, she encountered a woman in dusty veils and draperies who was inspecting the Pierce-Arrow with a lorgnette. The one faculty position left unfilled was irksome to Louise. She didn't see why it was less edifying for a nun to teach calisthenics than algebra, but the Archdiocese was not in agreement and she was having difficulty in finding someone to teach physical education.

"How typical," the woman sniffed, turning her lorgnette from the car to Louise. "What ostentation you Papists go in for—it's a wonder the seats are not trimmed in ermine! You carry yourself, I must say, with a certain distinction."

"Why, thank you."

"I am Mrs. Cornelia Van Pelt, widow, and may I ask where you propose to transport the young ladies of your school in this vehicle?"

"Well, actually—"

"To the opera, concerts, museums?" The gaunt, beak-nosed Mrs. Van Pelt trained her lorgnette sternly on Louise. "Such places, I'd imagine, are out of bounds for nuns."

Louise observed that the gauzy finery showed signs of wear and that the bridge of the lorgnette was taped with adhesive. It was her introduction to the segment of impecunious Hudson Valley aristocrats who eeked out an existence on the remnants of inheritances squandered by their forebears.

"Yes, that's true," Louise ventured. "If our students are to be given the cultural benefits of the city, it seems we must provide them with a chaperone."

"I confess to little acquaintance with Papists"—Mrs. Van Pelt waved the lorgnette—"but in other respects I am eminently qualified."

"Ah, then," laughed Louise, hoping to encounter next a gym teacher on the street, "here is your chance to be acquainted with us."

On a subsequent visit to the school to discuss her modest terms of employment, Mrs. Van Pelt was accompanied by her cousin twice removed, Miss Nina Osborne. A graduate of the Savage College of Physical Education, she was seeking a teaching position in that field and was hired on the spot.

With the opening less than a month away the pace accelerated, if that was possible, for Louise and the nuns. The *Catholic News* had front-paged the announcement of the opening, the city papers had printed it, and *The New York Times* had featured a photograph of Hightower in the Sunday rotogravure section. The inquiries had multiplied and Louise's calendar was jotted with appointments with the parents of prospective students.

The visits were as Connolly had described: Admitted to the chime of bells by Sister Léonie or Sister Colette and escorted up the royal-blue stairs, the parents, when Louise greeted them in the tower office, verged on speechless wonder. The fees set by Connolly at two thousand dollars per annum ranked Rosemoore among the most expensive boarding schools in the nation, but the dazzled parents seemed to accept it without a murmur. Perhaps they were distracted by the tea that Louise served them from a blue Canton service, or it might have been the Sargent portrait in the entrance hall.

In any event, the enrollment had doubled from four to eight, and the opening was still some weeks away.

TWELVE

Every afternoon at four o'clock Louise observed what had become a ritual for her. She scheduled her appointments so as not to be kept from her vigorous walk, uphill and down, across fields, and through the woods that encompassed the boundaries of the school property. It was the one interval of the day that she reserved for herself, a time for reflection and assessment. The yelping, nose-quivering Tyrone sometimes romped at her side and always some problem or other gave pursuit. The formal blessing of the school was to be held on August 15, the Feast of the Assumption, and she had invited Monsignor Hayes to officiate at the ceremonies. It was important to foster relations with the Archdiocese, and Hayes as Chancellor made an excellent conduit, but not until she broached it had Louise become aware of a secondary motive in having invited him.

"Then you'll accept?" she'd said on the telephone newly installed in her office. "And what of Father Regan . . . if not for him, we'd not have a school to bless."

"I'm afraid Sean isn't available," Monsignor Hayes had replied. "He's taken a leave of absence and is on retreat at a monastery upstate."

"Oh, I see . . . well, we look forward to your visit, Monsignor."

That the relationship with Father Regan had not ended but continued to exist on a subconscious level was most apparent to Louise on the afternoon walks. She took refuge from the disturbing realization by projecting herself into the future as she covered the school grounds. Coming down the porch steps, she envisioned a quadrangle of buildings across the drive and pledged herself to that endeavor. The gymnasium created from the stables had turned out attractively, with the original barn red retained, but even as she paused to admire it, Louise's glance would shift to the coach house across the yard. It was vacant, but she had assigned it a function. Moved to another site in a grove of pines up from the driveway, it would serve as a novitiate for the future nuns of Rosemoore. Often on her walks Louise tramped the fields to the imagined location where too a convent might rise, which the community of nuns would eventually require.

But just as often as she contemplated it, the future convent would jerk Louise back to the present and the problem of Bridget O'Shea, who had come to her with a request.

Although Bridget roomed in the attic and shared the lives of the nuns and Sisters, she was not a member of the community. No one had worked harder for the school than Bridget. She had joined with Sister Léonie and Sister Colette in the dusting, polishing, waxing, and scrubbing that kept the mansion in shining order. Since neither Sister spoke English, Bridget had taken it upon herself to instruct them in it. *"Fark,"* she would say, holding up that implement by way of illustration. *"Coop,"* she would say of a teacup, and *"sarcer,"* of its mate. To the extent that the Sisters had learned any of the language, they pronounced it with an unmistakable Irish brogue.

"If you'll excuse me, mum," Bridget had approached Louise after Mass one morning, "I'll not be needin' me wages no longer—I've saved the money to send for Ag."

"Now, Bridget, we've agreed—"

"If I was a Sister and belonged to God, I'd not be lookin' for wages ... and so, I ask for a holy veil and robes and vows to keep for the Lord God."

Louise had postponed giving Bridget an answer, and on her walks she debated the pros and cons of the plaintive request. She was determined, in establishing the American foundation of the Society, to eliminate the class system that she had disapproved of in

France. It was already in effect with the arrival of Léonie and Colette, but that was to be the extent of it. Weighed against this decision was the prospect of having to refuse Bridget what she so obviously longed for, and in doing it, to wound her tender and loving soul.

Louise was incapable of it, and a few days before the blessing of the school another ceremony was held in the chapel and attended by the community. In a white robe and shorn of her pigtails, Bridget O'Shea knelt before the altar. The lighted candle she held as she pronounced her vows to Father Anselm was a symbol of the light of faith. As Sister Bridget she then received from Louise the garments she had desired to wear. The black veils and robes had been sewn by the nuns, a gift of welcome into the community, but with the traditional apron of servitude omitted.

The ceremony of the blessing on August 15 was to retain for Louise a special poignance. She had scheduled it for five o'clock, when the shimmering summer heat had abated and the first shadows of dusk fell over the lawns. The candlelight procession that moved through the rooms of the mansion was led by Monsignor Hayes in a cope of cloth of gold. Two seminarians from Dunwoodie went in advance of him, incense wafting from their censers. Behind the Monsignor walked Father Anselm and Father Bede in gray monk's robes, and behind them were the nuns and the invited guests. Connolly Moore and his daughters, tanned from their summer at the beach, led the contingent of guests. Sister Matilda and Sister Clarita had traveled up from the convent on Waverly Place for the occasion. Joseph Slattery and his wife had turned out for it, along with Dr. and Mrs. Gavin, John Tyler, the architect who had drawn up the blueprints for the renovation, "Big Bill" Guinness, the contractor, and Takis Ariakian, whose wife was draped in a Spanish shawl. The lawyer, Jack Geoghegan, was present, anxious to catch an early train back to the city, and so was Rita Philbin, Connolly's secretary. Mrs. Van Pelt and Miss Osborne, as members of the faculty, felt duty bound to attend, wary though they were of popery. Bringing up the rear of the guests was Duffy, who had settled into his snug janitor's quarters in the basement of the gymnasium. Duffy's pipe was clamped in his mouth, unlit as a concession to formality.

The procession wound in and out of the rooms of the red-brick mansion, which had been christened Annunciation Hall. Clouds of incense floated up to the ceilings in the flickering glow of the candles. Upon each room, with a sprinkling of holy water, Monsignor Hayes invoked the protection of God against the malice and snares of the devil. In the chapel, Sophie's Virgin, restored to her pedestal, extended her arms to the sprinkle of water. The classrooms upstairs were blessed, and the infirmary, the tower office, and the bedrooms. The flickering line of candles halted at the back stairs. It was too narrow to accommodate the procession, and so Louise climbed with Monsignor Hayes to the attic, where he blessed the bare white rooms of the nuns.

Here was her abode, thought Louise, not the tower office but here in a bare cell with a crucifix as the only adornment. A strange disquiet took hold of her, as if the very act of the blessing, the holy water, the invocations, had called up the existence of sin in all its manifestations. No one was exempt from it, she thought, whispering her vows to herself as she went down the narrow stairs with the monsignor.

Descending the porch steps, the procession was met by a wagging, prancing Tyrone, yelping for admission into the ranks. With the Irish setter bounding ahead, the weaving line of candles moved across the shadowed lawns under the sunset sky to the hockey field and tennis courts. A breeze from the river blew at the sputtering candles, threatening to extinguish them. Next, the procession circled around the giant oak at the top of the drive and along the path at the side of the mansion to the gymnasium at the back. Monsignor Hayes blessed the coach house too for good measure, which brought the ceremony to a close.

When the guests thronged into the dining room, the supper that Mère Blanchard had prepared of turkey and ham, baked beans, and salads was set out on the sideboard. Appetites were hearty and the Spode plates were heaped full. Sister Bridget, her face a lighted candle, made the rounds with the silver tray of coffee, replenishing the cups. As the hostess, Louise circulated among her guests, moving from group to group, unable to shake off the sense that the evening was incomplete.

Everyone associated with the founding of the school was present, she noted, glancing around the resplendent dining room, and only then did the thunderbolt strike.

Everyone was present, but not the guest whose absence was a torment that would not leave her.

Sundays were no exception to the afternoon walks, nor were the sudden cloudbursts typical of a Hudson Valley summer a deterrent to Louise's brisk coverage of fields and meadows and woods.

One of her favorite haunts had been Tyrone's discovery. Plunging ahead of her into the woods, he'd vanished through the trees one afternoon, and Louise had followed his shrill yappings to a clearing at the edge of the woods. There, alongside a stream that cascaded from a rocky cleft, stood a derelict cottage. Moss grew over the thick stone walls and chipmunks scurried in and out of the ragged holes torn in the shingled roof. The windows were gutted and the scarred door was half collapsed on its rusty hinges. A rotted paddle wheel at the side of the cottage dipped inertly into the stream, which was crossed by a decrepit footbridge. Investigating it, Louise had ventured down a sloping path that led to the meandering stone fence that marked the school's boundary from that of Faircrest.

Despite the ravages of time and nature, the cottage had not lost its look of sturdy endurance, and Louise later learned from inquiries in Peekskill that long before the era of Hightower, dating back to the Revolution, the cottage had operated as a mill, grinding corn and barley for the local farmers. The wooded setting, the babbling stream, gave the ruined structure a storybook quality and had elicited from her a number of imaginative uses for it.

On this last Sunday in August, she lingered in the clearing, debating her choices. The cottage would make an ideal hermitage for the nuns, a sylvan retreat from the pressures of teaching, but it would be equally ideal as a studio for gifted art students, or perhaps as a . . .

The quick spatter of rain interrupted her musings. The cool droplets were refreshing after the long hot day, and Louise was in no hurry to reach the driveway from the woods, but then another cloudburst, heavier than the first, sent her scurrying up the drive. Halfway to the mansion she stopped, arrested by the figure of a man who had taken shelter under the giant oak.

Unaccountably, a trembling seized her, even before the man turned around and she saw who it was. She drew back, unconscious of the movement, as he started toward her in the rain.

"I rang the doorbell," Father Regan said, slicking back his hair. "Bridget said you'd gone for a walk."

The trembling grew worse. "Why didn't you telephone you were coming?"

"Didn't expect to, till I was on the train."

"Well, you might at least have—"

"I've only got a few minutes—a buggy from the station is picking me up." Instead of cleric's garb, Regan wore a black jersey turtle-neck and white duck trousers. "Don't worry, I haven't quit the priesthood," he laughed. "It's just I couldn't leave without saying good-bye to you."

"*Leave?*" She knew, from the panic in her voice, the nature of her feelings for him. It seemed ludicrous that she hadn't always known. "Where are you going?"

The rain had let up and Regan stepped closer, but still with a dis-tance between them. He looked thinner and his powerful body was tensed, as if something triggered inside him was ready to go off. "I've been getting in shape," he said, with a flash of the old mockery. "The workouts in the gym didn't help, so I took myself to a Trappist monastery . . . for a different sort of workout."

Louise had heard only the fact of his leaving. "Yes, but—"

"Maybe once I was in shape, back at Dunwoodie." He raked at his sodden hair and glanced mutely around at the campus. "But then came Rome and I . . . let's walk a bit, shall we?"

They walked up and down the driveway, each at a proper distance from the other, and Louise felt a stranger to herself. Emo-tions, sensations, churned in her that were newborn and overpow-ering. A part of her listened to Sean Regan evaluate his position, while another, wilder self yearned to hear quite another dis-closure.

"As a boy, priests were my heroes," Sean told her, stripped of mockery or swagger. "On the Lower East Side, when you couldn't pay the rent or were in trouble with the law, you went to the rectory for help. The priests were good men devoted to serving the poor. I went to the seminary wanting to be exactly like them, but Rome changed all that."

"When do you leave?" Louise asked. "Where are you going?"

He gave her a look of hurt surprise. "It's funny, but things like ambition and currying up to the rich and powerful—I'd have guessed that you've prayed for me to recant them."

The other self in her would not be usurped. "How soon do you leave?"

Regan's eyes blazed as he swung around to her. "I've made a terrible career blunder, you see. I've fallen in love with someone and can't persuade myself that I have a right to it."

Louise swayed and reached out blindly, as if for support. "It's true for both of us," she cried. "How did we let it happen?"

He stared at her in slowly dawning recognition. "It's happened with you as well?"

"Until a moment ago, I thought you'd stayed away because you couldn't bear my company."

"I couldn't," Regan whispered hoarsely. "But not as you thought."

"Coming up the drive, when I saw you in the rain . . . perhaps then I knew."

"It shows what a colossal pair of innocents we were." Regan laughed, but his jaw tightened in a ridge of muscle. "Dear God, M.G., what's to be done about us?"

Louise glanced around at the lawns and trees as though she'd expected to find herself on a crater of the moon. She looked at Father Regan, who stood apart from her on the driveway. "It was wrong, you said, ever to be certain of yourself."

"I said that?"

"Yes, but I didn't understand what you meant by it."

"It's still a tendency with me." Regan paused, measuring his words, aware of a shift in himself. "For instance, I was absolutely certain about tomorrow."

"You're to leave tomorrow?"

"I've signed up with a delegation to study missionary conditions in South America . . . at least, that was my plan."

"But not any longer?"

Regan sucked in his breath and a vein throbbed in his temple. "Where's that discipline of will I was so expert at practicing?" he asked. "It seems to have deteriorated."

Louise resumed her pacing, groping her way out of the abyss. "Is that unusual, I wonder?"

"Unusual for whom?"

"The priests of your boyhood—what if they experienced the same conflicts, the same temptations as you?"

Sean Regan moved from where he was standing. "It's likely enough."

"What if they had to repeat, over and over again, the vows they made as priests?"

He stepped in front of Louise, the warmth of desire radiating from him. "What if finally they made the choice of human love?"

"Well, then . . ." The closeness of him, the muscled body tensed in the black jersey, robbed Louise of her meager defenses. "*What? What then?*"

"Is it a monstrous offense for two people, whoever they are, to love each other?"

"Not if . . . they have a right to it."

"Right or wrong," Regan whispered to her, "all that's left in me is this hunger for you."

"I know . . . I know." Louise glanced up at the house as if to find it had vanished in a puff of smoke. "All at once, nothing else seems to matter . . . except that it *does*."

"Not for me."

"Everything we believe in and dedicated our lives to—it matters and always will."

"I've tried to tell myself that, but—"

"If not now, at this moment, what of later on? Can you really tell yourself it won't matter?"

They turned from each other, struck silent by the sight of the buggy from the station clopping up the driveway. In the ballooning silence, they watched its slow, swaying approach. Breaking the silence, Sean Regan turned to Louise, his jaw ridged in muscle.

"Then you regard it as a betrayal?"

"Before long, so would you, I think."

"If you want me to climb into that buggy"—he spread out his hands—"tell me to do it."

"I can't—I've not the courage."

Regan looked at her in an agony of indecision. "I—I've thought of South America, as an expedition to go looking for a seminarian who got lost in the jungles of Rome." He shuddered and drew in his breath. "Is there a chance I'll find him again?"

"I—I'll pray that you will."

"Maybe he wasn't lost, but wandered astray, and the shepherd who knows his flock, as they know him, will guide him back to where he belongs."

"Yes . . . *yes!*"

The buggy had pulled to a halt below the porch steps. Before going to it, Father Regan took inventory of the lawns and the grounds that stretched to the rim of the woods. He nodded approvingly at the towered mansion.

"What a beautiful school . . . and Rosemoore is a beautiful name for it. It's very classy, but then so are you, M.G." He held out his hand in good-bye, a gesture that he didn't complete. "I'd better make this fast, or I'll end by begging you to come with me."

"I'd go, if I could, God help me."

"I wish you all the success in the world, but be careful of what it does to you."

An eternity passed for Louise as she stood back while Regan climbed into the buggy. The driver jiggled the reins and the drowsy horse broke into a leisurely trot. Another eternity began when the buggy jogged into the woods and Louise was bereft of her last glimpse of it.

An eternity passed before she turned away and went up the driveway to the porch steps.

Mère Blanchard stood in the front hall, hands clasped in her sleeve. "I recommended to the others that they go to the chapel and pray," she said, to inform Louise that no one had watched from the windows. "He has gone, our friend from the ship?"

"Yes, he is gone." It burst out, not asking her permission. "It's as if he had died and I will never see him again."

"*Ma pauvre,* you did not know what it was between you?"

"But you did? Who am I, Solange? What's happened to me?"

Once before, when courage had drained from Louise at the sight of Ireland from the porthole, Solange had restored it. It seemed a distraught child that she gathered in her arms, whispering words of comfort and reassurance. "It is far we have traveled, but there is still far to go, *n'est-ce pas?*" The strained, rasping breathing made it necessary for her to pause and then go on. "The school must open in two weeks and you are the *Supérieure*. To whom else do we look with confidence to carry it out?"

"I will," vowed Louise, as she had on the night of the storm in Ballymar. "I can't fail you, I mustn't think it."

"We pray in the chapel and then you are to rest, for it is Sunday and I have cooked a delicious ragout of lamb for the supper."

"What would become of me if it weren't for you, Solange?"

"Ah, you would go on as you have, with courage."

In later years, Louise was to retain a jumbled recollection of the final two weeks of preparations to open the school. The cartons of textbooks to unpack, the medicinal supplies for the infirmary, the telephone calls from Connolly Moore, the interviews with parents, the registration of students and scheduling of classes, all had claimed her time and attention, but as with the centennial parade, they were to be jumbled together in her memory of the final two weeks. By contrast, the morning of September 4 would stand out in the awful glare of clarity.

When Mère Blanchard failed to appear in the chapel for Mass that morning, Louise was not alarmed. Solange had been deaf to all entreaties to lighten her workload, and if sleep had made her deaf to the awakening bell, so much to the good.

Sister Colette cooked the breakfast that morning. She was to assist in the preparation of the students' meals and was eager to demonstrate her skills at the range. The minutes ticked past and Solange's place at the table remained empty. With a twinge of foreboding, Louise went up the back stairs to the attic.

She knocked at the door, and when there was no response she went in.

Mère Blanchard lay in her cot attempting to drag herself up from the pillow. The tortured rasp of her breathing filled the little room. In the struggle to rise, the frilly nightcap had slipped from the gray-white shorned hair. Her creased face was bathed in perspiration and contorted with pain. She stared at Louise, vainly working her mouth in an effort to speak.

"I will telephone Dr. Gavin." Louise turned to race for the stairs. "He has a car and will be here before we—"

"*Non . . . non, ma chère.*"

"Please, I must hurry at once and —"

"Uhhh . . . uhhh." Solange collapsed against the pillow. "It is too late for the doctor," she gasped, rolling her eyes toward the doorway. "Was it not you, *ma chère,* who implored me to rest?"

"No, please."

Solange lifted a frail bony hand entwined with a rosary. "Do you see, I am not afraid? I have prayed to the Virgin . . . and her Son is coming for me."

Louise threw herself on her knees at the side of the bed. "Not yet, not yet."

"If I go . . . another will take my place." The breath wheezing from her, Solange lay back clutching the rosary, her eyes lifted at the ceiling. "I will ask God to send you many nuns for our school. How good of Him to let me travel with you . . . so far from the mouse that I was."

"Solange!"

With a muffled cry Mère Blanchard rose upright in the bed. A convulsion shook her and the breath that she gasped for would not come. The flailing hands made a last request and Louise, comprehending, reached for the crucifix above the bed and set it in the frail grip. She supported the dying nun in her arms as the breath rattled from her throat and the gray shorn head lolled back.

For all of her questing walks of the school property, her projections of the future, Louise had not thought of the need for a cemetery. The site she chose was a hill that sloped up from the grove of pines, where someday the novitiate and convent were to stand. For two nights the nuns kept a vigil before the pine coffin in the chapel. Father Anselm intoned the Requiem Mass on the morning of September 6, after which the coffin was borne over the fields to the solitary freshly dug grave on the hill above the pines.

It was the longest walk that Louise had taken.

On September 8, as scheduled, Rosemoore opened for its inaugural year. The enrollment by then numbered eleven girls. Four were entered in the lower school and the remaining seven were freshmen in the upper school.

The morning was bright and clear with the crisp tang of autumn in the air. The red-brick towered mansion looked as if it had always thus commanded the hilltop, elegantly preserved to the last glistening frill of gingerbread and the lustrous shine of the silver doorplate engraved with the signature *R.* The effect was not at all of a school but of a gracious and inviting home for those fortunate enough to afford such an establishment.

Connolly's Pierce-Arrow was the first of the cars to deliver the students. Boylan, the chauffeur, handed Flavin, Anastasia, and Monica Moore from the running board, each wearing the requisite white gloves with their royal-blue pinafores and white blouses. The three sisters appeared tense and strained, which very likely was attributable to opening-day jitters.

Behind the girls, as they went up the porch steps and Boylan circled the horseshoe on the drive, came the second car, a Vinton with New Jersey plates packed with suitcases, riding boots, and tennis rackets. It was followed by Mother Larkin in the school's Pierce-Arrow, who had driven to the station to collect a lone student from Ohio.

One by one, while Duffy attended to the luggage, the girls in pinafores went up the porch steps and into the entrance hall. Waiting there for them was the headmistress. She stood erect and composed below the carved-oak stairs. The Sargent portrait gazed down from the mantel as Louise smiled a welcome at each curtsy and white-gloved hand that was extended to her. She greeted each girl by name and then gestured her into the drawing room, where the faculty was assembled. No classes were scheduled for the opening day. In the drawing room, Sister Bridget served the girls milk and cookies and the faculty engaged them in conversation. The parents who had accompanied their daughters were served tea and coffee in the library. Chapel was set for ten o'clock, followed by a tour of the campus. Time was allotted for the good-byes to parents, and for getting acquainted, unpacking suitcases, and settling down in unfamiliar rooms.

Louise stood in the entrance hall until she had greeted the last student and parent. Her smiling composure suggested a tranquillity that she was far from possessing. Connolly Moore had not arrived, as expected, with his daughters. Jonah Reeves, the butler at Faircrest, had telephoned to advise Louise that his master was indisposed and unable to attend the opening. She had connected it somehow with the tension evident in the sisters when they had arrived . . . but what had afflicted Connolly?

The smiling composure belied the image of the white cross on the cemetery hill, and that of a steamship bound for Argentina, which haunted Louise as she stood in the entrance hall, every inch the vital and capable headmistress. No one was ever present to witness the moment when she turned to gaze questioningly at the Sargent portrait above the mantel. She felt a peculiar kinship with the portrait, as though a measure of the sadness inherent in it had been transmitted to her.

BOOK TWO

IV
THE FLOWERING

THIRTEEN

In 1922, a gala event was to coincide with the opening of Rosemoore for the fall semester. Work was finished on the first new building to go up since the school's founding, and the dedication ceremonies were to be held on the Sunday preceding the start of classes.

All schools are rumor factories and Rosemoore was no exception. The fact that the building had not gone up sooner had long been a subject for conjecture. As early as 1916, fewer boarding accommodations were available than the applications received for them. The old coach house was a possible boarding annex, but it had been moved to another site and remodeled as a novitiate. The war years would have canceled any building plans, but no such plans were known to exist and the Armistice of 1918 had not changed the situation. Certain individuals had espoused the theory that the school wished to preserve its exclusiveness by limiting the enrollment, but that was contradicted by the yearly increase of day students.

Still, something about the situation had not made sense. Rosemoore virtually exemplified the American success story, having achieved national prominence in a remarkably short period of time. It rivaled the convent schools of the Sacred Heart as the choice of wealthy Catholics for the education of their daughters. It offered amenities—a season box at the opera, summer travel in Europe—unrivaled by the Sacred Heart, but unlike those schools it had not grown by so much as a centimeter.

The decision to build, of course, rested with the Rosemoore Corporation, which was to say, Connolly Moore. In effect a one-man board of trustees, his decisions were not subject to public scrutiny. Conjecture was the only peephole into the chairman's motives and it could find no reason for the delay of the new building. The one other person who held office in the corporation was Mother Maguire, the headmistress, and it was inconceivable that she was behind the delay. If not, it indicated a conflict between these two strong personalities, but what lay at the core of it was anybody's guess.

With the announcement in 1921 of the projected new building, conjecture had taken a breather. By the summer of 1922, construction was near completion and the invitations to the dedication ceremonies went out, with an added fillip of drama.

It was learned that the Mother General of the Society had been invited as a guest of the school, but would she accept? Relations with Montpellier, less than cordial over the years, had not improved. The Mother General's coming, were it to materialize, was seen as an indication of compromise. To decline the invitation would widen the breach with the Motherhouse and render it that much more difficult to heal. Or she might come in order to exert her authority once and for all over a willful and rebellious stepchild in America. In either case, how would the stepchild greet her, by waving an olive branch or a battle flag?

If all schools are rumor factories, in this instance, the behind-the-scenes drama at Rosemoore extended to two persons who had not figured in any of the conjecturing. The invitations were mailed in August, a month in advance, to allow enough time for delivery, but both young women in question were, through happenstance, late in receiving them.

Agnes O'Shea's invitation was forwarded from a previous address and did not reach her until the week before the dedication. It lay on the hall table of the rooming house for a couple of days before she noticed it. In Ag's helter-skelter existence, mail was a rare occurrence.

Stuffing the invitation in her purse, Ag toiled up the flight of stairs. She worked as a waitress in a Times Square restaurant and her feet were killing her. Eight years had passed since she had left the orphanage in Cork to live with Bridget and the nuns at Rose-moore, and four years since she had made off for the bright lights and random diversions of the city.

Ag switched on the dim bulb in the frowsy room, kicked off her shoes, and examined her tired face in the dresser mirror. The powder and rouge did little to camouflage what was already a faded pretti-ness, wan and forlorn. She squeezed out of her skirt and blouse and pulled on a sleazy fuchsia-colored wrapper. Then she flopped on the bed with the invitation. The plucked eyebrows gave her a startled look as she tore at the envelope.

If Agnes O'Shea professed a creed, it was that life had cheated her. Early on it had landed her in the orphanage, then followed that with the humiliations of Rosemoore. Blooming princesses the girls were, and she was obliged to wait on them in the dining hall, they who had everything and she who had nothing. She had hated the morning prayers in chapel, the pious worship of God that had made Bridget the lowly servant of the nuns. Ag had rejected what she saw as Mother Maguire's pretext of concern for her welfare. She had balked at every attempt to provide her with an education. The day she was eighteen and could no longer be forced to stay at the school, Ag had fled to the city, which she felt had cheated her too.

The invitation rubbed at the hurt in Agnes as much as it fueled her anger. "Come back," it said in effect, "all is forgiven, we love you." Well, she had to admit that Bridget loved her to the ex-tent that anyone did. She'd let the months go by with Bridget not knowing if she was alive or dead, so why not be nice for a change and . . .

Ag traced a finger over the engraving and half made up her mind to attend the ceremonies. But then she thought of the princesses, them with everything and her with nothing. The anger boiled in Agnes, mixed with the hurt. She'd go up there, all right, but not for any ceremonies.

Owing to the fact that Lem showed up that night, Ag didn't get out of bed the next day until noon. He'd left ten dollars on the dresser, but why shouldn't he pay for what he'd done? She'd been saving part of what Lem gave her, and when she was ready to walk out on him, who would be cheating whom?

The anger stewed in Agnes as she pawed through her closet and selected a peach satin blouse, gored skirt, and feather boa to get dressed in. Damned if she'd go to work today, no, she'd go spring her surprise on Bridget, relishing the shock it would give her.

Ag skipped breakfast, since eating made her queasy, and splurged on a taxi to Grand Central as well as one at the Peekskill station.

"Rosemoore," she instructed the driver in a mock-fancy voice, but there was no fun in it, only rage. Ag suffered from asthma and warned herself not to get worked up or it would precipitate an attack. The taxi drove through the school gates and she made an effort to compose herself.

The effort was spent the moment she viewed the campus that had been the scene of her unhappiness. Stamping up the front steps of Annunciation Hall, she brushed past Sister Léonie, who answered the door, and flounced into the drawing room. Posed at the mantel, the feather boa slung over her shoulder, Ag demanded to speak with Bridget.

"We are all most busy, with the opening of—"

"Tell her it might be her last chance to see me," Ag said, which did the trick.

Ag strutted at the mantel while Sister Léonie went to fetch Bridget. She tightened her mouth when her sister appeared from the kitchen wiping her hands on her apron. It wouldn't do to let Bridget see how much she still meant to her.

"Ag, darlin', did ya get the invitation? It's for Sunday, but—"

"I didn't go around to the back, like the old days, and you'll not make me sit in the kitchen with you."

Bridget's face clouded with reproach. " 'Twas yer own doin' and no one made you . . ."

"I didn't come for a handout."

"Who says you did? Besides, it was always Rev'rind Mother who thought to—"

"The reason I came is . . ." Ag blurted it out, not as she'd rehearsed it. "I'm in the family way—you know, a bun in the oven."

"You—?"

"I'm pregnant." Ag had expected a surge of gratification at her sister's shocked reaction. Instead, it bore out the stark reality of her plight. "I've not been to a doctor yet, but I'm four or maybe five months gone."

Bridget crossed herself. "Thank God you've come to us. We'll go straight to Rev'rind Mother, she's awful busy with the dedication, but—"

"Take me to Her Highness—what for?"

Bridget was certain that her prayers for the wayward Agnes had been answered. "Sure, the babe is a blessing that will change yer life. We'll find a place nearby for you to stay and when the—"

"A blessing, did you say?" Ag's laugh was harsh and abrasive. "You'd like that, wouldn't you, a kid to raise in the love of God?"

"Listen to me, darlin'—"

"What a joke, sendin' me that invitation." Agnes yanked the engraved card from her purse and threw it on the carpet. "Come back, we forgive you, when it's you that needs forgiveness for keeping me where I didn't belong and never could."

"No one could tell you different."

"Me, who had nothin', well, now I've got somethin', and it's mine and I'm keepin' it." The constriction had started, the slow knotting in her chest like a rope strangling her breath. "You'll not any of you lay eye on my baby," Agnes gasped, clutching at the feather boa. "I'll cheat you out of it."

"Don't say ugly things, I beg you."

"Lem's been givin' me money—this time I'll buy the boat ticket, *back* to Ireland."

It took Bridget a moment to absorb the news. "Save us, you don't know a livin' soul there."

"It's my home, ain't it? The orphanage was more of a home than any I found in America."

"Ag, darlin', you wept for me to take you from it—why else did I stowaway as I did?"

"My mind's made up—I'm goin' back, the sooner the better." The assertion gave Agnes some satisfaction and eased her breathing. The rope unknotted and with it the fear of her predicament. "I'll send ya a postcard, Bridie, and let you know 'tis a boy or a girl. Meself, I rather favor a girl."

Bridget thought of her prayers, trusting in them to aid her sister. "Once yer mind is set, it's useless tryin' to change it . . . but will you not talk to Rev'rind Mother before you go?"

"Why should I? All she ever felt for me was pity." It wasn't true, but knowing that it wasn't goaded Ag into a wild lashing out. "You might tell Her Highness that I favor a girl for my baby—it'll be mine to teach and not hers. Everything she'd have her believe, I'll learn her the opposite."

Bridget was aghast. "You'd not raise a child deliberate bad?"

"Oh, wouldn't I? Well, that's to be seen, isn't it?" Ag looked at her sister, except for whom she was alone in the world. "You meant good, Bridie—I'm sorry it didn't turn out like you hoped."

"*Stay*, and let us look after you."

"I'll not be pitied, d'ya hear?" The rope knotted again and Agnes clawed at her chest. "See what it does to me, comin' here—the asthma starts up and I can't breathe." She lurched across the burgundy carpet, trailing the feather boa. "I want a taxi! Call me a taxi!"

"Ag darlin' . . ." The grieving Bridget followed her into the hall and did as she was asked.

Up the road at Faircrest, the door closed upon Monica Moore and the protective young man who was with her. They went down the portico steps and Monica turned for a last look at the manor house.

"I'm not sorry we came, are you, Billy?"

"At least we tried to make peace with your father."

Monica had grown into a soft, yielding prettiness that did not suggest the embattled defiance she had displayed in days gone by. "Father won't change his mind," she said. "I know it as surely as my own name."

Billy grinned. "What's your new name?"

"Mrs. William J. McNally, and worth any price I have to pay for it."

Billy tucked his wife's arm in his and they started down the long graveled drive. It was an error to judge Billy McNally by his bantam height and boyish appearance. He carried himself as if he were six feet tall, and his direct, self-reliant gaze was an accurate measure of his character. The summer that Monica was seventeen, she had met Billy at the Monmouth Beach Club. He was working as a cabana boy to put himself through college, and was not considered by Monica's father to be an eligible suitor for her hand. For four years, obstacles had been raised to break up the budding romance. Monica has been shipped to Europe for a protracted stay, and Billy was dismissed as an errant fortune hunter. She had been threatened with disinheritance and banishment from her home and family. Finally, when they could wait no longer for her father's approval, Monica eloped with Billy to Maryland. They had returned the day before from a weekend honeymoon in Atlantic City, and had come to Faircrest hoping for a reconciliation.

Salvio, the head gardener, was clipping the shamrock hedge at the oval in the drive. Few secrets were kept for long from the staff at Faircrest, and he put down his shears at the newlyweds' approach. Salvio's leathery countenance was creased with regret at the misery that had been inflicted on the young couple. He took the bouquet of white lilacs that he had concealed in the hedge and presented it to Monica.

"White for da bride, an' wishes of happiness."

Monica bit her lips and thanked the gardener who had sung Neapolitan songs to her in her pram. The hardest parting, second to that with her sisters, was with the men and women of the estate who had raised her.

"I'll miss you, Salvio—will you tell everyone for me that I'll miss them?"

"Yeah, I tell 'em."

Billy put a comforting arm around Monica and they continued down the driveway. She glanced through the mail that Jonah had given her at the door and opened the invitation from Rosemoore, which she showed to Billy.

"It's really a shame—we should all be together at the dedication and yet we won't be."

"But why is it? What makes your father act as he has with us?"

Monica sighed at the perplexing riddle of her father. "I don't know, but it's all to do with whether we love him or not. I couldn't give you up just to prove it."

"Well, maybe with time he'll feel differently about it."

She was free, thought Monica, as they neared the wrought-iron gates. The distant echo of a train whistle sounded over the hills and stirred a memory of her childhood.

"I was four when Mama died, so I don't remember her too well ... but she used to listen to the train whistles, and now I wonder if ... ?"

"What, honey?"

Monica walked through the gates of Faircrest. "Well, I guess she must have longed to get away too."

A taxi went past them on the road, but Billy's mind wasn't on taxis. The weekend in Atlantic City had made a large dent in his cash reserves. He'd insisted on the honeymoon, just as in Elkton he'd held off the wedding until he'd found a priest who would agree to marry them. Billy wanted nothing less than what was proper for his bride.

The newlyweds hiked the mile and a half to the trolley stop at the top of Main Street. "Here's the extent of my cash reserves," Billy said, waving the eight dollars at Monica. "Think you can manage till payday?"

"I haven't the least idea about money, but I'll try."

"Typical rich girl. Frankly, I worried about marrying you."

"You did?" Monica queried. "Not that I blame you, but why?"

They boarded the trolley, which went clanging down the steep hill into town. "Y'see, it started when your father called me a fortune hunter. Holy mackerel, I thought, maybe he's right. Is it her money I'm after?" Billy's arm slipped around the back of the wooden seat. "It had me worried, so I tried to think of you as poor, not a nickel to buy a Hershey bar . . . and it made me love you even more."

"But didn't you know?" Monica's voice trembled. "I *was* poor," she said, and Billy grabbed her in his arms and kissed her in front of all the trolley passengers.

They strolled the station platform, mapping out the future while they waited for the train. Billy's money had also gone to rent a walk-up flat in the Bronx, around the corner from his family. The furniture at present consisted of a bed and bureau, kitchen table and two chairs, and a sofa on loan from his parents, but Billy was confident of adding to it. "Won't take long," he promised. "I'm due for a raise in January."

"Your parents have been so kind."

"Can't you tell they're crazy about you? Mom's buying the works for the kitchen to start you on cooking lessons."

Billy's confidence in the future was boundless. He had been hired straight out of Fordham by the little-known but prospering Computing Tabulating Company. It had changed its name since to International Business Machines, which was indicative of a confidence equal to Billy's of what the future held in store. "Wait and see," he declared. "Someday I'll earn enough to send our daughters to Rosemoore."

"Oh, I'm sure of it."

Despite the bright optimism of their talk, one aspect of the future was avoided by the newlyweds. It had been pivotal to their elopement, but both felt too awkward and shy to discuss it. In the gaps of silence that ensued, Monica kept looking up the platform at the pale young woman with spots of rouge and frizzy hair who sat alone on a bench at the end. Monica frowned, trying to identify her, then finally went up to the bench.

"Excuse me," she said, "but aren't you Agnes O'Shea?"

The reply was short and pithy. "What of it?"

"I was certain we knew each other . . . and then I remembered Sister Bridget's joy the day you came to Rosemoore."

"Oh?"

"Were you visiting her today? Perhaps you don't remember me, but—"

"As if," Ag laughed, "I could forget the number-one princesses."

"Is that how you thought of us? It's the last thing I'd have called myself."

Ag shot her an accusative look from the bench. "You was princesses to me, with every sweet thing in life you could want."

"Not always." Monica turned and nodded down the platform at Billy. "That's my husband, but until a few days ago I was afraid we'd never marry."

Ag was suspect of what Monica had said, and yet she sensed that it was genuine. "All the same, I'll bet you wound up with a grand weddin' costin' a fortune."

"No, it wasn't the least grand. In fact, I didn't have a bridal bouquet until today." Monica regarded the white lilacs cradled in her arm and drew one out from the bunch. "I'd like it if you'd share our happiness."

Against every warring instinct, Agnes O'Shea took the proffered flower. She fondled the white petals and imagined herself as a bride, but the fantasy was of brief duration. "Share, did you say?"

"I just meant—"

"Ya needn't pretend with me." Ag got up from the bench and the hurt that translated into fury spilled from her lips. "We've nothin' in common, you and me, and you're a blitherin' fool to think it."

Ag was wrong in her estimate but unaware of it, and she threw the flower on the wooden planks in disgust. She stalked to the rail at the far end of the platform, jabbing at the frizz of hair.

Billy McNally hurried to his wife, who was retrieving the discarded flower from the wooden planks. Monica was pregnant, which had precipitated the elopement to Maryland. She shared that in common with Agnes O'Shea as well as their years at school and the invitation to the dedication of the new building. The station itself, the toot of the whistle sounding along the tracks, the train that chugged toward the station—all held a share in the future of Rosemoore and of those whose lives were linked to it.

FOURTEEN

"Listen," said Mary Elizabeth Devlin, who preferred to be called Lizzie, from the rear of the Cadillac. "No fooling, it's not going to work."

"The invitation said two-thirty. We're not late, are we, Frank?"

"Easy, sweetheart." Frank Devlin calmed his excitable wife. He swung off the highway and onto the country road that led to Rosemoore. "We've got a couple miles to go, so relax."

"Why am I nervous?" Marge Devlin gave a despairing tug at her silver foxes. Stone marten or mink would have been nicer but not so showy, she fretted. Ever since Frank had made it big in the gasket business and moved his family to the Strawberry Hill district of Stamford, Connecticut, Marge had done little but worry that she and her seven red-haired children would commit some social blunder. The Irish, she kept telling them, were descended from kings, though she suspected that these alleged monarchs were barefooted and had dwelled in caves. Still, Marge was determined to make ladies and gentlemen of her boisterous crew and today was a supreme effort in that direction.

"Mom, listen, to quote the old saying about a sow's ear—"

"Hold it a minute," Marge cried, at which Frank stopped the car to allow her the view of wrought-iron gates and velvet lawns sweeping to the manor house on the hill. Faircrest epitomized all that Marge had preached to her children and she spoke of it with a reverence worthy of a holy shrine.

"Can you imagine it? For Flavin's twenty-first birthday party her father imported four hundred guests by boat from New York." A devout reader of the society columns, Marge reserved for Flavin Moore the adulation usually bestowed on movie stars. "Of course, it was peanuts compared to her debut at Sherry's. The *Journal* gave it a whole page of pictures. I ask you, what Catholic girl ever got that kind of publicity?"

"The Blessed Virgin," Lizzie quipped.

"Don't be fresh, Mary Elizabeth, and we're not to gawk at Flavin if she's at the ceremony. It's not polite, but just think, baby ..." Marge adjusted the silver foxes. "You're going to the very same school where she went."

"Yeah, and that's the trouble." Lizzie leaned forward, skinny arms propping her chin. "It won't turn me into Flavin Moore. You can't make a silk purse out of a sow's ear."

"You are not a sow's ear." Marge reached behind to comfort her offspring. "What you are is a hooligan and it's the duty of Pop and me to make a young lady out of you. That's final."

The car started up again and Lizzie flung herself against the back seat. She stared in misery at her royal-blue pinafore and ached for the Levi's and sweat shirt that were her favorite garb. A lump welled in her throat as she thought of the parting that morning from her brothers and sisters and Rooney, the family's Irish setter. Frank Junior had once remarked that Lizzie was a dead ringer for Rooney and she could see what he'd meant: the same streaky red mane and long skinny legs constantly on the gallop. Lizzie Devlin was ideally constructed for such outdoor pursuits as climbing trees, scrambling over backyard fences, and playing stickball with her four brothers. While admitting the hooliganism, she felt that today was a stiff price to pay for it. The road turned, and as the gates of the school loomed before her, Lizzie swallowed the lump in her throat to keep from bawling.

"Here we are, baby. Isn't it gorgeous?"

Marge Devlin fell into a reverie as Frank followed the shiny cars that wound through the firs and evergreens. She remembered the parochial school on the wrong side of the tracks in Bridgeport that she had attended as a girl, a dungeon of a school set in a concrete yard bare of trees or greenery. The driveway curved up from the woods and the sudden vista of flower-splashed lawns and towered mansion set high above the river prompted Marge to give thanks for her good fortune. She aspired to the best for her children and Rosemoore was the best that money could buy, a Catholic boarding school possessed of what Marge designated as "class." She was hard pressed to define this quality, except to acknowledge that she herself lacked so much as an ounce of it. Flavin Moore, on the other hand, possessed tons of class, and when she made it into the society columns, so had the school of which she was a graduate. In Marge Devlin's view, you couldn't ask for fancier credentials than that.

Frank pulled into the parking lot and Marge panicked at the sight of the well-dressed guests who were streaming toward Blanchard Hall, the new building across the drive from the red-brick mansion. The number of mink scarves and capes on the women confirmed Marge's fears about the silver foxes. At least she'd picked the right car, she thought as Frank assisted her from the Cadillac. "Honest, it's all so classy, you'd think we were Episcopalians," she said, adjusting the foxes, her pinkie daintily crooked. "We'll leave the trunk till later. Come along, Mary Elizabeth, we musn't be tardy."

Lizzie hung back on the drive, trailing woefully behind her parents. She hadn't cried since the age of five, a proud record that she was on the verge of spoiling. She refused to cry, nothing could make her cry, vowed Lizzie, spying the giant oak at the top of the drive. Trees were her refuge and she did not hesitate to run for it and duck behind the gnarled, massive trunk.

Peering out, Lizzie observed that her parents were not yet aware of her defection. Poor Mom was having all she could do to get up the terrace steps without tripping over the silver foxes. After checking to see that a nun wasn't looking, Lizzie shinnied up the trunk, grabbed at a branch, and swung onto it. Curtained by the green leaves, she struggled with the lump in her throat. It eased up when she was able to shut her brothers and sisters and the adorable Rooney from her mind.

If boarding school was the price for her hooliganism, decided Lizzie, she might as well get some fun out of it. Straddling the branch and flipping her untidy red mane over her shoulder, she reconnoitered the rolling hills of the campus for signs of action.

The crowd of guests had proceeded into Blanchard Hall, from

which a burst of organ music indicated that the dedication ceremonies had begun. The campus was deserted except for a man who was coming up the driveway from the woods. He walked with a slight limp, Lizzie saw. Next, a big black car gunned past the man, narrowly missing him by inches. The car drew up below the oak tree on the drive and a chauffeur got out—a bruiser, in Lizzie's terminology. He opened the car door and from it crept a girl so wispy and thin that her pinafore looked as if it hung from a wire hanger. While the chauffeur removed her luggage from the car trunk, the girl stood quaking at the curb. She glanced up at the oak tree and in due course spotted the figure crouched in the branches.

"Hi, kiddo," Lizzie called down, not having much of a choice. "Well, tell me . . . how's tricks?"

"Hello," came the tremulous reply.

"What are you scared about?" Lizzie grinned down at the wispy girl. "I bet you're a freshman like me, but look at it this way: At least you won't get kicked out the first day for climbing trees. What's your name?"

"I . . . uh . . . it's Florence Giambetti."

"Italian, huh? Well, I'm Lizzie Devlin and back home I'm famous for climbing trees. That's what did it, thinking about home and my brothers and sisters. Say a prayer that I don't get caught, because then—oh, boy, here we go."

The burly chauffeur was approaching, but the girl headed him off. With a pluckiness that Lizzie would not have guessed at, she ran to her luggage stacked on the curb and distracted the chauffeur by counting it with him. The shrill barking of a dog signaled the next sequence of action. It streaked around the side of Annunciation Hall, an Irish setter, the very image of Rooney. Oh, rapture, thought Lizzie, borrowing from her favorite heroine, Dorothy of the Oz books, but then her heart gave a thump, for the dog bounded unerringly for the oak tree.

"Hey, listen, cut it out," Lizzie hissed at the dog, who was leaping and pawing at the gnarled trunk. "No fooling, I think you're adorable, but at this exact moment—"

She gasped in dismay and crouched down, hugging the branch. The dog's barking had caught the attention of the man whom she'd seen coming up the drive. He looked over at the tree and the dog, and decided to investigate. Moving closer, he peered up into the branches, which was Lizzie's undoing.

Down she toppled, spout over teakettle, and landed flat on her back in the grass, the breath walloped out of her. Zigzags of color exploded like firecrackers and waves of dizziness washed over her. After some moments had passed, her eyelids fluttered open. The dog was sniffing anxiously at her feet and the man was kneeling beside her. She looked up at him, and then it wasn't dizziness that kept her flat out in the grass.

"Are you all right?" he asked solicitously. "Hurt anywhere?"

It seemed wholly appropriate to Lizzie that angels bore masculine names, for here was St. Michael kneeling beside her, dark and beautiful in tweeds and flannels.

"I'm Stephen Jarvic, the new art teacher," he said. "Are you new here too?"

The jig's up, thought Lizzie. "It's okay if you've got to turn me in," she said.

"I think a few allowances should be made for the first day, but we ought to check for broken bones."

Lizzie Devlin blinked, startled as a finch, and scrambled to her feet, declining assistance. She brushed furiously at her mussed and snagged pinafore. "Honest, nothing's broken, I can tell."

Stephen Jarvic stood up, hindered by the stiffness in his left leg. He nodded across the drive at Blanchard Hall. "I'm sure there's a doctor among the guests in the chapel. Why don't we ask him to take a look at you?"

"No, I'm fine, see?" The dog chased eagerly in front of her, and Lizzie joined in his play. She raced to and fro to rid herself of the confusing emotions that she could not identify, "See, I'm fit as a fiddle," she protested, and ran up to Florence Giambettti at the curb.

"Listen, want to be friends, or would you rather think it over?"

"No, I—I'd like it," Florence asserted, despite the intimidating presence of the chauffeur.

"Back home, my friend Mr. Pizzaro lets me ride around on his ice wagon."

"Really? My grandfather used to have a fruit wagon on Mulberry Street—it was my fondest wish to ride with him."

"Well, that makes us a natural." Lizzie shot a quizzical glance at the chauffeur. "Why didn't your parents bring you today, or don't you still have them?"

"Oh, yes, but . . . they let Primo bring me."

"Who can figure out parents?" Lizzie exclaimed, pushing away the unwanted emotions. "C'mon, let's go sit on a bench and act ladylike."

Lizzie headed for a bench under a beech tree on the south lawn and didn't glance back. She sat conversing with Florence, the dog flopped at their feet. "What's he doing?" she asked her new friend. "*Him*, the art teacher . . . never mind, it's a mere bagatelle," said Lizzie, who liked the sound of the word though ignorant of its meaning.

Only by prodding himself did Stephen Jarvic cross the drive to Blanchard Hall. He'd arrived in his flivver in plenty of time for the ceremonies, but some contrary impulse had taken him through the woods to the abandoned cottage he'd discovered on an earlier prowl. He sought it out, he guessed, because it reminded him of his own state of disrepair.

Stephen's leg injury was the consequence of a grenade that had torn into it at Château-Thierry in 1918 in one of the bloodiest offensives of the war. Paris had been the dream of Stephen's youth in the Slovak farm community in northern Wisconsin where he'd grown up, a farm boy with a passion for sketch pads and charcoal pencils. He'd won a scholarship in art at the University of Wisconsin and had stayed on in Madison after graduation, teaching in a high school to earn the money for a year in Paris. The war had shipped Stephen overseas free of cost, and the grenade at Château-Thierry had shattered his dream as well.

He stood on the walk below the terrace of Blanchard Hall listening to the hymns and organ music that floated from the chapel. The frailty of the injured leg was contradicted by the lean, taut thrust of his shoulders, but a different kind of frailness shone in the dark face that had summoned the image of angels for Lizzie Devlin. Stephen listened to the singing and thought of the girl he had seen in the park while an inner voice urged:

Why must you keep on expecting the worst? You were ready for amputation, but Dr. Staples wouldn't give up until he'd saved the leg. You were terrified that in mind and spirit you were beyond healing, but Father Regan wouldn't

*quit until you were fit for release. The girl you were convinced you'd never see
again or learn who she was . . .*

The leg was hurting, but Stephen paced the walk below the terrace steps ignoring the darts of pain. Worse than the multiple sur-
gery and tortuous exercises was the psychological damage the war
had inflicted. He'd languished in the army hospital in Washington
for months until Father Regan had arrived to shake him out of his
lethargy and despair. The chaplain was famed among veterans for
his overseas work with the shell-shocked and wounded, but Stephen
had not experienced his rough therapy at first hand. By turn mocking and tender, dismissive and caring, the priest was fully committed to the injured men, and sensing it, they had responded
accordingly. To Stephen, a deeper bond had existed with Regan,
that of suffering. He knew little of the priest's background, but
it was as if he had been wounded too, though not on the battle-
field, and understood the havoc it wreaked on the spirit. Stephen
had received from Father Regan the strength of will to leave
the hospital that had become his jailer. After his release, he'd
gone to New York and enrolled at the Art Students League in an
attempt to recover his lost life. Often in painting class his hand
shook so badly that he couldn't hold the brush, but he'd stuck
at it and not heeded the demons that whispered of futility and
defeat. He'd looked for a teaching assignment to supplement
the disability pension from the army. Regan had given Stephen
letters of introduction to several Catholic schools in the city,
and one of the girls' academies had engaged him to teach drawing twice a week. Loneliness sometimes overwhelmed him and
drove him from his furnished room to wander the city, and one
afternoon in Central Park, one golden afternoon at the sailboat
pond . . .

Stephen turned from his pacing, aware that the singing in the
chapel had stopped. The jingle of the altar bell indicated that the
concluding rite of Benediction was under way. What foolishness, a
girl in the park whom he could not forget . . . expecting never to see
her again, a nameless girl, but then he'd taken Regan's letter to
Rosemoore and had encountered the Sargent portrait in the entrance hall. The resemblance was too striking to be a coincidence,
but how to ask the headmistress about it?

"I appreciate your seeing me," Stephen had said when shown to her office. "I ought to have written for an appointment, or tele-phoned—"

"Father Regan is an old friend, Mr. Jarvic. Nothing would have kept me from seeing you." Mother Maguire had been anxious for news of the priest. "We've all read of his exploits as a chaplain in the trenches . . . was it at the veterans' hospital in Washington that you met him?"

"If not for him, I'd still be in that hospital, like thousands of other men across the country. Some are too damaged ever to leave, and some can't take that final step back to civilian life. I couldn't have without Father Regan."

Mother Maguire, obviously moved, had shifted the papers on her desk. "You've come at an opportune moment, Mr. Jarvic. Our art teacher is to complete her degree requirements for a Master's in the fall, and we're looking for someone to take over her freshman and sophomore classes . . . if, of course, it would interest you."

"Yes, certainly." Stephen could not stem the question from his lips. "By any chance, is that a Sargent portrait in the entrance hall?"

"It's lovely, isn't it, although I've always felt . . ." The headmistress had paused and not explained her remark. "The portrait is of Mrs. Moore, the late wife of our benefactor. The school is named in her memory."

"I see . . . well, it's a stunning work." The question had been posed, but the answer did not suggest itself until Stephen, after discussing salary and what courses he would teach, got up to leave.

"The late Mrs. Moore—did she have a daughter, I wonder?"

"Yes, three of them, all graduates here, but what makes you ask?"

"I—I'm not exactly sure . . . it seems a shame, a woman of that beauty not having a daughter to inherit it."

"Ah, Mr. Jarvic, wait till you meet Flavin Moore. She is away for the summer, but she'll be here for the dedication of our new building in September."

"Is that so? Gosh, the world is smaller than it sometimes appears—I mean, I'll look forward to meeting her."

The singing in the chapel had resumed. "Tantum Ergo," familiar from Stephen's altar-boy days, was the closing hymn of the service. He held his breath as a nun came out on the terrace and hooked back the entrance doors. The chapel, which occupied a wing at the rear of the new building, was entered from the terrace at the front. Of the same red brick as the mansion that faced it across the drive, Blanchard Hall retained the Victorian character of the older building but with less clutter and a modernist expanse of windows. The Jamestown brick lent it a mellow patina of age, enhanced by the trellised ivy on the walls and the venerable trees it was set amid.

Bells chimed out over the campus, scattering jays and starlings into the blue sky. After a moment, guests proceeded to exit onto the terrace. The stylish matrons, the graying executive men, the poised young girls in blue pinafores, were as much a revelation to Stephen as was the opulent mansion on his first visit. The Slovakan farm women and men in cheap, mail-order calico and serge who had trooped with him into the weather-beaten frame church in Eagle River on Sundays were unrelated to the fashionable group of Catholics assembled on the terrace of Blanchard Hall.

The chattering groups and the air of casual assurance that they projected reminded Stephen of the summer people of Eagle River, the rich families from Chicago, Detroit, and St. Louis with big homes on the lakes, servants, motorboats, and big cars with chauffeurs to drive them into town for a movie or shopping. As a boy he'd thought of the summer people as belonging to a mysterious private club from which his religion and background excluded him. The families on the terrace impressed Stephen as a Catholic version of the same club, and he felt himself as much of an outsider among them.

A reception was to be given in Annunciation Hall, but the guests were not in a hurry to leave the terrace. While the younger children raced to frolic on the lawns, the parents moved from group to group greeting one another effusively. The girls in blue pinafores made up their own groups, trading breathless accounts of summer vacations. The nuns, whose graciousness was a far cry from the stern disciplinarians of Stephen's boyhood, filed out from the chapel and mingled with the girls and their families. As yet there was no sign of the person whom Stephen waited to glimpse, and it occurred to him that in view of her prominence and beauty, the guests were probably waiting to glimpse her as well.

He decided that he was correct when a news photographer stationed himself at the entrance doors focusing his Graphex. It brought an instant hush to the bright flow of chatter. The photographer, who was from the *Catholic News*, aimed his camera at the Archbishop of New York, resplendent in purple robes in the doorway. Patrick Hayes had succeeded to the title upon the death of John Farley in 1918, and his shyness was still evident as he posed for the cameras with Connolly Moore and his eldest daughter.

Her face was shaded by a lace mantilla, which she removed at the photographer's request. The flashbulb exploded and for an instant her face dissolved in the flash, but then it formed again, the face of the girl in the park . . . or was it the same girl?

Stephen stared at her in a turmoil of indecision. The girl at the sailboat pond had worn a middy blouse and skirt, typical of a music student, which, since she was studying a piano score, he'd taken her to be. In contrast, Flavin Moore's tailored clothes looked designermade and expensive. The ash-blonde hair was not tied with a ribbon and flowing down her back, but was drawn in a sleek chignon at the nape. She looked as if she had never ventured anywhere unchaperoned, certainly not to a common bench in Central Park.

And yet . . . something in her manner persuaded Stephen that Flavin Moore was the girl for whom he'd gone back countless times to the park, searching to find again.

The photograph taking wasn't finished, and he noticed how patiently Flavin held the pose, as if it were a duty she was obligated to perform. Another flash, and then she moved onto the terrace with the Archbishop and her father. The crowd made a path for them, and the guests who were closest to the Archbishop knelt to kiss his ring. As Stephen observed, Flavin and her father were paid a similar obeisance in the hands that reached to clasp theirs and in the smiles that competed for acknowledgment. Flavin again seemed to be performing a duty expected of her for which she had scant inclination.

Patiently, she threaded through the crowd, nodding, smiling, clasping the proffered hands. She reached the terrace steps in advance of her father and the Archbishop and, glancing up, her eyes met Stephen's. She was the girl from the park, beyond question it was she, but as Stephen returned her gaze, the cold fist of reality closed around him.

He stood below the steps, the outsider gazing up at a member of the club, the most beautiful and very likely the richest, and who was he, who other than an outsider? The frail, damaged hope that shone in his eyes contained no measure of worth or self-esteem. The dark, hollowed face held for Stephen no resemblance to a Caravaggio angel, only the rough look of a Slovak farm youth caught in a perpetual dream of thwarted longing. In the attitude of that youth, he turned away from Flavin Moore and went up the walk. The leg was shooting pain through his body, but it did not hinder his stalking retreat down the driveway, past the south lawn and the two girls who watched from the bench under the beech tree.

"What's wrong with him?" Lizzie Devlin asked Florence Giambetti. "He's sure in a hurry to get out of here."

"It's hard to figure out the things people do . . . listen, are you serious about us trying to be roommates?"

"Absotively." Lizzie spied her anxious parents descending upon her from the terrace, but even then her wistful gaze followed Stephen Jarvic to the parking lot.

Stephen's flivver, parked among the Lincolns and Packards and a spectacular emerald-green Rolls-Royce, attested as to who he was. He slid behind the wheel, massaged his leg, and switched on the motor. The guests had started across the drive for the reception at which Mother Maguire was expecting him, but he steered the car toward the woods. Classes were tomorrow and he wanted to review his notes and lesson plans.

As for the rest of it . . . the rest wasn't so awful, Stephen Jarvic told himself, swinging around the curve in the drive. The furnished room he'd rented in Peekskill was comfortable enough, and the tool shed behind the house might serve him as a studio. The woods brought thoughts of the ruined cottage for that purpose, but he rejected the idea as typically impractical. No, he'd speak to the landlady about the tool shed and haul out his easel and palatte and tubes of oils. He'd teach his classes and paint again . . . and keep safe in his heart the radiant image of the girl in the park, rather than let reality destroy it.

Not all the guests had crossed the driveway to the reception. Groups of parents and students were still congregated on the terrace, waiting for the nun without whose presence no school function was complete. She was the pulse, the heartbeat of Rosemoore, the driving force behind its success, eminent in her own right and as worthy of waiting for as Archbishop Hayes.

Reverend Mother, as she was called by everyone, was usually the first to move among the guests, welcoming them just as she had welcomed every freshman to enter the school since the opening day fourteen years ago. Yet for some reason she had not appeared from the chapel and the minutes kept ticking away. . . .

Louise stood at the altar rail of the blue-and-gold chapel, hands clasped in her sleeves for self-control, the one indication of what she was feeling.

"The frescoes?" inquired Mère Tissaud with maddening persistence, strolling the center aisle. "What is the origin of the frescoes?"

The duel had not let up since the Mother General's arrival a week earlier. "They are by an artist from Baltimore—quite lovely, don't you think?"

Mère Tissaud refrained from comment. Silence was the principal tactic she had employed in the duel, that and little demonstrations of authority. She had chosen this inopportune hour to inspect the chapel, simply to indicate that the prerogative to do so was hers. With her companion, the Vice-General Mère Guérin, she continued her leisurely tour of the aisles. "And the origin of the nuns' stalls?"

"A convent in Italy—Orvieto, I believe." Nothing had changed, thought Louise, except the names. Mère Tissaud was a carbon copy of her predecessor, who had died in 1915. The election of a new Mother General had been held within the thirty-day limit prescribed by the Society's constitution. Each house of the order had sent a delegate to Montpellier empowered to vote for the nuns of that house, but no allowance had been made for the thousands of miles that separated Rosemoore from the Motherhouse. As usual, the expense of a cablegram had been dispensed with. By the time Louise was notified of the death, the election had been held, depriving her of a vote in the outcome. Since then, Mère Tissaud had ruled from her distant throne chair in the aloof and arbitrary manner of old. She had looked upon Rosemoore as a rebellious stepchild, taking for granted the financial benefits of the relationship while perpetuating the injustices that had long existed.

But Louise had changed, if the Motherhouse had not, and the stepchild had grown into a prodigy. That, she thought, was the mistake that would be Mère Tissaud's undoing: her failure to recognize anything but the status quo as she conceived it to be.

"It is a jewel," the Mother General exclaimed of the chapel, gesturing at the gold-leaf columns and the mosaic arches that made graceful arabesques high in the ceiling. "Is it not a veritable jewel?" she asked of Mère Guérin, whose function was to nod assent when consulted. The Mother General trooped up the aisle toward Louise. "A jewel of such extravagance that, alas, it compels me to reflect—"

She halted before the Lady Altar and pointed, not at the Sienese Madonna that graced it but at the pedestal that stood below the altar. "Surely, that poor object does not belong among your treasures?"

"On the contrary." Louise turned to the wooden carving that was enclosed in a bell jar for protection. The years had almost worn away the stars on the mantle and girdle and made fragile the thin outstretched arms. Bits of paint had flecked away from the carved face but had not obscured the tenderness that illuminated it. "We think of Sophie's Virgin as a priceless treasure," Louise said, gathering courage from her words. "The girls at school all hurry to her with their petitions. If someone is ill, we carry the Virgin to her bedside. Many of our graduates who marry come with bridal bouquets to lay at her feet. Those who enter the novitiate bring her flowers on the day of first vows."

"What, do you claim miracles for your little Virgin?"

"No, not that . . . but faith is sometimes answered by a miracle." Louise turned to the Mother General in a sudden flash of swordplay. "However, you were saying about the chapel?"

"Pardon?"

"The extravagance—what did it compel you to reflect?"

Mère Tissaud's riposte was swift. "Let us not discuss it—today is for celebration and not for reproach."

"Reproach?" Louise asked, though she understood exactly the inference. "For me, do you mean?"

"*Ma fille,* it is a subject we must deal with, but at another time."

"Ah, yes, so we must." Turning, Louise was pleased to observe Mother Larkin hurrying up the aisle. It was four o'clock and she had timed her appearance to the minute.

"Gracious, Larkie, what explains your unseemly haste?"

Mother Larkin genuflected before the altar. "Excuse me for interrupting, but—"

"Yes, what is it?"

"The Archbishop." Mother Larkin bowed her head, a lowly subaltern. "He has remarked more than once on your absence at the reception."

"Bless the good man for noticing it." Louise turned with a smile to her superiors. "Are you famished for refreshment? Larkie, be an angel and take the Reverend Mothers over to tea."

Mère Tissaud, outflanked, delivered a parting thrust. "I will call a meeting at a suitable time . . . to pursue our discussion."

"Excellent, and be sure to sample the cucumber sandwiches. I'll join you in a moment."

Louise watched the chapel doors close upon the visitors from Montpellier. As she had estimated, the Mother General had not come to Rosemoore with the intention of mending fences. Nothing had changed, and the motive for the visit was exactly as Louise had surmised: to contest the ownership clause in the agreement that she had signed without her superiors' permission.

"Title to the property known as Hightower will be held by the corporation until such time as . . ."

Slowly, Louise glanced around the exquisite jewellike chapel. In her mind she emptied the new building and Annunciation Hall of nuns and students . . . all of the campus, empty and silent . . . of what value would it be then to the benefactor who, despite assurances to the contrary, still held the deed of title?

It was beyond her to fathom the reasons why Connolly Moore had not relinquished the deed. So touchy was the subject with him that she had ceased to bring it up, but now she was prepared to challenge him on it by initiating countermeasures of her own. *Without her, would there be a school?* Finally, Louise was ready to put that question to the test.

She knelt at the altar rail, both disturbed and stimulated by the strategy she had devised. Not a candlestick in the chapel belonged to the nuns, not a stone, a pebble, a blade of grass of Rosemoore was the property of the rightful owners. She had gone on trusting in the providence of God to settle it, but now she would assume that task herself, and would settle the injustices of the Motherhouse while she was at it. To win what was rightfully hers, she was ready to risk the loss of it.

Louise found it difficult at that moment to pray. It seemed hypocrisy to seek guidance when she was already committed to a course of action. The years had little affected the handsome face in the white fluted coif, but had cut between the winged brows a thin, vertical line that, as she knelt prayerless at the rail, grew sharp with the urgency of decision.

The furrow was smoothed away and Louise was again the serene and confident headmistress when she went from the chapel in her rushing stride to the guests who waited on the terrace.

The Rolls-Royce glided from the parking lot, the focus of interest to the guests who were departing in cars of lesser status. It took as much as two years for delivery of a Rolls, but Connolly had shortened the wait by going to England to claim his custom-made beauty at the factory. He could not resist the pleasure of beating the wait and sailing home with his prize in the ship's hold. The emerald-green shimmered with the depth of color of an Alpine lake as Boylan navigated the curve in the drive and his master leaned back in the cushioned luxury of the creamy leather seat.

"On the whole a notable day," Connolly remarked to Flavin, who sat alongside him. "Hayes is getting more princely with each public appearance. The red hat's a cinch for him, but the regal presence today belonged to Mother Maguire."

"Oh, I don't know," Flavin said, thinking of the difference the school had made in her life ... a second and happier home. "She was always so kind and approachable that I lost any awe I might have felt."

"Don't forget, I'm the one who pegged her as a winner." Connolly's hand went to his breast pocket for a moment. The dove-gray suit and gray Homburg were a perfect complement to his silver hair and the clipped black moustache flecked now with silver. He lowered his hand with what seemed like regret. "Well, the new building ought to satisfy her for a while. God knows, it cost me a pretty penny."

The Rolls glided out the school gates onto the road. "But you and Mother Maguire get along famously."

"Yes, we do, but ..." Connolly abruptly shifted the conversation.

"I want to thank you for accompanying me today. Unlike Stacey, you didn't storm off in a temper for the weekend."

"If you ask me, she enjoys her displays of theatrics." Flavin smoothed a gloved hand over the rose-point lace mantilla neatly folded in her lap. "I'm sorry that Monica wasn't with us. . . . Truthfully, Father, aren't you?"

Connolly stiffened. "The subject of Monica is closed—out of heart and out of mind."

"Then why have I seen the lights burn in your room late at night? I've noticed because I've not been sleeping too well myself." She waited for a response, and when it wasn't forthcoming, she went on with her entreaty. "Really, you know, Billy McNally is a decent young man. It's not as if they didn't ask for your blessing."

"You've heard me speak of your grandmother, but it illustrates my point about your sister." Connolly pressed the button that raised the glass between Boylan and the rear seat. "The first money I saved was to bring my mother over from Ireland. The first real home I could afford was for her to share with me, but she never set foot in it. She'd made her choice and it meant that she loved someone other than her son. God help me, your grandmother's long dead and gone, but I still can't forgive her for it."

"Monica loves you, I know that she does, and if you'd only—"

"You are provoking me, daughter."

"I'm sorry if I am, but—"

"The subject of Monica is closed." Connolly's voice was flat with finality. "A girl elopes because either her family disapproves or she is pregnant. I'll warrant it was the case with Monica. She has made her choice and I have revoked her trust fund, and that is the end of it."

Flavin turned and gazed out the car window at the road. She fingered the pearls at her throat, her mother's pearls, and fought the impulse to unfasten the sleek coil of ash-blonde hair that pulled at her temples. The hairstyle dated back to her debutante year and had created a vogue among the shopgirls who had copied it from the newspaper and magazine photographs. A minor vogue, thought Flavin, as minor as her talent for the piano. A minor life, for that matter, lunches and shopping and dinner escorts as interchangeable as her clothes, a life that had included three broken engagements and was going nowhere fast on a silken treadmill. *Age?* Flavin asked herself, and answered, *Twenty-six.* And then, *Occupation?* For that she looked at her father, who was her principal occupation. He sat ramrod straight, his frosty eyes fixed ahead, furious at her defense of Monica. If unchecked, his mood would follow a downward spiral well known to Flavin, whose job it was to divert him from it.

"Father, how about dinner in town tonight?" she suggested, as much in her behalf as his. "Jack and Charlie's is fun, or we might try the new supper club at the Ambassador."

Connolly made a show of rejecting the idea. "Speakeasies are hardly the place for you to frequent, and I've got a stockholders meeting to prepare for."

"We'll stay at the Plaza tonight—it will spare you the drive in the morning."

"Well, that's certainly a plus." The Rolls slowed for the turn into the gates of Faircrest, and Connolly pressed the button that lowered the glass. "Change of plans, Boylan, take us to the city." No one knew of the downward spiral better than he, and he turned to Flavin in gratitude for rescuing him from it.

"What would you say to Delmonico's—evening dress and a table at the window? For my money, it's still tops in town."

"I'll wear the Lanvin, if it's at the hotel."

Connolly had not lost his penchant for hotels as a means of contributing to his sense of well-being and importance. The year after his wife's death he had leased an apartment at the Plaza, which had recently opened, and he had renewed the lease every year since. Of any hotel he'd stayed at, the Plaza's standards and appointments were the most gratifying to his needs. The arrival of the Rolls at the Fifth Avenue entrance was the signal for a rush of bellboys to the curb. There was no luggage to carry, but each was rewarded with a crisp five-dollar bill. The progress through the glittering lobby drew as much attention as had the appearance of father and daughter on the terrace of Blanchard Hall. Mr. Willis, the desk manager, sprang to usher them into the gilt cage of the elevator and up to the apartment on the seventh floor.

"I'll want a room for my chauffeur for the balance of the week."

"Yes, Mr. Moore, one of our very nice servants' rooms."

Connolly's apartment consisted of a corner suite on Fifth Avenue, which he occupied, and a connecting two-room suite overlooking the park for his daughters. He was, as he often declared, an old-fashioned father, conscious of his duties. Any guests that his daughters entertained were required to enter by way of his door.

Connolly trooped through the rooms, throwing open the windows and connecting doors. Mr. Willis, hurrying off to reserve a window table at Delmonico's, collided with the valet summoned to press Connolly's evening clothes. For convenience's sake, he kept a full wardrobe at the hotel, a practice followed by his daughters. A maid was already in the bathroom, running the tub. He tossed his suit coat on the bed, pulled at his necktie, and boomed through the rooms at his eldest daughter.

"I realize you could have your pick of escorts for dinner, but will I suffice?"

Flavin stood at the mirror in her bedroom, unloosing the coil of hair. "Yes, of course, Father," she called back.

"Those broken engagements . . . I can't say I was sorry. The men weren't nearly good enough for you."

"No?" The hair spilled golden down her shoulders, and Flavin went to the window and looked out at the twinkling lights of Central Park. "I wasn't in love with any of them," she called through the rooms to her father.

"I tell you, I'm getting fed up with these damned stockholders meetings."

Connolly tipped the maid, who had come out of the bathroom, and sent her to attend to Flavin's bath. He kicked out of his trousers, shirttails flapping over his hairy legs. The joy had gone out of Shamrock for Connolly when it had become a public corporation in 1915. He resented the stockholders, whom he considered meddling fools. When George Hartford, his archcompetitor at the A & P, had offered to buy Shamrock outright in 1917, Connolly had been tempted to accept. He padded naked across the beige carpet to the bathroom, of half a mind to sound out the Hartfords again. It wasn't as if Shamrock belonged to *him* any longer. Besides, he had plenty to do just looking after his real estate and investments. Damn it, he wanted more time to enjoy his life—Connolly eased himself into the steaming tub—more time, above all, for Flavin, while she was still his to cherish.

The twinkling view of the park held Flavin captive at the window. When she was a child, the outings with her sisters along the winding paths had been invariably restricted by a governess. How she had envied the squads of children free to roam over rock and ridge as they chose. Later on, she had envied the couples strolling the walks arm in arm, and had woven a romantic fantasy for herself set in the park.

"I've run your tub, Miss. Are you wantin' any clothes pressed?"

"No, thank you."

Lingering at the window, Flavin thought of the young man whose eye had caught hers from the walk below the steps of Blanchard Hall—the gaunt young man, so alone and desolate, who had limped when he'd turned away with a scowl on the walk. She had wanted to find out who he was, but it had seemed awkward to inquire about someone glimpsed for a moment in a crowd. Well, it was too late to find out, Flavin concluded, and went to take her bath.

Connolly, wrapped in a Turkish towel, padded back into the bedroom. As he reached for a robe in the closet, he saw that the envelope had slipped to the carpet from his suit coat on the bed.

It shamed Connolly that in the envelope was the deed to Hightower that he had not turned over to Mother Maguire. It was hers and not his, and he'd intended to present her with it after the ceremonies today. Why had he reneged at the last moment? It made no more sense than his opposition to Monica's marriage when he could think of no valid objections to Billy McNally.

What was wrong with him that he could not let go of the deed? On the one hand willing to dispose of Shamrock without a qualm, and on the other . . .

Connolly retrieved the envelope from the carpet and wrestled with his fears. Once the deed was hers, what importance would he have for Mother Maguire? Those he loved, did they love him? How was he not to lose them, unless they were bound to him?

He slid the envelope into the drawer of the bed table and drummed his fingers on the marble surface. Very well, he'd take his chances with Mother Maguire and give her the deed, if he could bring himself to it. Connolly turned, knotting the sash of his robe, and looked at the doorway and the rooms beyond it toward his daughter's room.

"Getting dressed in there? The reservation's for nine o'clock."

"I'll be ready, Father."

"Since there's no young man in the picture . . . what would you say to a week of golf at Pinehurst after the stockholders meeting on Tuesday?"

"I'm only just back at my piano lessons, after the summer."

"Oh, c'mon, isn't your old man worth a canceled lesson or two? I count on you, Flavin, more than you realize."

"Yes, Father . . . I know."

"Then you'll give me a week on the links? Thank you, my darling."

Having prevailed, Connolly rang for the valet and demanded his evening clothes.

FIFTEEN

Louise took the folder of papers from her desk and followed her customary path between the door and the windows of the tower office. The Mother General had called a meeting for that morning, two days before she was to sail for France. Delay was another of her tactics, but it would not forestall what the papers revealed about the school's finances.

The eight-thirty bell drew Louise to the window and the bustling scene below. Nuns were crossing the driveway, en route to classrooms in Blanchard Hall. The mail truck was parked in the rear court of the new building and the driver, while he fished out the sack of mail, was gossiping with Sister Margaret, the postmistress. The school had grown sufficiently to merit its own post office in the basement of Blanchard Hall.

Mrs. Van Pelt stepped from her elderly Marmion in the parking lot. She had, as she would have expressed it, widened her horizons since coming to Rosemoore. Every Saturday she chaperoned the students who had elected to attend the afternoon performances of the Metropolitan Opera in the school's grand-tier box. As a consequence of this, she taught a course that she had entitled Glorious Opera: an Introduction, as well as much-needed classes in social etiquette. Mrs. Van Pelt's constant admonition, "Remember, you are Rosemoore girls," was a rallying cry among students, if somewhat of a joke. She had also widened her view of the Catholic Church, tutored by Father Anselm. "What drama, what intrigue!" she had enthused of the volume he had recommended on the succession of Popes.

Father Anselm, who had said the nuns' Mass earlier and heard confessions every Friday, was rattling out of the parking lot in the monastery car. Mrs. Van Pelt tossed him a gay wave of the hand and then, with Miss Osborne, the gym teacher, proceeded up the driveway. The two were inseparable companions and had taken to sharing a summer cabin together in the Adirondacks.

A noisy profusion of girls, fresh from breakfast in the twice-larger dining hall, spilled onto the terrace of Blanchard. Poor Solange turned into a building, the last thing that would have occurred to her, thought Louise at the window with a pang for her old confederate.

She looked down at the expanded campus and wiped the lively, thriving scene from her mind. She had envisioned the new building as the first unit of a quadrangle that would eventually include a new gymnasium and library, but that was the loss she was committed to risk.

Empty and silent, all of it ...

Seated at her desk, Louise examined the folder of papers, which supplied a record of the disbursements paid out by the school to date. She listed her findings on a yellow legal pad for use at the meeting. *Travis,* she jotted on the pad and circled it as a reminder.

Before she telephoned Henry Travis, of Travis and Hawes, Realtors, Louise went out to her secretary's office. It was an advantageous position for a nun, since the previous occupant, Mother Larkin, was the present registrar and assistant headmistress.

"I wonder whether the morning mail is sorted yet," Louise said to Mother Friel, her newly appointed secretary, who was filing correspondence at her desk and keeping an eye on the switchboard over which she presided.

"Yes, Reverend Mother, I shall inquire at once," the young nun replied and sped for the hall. As Claire Friel she had come to Rosemoore in her senior year and had entered the novitiate shortly after graduation. She was an efficient secretary, punctilious and smiling, but Louise sensed that behind the smile was a person to whom she had yet to be introduced.

Back at her desk, Louise reproached herself for suspecting that her calls were listened to from the switchboard. What evidence had she of it? She reached for the telephone, unwilling this morning to chance it.

"Mr. Travis? Mother Maguire here, calling to ask if—oh, really? Yes, that's precisely what I had in mind. A Fifth Avenue address?" Louise copied down the address. "Mr. Travis, I'm to be in the city on Wednesday. As I've explained, it must be treated in strictest confidence, but I'd like to look at the property. Say, two o'clock this Wednesday? Splendid, Mr. Travis."

The furrow between the winged brows was incised with tension, but Louise's step in the corridor was light and fleet. She understood why the Mother General had requested the library for the meeting: The tower office was not conducive to the authority she wished to exert. Again, it was a mistake in her calculations.

"Oh, golly," squeaked a gawky girl with flaming red hair who ogled Louise from the stairs and gave a wobbly curtsy. "Er, uh . . . good morning, Reverend Mother."

"Why are you not in class?"

"Well, see, I was, but I forgot my homework paper." The girl pulled an ink-splotched paper from her composition book. "Mrs. Van Pelt sent me back for it—'The Art of Pouring Tea,' " she added with a titter. "It'd be easier to write about the Eskimos, y'know?"

"What is your name, child?"

"Mary Elizabeth Devlin, but plain Lizzie suits me better."

"It has an honest ring," said Louise, whose encounters with her students were less frequent than in earlier years, and therefore prized. "I tell you what, Lizzie Devlin. Sunday afternoons I invite a group of girls to tea in my office. Why don't you come and pour for us next Sunday?"

Lizzie's freckled face split in a grin. "It's like asking an Eskimo, but I'll give it a try."

" 'I will'—that's the spirit, and now hurry off to class."

The brocade and velvet of the drawing room, the chandelier and Brussels lace curtains, posed for Louise, as she crossed the burgundy carpet, the question of ownership. She paused outside the walnut-paneled library, measuring herself against the two impassive figures seated at the table.

Mère Tissaud sat in a Windsor chair at the head of the oval table with Mère Guérin at her left. Louise entered, bowed to her superiors, and was motioned to a chair at the opposite end.

"Let us ask for divine guidance," said the Mother General in a sepulchral tone. She led the prayers, and then in a manner of speaking laid her cards on the table.

"A situation exists, my dear Louise, which I cannot permit to continue."

"You refer, I take it, to the agreement that I signed with Mr. Moore."

"Where you have failed, we will attempt to succeed."

"I see." Louise nodded slowly. "It is to be taken out of my hands?"

Mère Tissaud's smile was wreathed in benevolence. "The fault is no less ours. We did not supervise you as closely as we intend to in the future."

"Ah, yes." Louise placed the yellow pad on the table. "Here at Rosemoore, the future was the subject of a vote by the nuns . . . but I hesitated to upset your visit with the results."

"Upset our visit? Results?"

"The nuns have voted in favor of separation from the Motherhouse—to declare ourselves independent of the Society."

It was as if a cannon had exploded in the book-lined room. When she was sufficiently recovered to speak, Mère Tissaud fixed Louise with a baleful stare. "Must I remind you of your holy vow of obedience to the Society?"

"We felt it preferable to separate rather than to break that vow. It seemed inevitable, under the circumstances."

"What blasphemy is this? I confess I am scandalized by it."

"In view of my letters to you over the years, I find that surprising."

As a veteran of convent politics, the Mother General was less distraught than she appeared. The wind had shifted, sweeping away her objectives. She consulted in drafty whispers with Mère Guérin and availed herself of the water carafe while she reassessed her position.

"My dear Louise, if you bear grievances against the Motherhouse . . . however trivial, let us speak of them."

Louise stood up with the yellow pad. "Where shall I begin, with finances?"

It might have been a sharp pin that had jabbed Mère Tissaud. "Proceed, my daughter."

"Since 1908"—Louise consulted her pad—"the Motherhouse has received the sum of one hundred and eighty thousand dollars for the services of the nuns at Rosemoore."

"The agreement provides for it."

"If you dispute one clause of the agreement, why not the others?"

The Mother General exchanged a quick glance with the Vice-General and uttered a doleful sigh. "Since the war, the income from our vineyards has declined. Is it not true, Alphonsine?"

"*C'est vrai,*" echoed Mère Guérin with downcast eyes.

Louise resisted the bid for her sympathy. "From what I'm told, you are to close three of your schools—a declining enrollment, is it?"

The pill was bitter for Mère Tissaud to swallow. "*Alors,* we are forced to close them . . . a sad day for us."

The pain with which it was said deterred Louise, at least for a moment. "As daughters of the Motherhouse, we were happy to contribute to your support," she went on, "but to take from us half of our annual stipend, no, it was unjust and intolerable."

"Can we not discuss a solution?"

"It is too late—we have voted to separate."

The Mother General glimpsed a dim light in the tunnel. "Surely a larger share would alleviate your grievances?"

"Money isn't the only issue at fault. We have been denied from the beginning a voice in the Society and a vote in the elections."

"But my dear Louise—"

"Oh, I know! You abide by the rules of the constitution—to that I say it is high time you amended the rules."

Mère Tissaud glanced in a panic around the library, as though it had been invaded by looters. The lawns that stretched beyond the windows, the new building across the driveway, all she had seen during her visit, the affluence, the success, dictated the course she was obliged to pursue.

"What, tell me, Louise, would you consider a just share of the annual stipend?"

Louise circled the table in sober reflection. "As I've said, it is too late . . . but what if I were to advise the nuns that the Motherhouse had offered to accept a quarter of the stipend instead of half?"

The second pill was as bitter to swallow as the first. "The Council must approve it, but I will endorse what you suggest."

"It ought to allow for compensation for the years of disparity." Louise paused in her circlings and turned to Mère Tissaud. "I wonder, did you at last find a buyer for the property in Ireland that was such a burden?"

"A total loss, that property, not a buyer has turned up for it."

"Give it to us as compensation and it needn't be a loss." Louise returned to a chair at the table, but not to her designated chair. "Persuade the Council to think of it as an investment in good will."

"*Give* it to you? For what use?"

"Vocations," Louise replied. "Of the twenty-four nuns at Rosemoore, eleven are from our novitiate—an excellent record—but our growth depends on vocations. Imagine what a novitiate in Ireland would bring us in time."

"You have not the staff for it."

"We might, if you were to help us staff it."

The Mother General gathered the remnants of her authority around her like a tattered shawl. A transfer of power had occurred within the last minutes, and the nature of the duel she had waged was clear to her. It was a duel between the old and the new, the past and the future. Montpellier, however she lamented it, belonged to the past. Rosemoore was the future and she must either submit or be severed from it, but not without a last flash of sword.

"You talk of compensation," she rebuked Louise, "but you vote for separation."

"Then it leaves me with the task of nullifying the vote."

"And what else?" The Mother General signaled to Mère Guérin and they got up from the table. "It leaves you with Mr. Moore and the deed he has omitted to provide."

A class bell rang and Louise rose from her chair. "Yes, but I'm in the process of correcting that omission," she said, and followed the two from the room.

"Are you certain?" Louise asked on the telephone the morning that she was to drive the visiting superiors to the pier. "The fund is ours to spend as we choose?"

"Look, who stashed it away—Calvin Coolidge?"

"No, but I—"

"Listen, when did I give you a bum steer?" asked Joseph Slattery from his tower office in the Woolworth Building. Joe had traded the racetrack plaids for the muted worsteds of a company president. Slattery Associates had grown into a flourishing enterprise of senior accountants, junior accountants, secretaries, typists, and a mailroom boy who doubled as messenger. The client list boasted of blue-chip names like Warburton and Munn, but under the surface polish Joe was the same genial diamond in the rough who had guided Louise through the debits and credits of a score of ledgers.

"It's your money, thanks to no one but you and the nuns," he affirmed. "Raffles, teas, bridge parties, fairs—you did everything but pull off some stickups for it, am I right?"

"Fourteen years' worth, and rather on the order of stickups."

"Okay, so according to my records you've got a cozy balance of six thousand bucks, plus interest, sittin' in the Hanover Bank. It's strictly your business how you spend it."

"Mr. Slattery, were I to apply at the bank for a loan, a sizable loan, would they approve it?"

"All you gotta do is tell me, and I'll go to bat for you ... but you're not, are you?"

"Telling you?" Louise hesitated before she answered. If Mother Friel was listening at the switchboard, she had already said more than was wise. "At this stage, it's simply an idea under consideration, and of utmost confidence."

"Don't worry, I get the message. You can write a check on that money, if you need to. The Chief is down in Pinehurst swinging the clubs, in case it's useful to know."

"It is—and thank you."

Louise hung up the telephone and whirled into motion. It was ten o'clock, which allotted two hours for the drive to the city and minutes to reach the pier for the sailing. She collected her cloak from the Victorian brass coat-tree at the door and her purse and gloves from the bottom desk drawer. A breakfast tray was pushed to the side of the desk, the eggs and toast untouched. Little of consequence had transpired since the meeting with the Mother General. Louise had not yet informed the nuns of the outcome and the rumors were flying thick and fast. Even her closest confidante, Mother Larkin, was having to resort to guesswork, but all must wait until after the appointment with Mr. Travis.

"What's this, yer breakfast not ate?" clucked Sister Bridget in the doorway, making a beeline for the telltale tray. She reserved for herself the privilege of scolding her mistress, and woe betide anyone who poached on it. "I don't like this takin' yer meals on trays, with hardly a bite goin' down—'tis a one-way ticket to the graveyard."

Louise swung the black cloak around her and fastened the clasp at her throat. "Darling Bridget, I'm in a frightful hurry. Is Larkie downstairs with the car?"

"She is, an' the Rev'rinces are with her, sour as pickles." Bridget held out the wicker hamper, time-honored from the days before the school opened. "I've packed you a nice lunch for the city, since ya always find errands to keep you over."

Louise drew on her gloves and on second thought went to the desk for her checkbook. "If I go by Lewis and Conger, I'll bring you a new kitchen gadget."

"Or you might . . . no, you've enough on yer mind." Bridget said no more and lifted the macrame tray from the desk. If not a tray, it was a mop or broom or dust rag that she bore in her hands. A waif's look still clung to Bridget and she bordered on illiteracy despite her proximity to classrooms, but the years had made something else of her. Bridget was an institution at Rosemoore, beloved by the students for the simple offer of herself to their needs. She served their meals and made up their beds and visited the infirmary when one of them was ill. A refuge for the timid and lonely, solace for the homesick, Bridget found merit in the least of the girls, declaring that they were all of them a wonder. After class in the afternoon, the students flocked to the Pow-Wow, the tearoom in the basement of Blanchard Hall, as much for Bridget's presence as for the candy, ice cream, and soda pop she dispensed from behind the counter. Some of the students asked for her prayers along with the Tootsie Rolls and Baby Ruths, convinced that in her simple acts of kindness, the daily offering of herself, she was closest to God of anyone in the school.

"Well, I'm off," Louise said, the checkbook tucked in her purse. The cloak billowed behind her, but at the door the folds grew still. "I forgot, didn't I?"

"What's that, mum?"

She hurried back to the desk, where Bridget stood clutching the tray. "You've not heard from Agnes or whether she's left for Ireland?"

" 'Tis her babe I grieve for."

Louise thumbed her address book and jotted an address on a slip of paper. "I'll try that last rooming house and see if she'll listen to reason about the baby."

"Sure, I knew you'd think of it!"

"Merciful heaven, it's past ten o'clock and the ship sails at twelve-thirty!"

The drive to the city was enlivened by the clip at which it was made, but not by the two passengers in the rear seat mulling over their visit in dour silence. Up front, Louise's efforts at conversation flagged while Mother Larkin at the wheel pursued her guesswork as to what had happened at the meeting.

The royal-blue Chrysler, acquired last year in exchange for the expiring Pierce-Arrow, swerved up to the pier with ten minutes to spare before the *Rochambeau* sailed. All but one of the gangplanks were lowered, and before she went up it, the Mother General turned for her good-byes.

"*Au 'voir*, Louise . . . in parting, may an old nun offer her advice?"

"Of course, Mère Générale."

"It is God to whom we vow obedience, but when I was young and impetuous, I often forgot that my superiors were the instrument of it. To forget that is for a nun to fail, whatever her triumphs as a woman."

The ship's band was playing on deck. Obedience to what? Louise asked herself, waving with Mother Larkin in the crowd at the far end of the pier as tugs nosed the liner out into the river. "Why, it was highway robbery," she protested afresh. "Half the yearly stipend—I could not let it go on."

"Did you settle it at the meeting?" asked Mother Larkin, hoping for some tidbits. "What of the vote? Are we to separate?"

Louise paused in the crowd milling toward the street. Assailed by memories, she looked across the river at the pier where the *Kronprinz* had docked in what seemed another lifetime. How different it had turned out, different goals from those the steerage immigrants had awakened in her, and what had she to say about any of it?

"Knowing you," Larkie went on, "I'd guess that there's a master plan behind all this, but as to what it involves—"

"Patience, the cat is not out of the bag quite yet." Louise took from her purse the slip of paper with the address on it. "We have a two-thirty appointment uptown, but first we must inquire about Agnes O'Shea."

Brownstone rooming houses dotted with TO LET signs lined the block on West 103rd Street. The curiosity of those lounging on the stoops was piqued by the royal-blue Chrysler that pulled up at the curb, and even more so by the unlikely nun at the wheel. Another nun, stepping to the curb, marched briskly up one of the stoops and rang the doorbell. The sight was unprecedented on the block. So intense was the curiosity that several onlookers sidled up to the Chrysler and peered in the windows.

Easy does it, thought Mother Larkin, her gaze fixed on the distance. She recalled an expedition with Reverend Mother to B. Altman and gliding up the escalator past the stares of throngs of shoppers. Though somewhat menacing, today's throng was merely what to expect when in transit with the irrepressible headmistress of Rosemoore. To Larkie's relief, that person was briskly descending the stoop, not, however, to return to the car, but to proceed up a stoop a few doors away.

At last the ordeal was over and Louise, with a gracious bow for the curbsiders, climbed back into the car. "How typical of poor Agnes," she exclaimed, "to leave one rooming house for another on the same block. Thank goodness the landlady directed me to it."

"Then you saw Agnes?"

"Shall we lunch, dear?" Unperturbed by the window audience, Louise reached to the back seat for the wicker hamper. "Cheese and tomato sandwiches and a thermos of tea—Bridget packs a nifty lunch!"

"Well, did you?"

"Agnes, you mean?" The wax paper crackled in the passing of sandwiches. "We missed her by a hair's breadth. Yesterday, in fact, is when she quit our shores, as threatened."

"What is the sense of it? She doesn't know a soul in Ireland, and in her condition in the bargain."

"Let us don our thinking caps." Louise poured two cups of tea from the thermos. "If I were the girl, where in Ireland would I go? What amuses you, Larkie?"

"The idea of you as Agnes O'Shea, but come to think of it—"

"Exactly my reasoning." Louise ate her sandwich and sipped her tea. "The orphanage in Cork was home, after all, and would provide shelter until the baby is born." She finished the tea and brushed the sandwich crumbs into the wax paper. "I shall write the Sisters at the orphanage tomorrow, and now, Larkie, you may drive us to nine-eighty-two Fifth Avenue."

"*Where?*"

"We must strive not to be late for Mr. Travis, who awaits us."

Larkie restrained her queries and switched on the ignition. The cat was about to be sprung from the bag, the master plan revealed, and she doubted that any nun was as lucky as she to have found a school and a Reverend Mother of such exhilarating pursuits.

The mansion at the corner of Fifth Avenue and Seventy-eighth Street, and the gentleman who stood in front of it, were of a similar temperament. The mansion, in the elaborate style of a French château, was one in an assortment of Florentine palazzi, Palladian villas, and Bavarian castles that paraded in lavish formation up the city's queen of avenues. In wing collar, frock coat, and graystriped trousers, Mr. Henry Travis was of similar outmoded grandeur. Here and there a rude upstart of an apartment building interrupted the solid phalanx of ornamented cornices and turrets, to Mr. Travis's abiding regret. Although these upstarts were to his profit as a realtor, he mourned the passing of an era to which he had belonged.

Mr. Travis's acquaintance with Louise was limited to the telephone and he regarded it as perplexing. Not all nuns, it appeared, were hidden away behind convent walls, out of touch with the world, for here was one who followed the real estate ads in *The New York Times* and knew precisely the type of property she wished to purchase. Still, when the Chrysler drew up in front of the mansion, it was a dubious Henry Travis who went forward in greeting. Louise stepped to the pavement, tall, erect, a gloved hand extended to him, and the realtor's doubts abated. Here, emphatically, was a lady, and he was groomed in the protocol of ladies.

"A civic treasure," he said of the Ogden mansion, after having greeted the younger nun and turned with a flourish to the five-story limestone residence whose spired copper roof glinted in the warm afternoon sun. "Richard Morris Hunt was the architect. Codman did the interiors. The ballroom surpassed Mrs. Astor's and was the scene of glittering assemblies. I should hate it to fall to the wrecking crews."

"Might it?" Louise asked.

"In ten years, half the great houses on Fifth Avenue will lie in dust and rubble. Apartments will rise on the sites, which I will profit from, but I rejoice at every house that I secure for a consulate or legation ... and in your case, a school."

Escorting the nuns to the iron-canopied entrance, which fronted on Seventy-eighth Street, Mr. Travis produced a ring of keys and applied one to the grilled door. "As a school, it would have no equal in New York for magnificence."

After a tour of the ground-floor salons and a lecture on the moldings and stucco work, the nuns were conducted across the marble entrance foyer to the tiny elevator installed beneath the swanlike curve of marble stairs. The elevator cranked upward with a slight wheeze, imposing on Mr. Travis an intimacy with the nuns that compelled him to remark, "I am the grandson of a clergyman, the rector for many years of St. James's on Madison Avenue, where we continue to maintain a family pew."

"Oh?" Louise gave it a moment's thought. "You wouldn't by chance happen to know Cornelia Van Pelt?"

"Of the Tivoli Van Pelts? Indeed, we attended many a cotillion together. She was a Lindley before her marriage."

"Mrs. Van Pelt is on the faculty of Rosemoore, our school on the Hudson."

"Hmmm ... I seem to recall mention of your school now and again in wedding announcements."

The elevator cranked to a halt at the top floor and Mother Larkin, as the tour resumed, credited her superior with another in her string of conquests. Were the disposal of the property Mr. Travis's to decide, he might just as well hand it over and be done with it, but how did it fit into the master plan? Dutifully, Mother Larkin traipsed in and out of bedrooms, along corridors and down stairways, increasingly baffled. By every indication, Reverend Mother was considering the purchase of 982, which wasn't remotely feasible. For as long as the deed to Hightower was not signed over to her, it meant ...

"Young girls exposed to the classic refinements of the Ogden house—think of the influence on their taste," said Mr. Travis, descending the stairs to what he described as the piano nobile. "And now let me show you the crown jewel of the residence."

The upper stairs met the curving bronze rail of the foyer stairs in a reception hall that opened onto the mansion's most notable feature. It extended across the sixty-foot width of the house, conjuring up visions of satin gowns and diamond chokers, swallowtails and starched white shirtfronts, of orchids and gardenias and violins lifted in a waltz.

"What evenings this ballroom has witnessed." Mr. Travis gestured at the painted ceiling, thirty feet high, and the golden stage at one end where the orchestras had played. "Vanished, an era vanished and gone. . . . The future will have no place for private ballrooms."

Louise, who had said little during the tour of the house, advanced over the polished hardwood floor. She gazed up at the painted blue sky of the ceiling and the exotic birds of brilliant plumage that soared across the blue. "Must it vanish?" she asked.

"Surely, in terms of a school—?"

"Think of it, Larkie . . . every year, perhaps at Christmas . . . the Rosemoore Ball."

Mr. Travis was awestruck. "It is you who must acquire the Ogden house," he declared. "Not only that, but I will pledge every assistance."

"The price—astronomical?"

"Bargain of a lifetime." In his excitement Mr. Travis charged across the floor to the French windows that looked out on Seventy-eighth Street. "Ordinarily, a Fifth Avenue corner would fetch twice the price, but, you see, the parcel of land is too narrow for an apartment building and no adjacent parcels are available for purchase. The houses next door are owned by the De Meers sisters, Miss Lucrezia and Miss Althea, who wouldn't dream of selling. Also, and this is in the strictest confidence—"

"Have no fear, Mr. Travis."

"The Ogden heirs are old friends, but I will tell you that they are pressed for money. It is why the property is for sale."

"Ah, yes." Louise seated herself upon an apricot velvet banquette recessed into the mirrored wall. "What are they asking?"

"Five hundred thousand . . . half a million and worth twice that amount."

"Will you excuse us for a moment?"

"As I've said, you may depend on my every assistance."

After Mr. Travis had exited, Louise turned to Mother Larkin who was hovering in the doorway. "Your bewilderment is quite understandable. Speak up, you needn't hesitate."

"I won't then." Larkie ventured onto the polished hardwood. "Usually I'm adept at reading your mind, but today it is positively labyrinthine—I haven't a clue."

"Well, my dear Larkie, what if circumstances required us to give up Hightower? I doubt it will come to that, but ought we not have some place to go?"

Larkie was less startled than she had expected to be. "I've wondered for years when you would risk it," she said. "All or nothing was the alternative left to us."

"True, but I kept hoping that Mr. Moore would think better of his actions. I'm past that now; it's not to happen by itself."

"Yes, but . . ." Larkie knitted her brows together to examine the difficult equation. "If you don't expect to lose Hightower, only to risk it . . . then why this pretext today?"

"What pretext?"

"Am I mistaken or did I hear Mr. Travis quote you a price for this house of a half a million dollars?"

Louise lifted her eyes in contemplation of the birds soaring across the ceiling. "It wasn't idle fancy, the notion of giving a ball here, as a benefit, of course."

"I ought to have guessed it," said Larkie in a whisper. "You're thinking of a second school!"

"A Christmas ball in a mansion where the Irish servants were kept below stairs . . . a ball in the old style of elegance for a new generation of Irish." Louise's gaze transferred to her bemused listener. "Don't you agree it would raise a handsome sum each year, sponsored by the nuns for the benefit of the school?"

Mother Larkin was incredulous. "That's the master plan—*two* Rosemoores instead of one."

"Well, there *are* details to iron out." Louise stood up and dug into her purse for her checkbook. "Let us confer with Mr. Travis in regard to the assistance he is prepared to offer us."

The miles flew past on the drive back to Peekskill. Mr. Travis had assured Louise that the check for six thousand dollars would serve as a binder on the Ogden house, pending the approval of a mortgage. He had offered to commend her to the officers of the Bank of Fifth Avenue, his own bank, but she had thanked him for the kind offer and said that it wasn't necessary.

"I've only to say the word and Mr. Slattery will get us a bank," she advised Mother Larkin. "Really, how wrong of me to think we'd have no collateral to put up, when actually it is gilt-edged."

Larkie steered past the lumbering truck that slowed her progress. "Forgive my ignorance, but *what* collateral?"

"*Success,*" Louise replied, as if in answer to the misgivings that prodded at her. Far below, the river emerged from behind the hills, beckoning her homeward. "A school of unqualified success, achieved by us, for which we may take credit."

Not Connolly? Was Connolly not to be accorded some credit for it?

Bear Mountain, the sentinel of home, rose above the hills and the river widened, a blue cape flung down by a cavalier. The final miles of the drive were always the longest for Louise, but never more so than today. After the turnoff from the state road, her impatience was scarcely to be contained. It seemed interminable, the last mile before the school gates were to be glimpsed through the trees.

"I'd rather we kept today's transaction to ourselves, Larkie. The grapevine is already going full tilt about the Mother General."

"Nothing is busier than a convent grapevine—you'll have to call a meeting to quiet the wilder rumors."

"I can't until I know where we stand."

The road turned, and at the sight of the gates her heart beat faster and then thumped in alarm. The enormity of the risk she was taking swept over Louise, obliterating the earlier sense of victory within grasp. She closed her eyes as the car swung through the gates and up the winding driveway into the woodsy fragrance of firs and evergreens. What if she had miscalculated and the risk backfired? What if her beloved school were to be left empty and silent as the result of her strategy?

"Look, there's Mr. Jarvic coming out of the woods. Where does he go, for heaven's sake?"

"Pull over, Larkie. I must ask him about the cottage."

Stephen Jarvic turned at the sound of the motor. He wore khaki pants, a lumberjack shirt rolled up to his biceps, and muddied work boots. "You're an absolute lifesaver," he said to Louise at the car window. "It didn't look as if I'd find a studio after the landlady vetoed the tool shed."

"We're happy to offer you the cottage, but it's in such awful disrepair."

The dark taut face relaxed in a grin. "I'm rather experienced at salvage jobs. If I give it weekends, it ought to be in fair shape by winter, and then I'll finish up in the spring."

Spring ... by then where would they be?

"I've heard excellent reports of your classes, Mr. Jarvic."

"Well, thanks for telling me."

"Incidentally," said Mother Larkin when they continued up the driveway, "did you know that every girl at school has a crush on Stephen Jarvic? One little freshman is smitten to a painful degree."

The campus was bathed in the gold of late afternoon. Girls strolled the walks and were gathered in prim groups under the trees chatting with the nuns. Autumn was quick to descend on the Hudson Valley, and the trees were shedding their foliage. The leaves of the maples were tinged with crimson. Beech, maple, ash, sycamore, elm—Louise had committed to memory every variety on the property. Swift was autumn, turning the trees into bare scaffolds, and when spring dressed them again, what bereft scene would they witness?

Mother Larkin drew up to Annunciation Hall and switched off the motor, guessing the reason for the constrained silence that gripped Louise. "The vote against the Motherhouse was really a vote for you," Larkie said with quiet emphasis. "We are behind you, all of us, ready to follow where you take us. We are nuns and trials are our testing ground . . . and in that, you are the model we emulate."

"It's too late to reverse course." The furrow cut deep between the winged brows. "If it means that we are to start over, well, then so we will."

She was out of the car and up the porch steps in a single fluid motion. Before Sister Josie, the portress, could reach the door, Louise was on the stair landing. A group of students on the stairs broke into a rash of curtsies, which went unnoticed. The binder on 982 Fifth Avenue was secured and it remained to run the risk in full.

"The calls, Reverend Mother, and nowhere to reach you!"

Louise rifled through the message slips that Mother Friel handed to her. She felt her heart give a jolt. "Father Regan telephoned? From where?"

"The city." Mother Friel looked confused by the tense, anxious question. "He's the priest from the Paulists who is to give the Advent sermons."

"You may go, Friel, thank you."

"The day's mail, don't you—?"

"We'll go over it in the morning. It's getting toward dinner."

Louise closed the door behind her and hung up her cloak. She flicked on the desk lamp, deposited purse and gloves in the drawer. The light at the window was ebbing from the sky in purple welts. She sat at her desk and contemplated the yellow pad on the blue blotter. Dipping a pen in the inkstand, she took the pad and commenced to draft a letter on it.

It was addressed to Connolly Moore and the Rosemoore Corporaton in care of his attorney, John J. Geoghegan. The letter went through several revisions before she settled on the final form.

I regret to inform you of the decision made in regard to the Agreement, dated May 16, 1908, and signed by us as parties to it.

The corporation has failed to abide by the terms of the agreement, with reference to Clause 8. Accordingly, I have reached a decision in behalf of the nuns. It is our intention, at the conclusion of the spring semester, June 1923, to vacate the property known as Hightower . . .

Having taken the risk, Louise pondered the situation that had precipitated it. It had not surprised her to learn of Monica Moore's elopement: Connolly had driven her to it by his intransigent opposition. Sooner or later, Flavin and Anastasia would rebel, just as she, Louise, had rebelled, and yet . . . yet . . .

She read over the draft of the letter, unhappy with the cold, impersonal legality in which it was couched. It admitted not a shard of feeling for the man whose kindness to her and the school, with this one glaring exception, was immeasurable. Worse still, the letter was a device to get what she wanted, Hightower . . . and after that, the Ogden house.

The window was dark when Louise looked up from her desk. Connolly, she thought, had a dark side, as contrasting as night from day, and possession, the hand closed like a vise, was a component of it. Sorrow was another, the sorrow that in unguarded moments was revealed in his eyes, piercing and unassuaged. Ought she to tear up the letter and trust in God, whatever the outcome?

Louise went into the study that had supplanted the attic cell as her bedroom. The late hours at her desk, the meals on trays, were routine, but when the nuns had found her too often asleep at her desk, they'd insisted on the change and she had not protested.

The narrow room was furnished with the simplicity of the cell, or an approximation of it. The mahogany gleam of the daybed was muted by the washworn white spread, but folded at the foot was a goose-down quilt sewn by the nuns as a Christmas gift. A crucifix hung on the bare wall and the floor was bare, if you discounted the needlepoint rug the nuns had made for her. Louise had submitted to the lounge chair and ottoman slipcovered in chintz, but had refused to part with the old pine chest from the attic. The night table held her rosary, a French edition of the *Imitation of Christ,* from her novitiate days, and a tintype of Honora and Vincent Maguire, who were both now interred in the Columkill graveyard. Vincent had died of a stroke in 1910 and Honora four years later of diphtheria.

Switching on the lamp, Louise removed from the pine chest a biscuit tin as precious to her as the tintype. The contents were unknown to anyone else and were seldom taken out, except when her need was at flood tide.

"Sean . . . Sean." She whispered the name she had never spoken aloud, and sat in the chair and lifted the lid of the biscuit tin in her lap. *"Sean . . . Sean,"* she whispered and touched like a blind person the faded photo of the steerage deck, herself encircled by children and in the crowd behind, the young, irreverent priest whom she had loved and hadn't known she did. *"Sean . . . Sean."*

Item by item, Louise sifted through her meager trove, the postcards from Brazil, Argentina, Lisbon, that recorded Sean Regan's eventual journey back to Rome, and those from Rouen and Amiens, where as an army chaplain he had served in the trenches and field hospitals under enemy fire. The postcards ended with Paris and the Armistice, but Louise had cut out the newspaper clippings that had chronicled his work at Walter Reed Hospital in Washington with the war's damaged survivors, the maimed and crippled, the shellshocked and shattered, who in the irreverent, mocking priest had been sent a defender.

"Sean . . . Sean."

She read again, though it was learned by heart, the clipping from *The New York Times,* which quoted the speech he had delivered before Congress. It was an eloquent plea for the disabled veterans who were doomed to rot in hospitals, deprived of assistance to help them when they left. Regan's transformation from the young priest of relentless ambition had both thrilled and disturbed Louise. It was almost as if they had traded places in the turn their lives had taken.

"What is happening to me?" she asked of the steerage photo. *"Would you think me capable of such a letter to Connolly Moore?"* The photo was worn from handling, but it and the postcards were a means of con-

tact with Sean Regan. At their last meeting, he had stirred newborn emotions in her, wild emotions that over the years had resurfaced, at prayer in chapel, at student assembly, urging her to go to the priest that she loved, not as a nun but as a woman. The effort to resist had cost Louise white knuckles and vigils at the altar, and she was never wholly at peace with her sacrifice.

"Help me, Sean ... I'm at a crossroads and the letter is the signpost ... pointing where?"

Louise shut the lid on the biscuit tin and stored it in the pine chest. It occurred to her that the love she had sacrificed had only been transferred, bestowed in abundance on the school.

Turning off the light and going from the room, she went to her desk in the tower office and reached for the yellow pad. She tore the page from it, but not into bits as she had intended. At the last minute, something that would not be held back dictated that she write out the letter on the Tiffany notepaper, after which she affixed her signature to it and sealed the envelope for posting in the morning.

In the morning, refreshed from a night's sleep and an invigorating walk after mass, Louise was at her desk checking the calendar for the day's appointments.

A discreet tap announced Mother Friel's presence at the door. "While I go for the mail," she said, advancing on the blue carpet, "here is yesterday's lot to look over."

"Thank you, dear, such efficiency. We'll catch up with the replies later."

In the stack of mail was a bulky envelope addressed to Louise and postmarked, "Pinehurst." She slit it open and removed the sheet of hotel stationery. The paper was blank and folded in it was the deed of title to Hightower. Evidently, Connolly Moore had thought it was message enough to send her.

All of yesterday ... while she had conducted her clever negotiations with Mr. Travis and calculated the risk she would take ... all the while, the deed was waiting in the mail.

It seemed to Louise someone else, not herself, who took the letter to Connolly from the desk drawer and tore it up, letting the pieces fall in a drift into the wastebasket.

Over the next days the deed was made to perform a dual function. It served as collateral for the mortgage to secure title to the property at 982 Fifth Avenue, and for a bank loan to cover the expenses of opening a city branch of Rosemoore at that address.

The exhausting negotiations had involved daily trips to the city for Louise, meetings with bankers, documents to sign, and interviews with contractors. She was determined that 982 would open for classes in September, but it would require astute planning and scheduling. At the close of the week she called a meeting of the nuns to inform them of the exciting developments.

"You will share my happiness, I know"—Louise raised a hand to quiet the applause—"when I tell you that separation from the Motherhouse is no longer a necessity. On her recent visit, the Mother General agreed to concessions that erase the injustices of the past ... and will bring us the wonderful prospect of a novitiate in Ireland."

Ireland ... what had she forgotten about Ireland? she asked herself as she stood in the storm of congratulations from the nuns. Sister Bridget was among the last to approach her, shy and hesitant, a waif still in her veil and robes.

"I didn't forget," Louise said, clasping Bridget's hands. "I inquired about Agnes at the rooming house last week, but she'd left for Ireland the day before."

"Ah, don't I know you've got more important things to look after?"

"No, it *is* important," Louise insisted with peculiar urgency. "God would not think it unimportant, why would I? No, we will find her, Bridget, I promise you."

That night at her desk, Louise wrote to the Sisters at the Holy Child Orphanage in Cork, asking after the whereabouts of Agnes O'Shea. She stamped and mailed the letter herself in the post office in Blanchard Hall.

Sleep would not have come without it, and even then it was fitful and tossed with unsettling dreams.

SIXTEEN

F lavin Moore stood among the beaming fathers and doting relatives at the nursery window. "McNally," she said to the nurse when it was her turn, pressing against the glass when the baby was taken from the rows of bassinets and held up for her inspection. The tiny fists flailed the air and the puckered shell-pink face peered at Flavin as if trying to identify her. The moment was over too quickly, and it was somebody else's turn at the window. Flavin went along the hospital corridor, the vision of the baby floating before her, out of reach.

"He's beautiful, Monnie, and so alert, the way he looked at me."

Monica lay pale and fatigued in the cranked-up bed. The birth had been difficult and protracted, but joy shone through her exhaustion. "Isn't he perfection? I still can't believe he's mine." She reached for her sister's hand and held it. "I guess they'll call him a six months' baby, but I'm not the least ashamed. I think I did it on purpose so that nothing could stop the marriage."

Flavin drew up a chair at the bed and folded her white gloves over her black alligator bag. The white was picked up by the pearls at her throat and the black by the tailored suit from Milgrim. "We got back this morning—I wish it could have been sooner."

"You, but not Father." Monica sighed and plucked at the blanket. "He's never stayed in Palm Beach until April."

"He's such a contradiction, Monnie. All he thought of in Florida was you and the baby, but he wouldn't give in and come home a day sooner."

"Well, he's the loser, not Billy and me." Monica struggled up against the pillows, glowing through her pallor. "Every night when Billy comes we go to the nursery window, not saying a word, and just gaze at Acquin."

"I'm so glad for you." Flavin smoothed her gloves and smiled. "Acquin, what a lovely name."

"It's for Billy's uncle—you know, the missionary in China."

"Oh, yes." The coil of hair was tied with a black velvet ribbon. Flavin got up and went to the dresser to arrange in a vase the pink roses she'd brought. "It's all worked out for you, hasn't it?"

"Billy received another raise and I've given him a son. It scares me, how happy we are."

Flavin fitted the long, thorny stems into the vase, some with pink buds that were pushing open. "You've earned every bit of it."

"And you, Flavin?" Monica lay back on the pillows. "The last thing you talk about is yourself, but are you happy?"

"Let's see, what changes can I report?" Flavin carried the vase to the washbasin for water. "When I left the hotel, Father asked where I was going. 'To see your grandson at the hospital, where you should be going,' I told him."

"A new leaf—hurrah for you!" Monica applauded. "I'll bet it was the row with Stacey that's made you take a stand. Was it awful, threats and curses and everything?"

"Incendiary!" Flavin held the vase under the faucet, guarding the buds. "He ordered her out of the house, and she packed and left. Imagine our Stacey, commuting by bus from West Palm Beach and working at Saks."

Monica gave the facts some appraisal. "She must want to stay down there, which means a gent is mixed up in it."

"Let's hope he's not a blackjack dealer, like the one last year." Flavin set the roses on the dresser. "I admire her for taking a job. In fact, I've . . ."

"Yes, Flave?"

"Well, it started me thinking about my own future. You have Billy and a son, and when Stacey marries . . . I'll be the old maid of the family."

"You mustn't say it." Monica was aghast. "I can't bear you to say it, the best, the kindest, the dearest of us. It's Father's doing and you mustn't allow it."

"An Irish family isn't complete without an old maid."

"You're making a joke of it, but—"

"No, I'm not." Flavin's arms slipped around her sister, comforting her as she had in the dark when they were children. "We're an Irish family, no more and no less. The money was a freakish happening, but it hasn't changed who we are. In addition to old maids, Irish families have ghosts, as Father calls his memories . . ."

"Flavin, you—"

"Without me, he'd be left with no one, and I can't allow that."

"He's maneuvered you into thinking it."

"Oh, I expect that if I fell in love . . ." Flavin provided her teary sister with a handkerchief. "Remember the prince I always said would find me in the park?"

"A prince in disguise, but we were children then and we're not anymore."

"Exactly, there is no prince—three broken engagements testified to it." Flavin clicked the alligator bag shut. "You needn't weep for me. Quite aside from Father, I intend to have a life for myself."

"Like what?"

"You won't laugh if I tell you?"

"Don't be silly," Monica sniffled, "but a job at Saks just isn't up your alley."

"What would you say to teaching?"

"You, a teacher?"

"Of music . . . at Rosemoore." Flavin pulled on her white gloves. "The years of lessons wouldn't go to waste, and I'd really like to teach."

"Listen, I'm for anything that gets you away from *him.*"

"I've no experience, but I'm sure that if I went to Mother Maguire—"

"She can't say no, and if Father does, she'll help you with him."

"After all, what better friend have we than her?" Flavin swung the bag over her arm. "I'll go to her, Monnie, and ask for a chance to teach."

"*When?*" Monica shot back. "*Soon,* or you'll get whisked off on another trip for a week that turns into a month."

"Today—I'll go see her today." Flavin pressed her cheek against her sister's. "It's right to call a baby a blessed event. The nurse held

Acquin to the window, this tiny, miraculous new life to be valued, and I prayed that mine would have value too."

"Well, start upping your value and skip the old maid part of it."

Half an hour later, Flavin Moore was on a train to Peekskill without having advised her father of it. They were not to leave the Plaza for Faircrest until the weekend, but the servants had only just returned from Palm Beach, and she'd utilize the trip by looking in on them and then going over to Rosemoore.

To ride in a coach seat was a novel experience for Flavin. She hadn't been at all certain that the nine dollars in her purse would pay for the taxi to Grand Central *and* the train fare, and she felt clever at having a few dollars left over. She estimated that actually she'd ridden in a coach once before, and the memory of that day took up the rhythmic clack of the wheels.

Then, too, it was an April day. She was four years old and Mama, dismissing the maid, had dressed her in her pink Easter coat and bonnet and called for the carriage to drive them to the station. "Surprise trips are the best kind," Mama had said on the train, flushed with excitement. They were going to the city to visit Aunt Bea and Uncle Mike Nugent in the flat on Tenth Avenue where Mama had lived when she'd come over from Ireland.

"It's beyond your father that I would miss an old tenement flat, but it was so cozy and friendly, with the neighbors dropping in, and later when I kept house for my brothers." Mama was silent a moment. "They are my family and it's wrong, I tell you, to cut me off from them." Her voice had risen shrilly above the clacking wheels, but then she had smiled gaily at Flavin. "Surprise trips are the best, my darlin' Flavin. Of course, we can't stay too long and must think of the train back."

Flavin's memory of the visit was vivid with detail: the spotless kitchen of the flat and the delicious soda bread that Aunt Bea had served with the sugared tea amid the laughter and talk and the neighbors flocking in and out the door. The light was fading at the kitchen window when her uncles, home from work, had trooped in and escorted Mama to the upright in the parlor demanding songs, Irish songs. Her hands had flown over the keys, the uncles booming out the lyrics of the melodies, one after another, until Mama had frozen on the piano stool.

"Dear God, is it evening? I must let Connolly know that I'm in the city. If he has called the house and found me gone . . ."

"Ossining," the conductor shouted as the clacking slowed and Flavin looked out at the glinting river. It was her last and only visit to the flat, she remembered. Not long after, her father had purchased homes in Brooklyn for her mother's family, and they had moved to that inaccessible borough. Once a year in June, the aunts and uncles and cousins were invited to Faircrest for a day's outing, but the grandness of the house, the liveried servants in attendance, had made for little song and laughter. The invitations were stopped at her mother's request the year that Monica was born. A governess was hired to look after Flavin and Anastasia, and with the baby in a nurse's care, Mama had spent more and more time upstairs in her lace-hung bedroom, coming down in the afternoon to play the piano but absent from the dinner table at night. On weekends when Father was home, she didn't come downstairs at all.

"My beautiful Rose . . . what's gone wrong?" he'd asked, drawing Flavin upon his lap. "Every luxury a woman could want . . . what haven't I given her?"

"Peekskill," the conductor shouted, and Flavin hurried to the front of the coach, afraid that she would miss the station. The gabled roof poked up at the turn in the tracks, and she questioned when exactly the thought had lodged in her that she must compensate for all that grieved her father.

Deposited on the rickety platform, Flavin counted the bills in her purse and went over to the taxi stand. She had yet to arrive anywhere unaccompanied or without someone, a chauffeur, a man from Thomas Cook, a hotel representative, to meet her. It aroused a sense of helpless dependency, a failing that she intended to correct.

The charge for Faircrest, the taxi driver informed her, was fifty cents. "But don't worry, Miss Moore, I'd say your father was good for it."

"No, no, I've the money to pay," Flavin said and got into the taxi, which rattled away in a cloud of exhaust fumes.

The line of girls inched along the soda counter in the crowded Pow-Wow to give their orders and dig coins from pockets while keeping up a steady flow of chatter.

"Any news of the baby?" asked Lizzie Devlin, ordering three Cokes for which she plunked down a quarter and a dime. "It's just about due, isn't it?"

"Bless ya, we heard this mornin' from Ag—'tis a baby girl." Sister

Bridget set the Cokes on a tray and fished a nickel's change from the cash drawer. "She's thinkin' to name it Kathleen."

"Sure and begorra and the saints be praised," whooped Lizzie, mimicking a brogue. She eyed the milk bottle that Bridget kept on the counter for contributions to the African missions. "How much before I get to christen a black baby?"

"Why, with the nickels and dimes you've given—"

"*Au 'voir, mon ami,*" said Lizzie to her nickel, and clinked it into the bottle. "I want a girl baby, christened in honor of Kathleen."

"You're a wonder, Lizzie Devlin."

"I'm a big joke, you mean." Lizzie steered between the tables with the tray of Cokes, calling out hellos that were not returned. She lowered the tray onto the table at which sat her two best friends in the entire world and flopped into the chair next to them with a groan.

"It's definitely not working—you'd think by the eighth day I'd feel some relief."

Florence Giambetti and Eileen Birnbaum, who were Lizzie's roommates, received this announcement with the gravity it warranted.

"We'll renew it if you don't get results by tomorrow," said Florence.

"I'm game if you are," Eileeen declared, "but we mustn't expect a guarantee."

"Well, it's not like I'm asking for bosoms, which, ugh, I don't want."

Such a conversation was possible only among Catholic girls, for it referred to a novena the three were making to Sophie's Virgin to cure Lizzie of a well-known infatuation. The ninth day of the novena was tomorrow, which accounted for Lizzie's gloom.

"Let's face it, I'm not the least bit cured." She sipped her Coke. "Who do I think about when I wake up? S. J.! Who, when I go to sleep? Ditto!" She sat up, struck by a new and alarming aspect. "What if it's a sign that I'm intended to be a nun? I've heard of cases like mine who wind up in the convent."

"Nuns," said Florence, who was of pious inclinations, "go into the convent for love of God . . . and to save souls."

"Yeah, I sure can't imagine Reverend Mother going nuts over a guy."

The three girls sipped their Cokes while pondering the mysteries of the universe. They had dubbed themselves the Three Musketeers, sworn to eternal friendship, and were bound together by the differences that marked them apart from the typical Rosemoore student and her mannerisms. Florence Giambetti, as the only Italian at the school, was looked upon as "not fitting in." Italians were known to be gardeners or bricklayers, or they operated fruit-and-vegetable stores, or were head waiters in restaurants. It didn't boost Florence's rating that her parents had yet to appear at a school function. On Fridays the burly Primo showed up in a big black car to drive her home to Mineola, Long Island, for the weekend, returning with her on Sundays before the six o'clock deadline, and that was the extent of her family's contact with the school, except for the payment of fees.

Eileen Birnbaum, what with the dubious combination of her given name and surname, was also deemed not to fit in, but less calamitously than the mousy Florence. Eileen's mother, after all, had been a Walsh prior to her marriage to Stanley Birnbaum of Seventh Avenue. Her father's Jewishness was mitigated by his consent to rear Eileen in her mother's faith. With her jet-black hair, ivory complexion, and curvaceous figure, Eileen was a beauty, and she had scored highest in the freshman midsemester exams. These were definite points in her favor, had she sought favor among the girls. Instead, Eileen remained aloof from them, preferring the company of her two roommates.

It was difficult not to respond to Lizzie's infectious grin and slambang personality, but these were questionable assets. Clown, hoyden, climber of trees, gawky and freckled with streaky red hair flying behind her, Lizzie was regarded at school as a "character," good for laughs but outlandish, a joke, which was precisely how she regarded herself.

Lizzie pushed away her Coke. "Okay, I won't quit the novenas, but it isn't working and we've got to come up with some other cure for me. C'mon, let's go."

The Three Musketeers trudged up the outer basement stairs from the Pow-Wow. The April weather was chilly enough for scarves and navy chinchilla coats, but the sun's fitful warmth redeemed the chill, the dogwood trees were budding into bloom, and the campus was sprouting a springtime greenness. "Y'know," said Lizzie as the girls swung along the walk toward the terrace of Blanchard, "maybe if Mr. Jarvic got involved with someone . . . then maybe I'd ease up on how nutty I am about him."

"It has a certain logic," Eileen agreed. "You'd want his happiness, above all else, which would sort of act as a cure."

Lizzie's glance strayed to the parking lot, as it had on her first day at Rosemoore. The flivver was parked there, which indicated that he was on campus and where she might go looking for him. What she felt for Stephen Jarvic went deeper than a schoolgirl crush. She'd embarked on the novena to Sophie's Virgin to be relieved of the burden of loving him.

She stood back as Eileen and Florence went up the terrace steps with rosaries in hand for the chapel. "It's gotta be nine consecutive days or I'll blow it," Lizzie said, "but I'm not up to it today."

Both girls, perceiving where Lizzie was headed, showed commendable tact. "You won't blow the novena," Eileen assured her. "The Blessed Virgin overlooks minor technicalities. She's not a stickler for the rule book."

"We'll start on a second novena," Florence offered. "She'll grant your cure before we're through with her."

"Honest to Pete, I've got the best friends in the entire world," Lizzie crowed, and when the two girls proceeded into Blanchard and the chapel, her glance strayed back to the flivver in the parking lot and then swept over the hockey field to the woods. It was like the flu, she thought, aches and chills and fever, and you had to bear it for as long as it lasted.

She turned at the sound of ecstatic barking and held out her arms as Tyrone, the setter, raced toward her from the driveway. She knelt in the grass and wrapped her skinny arms around the muzzling animal, wishing that she'd confined her love to dogs. Well, anyway, at least she didn't pray for bosoms, like some of the girls at school. Think what problems that would bring!

"Hey, listen . . . want to go spying?" Lizzie asked of her other best friend. She got up and scouted the campus walks for vigilant nuns. The woods were off limits to students, but it hadn't stopped her before.

"Promise not to bark and give me away," she cautioned Tyrone, and set out with the dog across the hockey field to the line of trees in the distance.

*   *   *

Flavin tied a white silk scarf over the blond spill of her hair and went into the hall. The rooms that she had shared with her sisters opened off one side of the hall, across from the elaborate suite whose only tenant was their father. Beyond, the stairs curved to a landing, and then in a widening curve to the hall below.

The tug of a memory, like the tug of a rope, pulled Flavin back from the stairs. Snow frosted the window on the landing and she was nine years old, watching the priest climb the stairs with the holy viaticum. It was the week before Christmas and Mama was sick with pneumonia. She hadn't been outdoors, but even so she'd caught pneumonia. The doctors and round-the-clock nurses could not save Mama and now she was dying. One of the nurses knelt at the tinkle of the priest's bell, while behind him came Father, pale and shaken with grief . . .

Flavin grasped the banister and went down the stairs. Jonah was crossing the black-and-white squares with a tray of silver julep mugs. He turned as she reached the bottom step and noted her change of dress.

"You fixin' to play tennis or what, Miz Flavin?"

"With whom?" Flavin laughed, self-consciously. The middy blouse and skirt were originally a tennis costume, until she'd taken to wearing it in the city to her piano lessons. "I'm going for a walk over to school. You look tired, Jonah—I'm worried about you."

The mocha hands that held the tray were swollen at the joints with arthritis. Twice each year, the complex transfer of the household, to Spring Lake in June and then to Palm Beach in January, was Jonah's to carry out. Invariably, the houses were in perfect order for Connolly's arrival, but at the increased taxing of Jonah's strength. He was growing old: The grizzled head was turning white and the arthritic hands gripped the tray in pain.

"Don' you worry 'bout me," he chastised Flavin. "We be goin' home to Kentucky next month, with nothin' to do 'cept sit on the porch an' relax." The first two weeks of May were vacation time for Jonah and Clarice in the house in Keenland that Connolly had purchased for them.

Flavin relieved him of the heavy tray and carried it into the dining room. "When you come back, you're going to do less and let Della help you more."

"Yes'm, ah surely will."

She set the tray on the dining table in the forest of silver bowls, plates, tureens, and candelabrum. The opening of the house was the occasion for massive silver polishing, at which Ruby, Della, and Mamie were engaged in the kitchen. "We'd be lost without you, Jonah, but I won't let you wear yourself out for us."

Jonah, anxious to change the subject, narrowed his eyes. "What brung you up here today? Ah 'spect you didn't tell yo' Daddy, neither."

"You're right, I didn't." Flavin went up to him, thinking of the role she was prepared to assume and the responsibilities it entailed. "If he or Miss Philbin calls, say that I've gone for a walk."

"Over to da' school?"

"Yes, tell him that, and . . ." She touched Jonah's sleeve in lieu of an embrace. It would have embarrassed him, and such displays belonged to her childhood. "All I meant just now was that you are dear to us and we care about you."

Jonah smiled and pressed her hand. "Ah knows that right enough, an' ah'm fixin' to go on fo' many a year to come."

The house, she thought as she went out the door and down the portico steps, would benefit from more displays of affection. Well, the parade of grandchildren was off to a start with Acquin, and she, the maiden aunt, would bombard them with parties and toys and games. Father would not refuse her that pleasure, and he would benefit from a house grown warm with laughter and squeals and children climbing onto laps for kisses and hugs and storybook tales.

Flavin cut across the lawn to the hedged walk that skirted past the rose garden at the north side of the house. She waved at Salvio, who was trimming the thorny bushes, and called out the news of the baby. The vine-wreathed tunnel of the wisteria arbor brought her into the rock garden and its splashing fountains. The tennis courts were next, shaded by tall cypresses, and from there the ground sloped to the dark green stables and garage. Matt Hogan, the groom, was exercising a horse in the white-fenced paddock, cantering it around the dirt track.

From where she stood, the wind from the river whipping at the white silk scarf, Flavin's view was of fields and orchards that stretched to the blur of woods in the distance, which marked the boundary line of Rosemoore. As young girls, she and her sisters had been permitted on balmy spring mornings to follow this route to school, freed of the chauffeured car, and now she set out over the fields again, in the middy blouse and skirt that were a badge of independence, moving toward the future that she foresaw for herself.

It was not a future that distressed Flavin. What she had feared was a wasted life, the broken engagements, the music lessons that were constantly interrupted, often for months at a time. Yet she had persevered, picking up with Professor Steiner where she had left off, contriving one banner year to enroll at the Institute of Musical Arts for courses in theory and composition. She had studied music long enough to know that her talent at the piano was minor, but it had not marred her love of music nor abnegated the sense that it was a form of expression otherwise missing from her life. Flavin looked back on the year of her debut, the whirl of balls and cotillions, the brief celebrity of flash bulbs and society columns, as something dis-associated from herself, undertaken for her father's sake. For that she had exhibited herself, gowned and jeweled, in a box at the opera on Monday nights, the fashionable night to attend. "You ask who she is?" she had overheard a dowager in a diamond tiara whisper one night from the adjacent box. "A little Irish girl, Catholic, of course, and quite pretty in her way."

Yes, thought Flavin as she crossed the fields, that's who she was, an Irish girl with a passion for music who wore a middy blouse and skirt to Professor Steiner's, the dress of the other girls who were stu-dents, identifying herself as one of them. She had given as her ad-dress not the Plaza Hotel but 2 West Fifty-ninth Street, and after a lesson, strolling back through the park to the hotel, she had indulged in her romantic girlhood fantasy of . . . but not any longer, she was done with foolish illusions.

The blur of woods dissolved into a thicket of trees as Flavin moved closer. She sought out in the trees the chimney stub of the ruined cottage that on the walks to school had served to nourish her fantasies. The cottage had stood in abandoned ruin for as long as she had lived at Faircrest, but surely it was the secret dwelling place of her prince in disguise.

Flavin drew to a faltering stop before the meandering stone fence of the school property. She had not telephoned Mother Maguire to learn whether she could see her today, but why had she not? Perhaps it was all an illusion—the teaching, the house grown warm with the laughter and affection of children, and she in her old maid's chair at the fire—an illusion to mask the fear that underlined it, not so much of waste, but of her inability to oppose her father in the life that he had ordained for her.

She climbed over the fence in what was an act of defiance and followed the upward path through the trees. If she had a true friend in the world, that friend was Mother Maguire and she would go to her for help. The afternoon sun had fled, and the middy blouse and skirt were scant protection against the chill, but rebelliously Flavin unknotted the white scarf and let her hair tumble free down her shoulders. Then, as she reached the footbridge under which rushed the stream that cascaded from the cliff of rocks above, Flavin halted in disbelief and stared at the clearing on the other side of the bridge.

The cottage was not the ruined hovel that she had gone past on the morning walks to school. The shingled roof was repaired and the gaping windows were fitted with glass panes. The yard in front was shorn of weeds and furnished with a canvas beach chair and a metal table on which rested a tool box and some sketch pads and charcoal pencils. The tilted door of the cottage was made upright with shiny brass hinges. The door was ajar, and in the doorway, as Flavin looked on, appeared a young man in khaki pants and a lumberjack shirt who in turn looked at her.

"Hello," he said, and stepped from the doorway into the yard, shifting his glance away from her. The lean, dark face, the Slavic cheekbones . . . it seemed to Flavin that she had seen him before. He picked up a pane of glass and laid it on the table, and the slight limp to his movements told her where she had seen him.

Stephen Jarvic took a putty knife from the tool box and ran it along the edge of the glass. He held the knife with a perceptible tremble and his eyes would not stay fixed on it.

"I—I teach here at school," he said, glancing up with a dark flush and a glitter to his eyes. "I teach art . . . and in my spare time fix up this cottage for a studio."

"I live next door," Flavin said. "I've been away and came back this morning." She paused, and when he said nothing in reply, "We didn't meet, but I remember seeing you at the dedication ceremonies last September."

Stephen's voice was like a knife scraping over the glass. "Big crowd that day—it could be we saw each other."

She watched from the footbridge as he smeared the edges of the glass with putty, disinterested in conversation. "Do you know if Mother Maguire's in her office?"

"Hard to say—she's apt to be in the city, at the school on Fifth Avenue she's opening."

"When I was a student here, I always went to her with my problems. She certainly earned the title of Mother."

Stephen lifted the glass from the table, the muscles tensed in his arms. "I can't imagine you with problems."

"A few, now and then." Flavin ventured onto the path that sloped up to the cottage. "If I wanted to teach, for example, that would be a problem."

Stephen was crouched at a window fitting the glass in the empty pane. "Why would you want to?"

She looked at him with growing annoyance. "You oughtn't to make assumptions, when you know nothing about me. Oh, never mind, it's quite unimportant."

"No, you're right."

"Let's forget it." She turned on the path encircled by the woods, the trees darkening with the afternoon. "The day started off so well and now it's slipping away and I—forget it, it doesn't matter."

Stephen got up from the window, wiping his hands on his shirt. "I apologize for what I said, but as far as forgetting goes . . . I never could, where you are concerned."

She stared at him, uncomprehending. "Where *I* am concerned?"

"Days that slip away . . . I lost count of them in the hospital." He paced back and forth, the limp sadly evident. "Leg got smashed up in the war, months in the hospital, and then I came to New York . . . the Art Students League, figuring to get back to my painting."

"And did you?" Flavin asked. "I hope that you did. A form of expression like that, how awful to be deprived of it."

Stephen held out his hand, tipping the fingers like airplane wings. "Shook so bad I couldn't hold the brush steady enough to paint a stroke. Those were rougher days than the hospital, but it's funny how the littlest thing, if you hang on to it, can help get you through."

"For me, it's music that helps."

He moved toward her across the yard. "For me, it was a girl I saw one day in Central Park . . . on a bench at the sailboat pond."

"A girl? What girl?"

"She wore a middy blouse and skirt, and her hair streamed

like gold down her shoulders . . . seated on a bench, studying her music."

Flavin's hand went to the collar of her middy blouse. "You didn't speak to the girl?"

"I didn't think I wanted to." Stephen's eyes glittered and his voice was a husky whisper. "She was everything I couldn't paint, it was enough just to look at her. After that day, I kept going back to the park, the sailboat pond, the carousel, the lake . . . I never saw her again, but I couldn't forget her."

Somewhere in the woods a dog barked, startling Flavin who turned away, twisting at the white scarf. "But then last September, here at school . . . you saw her?"

"I'd learned who she was by then, and when she came out of the chapel with her father, the rich Connolly Moore . . . well, I made the wrong assumptions."

"I—I can't really blame you for that," Flavin said. "Sometimes I'm not sure myself of who I am, but I'm trying to find out."

"You're the girl in the park, it's as simple as that, I think."

"Is it?" She twisted at the scarf in a sudden panic. "I wonder, is this my white flag of surrender? You see, if I could teach, the music wouldn't go to waste, but . . ."

"What's to stop you from it?"

"As I said, a few problems." Flavin gripped the scarf and glanced around at the darkening trees. "Ghosts, my father's Irish ghosts, but that's nonsense, isn't it?" she laughed.

Stephen went toward her on the path that sloped up from the footbridge. "How is it that I couldn't forget you?" he asked. "Is it because I was meant to find you?"

"And you . . ." Flavin looked up at him, the slash of the cheek-bones, the Slavic tilt of his eyes. "I—I've known from long ago who you are."

The dog barked again in the twittering quiet, but neither of them heard it. Stephen stroked back the shining spill of her hair and Flavin lifted her face, and her arms went around him as his mouth came down hungrily.

That night, long after lights-out at ten o'clock, Lizzie Devlin lay awake in her bed, gazing out the window at the lemonade moon, transfixed by what she'd seen from her tree-perch in the woods.

It was a heart-thumper when Tyrone had barked, and heart-freezing when he'd let out another yowl. She had scrambled down and lit out of the woods, racing across the hockey field, breathless to tell Eileen and Floss what she'd seen—and think of what Flavin Moore's society-page fan would make of it!

Lizzie scrunched down in her bed, uncertain of why she hadn't spilled the beans to her friends nor phoned her mother in Stamford to give her the scoop. Maybe it was stupid, she thought, but it almost seemed that by revealing what had passed between Stephen Jarvic and Flavin Moore she would be guilty of betraying them.

To watch from the tree, was that a kind of betrayal? Lizzie didn't think so; after all, spying on lovers wasn't what she'd had in mind, it had just turned out that way. No, the betrayal would be to tell of something private and sacred that happened between two people. She'd keep quiet about it, mum was the word.

Lizzie yawned and hugged the pillow as sleep crept up on her. One thing she'd never doubt again was the power of a novena. She'd prayed for a cure and Sophie had answered her prayers. Maybe she still loved S.J., but the burden of loving him wasn't hers to bear alone.

She would have liked to muse about Flavin Moore, turning over her impressions like pictures in a movie magazine, but before she could, Lizzie was fast asleep.

V
THE DINNER PARTY

SEVENTEEN

Christmas at Rosemoore began officially with Advent, the twenty-four days preceding the feast itself. Nowhere is the approach of a holiday greeted with more excitement and anticipation than at a school, and in particular a boarding school. The bookstore at Rosemoore was stocked with Advent calendars, made with little cardboard windows to open for each of the twenty-four days, and the supply was quickly exhausted.

"One less day to wait," was the jubilant chorus in dormitory rooms as another cardboard window was opened and the girls hurried to their own windows to look for signs of snow.

The first snow had fallen the week of Thanksgiving, a light powdering of the trees and hills, short-lasting. It wouldn't be Christmas without snow, and all through the day the girls consulted the gray skies for portents of it. In the chapel, Sophie's Virgin was besieged with requests for thick, fleecy white flakes, not a blizzard, of course, which would jeopardize the journey home for the holiday recess. What else was Christmas intended for but to go home to families, gifts piled under the tinseled tree, parties, and boys?

With the recess two weeks away, long-distance calls to home proliferated, as did the postal money orders in student mailboxes. A passenger agent for the railroads arrived on campus and set up a table in the gym, taking reservations for pullman berths to Cleveland, Detroit, Chicago, Denver, Kansas City, and Little Rock. It was said of Rosemoore girls that the Twentieth Century Limited, the crack, extra-fare express train to Chicago, stopped at nearby Harmon for their convenience, eliminating the necessity of a trip to Grand Central to board it.

The money orders were for the purpose of shopping as well as pullman berths. Mrs. Van Pelt had her hands full, to say the least, on her Saturday excursions to the city. The opera-goers made up a small percentage of the group that she chaperoned, sufficient to warrant the hiring of a bus and the enlisting of Miss Osborne to help out. Immediately upon the bus's arrival at a garage on West Forty-fifth Street, Mrs. Van Pelt lined up the navy chinchilla coats in smart columns of two on the sidewalk.

"Deidre, Constance, Maryanne, Rosalind, will come with me," she called forth the opera-goers. "The rest of you, indifferent as you are to the splendors of *Tristan*, will proceed on your shopping rounds with Miss Osborne, but remember this, I pledge you," said Cornelia Van Pelt, in her venerable British tweeds. "Whether in Lord & Taylor or Woolworth's, remember that you are Rosemoore girls and conduct yourselves accordingly."

With that, one navy chinchilla column marched off to the Metropolitan Opera House and the other to Best & Company, Arnold Constable, Lord & Taylor, and Woolworth, winding up at Schrafft's for sodas and hot chocolate and toasted cheese sandwiches. The two columns met at the garage at six o'clock for the sleepy ride back to school, and not only on that day but for years afterward, in the blessings and vicissitudes of life, the girls remembered who they were, Rosemoore girls, marching straight and proud.

As each Advent window was opened, the wait for holiday recess grew shorter and, correspondingly, the excitement mounted. The nuns exerted themselves to maintain a semblance of discipline in the classrooms, and the talk in the dining hall focused on the two events that were to bring the long wait to a climax: the lighting of the tree in Annunciation Hall, and the caroling that dated back to the first Christmas at Rosemoore and had been held every year since. So had the Christmas pageant, which was performed the night before the start of vacation. It was to be given this year of 1923 a more ambitious production. Young Mother Fitzgerald, as part of her course requirements for a B.A. in English, had written a dramatic compo-

sition entitled *Whither Goest?* It chronicled the misadventures of the
Wise Men, not disclosed in scripture, on their journey to Bethlehem.
Tryouts for the large cast had taken place in early December and
daily rehearsals were in progress, though not to the satisfaction of
the entire cast.

"It beats me why we didn't get picked for the Wise Men," said
Lizzie Devlin, huddled at a table in the Pow-Wow with her two best
friends in the entire world. "We'd have given some zip to the action,
but look what we're stuck with!"

"Well, you must admit that Eileen is the perfect choice for Mary,"
Florence Giambetti vouched. "I mean, after all, the mother of Our
Savior . . ."

"Yes, that's true, for once she'll be Jewish, but has she a single line
to speak? No, all she does is sit in the stable in the last scene and look
holy."

"The last scene is a *tableau*," Eileen Birnbaum countered. "Nobody has any lines to speak—Fitz said it would spoil the effect."

"Oh, wow, a swell effect Flossie and me are gonna make," yelped
Lizzie, "as the front and rear ends of the donkey in the manger."

"Cheer up, you'll probably steal the show, and then it'll be
Christmas and *maybe*—" Eileen leaned closer so as not to be overheard. "Maybe it'll bring some interesting developments."

The gloom fled from Lizzie's freckled countenance. "With F.M.
and S.J., do you mean? Oh, do you think so?" It had thrilled her,
upon returning to school in September, to learn that Flavin Moore
had joined the faculty as a music teacher. To outward appearances,
however, her relations with Stephen Jarvic were those of fellow
teachers, nodding politely in the halls and on the campus walks.
Lizzie knew better, or thought that she did, and to verify it had re-
sorted to her forays into the woods. There, meeting in the shelter of
the trees, the privacy of the cottage, the lovers had expressed their
actual relationship . . . but why the need for secrecy? Lizzie could
not imagine why, but it worried her sufficiently to confide in Floss
and Eileen. Amazingly, the latter had come up with a likely explanation.

"It's perfectly logical," Eileen stated again at the table in the
Pow-Wow. "Since we know that the sister had to elope on account of
the father, which I got from Fitz who was her classmate—then
maybe F.M. will have to resort to it."

"What better time to elope than the Christmas recess," Lizzie crowed, banging the table. "Three whole weeks for a honeymoon, and we'll have been onto it before anyone else at school!"

The thought was intoxicating, as was the cloak of secrecy and intrigue, like a Philo Vance mystery. The Three Musketeers concentrated on their mugs of hot Ovaltine until Lizzie was seized by a related thought. "Speaking of recess," she said to Floss, "did you ask your parents yet?"

"No, not yet."

"It'd be a shame to miss it," said Eileen, who had invited her friends to spend a holiday weekend at the Birnbaum's Park Avenue apartment. "If you want, my mother can call your parents."

"Oh, no." Florence's dark eyes widened in distress. "It wouldn't change whether I go or not . . . which I guess I really can't."

"It's all right," Eileen consoled her. "You'd come, if it was up to you."

Lizzie patted the smear of Ovaltine from her mouth, mindful of etiquette class. "You and me, Floss, we're the front and rear of a donkey," she observed as they left the Pow-Wow for rehearsal, "so why won't you give us the lowdown on your family?"

"I would, I would." Florence hurried after her friends, who were precious to her since she had no others. "Honest I would, if I knew what it was."

During the welter of pre-Christmas activities that enlivened the school routine, little was known of the one that engaged Louise in the tower office. Rumor of it was rampant among the nuns, but as yet it was unconfirmed.

"I'd have to think about it," said Sister Pauline, the cook, when she was summoned to the tower office. "You're asking what I'd serve a dinner party of *men*?"

"Yes, of men." The mass of papers on Louise's desk were all related to the question she had posed. "Imagine that Mr. Rockefeller had invited a group of business associates to Pocantico Hills—what menu would you propose?"

"I'd give 'im a choice." Sister Pauline had cooked for the junior Rockefellers before switching to God's employ, as she thought of it. Like her, several of the sisters had been servants on Hudson Valley estates, drawn to Rosemoore by a sense of unfulfillment and dislocation in their lives. "Something in the beef line—tournedos of beef with Madeira sauce," Pauline suggested, harking back to the Rockefeller days. "Potatoes Anna, men are fools for potatoes, and a nice puree of peas and chestnuts."

Louise held her pen over the tentative guest list, deliberating. "Thank you, Pauline, I'm sure we can rely on you."

Sister Pauline ignored the signal to withdraw. A summons to the tower office was as rare as one to Mrs. Rockefeller's study, and she wanted full value out of it. "Did I hear you say when the party's for?"

"No, but it's for Saturday, the twenty-eighth of this month."

"With naught but men for guests?"

Louise glanced up in amusement. "The grapevine will have to content itself with that tidbit. I'll want to look at the menu when you've completed it."

"Yes, Reverend Mother."

Sister Pauline exited, not much wiser for her efforts, and Louise appraised the nettlesome list of names. The eighteen men on the list all had daughters at Rosemoore. John Snyder was a director of the American Export Line, and Kevin Keogh, a stockbroker with a seat on the Exchange. Walter Cronin, vice-president of the Merchandise Mart, Edward Morehouse of General Motors . . . she checked off the names that represented a potential safety net against debt.

Louise's desk lamp was kept burning into the night by financial problems, to which the strew of papers on the desk attested. Louise went over the figures again, though they were inked indelibly in her mind. The mortgage payments for the Ogden property would amount to $38,000 by the end of the fiscal year in June, the first of twenty years of payments. The annual cost of the bank loan to refurbish the mansion and equip it as a school was $9,500. The operating costs for both schools totaled $196,000 for the year. The Society's expenses, including the education program for the nuns, medical bills, and the costs of the novitiate, amounted for the year to $74,000. Each year, as was customary, the Archdiocese imposed a tithe on Rosemoore: With the opening of Fifth Avenue, it had been increased to $50,000. Aligned against these figures was the income of $326,000, derived from the student fees at both schools. The debits, when subtracted from the credits—shades of Joe Slattery!—showed a deficit of $41,500.

Louise cast the papers on the desk. It would take years before

Rosemoore–Fifth Avenue was a paying proposition. As a day school it was less expense to operate, but unlike Peekskill it was comprised of upper and lower schools. (*"The finished Rosemoore girl,"* stated the royal-blue catalog, *"will have progressed through the primary levels to the college preparatory classes."*) The inquiries from parents had started as soon as the mansion's acquisition was reported in the press. The school had opened to a fanfare of publicity, with an enrollment of eight students in Form One of the lower school and a freshman prep-school class of seventeen. Each year, as one class advanced to the next level like stepping-stones, another class would be added, but it would require four years to fill the upper-school ranks and twice that for the lower school. Only then would the balance sheets indicate a profit of any substance.

Renew the bank loan? Take out a second mortgage? Having ruled out any transaction that would increase the indebtedness, Louise paced back and forth at the window bay. The need was for a new source of income and the dinner party seemed the best answer, but she wished that she could talk it over with Larkie. She knew when she'd appointed Mother Larkin the headmistress at Fifth Avenue that she'd miss her. Somehow with Larkie she felt her old self again, before the years had wrought the changes in her.

The shouts of play from the campus and the beloved view of hills and sky went unheeded at the window. Louise was not conscious of someone's presence in the room until a voice addressed her.

"It's four o'clock, Reverend Mother, and I've come to scold you."

It took a moment for Louise to respond. "Quite right, Friel, I've not taken my daily walk, which I blame entirely on the dinner party."

"But it's a marvelous idea." Mother Friel glanced at the paper in her hand. "I daresay you've already composed the invitation."

"No, but have you given it a try?"

"It's not worth your attention."

"Nonsense, let me see." Louise was given the paper, on which in elegant Roman script a sample invitation was inscribed.

Reverend Mother Louise Maguire
and
The Society of the Holy Virgin Mary
request the honor of your company

THE FAITHFUL

at the inaugural dinner of
The Knights of Rosemoore
Annunciation Hall
Saturday evening, 28 December, 1923
at eight o'clock
Black Tie
R.S.V.P.

"Really, it's spendid," Louise exclaimed, reading the invitation again. "How inventive of you, to think of the Knights of Rosemoore."

"The pope has his Knights of Malta, why not some for our own?"

"Well, it certainly indicates the spirit we hope for, but as to my name on the invitation—"

"Your name, Reverend Mother, belongs on everything associated with Rosemoore."

Louise was not deceived by flattery, but neither was she immune to it. She gave her secretary the list of names, thinking that she had misjudged her. "Let's take the plunge, Friel, and send invitations to all eighteen of these gentlemen. Some are bound to accept."

"All eighteen, I'll warrant." Mother Friel folded the list of names and her pale-lashed eyes grew bright with reminiscence. "My family entertained rather often at our home in Brooklyn—I was raised on black-tie dinners as a girl."

Louise took her cloak from the coat-tree. "Well, then, you'll be invaluable in planning our dinner, on which so much depends."

"Before you go, Reverend Mother, the letter from Cork still wants a reply."

Louise turned from the door. "Sorry, but you'll have to refresh my memory."

"The letter from the orphanage, saying that Agnes O'Shea had run off to Dublin with her baby."

"Oh, yes." Louise wrapped a shawl over her cloak for extra warmth. "Fresh worries for Bridget, but I don't see what we're to do about it."

"I'll reply for you, thanking the Sisters for telling us."

Louise chose a volume of spiritual meditations from the bookshelf for her walk. "Excellent, Friel, you handle it for me."

Piano scales accompanied her down the carved-oak stairs. One of

Flavin's private lessons in the music room, estimated Louise. She
had not been eager to lend her support when Flavin had come to her
last spring. She felt that she had forfeited her right to ask concessions
of Connolly, but now she was glad to have interceded for Flavin
with him. He'd reacted as though the teaching were a move he
ought to have thought of himself, and so Louise had performed a
good deed at minimal cost.

The biting cold assailed her as she stepped onto the porch. The
blustery gray skies were a clear forecast of snow, and the groups of
apple-cheeked girls cavorting on the lawns seemed already on holiday. Some of the girls curtsied as Louise came down the porch steps,
but then went back to their play. She commenced her brisk turn of
the driveway, remembering the old days when students had flocked
like chickens around her skirts. At night sometimes Louise strained
to catch the laughter that was to be heard coming from the dormitory rooms. The freshmen still roomed in Annunciation, but it had
once housed all of the girls, and nightly peals of laughter that lasted
until lights-out. Of course, the new accommodations in Blanchard
had increased the enrollment by fifty and the income by . . . $35,500.
Louise multiplied the figures swift as a tabulator.

"Mother Maguire?"

She looked up from the volume of St. Francis de Sales. Flavin
Moore, in a cherry-red cadet coat with brass buttons, was coming toward her from the porch steps. She held a pigskin music case in her
arms as if it were a prize awarded for perseverance. The experience
of teaching, the give-and-take with her students, had coaxed Flavin
from the stiff formality that had inhibited her since childhood. Her
jaunty stride was a reflection of it, but her smile as she approached
Louise was tinged with anxiety.

"Wrong moment for a Christmas appeal?"

"Why, of course not, my dear. The era seems to have passed when
my girls rushed up with their confidences."

"You've become such a commanding figure of authority . . . it's
made all of us a bit shy."

Louise resumed her brisk pacing. "But not you, Flavin, I trust.
Now, what's this Christmas appeal, as you phrase it?"

"You won't be surprised if it's to do with Father? Christmas is a
difficult time for him—" Flavin fell into step with the commanding
figure of the nun. "He can't help associating it with Mama's death.

I'd hoped for a family reunion this year, all of us together, but he won't hear of asking Monica and Billy to the house or bringing Stacey up from Palm Beach."

"Patience," Louise counseled, of the virtue she had abandoned with Connolly. "He has another week to change his mind."

"I know, and he's been a dear about having to stay in the city without me."

"Well, there, he approved of the teaching when you least expected it."

"Yes, but you see—" Flavin's anxious glance went to the parking lot and the flivver that was its solitary occupant. Stephen had stayed after class to work on the scenery for the Christmas play, but the curl of smoke rising above the woods indicated to Flavin where he'd gone.

"Your father, my dear Flavin, has reserved for you a special place in his heart, and—"

"Help me, Mother Maguire."

The urgency of the plea shook Louise from her complacency. "What is it, child? What's wrong?"

"No, not wrong—wonderful!" Flavin hugged her music case, torn between rapture and despair. "The most wonderful thing of my life, but I dread telling Father about it."

Caution nudged Louise as she considered the importance of the dinner party. "Why not, if it is nothing wrong?"

"I love my father and if I were to tell him . . ." Flavin turned and looked at the girls playing tag on the lawn. She sensed that Mother Maguire was not disposed to hear her out. "Are you to be at the Christmas play?" she asked instead.

"Would I dare to miss it, but we were speaking of—"

"I'm to provide the piano music—dress rehearsal's tomorrow night and poor Mother Fitz is a bundle of nerves."

"Flavin, dear—"

"Perhaps I'm mistaken about Father. As you say, he didn't raise the slightest fuss about my teaching."

"Time and patience, my dear."

"Yes, perhaps that will do it . . . well, I'd better be on my way."

Louise watched the cherry-red coat move across the hockey field. She recalled that Flavin often walked to and from Faircrest, taking the shortcut through the woods in preference to driving. The red coat was a tiny stroke against the brown field when Louise noticed the smoke that curled from the chimney of the cottage in the woods.

The most wonderful thing . . . ?

With an effort Louise focused on the volume of meditations and paced the driveway. The Knights of Rosemoore, what a clever device for the dinner party. Connolly's invitation must, of course, be hand-delivered . . . and next year at Fifth Avenue, thought Louise in her pacing, the first Christmas Ball . . .

"So then," Connolly said at the candlelit table as Jonah served the dessert of baked caramelized apples and Bavarian cream, "I decided that if I was lonesome for my daughter, I'd drive up and take dinner with her."

"It's too bad that I have to rush off to rehearsal."

"Must you?" Connolly gazed down the gleaming length of the table at his daughter at the opposite end. She had been twelve, he remembered, when he had conferred upon her the hostess's chair. "I should think the nuns might allow me the pleasure of your company, since it is mine less often these days."

"We'll have loads of time once the recess starts, but tonight—" Flavin got up from the chair, her dessert untouched. "I really must go, Father."

"The sparkle in your eyes, the roses in your cheeks—teaching seems to agree with you."

She swept back her hair and started from the table. "Rehearsal's apt to last till all hours, so perhaps you oughtn't to wait up for me."

Then she was gone into the hall, and Connolly pushed away the dessert bowl and listened to the click of her heels on the stairs. He had not moved from the table when she was back again, buttoning the cherry-red coat and tying the white silk scarf under her chin.

"I promise to make it up to you over the holidays, Father—your every wish will be my command."

"Why is it, with a drawerful to choose from, that you always wear that particular scarf?"

"It's the French aviator's scarf you gave me in Paris." She leaned over the chair and kissed her father. "I'll make it up—I promise."

He felt her breath warm on his face and wanted to keep her with him, but it was an urge that he knew he had to resist."

"Away with you, Mary Flavin, begorra."

"If your light's on when I come in, I'll give a tap at your door."

Let her go . . . you've made a good start of it, don't wreck it now . . .

Connolly sat in his chair and listened to the crunch of the gravel as Flavin's car drove away. He'd wanted to tell her of the negotiations for the sale of Shamrock before the papers got wind of it, but it would have to wait until breakfast. He looked up to find that Della had entered and was setting the silver tray of coffee on the sideboard.

"What's happened to Jonah?"

"He . . . well, suh, Jonah be feelin' poorly, an' Clarice make him lie down fo' the night."

Negro servants, thought Connolly, were like silent ghosts moving through the house. "The arthritis acting up?"

"He jes' feelin' poorly."

Connolly made a mental note to take Jonah to the city for a checkup. He stood up and threw his napkin on the table. "I'd like my coffee in the library, Della, then why don't you wash up and turn in?"

He crossed the black-and-white squares of the hall and stood in the doorway of the music room. It wasn't to be the musical evening he'd planned of Flavin and Chopin, but a book and his favorite chair in the library were not a bad substitute. He stood in the doorway staring first at the Beckstein and then at the Dutch landscape on the wall where the Sargent portrait had hung, which was one less ghost to confront him.

The silent Della had left his demitasse on the drum table next to the tufted-leather English club chair and then had disappeared. Connolly surveyed the shelves of books that reached from floor to ceiling, the matched sets of morocco and calf, the first editions and folios, and selected *David Copperfield* for the night's read. By far Dickens was his favorite author, but when he'd settled back in the club chair in the cone of light that poured from the claw-footed floor lamp, ghosts swooped out at him from the opened pages.

The bachelor rooms on West Twenty-sixth Street . . . the shame of Gordon Morris having to teach him to read, and it hadn't made him a gentleman, that and all the rest of it . . . the awful struggle up from McGreevey's back room, half-starved and huddled on the floorboards with rags for warmth and no one to love him . . . no one until he found Rose . . .

The book slid to the carpet with a soft thud and Connolly got up from the club chair. He crossed back over the black-and-white squares, past the portrait of the papal marquis, the impostor who didn't fool him. The lights in every room were ablaze, in keeping with his longstanding instructions, but it was darkness that he sought going up the soaring curve of the stairs. The evening, once started upon a downward course—*"Sorry to rush off to rehearsal"*— must follow to its predestined conclusion.

The slam of the bedroom door, loud and sharp as a pistol retort, was the sound of Connolly's retreat from his life. The shadows that masked the big square bedroom did not hinder his passage through it into the dressing room. From accustomed touch, he extracted the key, hidden in the wardrobe, that unlocked the black-lacquered mother-of-pearl cabinet. Prohibition had made no dent in Faircrest's stock of liquor and wine. At regular intervals a Shamrock truck traveled to the Canadian border and returned with bootleg cases of whiskey and Krug champagne, some of which was delivered to the suite at the Plaza.

Connolly tore off the seal on a bottle of Bushmills and lifted it with trembling hand to his lips. The darkness he sought would be swift but irreversible, and he lowered the bottle in a last grasp at sobriety. As inevitable as his ultimate fall was, he had succeeded in eluding it for months at a stretch, sometimes by pursuing another form of release.

The evening was still young; it wasn't too late to drive back to the city. Mimi Lamont was a showgirl, lazy and bubble-headed with a lush and tireless body. Connolly was above bringing his whores to the Plaza, unlike some men he could name. Mimi had no complaints about the money she received for his visits to her apartment, and she didn't object to his roughshod lovemaking, but craved it, in fact.

Connolly switched on a light in the dressing room. Shakily, he relinquished the bottle, setting it on the cabinet. A press of a button on the telephone would summon Boylan and the Rolls, but was it worth it? The brief spasms of release with all the Mimis over the years, were they worth the guilt and remorse, the out-of-the-way confessionals to seek absolution for his sins? If Rose had been a lustier wife and not the eternal, everlasting virgin, cringing behind her locked door . . .

Seizing the bottle, Connolly held it glued to his mouth. The effect was instantaneous, a quivering release that cried to be fed, and he didn't quit until he'd satisfied it. The whiskey coursed like liquid fire through him, heating a rage in his blood. He turned, cradling the bottle, and appraised the door to the connecting rooms. It had not been locked for years, but he kicked it open as though to rip the lock from it.

The light from his dressing room spilled into that of his wife's. The mirrored closets in which her clothes were preserved glinted in the shadows. Connolly took a thirsty swig from the bottle and advanced to the inner sanctum of the shrine, the unholy shrine, that he'd kept in memory of his wife. The windows of the bedchamber were shuttered and dark, and the air was stale and musty but faint with the lingering fragrance of lavender water. The room was hung with lace; swags of it were draped in a canopy over the postered bed.

Rose . . . forgive me, Rose . . .

Connolly pushed back the lacy swags, fragile as cobwebs, and fell onto the bed, sloshing whiskey on the coverlet. Christmas wasn't celebrated the year that Rose had died, and in his grief he'd turned to his eldest daughter for solace. At the dinner table tonight, Flavin was the image of the young Rose . . . the sparkle of her eyes, the bloom of her cheeks.

He lunged up from the lacy pillows, convinced of what he had vaguely suspected from his daughter's manner at the table and her eagerness to leave for the rehearsal. What at school was the magnet that had drawn her away from her father?

Why the sparkle and bloom?

Connolly groped to his feet with the bottle, no longer wanting release. Alarm battled with his rage as he stumbled back to his rooms and pressed the button on the telephone that connected him with the garage.

"Is that you, Boylan?" he demanded. "Listen carefully, you are to take the car, not the Rolls, the estate car," he specified, "and you're to drive up the road to Rosemoore, as far as the gates . . . there's something I want you to find out for me."

It snowed the morning of the Christmas play, with flakes as thick and fleecy as the students had wished for. Hurrying through breakfast, the girls flocked outdoors, saluting the snow with waving arms and shrieks of glee. The 8:55 bell rang, but no one who was late for class risked a demerit. It was the day that the nuns received their Christmas gifts from the students, boxes of Caswell and Massey unscented soap, boxes of writing paper, also unscented, plain black gloves and umbrellas, books of poetry and the lives of the saints—how could you get a demerit when you showed up with a gift?

The nuns had exhausted the time-honored strategies of vocabulary drills and history quizzes to stem the tide of giggles and tomfoolery, and as a last recourse they invited a discussion of religion, all questions welcomed.

"What if I went on summer vacation," asked Tookie Fennelan, who was in Lizzie's class, "and I had to walk five miles up a mountain to get to Sunday Mass—would I still have to go?"

"Let us examine your question, Tookie. Is this mountain you refer to the Jungfrau, and what is a church doing at the top of it?"

"I don't know—a tourist attraction, say."

"It strikes me as a dubious attraction, but you are a creature of boundless energy. The walk *up* the mountain would be an appropriate penance and the walk *down* a happy reward for your fidelity to Holy Mass."

"Okay, but what if—?"

"Yes, Tookie, what if you vacationed in the jungles of Borneo and were captured by cannibals? Next question, please."

By three o'clock the snow had spread a blanket of ermine over the campus. Snowball fights erupted and a succession of navy chinchilla coats rolled down the hill above the hockey field, collapsing in laughter at the bottom. The wait was almost over, home and families were two short days away. Tomorrow night, the carols and tree lighting, and tonight was the Christmas play!

The snowfall ended at dusk, when the lights on the driveway winked on and Lizzie Devlin was to be seen plowing across the hockey field with Tyrone. The setter leaped and bounded in the snow, entranced, but Lizzie trailed behind, encumbered by more than her soggy, encrusted boots. Study Hall was at five o'clock and she'd be late if she didn't hurry, but it didn't spur her lagging steps as she made for the driveway.

"Off you go, sport." She dispatched Tyrone onto the walk that skirted around to the back of Annunciation, where, after a bowl of choice scraps and the fondlings of the Sisters in the kitchen, he would retire for the night to his warm quarters in the basement.

The chapel bells chimed the hour, of no incentive to Lizzie's dawdling. A crew of Peekskill high school boys, supervised by Aloysius Duffy, were shoveling the driveway clear for the cars expected for the night's performance of *Whither Goest?* It seemed to Lizzie a pertinent query as she watched the shovels toss the snow and debated whether to go straight to the gym, where Stephen Jarvic was finishing up the scenery for the play. Oh, how she longed to be home in Stamford with her family, spared for the holidays of worrying about the fate of the lovers after what she'd just seen in the woods.

Lizzie put off telling Mr. Jarvic about it and trudged in her soggy boots up the stairs of Blanchard to her room. She skipped the study period entirely and ran the water for her bath. She doused it with Eileen's Shalimar, borrowed from Mrs. Birnbaum, and luxuriated in the steamy bath clouds and delicious scent. At least, as the rear end of the donkey, she'd smell like a million bucks.

The performance of *Whither Goest?*—the world premiere of the drama—was scheduled for an eight o'clock curtain, barring delays, which at seven-thirty looked to be of considerable duration.

The stage of the raftered gym, which also functioned as the school auditorium, was in a frenzy of last-minute crises. The rented costumes from Eaves had arrived that afternoon, a day late, and some accessories were missing. Mother Fitzgerald, both author and harried director of the play, sat under a cutout palm tree fashioning a crown for King Balthazar from a gold candy box. Half-dressed members of the cast wandered onto the stage to report other missing items, such as St. Joseph's beard and the mate to a shepherd's sandals. In the wings, Mother Donlan, the stage manager, was cuing King Melchior, who had suffered a memory lapse. The starry-night backdrop of Bethlehem that Stephen Jarvic had painted was hung but not yet dry. The light board had blown a fuse and Stephen was up on a ladder testing the grid lights. Lizzie Devlin, not yet in costume, stood below with his tool box, thinking that what she had to tell him couldn't be put off any longer. It was painful, having to confess her spying activities, but there was no choice now that another spy was involved.

Lizzie peered up the ladder. "Mr. Jarvic, I've got something to confess."

"*You*, Lizzie?"

"You know how I like to go tramping around with Tyrone . . . this place and that."

"Yes?"

"The woods are off limits, but one afternoon last April it's where we went . . . to that cottage you were fixing up."

Stephen looked at her from the ladder. "What are you trying to tell me?"

"I—every so often I've gone back there, not for any bad reason."

"For what, to spy?" Stephen was more dismayed than angered. "Certain things are private, Lizzie, and I've thought of you as my friend."

"I *am* your friend, it's why I'm telling you this, because—"

"Secrets aren't very praiseworthy, but when it's in consideration of . . ." Stephen jumped down from the ladder, his dark brows forked together. "Why did you pick tonight to tell me?"

"Well, I'm going home Friday and I worried that if I kept quiet about what I saw—"

"Where—at the cottage?"

"Balthazar!" called Mother Fitz, waving the candy-box crown. "Where is he? Hurry someone and take Balthazar his crown. Are the lights working, Mr. Jarvic? Will this play ever get on?" She peeped anxiously through the curtains at the audience filing into the rows of fold-up chairs. "It is my last fling as a dramatist—I'm switching to the Romantic poets. Clear the stage, everyone, and let Mr. Jarvic finish the scenery. Steep yourselves in the ancient lore of the stars and prophecies!"

The curtains parted fifteen minutes late and the drama, which focused on the interminable wanderings of the Wise Men, got under way. Lizzie was confined for most of the performance to the locker room below the stage in the company of Mary, St. Joseph, shepherds, and angels, who were not to appear until the final nativity scene.

Draped in a blue mantle and cradling the infant Savior—an Effenbee doll—on her lap, Eileen Birnbaum made an ideal Mary, as had been predicted. "I didn't use a dab of eye shadow or rouge," she fretted, "but what about my lipstick?"

"It's the merest blush," Florence Giambetti assured her, engulfed in the donkey costume, the rear section of which dangled from her lap. "I like your beard," she complimented St. Joseph, whose chin was pasted with crinkled strips of brown crepe paper. "Let's hope it stays glued."

Lizzie, who sat next to Floss on a locker bench, was preoccupied with listening to the dialogue that, delivered in a shout, could be heard from the stage. She questioned that such gabby wise men would have ever reached Bethlehem, stopping off as they did to hold forth on everything but the price of eggs. A play, in Lizzie's opinion, ought to be action packed, with a thrill a minute and a rousing ending to cheer, not like in real life, when you could never be sure of the ending. Lizzie listened to the Christmas music that was being played on the gym piano between the scenes. During the final rehearsals, when Flavin Moore wasn't stealing looks at Stephen Jarvic, he was stealing looks at her. The girls were catching on and the whispering would start, so maybe it didn't matter what she'd seen at the cottage—the secret wasn't to last for long, anyway.

"Mary, Joseph—come, we're ready for you." Mother Fitz hastened down the locker-room stairs. "Eileen, don't forget the Christ child, and you, Tookie, what possessed you to wear those tennis sneakers?"

"It was an emergency," Tookie Fennelan, who was garbed as a shepherd, a well-fed shepherd, explained. "One of my sandals was missing."

"Remove the sneakers this instant and go barefoot—and where's the rear half of the donkey? I want no antics from you, Lizzie Devlin."

Lizzie climbed into the rear of the costume, which joined her to Florence, and together they trooped up the stairs to the stage wings. The curtains whooshed closed and the actors in the nativity scene took their places on stage. Mary sat on a stool at the manger holding the infant, with St. Joseph at her side and flanked by angels with cardboard wings. The Wise Men and shepherds knelt before them, while in the manger the donkey grazed on crepe-paper tufts of hay. Zippered into the costume, Lizzie felt a budding excitement as she bent over and hung on to Florence, and the curtains whisked apart to a wave of applause.

The sound of applause, the magic of the stage, were responsible for what followed. In the midst of the reverent tableau, to the piano strains of "Silent Night," the rear of the donkey gave a wiggle and swayed to provocative effect. The initial reaction came from one of the Wise Men and a shepherd who tittered. Mary and Joseph, closest to the mischievous beast, were clearly stunned. The reaction spread to the audience in an outbreak of giggles that swelled into shouts of laughter, which seemed to encourage the donkey to new feats of terpsichore. Backstage in the wings, Mother Fitzgerald called for smelling salts.

Lizzie would not have denied that the laughter was heady music. It was one thing to get laughed at in everyday life, but quite another to capture it on a stage in front of an audience. It touched a new chord in Lizzie of self-discovery, but as she wiggled and swayed and executed a comic two-step, she did it as much to banish from her mind the image of the man she had seen stealing from the cottage with the white silk scarf gripped in his hand.

EIGHTEEN

The blizzard that nobody had requested stormed from the sky the day after Christmas and whirled through the night. The sky was clear when Louise looked out the tower window early on Friday morning, but the walks were buried in glistening drifts and the driveway was a toboggan of snow. The blizzard had left the campus snowbound, threatening the dinner party for Saturday night.

Rather than face the canceling of the dinner, Louise turned to her immediate concerns. The telephone lines had survived the storm and a call to the monastery at Crugers verified that the monks were snowbound and unable to say Mass for the nuns. Prayer was the next best thing, and a galvanized Duffy was put to shoveling a path to Blanchard and the chapel.

It was a makeshift arrangement at best that housed some of the nuns in Blanchard and others in the attic and nooks and crannies of Annunciation. This morning, the novices were isolated by the blizzard in the coach house far down the driveway, which was impassable. As the nuns gathered in the chapel, it pointed up for Louise the need for what she had wanted to build for years, a convent for the nuns adequate for both the present and the future.

The soft chant of psalms and litanies that rose and fell in the chapel were at harmony with the peace and quiet of the snow outside. Apart from the respite from classrooms and students, the Christmas holidays provided the nuns with a time to renew the spirit that bound them together as a community of women vowed to the same ideals of sanctity.

Louise, who led the prayers from her stall at the front, was overtaken by distractions. Her mind wandered so frequently in chapel that her awareness of it was dulled. She fought against the near certainty that the dinner party would have to be called off . . . no, she would not permit the deficit to go unsolved.

The driveway was an affront to Louise when prayers had concluded and she inched along the slippery path through the snow in the convoy of nuns. "It will turn to solid ice by tomorrow," she lamented to Mother Tracy, who taught Latin and a senior course in botany. "We must get the snow shoveled off before it freezes over."

"Imagine if one were a sleigh," Mother Tracy proposed, whose fancy was not grounded by her schooling in the classics. "What sport to coast clear down to the gates and beyond."

"Yes, but imagination won't produce the boys from town to clear the driveway."

The holidays absolved Louise from breakfast on a tray at her desk, but she had little appetite for the rare treat of waffles and maple syrup that she was served in the company of the other nuns in the dining room of Annunciation. To linger over coffee was as rare a treat, but it was cut short by Sister Pauline's appearance from the kitchen.

"Park and Tilford was to deliver the provisions from the city today, but I guess with the snow you'll have to cancel the dinner party."

"Not yet, Pauline."

"But how in the name a' God—?"

"I've not given up quite yet, thank you."

Refusing to concede defeat, Louise left the breakfast table for the tower office. She went over the guest list as if to conjure the men's presence at the dinner by grit of her determination. Of the eighteen invited, four had declined, an excellent response. Two were to travel by train from Chicago and Detroit, and should the Westchester roads be snowplowed by tomorrow . . . but what assurance had she of it?

Louise did not hear the jingle of bells on the driveway. As loathe as she was to the task, the guests must be notified by telegram of the dinner's cancellation, and without delay. She was composing the odious wire on the yellow pad when the jingling reached her ear. She listened for a moment and then a glance from the window sent her flying down to the porch.

Coming up the driveway, pulled by a horse in jingling harness, was a vision out of a Russian novel—a scarlet sleigh with fur-lined seats and curl-tipped blades that sliced through the crusted snow. Connolly Moore's Persian-lamb cossack hat and mink-shawled greatcoat made of him a grand duke driving to the Winter Palace in St. Petersburg. He pulled at the reins and the snorting horse, breath fogging the air, pranced to a halt below the porch steps.

"You didn't cancel?" Connolly boomed at Louise, handing down a large steamer basket. "What sort of Knight would I be if I didn't help to gather the other Knights at your dinner table?"

"The sleigh, wherever did you—?"

"Ariakian, where else? He alleges to have bought it from a Romanov, no less." With a bow to the nuns who had collected on the porch, Connolly marched into the entrance hall, divesting himself of fur hat and gloves, stamping the snow from his shiny boots. "Don't ask me about Christmas—I endured it, let's leave it at that."

As he spoke, he looked up at the Sargent portrait above the mantel. "It's always a bad time for me . . . and somewhat lonesome for Flavin, with just the two of us at Faircrest." He swung around from the mantel and relieved Louise of the steamer basket. "You, as a nun, might feel obligated to comply with the Prohibition laws, but not I." He set the basket on the table and whipped the checkered cloth from the magnums of Krug. "How many guests are you expecting?"

"I doubt that I can reasonably expect any of—"

"A phone call to the right person will take care of the snow." Connolly flung open the door and boomed at the nuns who were admiring the sleigh. "Can any of you manage the horse? Bessie's a gentle soul—take her for a ride and set those bells to jingling!"

He turned to Louise and the swashbuckling ebullience drained from him. "What was I saying?" he asked, glancing around as if to recover his bearings. "As for the champagne, let's not forget a singular fact in that regard."

"Oh, yes?"

"Dom Perignon, who invented it, was a monk, which ought to sit well with you . . . and having braved the cold, your guests are entitled to some refreshment, are they not?"

Louise gave a sigh. "Since when have I won an argument with you, Connolly?"

He threw back his head in a roar of laughter. "Oh, I'd say we were a good match for each other, with wins and losses on both sides." Of a sudden, the laughter ebbing, he made for the stairs. "Listen to me go on, and the phone call forgotten. Well, let's get to it, my laddie."

He vaulted up the stairs and Louise followed behind, remembering Connolly galloping up to the porch on the black charger to invigorate her anew for the hard toil of founding a school. Disposing of obstacles, turning mountains into molehills with dashing aplomb, were the turbulent shifts of mood simmering in him even then?

She found him at her desk in the tower office grappling with the telephone, jiggling the hook in vexation.

"I want Albany, but all I get is an infernal buzz."

Louise went to the switchboard in the outer office and plugged in the long-distance line. She listened while the operator rang the governor's office in Albany. The call went through several intermediaries before it reached Alfred E. Smith, who this year had been elected to his second term as governor of New York State. With Smith on the line, Louise put the ear set down and waited for the click of the telephone in the tower office. Then she rejoined Connolly, whose mood was again at a peak of elation.

"How would you like a squad of state troopers to clear your driveway?"

"You've arranged for it?"

"Not me—Al's the fellow who did it. Extra crews to plow the roads and the troopers at one o'clock, so you'll want to have pots of coffee and doughnuts ready, like the old days, when the workmen were swarming over this place."

"I'll write the governor and thank him."

Connolly appeared not to have heard her. The elation was gone, and he sat drumming his fingers in a tattoo on the desk. "Al's the best damned governor the state's ever had, and mark my words, someday he'll be president, whereas I . . ."

He stared at the deep-blue carpet as though the future were woven into it. "I'll tell you what's in store for me, unless I mend my ways . . . a lonely and despised old critter, that's what I'll become."

The nuns had taken him up on the sleigh ride, and the jingling bells lured Connolly to the window bay and the view of frosted hills and icy river and the distant chimneys of Faircrest. "The snow made a prisoner of Rose," he said in a distant voice, "but I daresay she was always that in her mind, the whole year through. You see, the difficulty was that I—I—"

He swung around to Louise, his fists clenched in an effort to speak of what haunted him. "How must you have felt when I held on to the deed to Hightower?"

The question caught her ill prepared. "The only recourse was to wait . . . and to pray," she answered, and branded herself a liar for it.

"It's a sickness, I realize that, but what's the cure?"

"The cure for what?"

Connolly strode the carpet, the greatcoat flaring out behind him. "It's a sickness to hold on to everything, wanting it to belong to me. Money can't buy people, they're not chattel, you can't own them. The difficulty is in letting go . . . it lost Rose to me, and two of my daughters since, and a grandson I've never seen, and if I'm not careful with Flavin . . . it's God she belongs to, isn't it?"

"All of us." Louise folded her hands tightly in her sleeves. "We all belong to God . . . and to Him we must account."

Connolly paused in his striding and looked at Louise. He started to reply but the wheels shifted within him, away from the discussion. "Clever idea, the Knights of Rosemoore," he said in a lightning shift back to a former subject. "It has, like my shamrock, the right connotations."

"Of what? I'm not sure that I—"

"Where's the guest list, if you'll allow me a gander at it?"

Louise went to the desk with some hesitation and gave him the list, which elicited a whistle of appreciation and compliments on the astuteness of her selection.

"You've bagged yourself a choice catch, and you may rest assured"—Connolly whacked at the paper—"each of these gentlemen will bring his checkbook. Set a figure yet, have you?"

She flushed with embarrassment. "We are faced with a deficit this year of several thousand dollars and no means of raising it."

"Go to the banks for your deficit and let me hear what you *want* out of the evening."

"It hasn't occurred to me that I . . ." Louise stiffened and the wheels shifted in her. "I want a convent for my nuns," she said, and as an afterthought, "with a wing for the novitiate."

"Didn't I say we were a good match?" Connolly laughed. "Always know what you want and go for it. I'll lead off with a check for ten thousand and just watch the men follow suit."

It was someone else, not Louise, who had said that she wanted a convent. Going down the oak stairs with Connolly, some other person listened and paid little heed as he spoke of his daughter.

"Palm Beach won't be the same without Flavin. I might pass it up this winter."

"Might you?"

"She's a wonderful travel companion. By jove, the trips we've had together—why, on one occasion we weren't taken for father and daughter."

"Really?"

"The south of France it was, Nice or Antibes, I forget just where." Connolly bounded onto the landing with youthful vigor. "I was having breakfast on the hotel terrace, and what do you suppose the waiter asked?"

"Yes, what?"

He collected his fur hat and gloves from the hall table. "The waiter asked why my wife wasn't at breakfast with me . . . and I was flattered enough not to bother to correct him."

Louise and not someone else stood on the landing dumbstruck while Connolly pulled on his gloves and nodded at the basket of Krug as though he had said nothing of import.

"Be sure to serve the champagne properly iced—it makes all the difference."

She held on to the stair rail. "Before you came, I was drafting a wire to cancel the dinner."

"Easily solved—tear it up."

She went after him onto the porch, the wind swooping up her veil. The sleigh was jingling up the driveway packed with nuns. Connolly turned with outstretched hand and Louise asked, "Is Flavin enjoying the holidays? It must please you to see her so happy with her teaching."

"I'm pleased to think that I'm trying to let go of her. Now, don't forget the coffee and doughnuts for the troopers."

As Connolly went down the steps, the sleigh coasted up in a spray of snow. The nuns surrounded him, chorusing their thanks, and on the porch Louise watched him climb into the sleigh.

With a crack of the whip the horse cantered away, and shivering, Louise went back into the house.

The snow that Saturday evening lay in frosted banks along the driveway, glistening in the clouded moonlight. The towered mansion was a carnival of lights, harking back to a bygone era of gala parties and dances, and carriages rolling up with gentlemen in top hats and ladies in satin and jewels.

Anxiety beset Louise as she made a final tour of the rooms. The guests were due to arrive at any minute and it was futile to wish that it were not so. Tonight, she knew, was a turning point in the growth of Rosemoore, as had been the opening of the Fifth Avenue school. The group of men assembled for dinner were to be involved in more than the deficit or the financing of the convent. A commitment was expected of them, a pledge of support for the future, and this evening was to be the first of what she envisioned as annual dinners.

A hickory fire blazed in the drawing room, heightening the sparkle of the chandelier and the richness of the brocades and velvets. Louise made a swift passage through the room, checking the ashtrays and dishes of salted nuts on the lamp tables. If she nurtured a wish, it was for Mother Larkin to be with her to receive the guests, but that too was futile.

The dining room was agleam with silver and china and crystal, resplendently set off by the dark walnut paneling. Silver candelabra bestrode the embroidered banquet cloth which the nuns had made as their contribution to the dinner. The sixteen places (Father Anselm and Father Leo were to lend the table a priestly tone, and the nuns, of course, were not to be at table) were set with the Spode china and the Gorham flatware. The centerpiece was a silver epergne entwined with red roses from the Faircrest hothouse.

"Why, Friel," Louise exclaimed. "What an invisible presence you are."

Mother Friel moved quietly from the sideboard. "May I hope that the table won't disgrace you?" She was holding the place cards that she had decorated with the school crest and inscribed in her Roman script. "Days of preparation went into the formal dinners we gave at home," she said of the fiction she had created of her family background. "The house was a perfect setting for parties . . . but so were all the houses on Clinton Avenue."

"Yes, you've spoken of it."

Mother Friel went from chair to chair setting out the place cards. As a girl on a Brooklyn fire escape, she had dreamed of such houses, far removed from the dreariness of her life. She had dreamed of Rosemoore from the accounts in the newspapers, and the bequest of a maiden aunt had bought her a year at her dream school. Her only means of staying on was the novitiate, and Claire Friel had availed herself of it. "I never expected to find use for these talents as a nun," she remarked to Louise.

"Well, here at any rate." Louise was at the pantry doors when a nagging thought prodded her. "By any chance, did you forget to ring Larkie and ask her up for tonight?"

Mother Friel's expression was as bland as a baked custard. "You'd want her with you, of course. Larkie is everyone's favorite . . . but are you positive you asked me to ring her?"

"Perhaps I didn't and, really, your table is lovely."

In the kitchen Sister Pauline was stirring the simmering copper pots on the black-iron stove. She pulled the pan of roasting tenderloin from the oven and basted it with the hissing juices, her face lobster-red from the clouds of steam.

"I won't like it if the dinner's late," she declared as she would have to Mrs. Rockefeller. "It'll ruin the beef and I won't answer for the Potatoes Anna."

"Promptly at eight, we'll keep our fingers crossed."

The kitchen was a beehive of industry. The Sisters were kneading dough, rinsing salad greens, grinding coffee, and separating eggs for the dessert of Floating Island. The magnums of Krug, nested in a tub of cracked ice, were a subject of lively discussion.

"Like Ma used to say about Pa"—Sister Genevieve gave each bottle a hearty twist—" 'Let the man enjoy his drop,' she used to say, 'being that he's worked hard for it.' "

"Ha!" snorted Sister Pauline, basting the roast. "I wouldn't mind a drop or two myself."

"I want to thank all of you for your splendid efforts," Louise addressed the Sisters. "A great deal depends on this dinner and . . . "

The words trailed off, and she went over to Bridget, who was pressing butter molds of rosettes. There was a moment of awkward silence on Louise's part before she spoke of what she could not dismiss from her thoughts.

"Has Agnes written from Dublin? You ought to have heard from her by now."

Bridget did not look up from her molds. "No, yer Rev'rince, but Ag ain't much for writin'. She's what she is, no better nor worse. If it wasn't for Egypt, I'd be that despairin' of the baby."

"Egypt, you say?"

"Where they fled, y'know, with the Infant." Bridget's eyes, when she looked at Louise, reflected her worry and apprehension, but in them was the shine of belief. "A land of strangers it was, an' Joseph and Mary fearful of danger, but no harm came to the Child . . . and so I pray it won't to Ag and her babe."

"Reverend Mother—a car is coming up the drive."

"Thank you, Friel," Louise said to her secretary at the pantry door, and hurried past her back through the drawing room. The antler-horn chandelier was a bonfire of light in the entrance hall. Mother Tracy and Mother Shearin, who were to be hostesses with Louise, stood waiting at the cloakroom to receive the hats and coats and mufflers.

"You must tell me," she said to them. "Is there a romance going on between Flavin Moore and Mr. Jarvic? What amuses you that I should ask?"

"You are the last on campus to ask it, Reverend Mother."

"I am? Then it's true?"

Louise braced herself at the sound of the car pulling up outside. She stood at the mantel below the portrait, tall and erect, and felt the stab of a headache. The doorbell chimed and was answered by Mother Tracy, who smiled in welcome.

"Good evening, Mr. Cronin, may I take your coat?"

"Mr. Cronin—" Louise extended her hand and smiled. "How good of you to travel the miles from Chicago to attend our dinner."

The cars and the guests followed in swift succession. John Snyder, Kevin Keogh, Francis Coleman of Standard Oil . . . the headache stabbed, but Louise smiled and extended her hand, each name ready on her lips as the guests approached. At some point Mother Friel had joined her in the greetings, as if it were her customary function. With each chime of the doorbell Louise looked for Connolly to appear, but in vain.

These were the men that he'd told her of the day he'd brought her to Hightower, Louise remembered as she moved into the drawing room, men on the rise, proud to be Catholics, demanding their rightful place. They made a handsome assembly, well tailored in tuxedo jackets and wing collars, warming themselves at the blazing fire, greeting one another and performing introductions, which were unnecessary since each man seemed to know or know of the others. If, as Connolly had said, each had brought along his checkbook, it was because of who he still was in essence. The deference accorded the nuns and the two priests was evidence of it. In their company, the men were boys doffing their caps again on a school or a rectory doorstep in a gesture of allegiance. It was this common identity, this shared heritage, that had summoned the men to Rosemoore on a cold winter night, secure in what they had achieved and prepared with checkbooks to demonstrate it.

The iced champagne was served in crystal tulip glasses on silver trays, heightening the gusto of the men and their spirit of camaraderie. Louise's headache had worsened, in ratio to the liveliness of her manner. At eight-thirty Mother Tracy beckoned her aside to whisper that Sister Pauline was threatening to throw the roast in the sink and the Potatoes Anna with it. Hearing the chime of the doorbell, Louise turned to the archway and saw Connolly in the entrance hall.

He flicked off a scarlet-lined cape and was nothing short of magnificent in the gold-embroidered tunic and satin-slashed trousers of a papal marquis. The effect was startling to Louise, and unnerving, as if he had stepped out from the portrait at Faircrest to join that of his wife above the mantel. Suddenly, as Connolly moved toward her, the sorrow that she had first glimpsed in the Sargent portrait flashed in his eyes. *Sorrow for what? What was the sorrow that had lived on, haunting him through the years?*

"Good evening, Connolly." Louise smiled and extended her hand. "May I present our guests to you?" She escorted him into the drawing room, to the men, the Knights of Rosemoore, for some of whom he had been the role model. "Think of Mr. Morehouse, traveling from Detroit to be with us this evening . . . and of course you must know Mr. Keogh . . ."

The headache was a knife stabbing at her, but Louise was confident by the time she announced dinner that the deficit was no longer a problem and that the convent was to be hers.

*   *   *

Connolly sank back into the cushioned depths of the Rolls. He listened to the faint rattle of the tire chains as the car plowed along the driveway. The dinner party was over and Mother Maguire had received her bank checks of ten thousand dollars each, but what had the evening given him?

The moon has scudded behind the clouds and a mist was rising from the river. At the curve into the woods, Connolly peered out at the dark trees swaddled ghostlike in skeins of snow. The blizzard had ruled out the meetings at the cottage, it had relieved him to know.

"Well, Boylan, what's the report for tonight?"

The chauffeur navigated the winding, slippery drive. "Well, sir, 'twas like this: After droppin' you off at the school, I swapped the Rolls-Royce for the Nash, an' I parked in a clump a' bushes near the gates."

"You can skip the details and get down to where she went."

"Yes, sir, that I will." Boylan disliked having to edit the report of his findings; it lessened his sense of self-importance. "The long and short of it is, Miss Flavin drove her Aston Martin to the roomin' house where himself lives."

Connolly grasped the suede hand strap. "My daughter went up to his room?"

"Not a bit of it, sir. A toot of the horn and out he comes and gets in the car an' it's off to that tavern on Main Street for hamburgers and beer. A' course," Boylan added, taking his revenge as he swung onto the icy road, "who's to say of the carryings-on at the cottage between the pair of them?"

Connolly sat back, reluctant to pursue the exchange any further. Locked in the mother-of-pearl cabinet in his dressing room was the white silk scarf that Boylan had pilfered from the cottage. A week had passed, but Connolly had not confronted his daughter with the scarf, for then nothing would be the same between them ever again.

Let go of her, or history will repeat itself, a twice-told tale of woe ...

He stared out at the snow-ridged road, hating the winter as his wife had hated it, but why must he stay imprisoned by it? He needn't be if he went to Palm Beach instead of calling off the trip. The plan was to wait for the school recess in the spring, when Flavin would go with him. Was it beyond his capacity to leave in January, beyond him to let her be free, once and for all?

The Rolls moved over the icy road with a rattle of chains, and a burden was lifted from Connolly, a weight heavier than stone that he had borne since his wife's death. It was he who was not free, but once he was unburdened of the past, a new life would open up ... a reconciliation with Monica and Stacey ... Flavin set upon a path of her own unhampered by him ... and for himself, peace, *peace* at last!

The big headlights picked out the Faircrest gates from the darkness and Connolly was transfigured by a vision of peace as radiant as the heaven from which he had judged himself eternally barred.

"Tonight ends it," he instructed Boylan as he turned in at the gates. "From now on, we'll forego your reports."

"As you wish, sir."

"Yes, I wish it."

Layers of mist from the river rolled over the snowy lawns and swathed the blaze of lights on the hill. The car circled around the shamrock hedge, which was buried in snow. As it neared the portico, the lilt of Flavin's piano drifted from the house. She was at home and the game of hide-and-seek was ended.

"Are you wantin' me in the mornin', sir?"

"It's likely I'll drive to the city after Mass, just myself, but I'll let you know."

Jonah was at the door to take Connolly's cloak. "You're not to wait up like this," he scolded him. "Neither Flavin nor I can get you to change an iota. We can't afford to lose you, Jonah—you're what holds us together."

"Yessuh." Jonah went off with the cloak, fretting that old dogs could not be taught new tricks.

Connolly warmed his hands at the fire grate in the hall. The piano music had stopped for a moment and then continued. He didn't have to be told why his daughter had not rushed out to him, and he crossed the black-and-white squares to the music room to make amends.

"No, please keep playing, it soothes the savage breast."

Flavin lifted her hands from the keys. The heather cardigan and skirt brought out the blue of her eyes, which shied from her father in the doorway. "How was the dinner at school?"

"Mother Maguire has captured herself a Round Table of Knights ... and your evening, was it pleasant?"

The tumble of hair was held in check by a gold barrette. "I—I drove into Peekskill ... nothing very much to report."

"Are you sure there isn't?"

Flavin caught her breath. "If there were, would you want to hear it?"

"Yes, I would." Connolly loosened the stiff tunic collar and went to sit in the green silk needlework chair across from the Beckstein. "It's wrong to feel bad for my sake, and I'm responsible for it, just as I was with . . ." He leaned back, his head silver-white against the green. "The Schubert song about the garden at the end of summer . . . would you play it for me?"

"You mean . . . ?" Flavin drew from the keys the bittersweet melody of lost summers and vanquished dreams, but it was not the melody that Connolly heard as he listened.

> *The pale moon was rising above the green mountain,*
> *The sun was declining beneath the blue sea . . .*

"That first glimpse of your mother at church, she stole my heart at a glance . . . and in return I broke her heart," he said with a shudder. "I asked for her love, and when she gave it to me I destroyed it. I took a box at the opera to show her off and she sat in the box like a housemaid, and I let her know it. She loved her family, for they spelled home to her, and I wasted no time in cutting her off from them. It all had to be mine. She wanted a home in Faircrest, but I wanted a showplace, so it became what I wanted . . . and then I did worse to your mother."

The music had stopped. Flavin stared at her father, her hands frozen on the keys. "Please don't go on—what's the good of telling me this?"

"It's to free you, don't you see?" Connolly spoke in quick short breaths, devoid of emotion spent long ago. "She loved her babies, but I handed them over to nurses and robbed her of motherhood. Summers at the beach I'd find her gazing at the sea, longing for Ireland and home. It all had to be mine and I reviled her for it. She didn't love me, I said, and I filled her with shame at her failure. By then Faircrest was her prison, and she fled to her rooms to hide her shame from her children. She grew confused, mixed-up, the poor thing, and one winter night, the week before Christmas—"

"No, Father, please."

"I woke up, convinced that she was in harm in some way. The door between the rooms, Rose kept it locked, and when she didn't answer my poundings I ran down the hall to her bedroom . . . and the bed was empty."

"No, I don't want to hear any more."

Connolly's eyes were fixed on the window and the scene it framed of snow and mist. "I pulled on some clothes and went outside to look for her. She'd gotten almost as far as the gates . . . and was lying in the snow in her nightgown." Getting up from the wing chair, he moved past Flavin at the piano and stared out the window at the snow. "I can't know for certain, but I imagine that some noise awakened her, a train whistle perhaps, and in her confusion she conceived the idea of going to the city to visit her Aunt Bea and Uncle Mike. It was something like that, and I—I—"

He turned to Flavin, pantomiming the actions that he described. "I gathered her up from the snow. She was unconscious and I carried her up the drive and into the house and up to her bed. I couldn't get hold of a doctor till morning, but Rose was beyond any doctors by then . . . she died two days later of lobar pneumonia."

"It's over with," Flavin cried. "Dear God, let it be over with."

"But it isn't," Connolly said, turning back to the window. "It isn't over with, not for a day or a night since she died. The bequests to the church, the school in her memory, nothing has erased the memory of what I killed as surely as if I'd plunged a knife into her broken heart."

Flavin looked at her father, wanting to go to him with words of some kind, but no words came and she was powerless to move.

"Memories are my ghosts," Connolly said, staring out at the shrouded mists. "They followed me from Ireland, the sting of my father's strap and my mother's tears, but it's Rose's ghost that every breathing moment stays with me."

"You've told of what happened—isn't that a help?"

Connolly's stance shifted at the window. "It is for a start, and letting go of you is next."

"Father, we—"

"This young man, is he worthy of you?"

The words spurred Flavin up from the piano bench. "We love each other, Stephen and I, and I've hated keeping it from you."

Connolly turned from the window, less beleaguered by the mists. "It's a blow, as you surmised, but I'll attempt to recover from it. When am I to meet the young man who's stolen your heart?"

"Soon, it can't be soon enough!"

"Well, let's see what we can arrange." Connolly strode musingly away from the window. "You'd hoped for a family reunion at Christmas . . . would the New Year be too late?"

"All of us, do you mean, and Stephen too?"

"I'll get on the phone tomorrow with your two sisters. We'll celebrate New Year's Day at the Plaza, Billy and my grandson and your Mr. Jarvic, all of us."

"Oh, Father, really?"

"Yes, by jove, and I'll have an announcement to make by then— the sale of Shamrock, lock, stock, and barrel, or very nearly."

The news stunned Flavin, but with it she felt a jog of uneasiness. "Since when has this been going on?"

"For months, back and forth with the Hartfords. The stockholders still must vote on it, but that's a mere formality."

"I—I'm bowled over," Flavin said, brushing at the tumble of hair. "You'll be lost without Shamrock to occupy you."

"Or found." The wheels were turning in Connolly's mind, as they did when he wanted something. Florida next month, but not alone, and after that . . . "Do you love me?" he asked his daughter. "You needn't answer, but I'd pay any price to hear you say it."

And then he waited for her answer.

NINETEEN

The Plaza on New Year's Day was at its most crowded and festive.
The guests in evening clothes returning from parties imparted a
night glamour to the lobbies that were still decked with Christmas
holly and wreaths. From breakfast onward, the velvet ropes were up
in the Edwardian Room and the Palm Court, with long queues
waiting for tables. Lunch in the Oak Room was a New Year's tradition among the select clientele for whom the tables were reserved,
and not available on this day to the outsiders who strolled in from
hansom rides in the park.

Connolly's table in the Oak Room was in the rear corner to the
left of the entrance. It was *his* table, as the corner table to the right
was held for George M. Cohan, the Broadway song-and-dance man,
whenever he chose to claim it. In recent months, Connolly had
dined alone more often than not, and of considerable interest to
those lunching in the Oak Room was that all six places at his table
were occupied, with a high chair completing the family group.
To the hotel residents who were at lunch, it had appeared that
the Moore family was on the brink of dissolution, but here were
Monica and Anastasia, reunited with their beaming father. The
baby in the high chair was identified as Connolly's grandson, and
one of the young men at the table as Monica's husband, restored
to grace. It was speculated that the other young man, the dark, in-

tense young man, was Flavin's suitor . . . a prospective son-in-law?

How nice, how appropriate for the New Year, the luncheon guests agreed, that Connolly's family was gathered together in harmony, the rifts of the past forgotten.

After lunch, upstairs in the seventh-floor apartment, the air of harmony continued to prevail, though with an underlying tension. In the huge gold-and-white parlor of Connolly's suite, which over-looked both Fifth Avenue and the park, he uncorked a bottle of Krug to toast the sale of Shamrock Markets, to be announced in the next day's newspapers. Billy McNally's constraint was apparent as he politely raised his glass to his father-in-law. The sudden paternal benevolence was as mystifying to Billy as the paternal wrath had been a year ago. He was wary of Connolly's changing moods and the effect they would have on Monica and his son . . . and the money! All at once, Monica was to receive a yearly income from her trust of twenty thousand dollars. It amounted to twice Billy's salary at IBM.

A glance at his wife was sufficient reassurance for Billy. Monnie sat rocking a bleary Acquin to sleep in her arms, as unconcerned as her baby with money and trusts. Soon he would take them home to the Bronx and the ordinary routine of their lives would resume, the going to work and coming home, the Sunday outings on the Con-course, and he'd disassociate himself from Monica's income. On that point Billy wasn't as certain as he would have liked to be. Nothing in life was free in Billy McNally's experience. When money was in-volved, it involved whomever it touched and changed lives of its own accord.

Stephen Jarvic stood at the gold-draped window with Flavin, watching the lights wink on in Central Park. He felt shabby and unkempt in his brown herringbone jacket and gray flannels, the wrong clothes for lunch at the Plaza. At least the hiding was over with, and he couldn't say that Connolly had been less than cordial to him, but at what price?

Dreading the price that had been asked of him, Stephen set his glass of champagne on the windowsill. Leaning over while Connolly held forth on the humble origins of Shamrock, he whispered in Fla-vin's ear.

"I'll get my coat," she said and, in what was an unusual gesture for her, went from the room in the middle of her father's speech. She hurried into the bedroom, which was made infinitely more colorful by the presence of her sister, arrived yesterday by train from Florida.

Somewhat hastily, Anastasia Moore hung up the telephone in mid-speech, fitted a cigarette into a long jade holder, and ignited it with a Cartier lighter. She was stretched out on one of the twin beds in the Chinese lounging pajamas she had worn at lunch in the Oak Room. "I can't *express* my amazement over Stephen," she declared, reaching for a sip of her champagne. "He's the sexiest thing imaginable. Who'd have thunk it of you?"

"Am I to take that as a compliment?"

"Of the highest order." The pajamas and the cirgarette holder, along with the jangly bracelets, kole-lidded eyes, and shingle-cut hair, made up the exotic image that Stacey had devised to compensate for her plain, square-jawed face and stocky figure. "What bliss to wallow in luxury again, after the squalor of West Palm Beach," she ruminated. "Have I you to thank for it, Sis, and where are you going?"

"To the park with Stephen." Flavin belted her polo coat and went to the dresser for a scarf. "And who was that on the phone just now?"

Stacey got up from the bed and polished off the rest of her champagne. "I know you won't tattle on me, but promise you won't laugh?"

"I keep thinking I'll find my aviator's scarf, but it seems to be gone for good. Why would I laugh?"

"At my motorcycle cop, who, incidentally, is gorgeous." Waving the jade holder, Stacey paraded around the bedroom, teetering slightly on her sling-back high heels. "Palm Beach is where you go to nab a rich husband, am I right? Well, I got nabbed by Dave for speeding on the causeway last year and, bingo, that was it. He's got a wife and kids in Tampa, but I'm a fat, dumpy girl nobody's looked at twice, and I hopped into bed with him fast. I guess it makes me the family floozy."

"You're nothing of the sort and he's lucky to have you."

"Well, to level with you, Dave was looking to tie up with a rich dame. It's what he figured me for, but when I walked out on Father and he cut off the trust and I had to go to work at Saks . . ." Stacey mashed out her cigarette. "Well, I was scared that Dave would throw me over, but he let me move in with him . . . maybe because I'm good for laughs."

"Oh, Stacey." Flavin hugged her sister. "I'm so glad we're all together again."

"Of course, with me back in the chips, it's probably when the trouble starts . . . but how did you pull it off with Father?"

"What?"

"Sweetie, he'd never reverse himself like this unless he wanted something out of it, so what did he ask for?"

Flavin turned away, knotting a chiffon scarf under her chin. "Not so very much, compared to what I've been given," she said, and went into the drawing room. Her father was launched into a rousing account of the sack of stolen silver, and she committed the rare offense of interrupting him.

"Stephen and I are going for a walk in the park . . . the scene of the crime, as it were."

Then, with Stephen, she was in the gilt cage of the elevator, the two of them escaping from the perfumed lobby thronged with New Year's guests out into the cold, bracing air. They didn't wait for the light, but dodged through the traffic of Fifty-ninth Street to the park entrance at the corner.

"A year isn't so terribly long," Stephen reasoned. "Not in terms of a lifetime."

"Right at the moment it seems like forever, but we'll get through it."

The afternoon light was waning swiftly into dusk, but the park was still crowded with holiday celebrators. From the skating rink, the sheep meadow, and the carousel, they converged on the walk that Flavin and Stephen followed to the zoo—family groups, boys and girls in mackinaws with ice skates slung over shoulders, and the young couples whom Flavin had once envied. She held on to Stephen's arm, her head nestled against his trenchcoat collar, savoring each ticking minute that passed, loathe to acknowledge its passing. Jonah was closing up Faircrest and packing the mountains of luggage for the season in Palm Beach. Flavin was to leave with her father on the Saturday *Florida Special,* but it would be longer than the winter season before she returned to Faircrest.

"I couldn't say no when he asked," she explained for the hundredth time. "In so many ways, my father is a pitiable man, closed off and lonely, and he looks to me for companionship. A year isn't that great a sacrifice, when you're the reward for it."

"I can't honestly hold it against him for not wanting to lose you."

"The year will go quickly, I know it will."

They fell into a drifting silence, neither of them speaking until the snow-crusted walk had brought them to the sailboat pond at Seventy-first Street.

"I'm not sure of which bench," Flavin said, but Stephen remembered and led her around the dark shimmer of water to the far side of the pond.

"Here's where I saw you that day studying your music, so quiet and gentle and enchanting."

"If I was that enchanting, why didn't it embolden you to speak?"

"Well, see, I was saving it for now." Stephen's voice was husky and urgent and his eyes glittered in the gathering dusk. "It's sort of cold and not summer, but would you sit there again?"

"I . . ." Flavin sat on the bench, responding to his urgency, and from his trouser pocket he took out a jeweler's box.

"The suite at the Plaza and the lunch that must've cost a month of my salary—rich and poor, it's mixed me up all over again. I feel as if I'm giving you a cheap little trinket, but it's—" He opened the box on the flashing glint of the ring. "It's from Tiffany, the tiniest they had, maybe, but it's huge with my love for you."

"Stephen, Stephen—" Flavin brushed at her eyes. "How can I bear to leave you?"

He drew her up from the bench. "Got to do it proper." He laughed shakily, taking her hand and slipping the ring on her finger. "There, for richer or poorer, in sickness and in health, till death do us part."

"Till a year—and a lifetime."

They wandered back along the walk that followed the dips and turns of the park's traffic drive. Dusk had turned into night and with it the family groups had gone. The paths were deserted, except for a sampling of couples and old men on the benches in the lamplight. As they walked under the bare trees patched with snow, Stephen talked of the future. He'd written to a former professor of his at the University of Wisconsin who was presently the dean of the Fine Arts School, and had inquired about the chances of an instructorship. "It'd pay peanuts, but I could pick up extra money with private classes and work on my paintings to sell."

"I'd like that, a university town, and I'll help out with piano lessons."

"Madison's a pleasant town—the university has a terrific program of concerts and art exhibits and theater."

"We'll settle down and raise flowers and babies—you want children, don't you?"

"You bet, a slew of girls as lovely as their mother."

"No sons?"

"Oh, a couple of sons, but no wars to smash them up."

In meandering fashion they came to the stone bridge that arched over the duck pond at the Fifty-ninth Street end of the park. "We'll part here, if it's all right with you," Flavin said, lifting a hand to Stephen's gaunt cheek. "It would be easier for me."

Stephen caught at her hand. "Why easier?"

"I'll pretend it's the footbridge to the cottage and that I'm only going home to dinner."

"In that case, we needn't say good-bye."

"I've never told you, but—" Flavin turned and gestured at the Plaza Hotel, a wedding cake of lighted candles glowing in the night sky. She counted the floors to seven and picked out the windows of her suite. "When I was a child, I used to gaze down at the park from my bedroom window," she said. "It seemed a magical place and I dreamed that someday a prince in disguise would find me there."

Stephen pulled her against him. "A soldier back from the war, and do you know what you've taught him?"

"No, what?"

"Because of you, I'm not afraid anymore of things getting smashed up . . . or of a year to wait for my happiness."

"It's not good-bye—we won't say it."

"You'll wear the ring and not take it off?"

"Always—forever." Flavin ran from the bridge, past the frozen waters of the duck pond and up the rock-ridged steps to the street, not looking back. She rushed through the crowded Plaza lobby, and in the gilt cage of the elevator she kept her head lowered to hide her tears. She hurried past her family in the gold-and-white parlor and closed the bedroom door behind her.

It wasn't good-bye.

She held the ring to her lips and looked from the window. Night enveloped the park, but strings of lights traced out the network of paths and a lamp shone dimly on the bridge and the solitary figure in the trenchcoat who stood gazing above the dark frieze of trees at the hotel.

The holidays at Rosemoore did not officially conclude until the second Monday in January, when classes resumed. Over the weekend, by car and train, the students returned to the campus, not as jubilantly as they had departed but with the glad knowledge that the halfway mark in the school year had been reached. Term finals were less than a month away and the drudgery of cramming for them was imminent, but spring would follow, and the excitement and festivities of June commencement, and then, best of all, summer vacation!

The girls were not long in settling down to their books and crowding into the Pow-Wow after classes to relieve the tedium of studies. One startling bit of news that circulated among them had to do with Cornelia Van Pelt. She had chosen Christmas Eve and the monastery at Crugers for her reception into the Roman Catholic faith. "The historical evidence convinces me that it is the one true Church," she had informed Father Anselm, but the explanation was simpler than that. Having listened for years to the buzz of talk by her students of the miraculous powers of Sophie's Virgin, Cornelia had made one afternoon a surreptitious visit to the chapel. She could not account afterward for the emotion that had gripped her as she stood at the back of the chapel urging herself to leave, yet staying. The chapel was empty, except for a Sister who knelt before the little statue in the bell jar. Bridget O'Shea was of such inconsequence that Cornelia would not have known her by name, but something in Bridget's attitude, the utter belief and trust with which she prayed to the Virgin, had communicated itself to Cornelia Van Pelt. Faith was a gift, Father Anselm had said, and from that day on Cornelia had felt herself a recipient of that gift.

In the tower office, Louise was enmeshed in a variety of plans and negotiations. John Tyler, the architect of Blanchard Hall, had submitted a drawing of the new convent for her approval. She was anxious for construction to start in the spring, but was in a quandary over the drawing, which depicted a separate building, rather than a wing, for the novitiate, joined by a cloister to the convent. Tyler had said that it would add forty thousand dollars to the costs, but Louise was intrigued by the idea. If the future yielded all that she hoped for, and she was confident that it would, the novitiate was worth a building of its own.

After a day or two of what she regarded as dillydallying, Louise instructed Tyler to go ahead with the blueprints. Her decision was typically audacious in that it would require some artful juggling of finances. Late into the night she contended with the figures on the yellow pad, moving them this way and that.

The inaugural dinner of the Knights of Rosemoore had netted the stunning amount of $140,000, less stunning when the deficit was subtracted from it. The contractor's estimate for the new buildings was $210,000, and he had specified a payment before construction of $25,000. Tyler's fee of $10,000 would have to be paid, further shrinking Louise's capital.

All in all, the juggling taught her valuable lessons in finance, at which she was an apt pupil.

She elected to go to the banks for her deficit, as Connolly had recommended, but she shopped around, comparing the interest rates. When Union Fidelity quoted 3 percent, she closed a loan with that bank for $40,000. With the deficit out of the way, it gave Louise, at least for the present, the use of the $140,000. She prevailed upon Tyler and Big Bill Guinness to accept half of what was due them now and receive the balance in six months. She calculated that she had six months to turn a profit from her money, and longer for some of it.

Louise deposited $50,000 in a savings account at Union Fidelity. At 6 percent interest, it would pay for the cost of the loan and net her $1,000 in six months. She kept a reserve fund of $10,000 in her Peekskill account to meet the initial construction costs, and invested the remaining $50,000 in the stock market. She made an appointment with Kevin Keogh at his brokerage office on Pine Street; he assured her that, even with minimum-risk investments, the market would increase the $50,000 in six months' time by one quarter or better.

She took to following the stock-market returns in the newspapers to check on her portfolio, and to commemorate the generosity that had made it possible, Louise designated the library in Annunciation

Hall as the Knights of Rosemoore Room, with a bronze plaque to signify it at the door. She sent to each of the Knights a miniature plaque, suitably mounted, as an expression of her gratitude. To Connolly in Palm Beach went the cast of the plaque, gold-leafed, and a letter of special warmth and affection.

"Enjoy the bright sun and balmy ocean breezes," she entreated him. *"Do please tell Flavin that we miss her at school and will hear of nowhere else for her wedding next spring but our chapel."*

Louise gave prayerful thanks for the working out of what she had needlessly feared to be a calamitous situation. She chided herself for having interpreted a father's love for his daughter as excessive and inordinate.

The groundbreaking ceremonies for the convent and novitiate were held in April during Easter recess, a particularly busy time for Louise. The calendar on her desk burgeoned with appointments with parents coming with their daughters to look over the school. Louise herself conducted the visitors on a tour of the campus. Always the visits were climaxed by tea in the tower office, served in the blue Canton china at the rosewood table. It was frequently this gracious ritual that swayed the parents in favor of Rosemoore as the ideal, indeed, the ultimate, school for their daughters' grooming.

It rained the day of the groundbreaking, which took place in the grove of trees a secluded distance from the driveway. Above the projected site sloped the hill of the nuns' cemetery. This hill of Calvary, as it was named, bore four white crosses, two of them for novices died so young. The overcast sky was sullen with rain and the earth that Louise spaded up with the gaily ribboned shovel was sodden.

She was distracted to a degree from her joy in her achievement, won against formidable odds. For two months her irate letter to Montpellier had gone unanswered. The old story was repeating itself, as before. The Mother General, safely removed from proximity, had reverted to her policy of evasion and delay. Louise by her own instigation had secured the adjustment in the yearly stipends, but the question of the property in Galway was unresolved.

Louise wanted it! She wanted a junior novitiate in Ireland, wanted the vocations it would provide. If the future was to yield all that she hoped for, and she was confident that it would...

She stood below the hill of Calvary and spaded up the sodden earth, determined to win what she coveted, not for herself but ... *who?*

Who, if not for herself?

BOOK THREE

VI
THE HOMECOMING

TWENTY

Who was the girl perched in the oak tree watching the dawn break over the campus of Rosemoore? Was it the echo of last night's applause that had pulled her from sleep, or the expectations that beat within her and would not lie still until the wake-up bell?

She held her breath at the roseate pink infusing the sky and the fiery ball of the sun rising above the river and purple hills . . . the wonder of night turning into day. All but a trace of her gawkiness was gone, transformed into a coltish grace, apparent in the drape of her body on a limb of the oak. As Jo March in *Little Women,* the spring play last night, Lizzie Devlin had been a sensation, a whirling dervish of tomboy foolery and aching young womanhood that had made her audience laugh and cry and thunder applause at the curtain. She had cropped her hair for the role, but not entirely to conform with Jo's famous visit to the barbershop. Cropped short, the flaming hair would attract less notice, or so she had calculated, put off by the whistles that sometimes pursued her on the street. Alas, the cropped hair, curled at the nape, enhanced the striking hollows of Lizzie's face and contributed to her allure.

She listened to the chant of the nuns in the chapel, alert for the Communion bell that would signal the race back to her room before the nuns filed out. The four years at school had honed to an art Lizzie's skill at eluding detection on her many escapades. Was it really four years since the lump-swallowing day that her parents had delivered her to Rosemoore? How swift and fleeting the years, and in a month she would graduate, Class of '26 . . . to what new expectations in lieu of the old?

It takes time for the ugly duckling to realize it has turned into a swan, and as yet Lizzie had not done so. She knew that when she was on a stage a transformation occurred and she became the person in the play, but she didn't relate it to her own self. As far as Lizzie was concerned, she was now and forever the duckling and her expectations were not for herself but only for those she loved.

As the light spread across the sky, Lizzie scanned the woods for Tyrone to come trotting into sight. As a breed, setters were prone to run off, winding up miles away, and Tyrone was no exception. In four years, Lizzie had lost count of her expeditions in search of the animal, but the longest he'd ever been gone was two or three days. Now it was a week since he'd taken off, with no sign of him despite her searchings.

If he didn't show up today, then he will tomorrow, Lizzie told herself. She preferred not to dwell on the specter of Tyrone run over by a car or truck. Today, after all, was a doubleheader for expectations! Classes were to be suspended at noon in honor of the homecoming of Reverend Mother Maguire. The girls in white dresses were to line the driveway to cheer her victorious return from Montpellier. While Lizzie rejoiced for Reverend Mother and the nuns, it was the other homecoming for which she had waited more than two years.

Two long years for S.J., two years of letters with foreign postmarks, of waiting as Lizzie had, veering between hope and despair but not giving up, hanging on as she had, and today F.M. was coming home.

Well, at last the happy ending, sighed Lizzie. After today she would no longer have to worry about the fate of S.J. and F.M. It was enough bounty for one day, and she'd be perfectly content if by tomorrow . . .

She shut from her mind the screech of brakes of the onrushing car as it ran over Tyrone . . . after all, nothing in life was certain until it happened. By the same token, not until F.M. and S.J. were in each other's arms ought she to count on it.

The Communion bell rang in the chapel, and while it might have toppled the duckling from the tree, the swan cleared the branches in a graceful leap. Lithe as the spring air, a sylph in a nightgown flying across the lawn, fresh as the morning, Lizzie vanished up the steps of Blanchard before a single nun had filed out.

The girls in blue pinafores were by 1926 an accustomed sight in the exclusive reaches of 982 Fifth Avenue. The residents of the neighboring apartments and town houses, from what they observed of the girls, pronounced them to be charming and well mannered, though of the wrong credentials. They were not Brearley girls, or Spence or Chapin or Nightingale-Bamford girls, it simply had to be faced. In a district with the heaviest Social Register listings in the city, the churches of importance were St. James Episcopal and Madison Avenue Presbyterian. No slight was intended toward the Jesuit church of St. Ignatius Loyola on Park Avenue, or St. Vincent Ferrer on Lexington, both were perfectly respectable, but ... well, they didn't belong in the same category. Neither did Rosemoore, and nothing could be done about it.

On this Tuesday morning in May, Miss Althea De Meers of 1 East Seventy-eighth Street peeped through her lace curtains at the iron-canopied steps of the school. It was eight-thirty and the morning procession of girls was under way, in white dresses rather than the pinafores. Althea knew that the dresses were ordinarily worn on feast days, but today was a special occasion. She was acquainted with a number of the school's practices, but it was necessary to keep what she knew to herself.

Early some mornings at her parlor window, Miss Althea waited to glimpse the Jesuit priests who came from St. Ignatius to say Mass for the nuns. The infamous Jesuits were the reputed agents of the Pope, and it was deplorable of her to display an interest in them or in the nuns.

The lace curtains fell and Althea hurried away from the window of her handsome brick Federal town house. Miss Lucrezia De Meers occupied an identical house next door at No. 3, and made it her business to keep informed of her sister's activities. Heiresses to a silver-mine fortune wrested by their grandfather from the Colorado hills, the sisters were of such clashing temperaments that they maintained separate residences. The arrangement had failed to provide Althea with the independence she had sought all her life. She had grown up indentured in effect to her mother who, before her death, has passed her like a parcel to her elder sister. Lucrezia was still the boss, interfering, meddling, dictating at every opportunity.

Goaded by that realization, Althea resumed her watch of the girls in the white dresses. It was useless to deny her interest in all of it or the reason for it. One summer in Maine, years ago, Althea had fallen in love with the sports instructor at the Bar Harbor resort where she was staying with her mother and sister. Frank Harrington was a star athlete at Holy Cross, the Jesuit college in Massachusetts. Frank was everything a young girl dreamed of, but he was Irish and Catholic, and that had sounded the note of doom. Mrs. De Meers, warned of the affair by Lucrezia, immediately packed and departed with her daughters for Switzerland. The following summer it was Baden-Baden, and Maine was dropped from the De Meers's itinerary. Althea never saw Frank Harrington again. As an heiress she was not without suitors, but no young man had touched her heart as had Frank, and she felt cheated of the happiness she might have found with him.

She watched the girls proceed up the steps of Rosemoore–Fifth Avenue. She had been cheated of Frank Harrington, and now, all these years later, the faith that had separated them had moved next door. So compelling was the attraction for Althea that for weeks she had been engaging one of the nuns in sidewalk conversation, which was how she had learned of today's homecoming.

The last few tardy girls marched up the steps and Mother Larkin, the nun to whom Althea De Meers had spoken, appeared in the entrance. She stood with hands clasped in sleeves, intent upon the flow of traffic on Fifth Avenue. It was a banner day for the Rosemoore nuns and Larkie was hard pressed to contain her excitement when from out of the stream of cars and double-decker buses, the royal-blue Packard limousine turned the corner. The election at Montpellier had transferred in one stroke the seat of authority to America. No longer was Rosemoore the stepchild of the Society, but its ruler. As the Packard drew to a halt and the chauffeur hopped to open the car door, Larkie went to the curb, the first to welcome home the new Mother General.

"You're in for it," she warned as Louise alighted from the car. "White dresses, student assembly, the whole kit and caboodle."

"Sheer bedlam at the pier, and you are to subject me to fresh indignities?" Louise moved across the sidewalk in a swirl of skirts and veil, carrying the fitted leather writing case that traveled with her.

The curve of her lips, like a bow pulled taut, had tightened in a thin line, relieved at the moment by the gaiety of her smile. "As you know too well, I am the victim of a conspiracy."

In the marble foyer as she entered, a Sister fell to her knees, and Louise restrained herself from pointing out that she was not the pontiff. "The sealed ballot is what did me in," she said to Larkie. "Really, you might have hinted at what you were up to."

"Sealed ballots are prescribed by our constitution. Besides, you won in a landslide."

"I went to Montpellier to assert our right to vote in the election, not as a candidate myself."

"You were Rosemoore's candidate, every last one of us, and now you must submit to acclaim, Mother General."

"The lamb to the slaughter!"

Steeled for the ordeal, Louise proceeded with Larkie up the bronze-railed stairs. The return to the Motherhouse had been a wrenching experience. Immediately upon receipt of the notice of Mère Tissaud's death, Louise had embarked for France, determined to have a voice in the election. As the delegate from Rosemoore, she had taken with her the sealed ballot of the nuns, which committed her to their choice. She had arrived in Montpellier within a day of the election. It was as if, in the cold stone corridors and drafty chambers, she had searched for the young nun she once had been, a failure, but resigned to failure should God ordain it for her, since from it would come the victory of her soul over her life. That young nun who had given up home and family for the convent in the belief that God willed it did not exist any longer. The search was in vain and had yielded only a sense of irredeemable loss. Given that loss, it had impressed Louise as an action rich in irony when she had been voted the new Mother General.

At the entrance to the ballroom stepping forward, a child of the kindergarten class presented the Mother General with a bouquet of roses and a trembling curtsy. A pitch pipe sounded and a sea of white dresses rose from the gilt chairs in a burst of song.

> *This is the month of our Mother,*
> *O, blessed and beautiful May . . .*

Louise relied on her sense of humor to get her down the aisle. The hymn being sung was not in praise of her, but of the Blessed Mother, a distinction that the girls seemed not to have made. She stood on the stage buffeted by the waves of song, and a thorn from a rose in the bouquet pricked her black glove.

"Thank you for your kind and loving tribute," she said to the sixty-eight girls of the upper and lower schools arrayed in the gilt chairs. The stepping-stones had advanced as planned, and next year the upper school would turn out its first class of graduates. Rose-moore–Fifth Avenue was an unqualified success, underscored by the prestige of the Christmas Ball. The first such gala, organized by the Ladies of Rosemoore, sponsored by Coty perfumes and catered by Louis Sherry, had been attended by a representative group of New York's wealthiest Catholics. Under consideration was the idea of presenting each year at the ball the previous year's graduates as debutantes bowing to a new wing of society.

Success? Was she to speak of success, Louise asked herself, gazing at the sea of white dresses. She had sailed into New York harbor that morning for the second time. At the pier where in 1908 no one had waited for her, she had been accorded the Courtesy of the Port and whisked through customs. Instead of a trolley, a Packard limousine had conveyed her across town. Granted, it was the school car, reserved for guests and dignitaries, and Tommy Phelan was really Duffy's assistant who doubled as chauffeur, but what misgivings it had aroused in her!

"It is a tribute that is quite undeserved." She went on with her speech, the prick of the thorn in her flesh. "Success is not measured by high office, but by the good that is accomplished with it. My children, if we nuns have not taught you the great lessons of charity and love as preached by Jesus, then we have taught you nothing of value." She gazed in appeal at the rows of girls possessed of every material comfort and advantage. "You must never forget the Lord's command to feed the hungry and clothe the naked, but remember too that poverty can dwell in the richest house . . . and by your response will God measure your success."

She looked at the rows of sober young faces, not wanting to send them away on a dour note. "Since it is better to give than to receive," she said, "let me declare a school holiday, effective this very minute," and she was given a salvo of cheers.

Over tea in Mother Larkin's office, Louise broached the subject uppermost in her mind. She went at it by taking from her writing case a pencil sketch of a cardigan jacket and checkered skirt, stylishly drawn.

"What do you think of this for a school uniform, Larkie? The pinafores are getting a trifle outmoded."

"It's very chic, but who did you get to design it?"

"The woman in the next deck chair on the *Leviathan*—Madame Chanel. She told me of how she was reared in a convent and loathed the uniforms, and I invited her to strike back."

"Why don't we ask B. Altman to run up a sample model?"

"Yes, why not?" Louise returned the sketch to the writing case. "I mentioned, didn't I, that Connolly Moore and Flavin were passengers?"

"Thank God," said Larkie, crossing herself. "When you spoke to the girls of poverty in rich houses, it was Flavin I thought of."

"Connolly was ill in Rome and later on in London . . . though it doesn't explain the awful delay in coming home."

"Two years, all told—it looked as if the wedding would never take place."

Louise set her tea on the desk. She had boarded the *Leviathan* at Cobh, after a hurried trip to Ireland to inspect the Galway property. The steward had escorted her to a state-room in first class— Connolly, it seemed, had learned that she was boarding the ship and had arranged for the state-room. For the six days of the voyage he had stalked the decks and Flavin had appeared pale, tense, and at the breaking point. "I've promised the chapel for Saturday," Louise said, getting up. "Flavin has but three days to wait for her wedding—and now I must be off to face the hosannas at Peekskill."

Mother Larkin accompanied Louise to the car. As they crossed the sidewalk, Miss Althea De Meers scurried out of the house at No. 1 in a trailing morning gown of velvet and lace. Her eyes were wide with agitation as she confronted the two nuns, and for a moment she was incapable of speech.

"I—I must tell you my story—it's not by chance that you've moved next door, I can't help feeling."

"Good morning, Miss De Meers," Larkie said. "May I present our new Mother General, of whom we spoke yesterday."

"How very strange, a nun who is also a general. Frank Harrington never mentioned anything like that to me, though we often discussed the clash of our religions."

"Althea, stop this ridiculous display at once and come inside."

Miss De Meers turned slowly toward the house at No. 3 and the woman who stood imperiously in the doorway. "I am not a child, Lucrezia, to be scolded and ordered about," she said, a hand fluttering to her bodice as she turned back to the nuns. "Perhaps one day soon you will hear out the story of Frank and myself?"

"We are your neighbors and you are always welcome at Rosemoore." Impulsively, touched by the mute plea that was inherent in the tremulous Althea, Louise presented her with the bouquet of roses. "Will you accept this, please, as a token of our meeting?"

"How very kind of you!" Miss Althea pressed the bouquet to her bodice and trailed back to the doorway of No. 1. "It is a sign from Frank," she exclaimed, watched by her indignant sister. "The last evening we spent together, Frank brought me roses . . . what else is it but a sign?"

Then Miss Althea went into her house and Louise settled into the cushioned depths of the Packard for the drive to Peekskill.

A bellboy trundled another cart of luggage into the suite at the Plaza. Sweeping off his Panama hat, Connolly halted him with a Malacca cane and called into the bedroom, "Flavin?"

"Yes, Father."

"I'd appreciate knowing whether you want the steamer trunk, or—" He swung around as his daughter came from her room, each taking measure of the other. "Or is it to go to the basement for storage?"

"As you like." Flavin motioned to the bellboy. "The small Hartmann case, please." He pulled the suitcase from the cart, which she took from him and then started past her father.

"Amazing the Koh-i-noor wasn't stolen." Connolly nodded at the engagement ring. "What with the hotel thieves that abound in Europe."

"I was willing to risk it."

"Where are you going and must I remind you I'm due at Dr. Wilson's at eleven?"

Flavin gripped her suitcase. "I just spoke to Stephen at school. They're to have a welcome home for Mother Maguire and then we're driving to White Plains for our marriage license."

"Store the trunk," Connolly instructed, waving out the bellboy with a five-dollar bill. He closed the door, ignoring his daughter, and threw the cane and hat on a chair. "I've asked that you allow me to give you a suitable wedding. By that I mean the cathedral, Cardinal Hayes, and a proper complement of guests."

"You're still at it, aren't you, Father?"

"I won't point out that as a man of some prominence in the Church—"

"Two years or a lifetime, it wouldn't matter to you." Flavin's voice shook with accumulated outrage and frustration. "You'd keep at it until nothing was left in me to stand up to you, but it isn't going to happen."

"That's it, accuse me of a dastardly plot to thwart your marriage."

"You said it, not I."

Connolly went around flinging windows open on the warm, humid air. "Tell me, was Jonah a part of the plot? Did I go to him in Palm Beach and say, 'Look, old man, if you were to die, it would compel Flavin to stay on and straighten out the household'?"

Flavin shut her eyes, loathe to contemplate the last months. Jonah had finally agreed to nap in the afternoons, taking his rest in the servants' cottage behind the big house on South Ocean Boulevard. Late one afternoon last March, when he'd failed to appear at the house, she had found him lying in eternal rest in the cottage. For all these years, two families had lived together, that of Jonah and Clarice, Ruby, Della, and Mamie, side-by-side with Connolly's family. Jonah's family had gone with his coffin on the train to Kentucky, and with them had gone the home they had created for Connolly.

"Well?" Connolly demanded. "Was that my wicked scheme to ensnare you?"

"No, but you used Jonah's death to suit your purposes."

"Our home, such as it was, went with Jonah, he took it with him, and I was trying to put it back together."

"If that's true, why did you keep me in Palm Beach interviewing servants when you had every intention of selling the house?"

"Not at that point, with the question of Faircrest still to be settled."

"You went to New York to settle it, but Stephen was in New York, so of course I stayed in Palm Beach."

"Was I not to have one house left to me? I'd give them away, lock, stock, and barrel, but not Faircrest." Connolly stalked from one end of the huge room to the other. "Am I to be consigned to hotels for the rest of my life? Hotels are for transients, no matter how long you live in them. By God, I wasn't about to be robbed of Faircrest."

"Yes, and you came back from New York with a heart condition, so you said, and tickets for a Mediterranean cruise. What luck that the ship was to call at Nassau."

"I take it that you dispute the doctors and the cardiographs."

"What's the good of this?" Flavin cried, and went to the door with her suitcase. The months were a jumbled blur in her mind of cities and trains, porters, luggage and carts, and hotels. The cruise had terminated in Piraeus, and from there, Venice, Rome, Taormina, Cannes, Paris, and weeks in a London clinic to forestall the passage home. "I never left you," she said to her father. "Why didn't I? I wanted to, a hundred times, but I thought that if I could last it out ... it would be my wedding gift to you."

Connolly turned ashen under his ruddy glow. "I—I can't lose you," he said in a hoarse whisper. "All my life, I've felt alone, but not with you. Is the pain in my heart less real because a stethoscope can't hear it?"

"You're not losing me."

"The past can't be changed, but it's you who makes up for it." Connolly went to the mantel and stared up at the gilt mirror above it. "The ghosts are always there and I'm the same poor lad who ... it's futile to describe it for you." Futile, he knew, to describe the terrifying nights when the cold and the dark formed a black abyss of nothingness and the only escape was the bottle. "With you, Flavin, I can bear the ghosts, if I can't be rid of them."

"Or is it that you won't let go of them, as you won't of me?"

He turned from the mirror and looked at his daughter. "It oughtn't to come as a shock that you've joined your mother and sisters."

"You can't mean what I think you mean."

"Why should I expect you to be any different?" Connolly tore off the jacket of the immaculate gabardine suit as if the smell of the stableboy clung to it, and hurled it contemptuously on a chair. "When I'm alone with myself, I know who I am, and it's nobody to love, nor is it the fine gent that I put on a show of being. He fools others, that pious fraud, but he doesn't fool me."

Flavin lowered her suitcase in a final attempt at conciliation. "I ordered my bridal gown in Paris," she said. "Three days isn't much time to plan a wedding, but I'll manage somehow ... Stacey and Monica as bridesmaids and Acquin, your grandson, as ring bearer. Mother Maguire's promised us the chapel for Saturday ... and you, Father, will you take me down the aisle?"

Connolly stood at the window, staring down at the park. "Are you leaving? Go, if you are."

"Will you, Father? Oh, let it be a happy occasion."

"Boylan is downstairs with the car, if you wish it."

Flavin picked up her suitcase. "No, I—I like taking the train."

"You'd better phone Horace and Jetta to expect you at Faircrest. They're a sorry comparison to the likes of Jonah."

"No one is like Jonah." She crossed slowly to the door. "Are you driving up later?"

"Depends on Dr. Wilson—his diagnosis is apt to be more disturbing than yours."

"I'm sure not." *Leave or you will never leave,* Flavin urged herself, and, opening the door, went out.

The warm air wafted in the car window, unrefreshed by the Westchester hills, and of a sudden Louise gave up her efforts with the writing case.

She had wanted to get a head start on the monthly newsletter that, as the Mother General, she intended to send out to the houses of the Society in France. The ties must be strengthened with France and union forged out of the years of separatism. To further this goal, Louise had committed herself to an annual month's tenure at Montpellier. When the junior novitiate in Galway was launched, that too, she foresaw, would require a yearly visit. Clearly, the demands of her new office would mean relinquishing her office of headmistress, a blow to the cherished ties with the nuns and students.

It was habitual for one whirring thought to succeed another with Louise, but these reflections had not prompted her to close the writing case abruptly, nor was it the drafts of warm, humid air. A moment ago at the traffic light, glancing out at the city-bound lane, she had observed a Packard of the same model as hers. A chauffeur was at the wheel and in the back a gray-haired executive was hunched over a writing case, absorbed in his business papers. A copy of *The*

Wall Street Journal, to which Louise subscribed, was folded next to the man on the cushioned seat . . . and what precisely was the distinction, if any, between the two of them?

Louise grasped the hand strap at the window, thinking of her speech to the girls. *"Feed the hungry and clothe the naked . . ."* She knew of one instance when she had heeded that call and not turned her back on it. The consolation was small, but she sought it by pressing the button that lowered the glass between the front and back seats.

"That variegated family of yours, Tommy, are they all faring well?"

"Bless 'em, they are," said Tommy, keeping a vigilant eye on the road, enjoying as he did the chauffeuring in preference to his janitorial duties. A confirmed bachelor, Tommy immersed himself in the goings-on of his numerous relatives. "The Aunt made a killin' at the racetrack last week—a forty-to-one shot, praise God, to the tune of eighty greenbacks."

"Heavens, forty to one!" Louise was unacquainted with the relatives' given names. Tommy referred to them simply as the Aunt, the Uncle, the Niece, the Nephew, and so forth. "And the Uncle, how is he faring for himself?"

"The one that got thrown in the drunk tank, or the one that got gassed in the war?"

"Yes, that uncle . . . is he still with Father Regan in Yonkers?"

"It's nothing less than a miracle, the way it happened." Tommy paused to negotiate the traffic of a busy intersection at White Plains Road. "Them poor men, crippled and half blind, gassed and shot up—if it wasn't for Father Regan, they'd be rotting in veterans' hospitals, good as dead."

"I envy him such a mission, providing a home for those men."

"You ought to visit there sometime, Reverend Mother, it'd warm your heart. The house is sort of ramshackle and could use a paint job, but it's on a shady little side street, with neighbors and kids for the men to get to know and stores around the corner. Father Regan don't fit the usual notion of a saint. He's rough on the men and won't listen to excuses, but he gets them up and out every mornin', some to jobs who can work. They're *alive* because of him, and that's something terrific for a priest to do, like Jesus raisin' up Lazarus from the tomb."

"And each month . . . the money order comes in the mail?"

"It hasn't failed yet, ma'am," Tommy declared. "That's the miracle part, if you ask me. Father Regan started the house on a shoestring, and just when it looked like he'd go broke, the money order started to come in, every month, but from who? Nobody's found out yet, not the men, not Regan, not nobody so far."

"Well, isn't that best?" asked Louise, making promises to herself. "It's best for the giver to remain anonymous . . . and pleasing to God, I should think."

"Ma'am, that's expressin' it real nice."

The wedding would take place on Saturday. Louise promised herself that and more as the hills of home and the thorns of acclaim grew closer with each passing mile.

The front porch of Annunciation Hall was draped in blue-and-white bunting and the railing bedecked with the same tricolor flags that had been distributed to the students. The emblazoned *R* of the school flag flew from the mast over the porch steps and sprinklers played on the lawns, spraying the green with glistening arcs of water. As yet, the nuns and Sisters, the secular faculty and honored guests, had not assembled for the formal welcome, but Mother Friel, who had taken charge of the ceremonies, made frequent appearances to check on the decorations.

The signal had not yet been given to form ranks on the driveway, which left the girls in white dresses to collect in breathless groups or to stroll back and forth in the bright May sunshine, twirling the flags in keyed-up excitement. The white dresses endowed the occasion with the solemnity of a feast day, but the prevailing mood was that of a holiday, stretching, it seemed clear, to June and summer vacation.

As usual, Lizzie Devlin was out of kilter with the prevailing mood. She strolled back and forth with Eileen Birnbaum and Florence Giambetti, atwitch with nervous expectancy.

"Give us a repeat," she said to Tookie Fennelan, who had tagged along, her customary fate both at school and at home. "The whole thing, starting when he was called from class."

Tookie sucked in her breath, agog at having the spotlight, and repeated her account of how S.J. had been called to the telephone from art class that morning. "No kidding, a smile from ear to ear when he came back. Who else could it've been but F.M.?"

"But he didn't *say* it was her." Lizzie shot a nervous glance at the flag-bedecked porch. For months the school had buzzed with speculations of the interrupted romance and its outcome, but no one knew as Lizzie did of the havoc it had wreaked on Stephen Jarvic, the despondency between the letters with the foreign postmarks, the downtrodden gloom when the separation had extended into a second year. The girls had sighed at the *tristesse* of it all, but no one had fought as Lizzie had to disperse Stephen's gloom with jokes and banter and visits to the cottage in the woods, which had become his solitary retreat. She would not be satisfied today until he came onto the porch and she was given the evidence of his smile. "I wish he'd *said* it was F.M.," she moaned, her eyes cast downward. "Then we could all relax and get set for the wedding."

The girls turned at the porch steps and headed back up the driveway. "All this stuff about the wedding night," giggled Tookie in a bid to retain the spotlight. "My cousin Betsy says it's nothing like you think . . . I mean, if you want to hear the details."

Lizzie, Eileen, and Floss were less than eager for the details. "Mind you, Tookie," Eileen pointed out, "we're not interested in any conversation that smacks of indecency."

"Well, excuse me for not letting you stay dumb and ignorant on the subject."

Eileen's curiosity got the better of her. "You may proceed, but we'll stop you if it gets out of hand."

"It wasn't even night at the hotel," Tookie lamented. "Catholics get married at morning Mass and the latest the reception lasts is maybe four o'clock—it was *daylight* when Betsy and Chuck got to their room."

"The bridegroom's name was Chuck?" asked Lizzie. "How could Betsy get serious about a guy named Chuck?"

"He happens to be doing extremely well in the insurance business," Tookie snapped, momentarily diverted. "Anyway, the first thing he did—no, that's wrong. *First,* he sent the bellboy for a bucket of ice, for the champagne they'd swiped from the reception, and then he went down to the lobby for a pack of cigarettes—can you guess why?"

Eileen added to her reputation for braininess. "To allow Betsy the privacy to undress?"

"It was almost the worst, she says, picking out what ensemble to get into, the peach, the blue, or the pink with the marabou trim. Well, she decided on the pink, and all at once Chuck was back in the room, big as life, uncorking the champagne."

"Then what?" Lizzie inquired. "The lobby was out for Betsy, in the pink and marabou. Where did Chuck take off his duds, in the bathroom?"

"Betsy says to always bring magazines, *Vogue* in her case, which she read or anyway pretended to while he, er, uh, washed up . . . well, finally he came out of the bathroom and there they were, looking at each other in the broad daylight."

"Maybe," said Lizzie, slowing her pace, "we've come to the part where we should stop . . . but since we've all got to face it someday, you might as well go on, Tookie."

"Go on to what?" Tookie Fennelan blinked. "Betsy didn't tell me that part—it was too sacred, she said."

"Too *sacred?* Well, of all the—"

Destiny, that day, did not intend the enlightenment of Eileen, Florence, and Lizzie on "that part" of the bridal night, or, as it was for Betsy and Chuck, the bridal afternoon. Striding officiously onto the porch, Mother Friel emitted a blast of whistle worthy of a drill sergeant, and a flurry of white dresses hastened to form ranks along the driveway, hushed and expectant.

The three who were sworn to eternal friendship stood grouped with the seniors, aware as never before of the fleeting nature of time. White was the color of graduation as well as of feast days, and waiting in the closet for each was the billowing puffed-sleeve organdy, sashed in royal blue, that she would wear with a coronet of red roses in the graduation march.

As they stood in the white line, tricolor flags poised for waving, Lizzie, Floss, and Eileen practiced an art that was indigenous to convent schools. Eyes leveled ahead, postures erect and ladylike, they spoke to each other sotto voce, without any perceptible movement of the lips.

"Hey, Eileen, count 'em up . . . it's exactly nineteen days."

"Till commencement."

"Well, doesn't it throw you into a panic?"

"Yes and no, I'd have to say both." Eileen Birnbaum's blue-black hair fell to her shoulders, a lustrous frame for her creamy Irish complexion and the dark, somber Jewish eyes that posed the ancient questions of her father's race. "I am a Catholic and I am a Jew," she had told Lizzie and Floss, "and I shall build a bridge over my divided faiths." Eileen was to attend Barnard College in the fall and had chosen, to the consternation of one side of the family and the astonishment of the paternal side, to major in Hebrew Studies.

"I can't wait to get at it," she confided to Lizzie.

"At what, kiddo?"

"The Torah, of course." Eileen Birnbaum, class valedictorian and worshiper at two altars, gazed from the white line at the future that she had carefully plotted. After graduating from Barnard, she intended to continue her studies at Catholic University, delving into the theology of Thomas Aquinas, Augustine, and the other doctors of the Church, but of what was to follow that step, Eileen was less certain. Young men might well prove a distraction, she conceded to herself. Who but she had encouraged Tookie to reveal the details of the wedding night? It was true, a young man might enter the picture ... and the bridge she wanted to build, could she really ford the chasm gorged out by centuries of division?

Eileen Birnbaum stood in the white line cutching her flag, conscious of time and the hour glass, and was suddenly uncertain of her careful hypothesis, to which only time held the answer.

"Hey, Floss," Lizzie asked, "does graduation scare you?"

"Yes, and it's getting worse." Florence Giambetti's white dress hung from her as from a wire frame. She looked not a day over fourteen, as wispy and sallow as when she'd arrived at school. The restricted routine of her life had not changed. Primo and the big black car trundled her home on weekends and holidays, but an incident last summer had profoundly affected her thinking, crystalizing all that she had sensed and tried not to believe about her family's business dealings. Last summer at the Giambetti compound in Mineola, looking one day for Primo, she had encountered him in the garage, a revolver strapped to his chest, stuffing bundles of hundred-dollar bills into a suitcase. Nothing was said between them as Primo loaded the suitcase into the car trunk. She had left the garage, a silent trespasser, but on that and subsequent nights, Floss had lain sleepless in bed, piecing together the furtive comings and goings in the house, the whispers and footsteps, and the terse allusions to nightclubs and B-girls, betting parlors and slot machines, policemen and lawyers and judges.

Florence was by nature of a deeply spiritual inclination. It had been the motive behind her asking to go to a school conducted by nuns. Like all the Giambetti women, she had been drilled in passivity. The fact that she had been born to middle-aged parents, with brothers old enough to be her uncles, had isolated her from other children and retarded her growth as an individual of wants and needs. The one instance when Florence had asserted herself was in badgering her family to send her to Rosemoore. During the sleepless nights of last summer she had conceived of a bolder act, which she had resolved to attempt to carry out. It would require great courage, but she would beseech God's help and He would would provide it.

Outwardly as timid as before, Floss had returned to school for her senior year, getting up in the morning darkness to attend the six-thirty Mass of the nuns. She was not alone in this practice, but few students were as faithful in carrying it out. It was as if a wick were ignited in Florence, a flicker that over the months had burned to a vibrant flame ... but, oh, how prey it was to snuffing, how hidden she must keep it, not daring to confide in her two best friends in the world, not today nor tomorrow, not for years after graduation ... and then what?

"Oh, Lizzie." Florence clasped the tricolor to her breast. "You won't forget me after graduation? You'll remember the Musketeer who wasn't brave but wanted to be?"

"Listen, we'll always stay friends," Lizzie vouched, eyeing the starchy assembly of nuns on the porch. "We'll always remember our days together and all that went on here at Rosemoore."

"Always," vowed Eileen, detaching herself from thoughts of young men.

Lizzie picked out Stephen Jarvic on the porch, who was standing off to one side with Mrs. Van Pelt and Miss Osborne. He was smiling to beat the band, the kind of smile that would not go away. It seemed to confirm the telephone call, but nothing, Lizzie reminded herself, was certain until it happened.

Lizzie's eyes slid to the woods. Tyrone was still missing and until he turned up she would not rest easy. The same held true for S.J. and F.M: Not until the lovers were married would she trust in it to happen. For that matter, not until the blue Packard curved up the driveway would she be assured of Reverend Mother's homecoming.

After all, a smashup on the road was no less a possibility than Tyrone getting run over. No, she would not rest easy yet.

Love, thought Lizzie Devlin in the white line of dresses, was as fraught with danger as a highway. Last summer on Cape Code, college friends of her brother's had camped nightly on the Devlin porch, plying her with invitations to the movies and the dances at the yacht club. She had spurned every last one, racing off instead to usher at the Falmouth Playhouse, where her days were spent painting scenery, selling tickets, and rounding up props. Miss Laurette Taylor had appeared for one week at the summer theater in *Peg O' My Heart,* the play that long ago had made her a famous Broadway star. Lizzie, for one glorious week, had walked onstage in the crowd scene as a barefoot Irish maiden in a shawl. To her bewilderment on the final night, Miss Taylor had scowled at Lizzie throughout the scene. *"There,"* the actress had stormed after the curtain, pointing an accusative finger. "I'm too old for it, but *there* is your Peg, that impudent baggage with the bare feet and shawl." She had flounced off to her dressing room, only to relent and dispatch the stage manager with a gift for Lizzie of a bracelet of moonstones.

Now the delicate bracelet shimmered on Lizzie's wrist, from which it was seldom absent. The stage was her haven, where she was someone else, at least for the course of the play. Love of the kind she'd witnessed between S.J. and F.M. was all too real and painful, a force of nature, a cyclone that struck those who were not wary of it. Thanks, but it was not for her, vowed the duckling who would never entirely believe in the change that had made her a swan.

The duckling and not the swan gave a yelp and bolted from the line of girls. Loping up the driveway, the worse for wear, his fiery coat matted and prickled with briars but wagging his tail, was Tyrone. Behind him at the curve in the drive the blue Packard appeared to a ringing of cheers and a waving of flags. Well, thought Lizzie as she ran, the new Mother General, from what she knew of her, would not have wanted too solemn a homecoming.

Heedless of her white dress or the approaching car, Lizzie flung herself at Tyrone, scratching her knees and tolerating his gamy smell and slobbering tongue. She looked up then, hearing the shout, and surrendered to her expectations.

THE FAITHFUL

If a remnant of solemnity lingered on the day, it was dispelled by Stephen Jarvic's joyous shout from the flag-draped porch of Annunciation Hall. It was not for the approaching car, but for the young woman who was running across the hockey field to meet him with outstretched arms.

TWENTY-ONE

There was a ....

In the cottage doorway, Stephen pulled Flavin to him in an out-pouring of pent-up desire and longing.

"I'll never let you out of my sight, not for a day."

"Nor I you—and I never took off your ring."

He lifted her hand to his face and raked the ring across it. "Blood of my blood—" He touched her finger to the fleck of crimson. "Flesh of my flesh, life of my life—"

"For always."

Then Stephen let his mouth and hands speak for him, until he released Flavin with a shaky laugh and produced some papers from his wallet.

"Here's my blood test, proof of age and citizenship—and yours?"

"The ships's doctor did the blood test and I've my passport with me."

"All set for the marriage license." He locked her in his arms and brushed back the spun-gold hair. "Want to take a look at our home for the next month? I'm proudest of the plumbing."

Stephen led her by the hand across the stone floor that shone from waxings and polishings. It had taken him most of last summer to build the extension onto the rear of the cottage. The raw pine roof made an arch over the little kitchen, which was equipped with a stove, a zinc sink, an icebox, and a cupboard. "As for other conveniences—" He threw open the door to the bathroom, which included a claw-foot tub and a shower. "Every item is from the junk dealers, and not the luxury you're accustomed to, but—"

"It's wonderful." Flavin wandered over to the old curved-back sofa that was drawn up to the rough stone fireplace. The frayed plush was covered with a paisley spread. Behind the sofa a pine trestle table stood on a hooked rug. A pewter jug full of wild flowers bloomed on the table and above it, from the cross-beamed ceiling, hung a brass gas lamp.

"Well?" Stephen inquired with a grin. "No electricity and somewhat rustic, but will it do?"

"It's about to undo me." Her voice shook and she held on to the ring with a trembling hand. "The months went by, each longer than the one before . . . thousands of miles away . . ."

"I tried to paint your portrait." Stephen went over to the easel set up at the window. A canvas was propped on it, bare except for a few strokes of charcoal. "I thought that if I had your portrait, it would bring you closer, as if you were here with me."

He crouched down and thumbed through the canvases stacked against the wall. He passed them to Flavin, still lifes and landscapes of brilliant colors divided into cubist shapes and planes. "Finished these, and some that I've sold, but I couldn't capture you at all. I figured maybe the Sargent portrait was stopping me, but it wasn't that."

He stood up and nodded at the canvas on the easel. "I couldn't get a picture of you in my mind's eye. He turned to Flavin, his eyes flashing with intensity. "I'd lost my image of you, and the old nightmares started up, but I wouldn't give in and take the canvas from the easel. Each letter you sent, I'd bring it here to read, and it made you real again. I worked on the cottage as if tomorrow you'd walk in the door. The bad times, I'd go help out Father Regan at the house in Yonkers, and when I left those men, I knew how blessed I was, and that I only had to wait and you'd come back."

"We've lasted it out, haven't we?"

"And when I try your portrait again . . ." Stephen traced the charcoal lines on the canvas. "It won't be another Sargent, but I'll paint glory into it."

"Stephen!"

"Nothing less than glory!" He took her in his arms, her head rested against his shoulder. They rocked in each other's embrace, and then with the same thought sprang apart.

"The license!" Flavin exclaimed.

"White Plains—the bureau closes at four, I checked."

They hurried from the cottage and through the woods to the hockey field. Halfway across, Stephen came to a halt and smacked his brow. "Stupid car's getting fixed—I've been hitching rides with Cornelia Van Pelt."

"No car?"

"A practically brand-new Chevy for the wedding trip, but the stupid carburetor's on the fritz."

"What wedding trip?"

"Right now, I can't even get us to White Plains."

Flavin started back across the hockey field. "We'll simply use my car, provided that Matt has a set of keys."

They doubled back through the woods to the cottage, crossed the footbridge, and went down the twisting path to the school boundary, and Stephen, lifting her over the mossy stones, felt a sudden plunge of emotion.

"All this wealth"—he set her down on the privileged acres of Faircrest—"and I'm asking you to live in a patched-up cottage?"

Flavin surveyed the sweep of field and meadow, the green rolling hills set high above the river. "It looks the very epitome of a country estate, and in many ways it was . . . but a shadow lay over it always."

"A shadow of what?"

"Of what?" She frowned and shook her head. "I didn't know what as a child, but now I'd say it was the secret unhappiness that was everywhere."

"You've said so little about it." His arm slipped around her from behind. "If you wanted to you would, I figured."

"We mustn't expect my father at the wedding," Flavin said. "Unless I'm mistaken, he won't come."

"It's *him,* as if I need you to tell me."

"We've lasted it out, that's all that counts, and I refuse to spoil another breath of this beautiful day by thinking of it."

She clasped his hand and, running, they crossed the sunlit meadows and expanses of greensward until the manor house was in view, the chimneys and then the white columns, but Flavin headed away from the house, toward the elm-shaded complex of stables, paddock, and garage that lay a distance below.

Mattie Hearns, the groom, was dozing in the sun, his chair tipped back against the dark green stables with one of the setters sprawled at his feet. He got up at the sound of Flavin's approach and went to greet her.

"It's that grand to have you back, Miss Flavin. Seemed like your travels was never to end."

"Yes, to me too." Flavin stroked the nuzzling dog that had bounded up. "Mattie, I'd like you to meet Stephen Jarvic. By any chance, are the keys to the Aston Martin handy?"

"Well, now, let's take a look for ourselves."

As they went past the stables another dog loped out, and in the shadowy stalls Connolly's black charger reared up, beating a tattoo of hooves. The white clapboard garage was as big as a house, with space for six cars and rooms above for Boylan and Mattie.

"Here you go, Miss." He plucked some keys from a rack. "Tank's full up, like we always keep her."

The yellow sports coupe and the estate car were the only occupants of the six spaces. "Thank you, Matt. I'll park up at the house when I get back this evening."

"Would ya happen to know when Mr. Moore is comin'?"

"He didn't say, but I doubt it'll be tonight." Flavin went over to the coupe, away from the space reserved for the Rolls. "I'm sure Miss Philbin will let you know when to expect him."

"Something else, Miss." The groom shifted his boots uncomfortably. "It's not for me to say, but that butler and his wife, Horace and Jetta—a nasty pair, and I'd watch out for 'em."

"Oh? Well, thanks for the warning." It was not her problem, thought Flavin, and handed the car keys to Stephen. "Care for a turn at the wheel?"

They drove with the canvas top rolled down and the yelping dogs chasing behind. Stephen swung around the shamrock oval in a crunch of gravel, and the wind caught at Flavin's hair. She suspected that she knew where and how her father would spend the night. Was it the Follies girl or a newer diversion? She didn't remember exactly when she'd learned about the women, before or after she'd known of the periodic drinking behind the locked door.

"Are you okay?" Stephen asked with a touch of anxiety.

"I'm fine, perfectly fine." The car scudded through the gates and she rested her head against the leather bucket seat, the wind whipping at her hair. "I think you'll be pleased with my bridal gown. It's from Callot, ivory peau de soie, very simple, all in the cut."

"A knockout, just like you."

"Is the wedding trip to be a surprise, or may I ask about it?"

The yellow coupe spun along the post road in the light flow of afternoon traffic, and Stephen described the wedding trip that he'd mapped out for July. He'd gone last summer to visit his parents in Wisconsin, and since they were unable to attend the wedding, he would take his bride to meet them. "It's just a plain old farm, y'know. Mom and Dad speak with a Slovak accent and are shy with strangers, but you can count on a warm welcome and the best strudels you've ever tasted."

"Your mother won't know what to make of me, this girl from New York who annexed her son."

"She'll wait for Sunday and show you off to the farm women at church. I was named for St. Stephen, and my mother will tell her friends that you are the reward for it."

"You *are* her reward—and mine!"

"My brother's farm is down the road. We'll go there for a picnic and to the lake for a swim, and then on the route back ..." Last summer, too, Stephen had called on his former professor at the university in Madison, who was now chairman of the Fine Arts School. "I showed him some of my paintings, very encouraging response, I must say. Lindner can't promise anything, but he said that a vacancy is coming up in the department and he'd be glad to interview me."

"It's all to work out—I know it will," Flavin said, gazing at the tiny flash of her ring. "What time is it? It can't be getting close to four."

"Relax, we're nowhere near it."

It was one minute before three by Stephen's watch when they pulled into the parking lot across the street from the county courthouse in White Plains. They had a full hour to get the license, but Flavin climbed the couthouse steps as though not a minute was left for it. The bureau was at the end of a long corridor, and she paused outside the frosted-glass door to comb her wind-blown hair. She made the sign of the cross as if she were entering a church, and took Stephen's arm and went in.

A line of couples extended from the window grille at the rear of the room. Globes of light glared from the ceiling and a row of benches ran along the wall. At the windows were counters for filling out the application forms available at the door.

Flavin made an error in the space provided for her name. Without thinking of it she wrote "Rose Flavin Moore" in the space and was embarrassed to account for it to Stephen.

"When I was little, I used to mix up my name with Mother's. The two were so alike to me—interchangeable."

"I don't wonder," Stephen laughed, and went for a fresh application.

The wait in the line seemed an eternity to Flavin. She stood with Stephen, papers in hand, behind a diminutive Chinese couple, and while she could not think of any last-minute barrier to the license, she felt that one would crop up. Each couple, when they reached the window grille, submitted their papers to the clerk for inspection, and not all passed muster. The proof of age or citizenship was deemed insufficient, or the clerk spotted an error or omission in the application, and the couple was dispatched from the window to correct it.

The line inched forward and Flavin's anxiety mounted with every tick of the clock on the wall. Her blood test might not be valid since it was performed at sea. She examined her passport, the pages stamped over the years with the entry and exit seals of dozens of countries. What if the clerk were to find some illegality in it?

Ten minutes, fifteen, twenty-five ... and then the eternity was over for Flavin. She turned from the window in a flood of relief at the license that Stephen tucked proudly in the breast pocket of his seersucker.

"I was convinced that something or other would go wrong," she confessed. "Why, when there was no reason for it?"

"Past history."

"Yes, I expect so." The delicate face turned grave with reflection. "The past doesn't go away that easily ... Stephen, listen to me." They went along the corridor. "We've got three days to prepare for the wedding," Flavin outlined. "First thing tomorrow, I'll get busy on the phone with my sisters and talk to Mother Maguire about the chapel and call the florist—I'll take care of everything, but not today. Let's keep today just for us."

Spread before them as they came down the courthouse steps into the May sunshine was the burgeoning downtown sector of White Plains, Westchester's county seat. Trains shunted in and out of the railroad station a few blocks away, citizens lounged in the leafy courthouse square, and suburban matrons with shopping bags conducted themselves placidly along the sidewalks. At the corner, a Good Humor vendor was dispensing ice cream sticks from his wagon.

"Vanilla or chocolate?" Stephen asked. "What's your choice?"

"A choice, where chocolate is concerned?"

Sauntering along Mamaroneck Avenue, the main shopping street, they nibbled at the ice cream sticks and browsed in the shop windows. It seemed utterly special to Flavin to walk hand in hand with Stephen in the jostle of shoppers, belonging to the crowd and not isolated from it. The sense that at last her life belonged to her was dazzling to contemplate.

"In July, when we visit your professor," she said, as they inspected the bright-jacketed summer fiction in a bookstore window, "it might be a good idea to look at houses for rent."

"In case, you mean?"

"Well, there's a chance you'll be offered the vacancy."

"You're right." They moved on to a housewares shop, the window shiny with kitchen cabinets and chrome bathroom fixtures. "If I get the vacancy, we'll take a house and not worry about the rent."

"We might not have to worry, if Father doesn't revoke my trust ... or would you rather I not accept it?"

Stephen laughed and took her in his arms. "Actually, no, I wouldn't, since I can't quite see you getting along on a pittance."

"Oh, I wouldn't mind."

"No, but maybe I would."

"I'd make sure that you didn't."

"I know ... I know."

It was all predestined, this day with Stephen, the very walk they were taking, Flavin mused to herself. On the next block, when she spied the dresses in a bridal-shop window, she was certain of it.

"Look!" she exclaimed, gesturing at the mannequins in the window dressed as bridesmaids in pale mauve chiffon, with flowing skirts and filmy hats tied with mauve streamers. "Wait and see, they'll have sizes for Monica and Stacey, I just know it," she said, and hurried with Stephen into the shop.

The saleswoman advised her that the dresses were available in a range of sizes and could be ordered for delivery by Thursday afternoon. Dresses, hats, slippers dyed to match, all could be ready by Saturday, she confirmed. "And what of a gown for the bride?"

"I've bought the gown, but I'll want two of the dresses, sizes ten and twelve."

"Let me call the manufacturer, to be on the safe side."

They waited while the saleswoman disappeared into the back of the shop. Again, Flavin was beset by anxiety, as though her life and not the dresses hung in balance by a precarious thread.

"Success!" trilled the saleswoman, bustling from the rear. "Ten and twelve are yours, my dear. Now, if you will kindly give me a small deposit . . ."

"Would you mind a traveler's check?"

The sky was streaked with pink and blue and the ball of the sun was sinking in the west when they came out of the bridal shop. They continued along Mamaroneck Avenue and Flavin halted at the telephone booth at the next corner.

"I really ought to call and see that Father's all right," she said.

"Yes, maybe you'd better."

Stephen supplied her with coins for the slot, but the suite at the Plaza was silent to the repeated rings. Flavin telephoned Dr. Wilson's office and was told that Mr. Moore had canceled his appointment. Miss Philbin at Connolly's office reported that she had spoken with him that morning, but that he hadn't visited the office or informed her of his plans. Boylan had checked with her at noon, she said, and was waiting at the Plaza with the Rolls.

"I'd imagine that your father is in the city, but as to his whereabouts . . ."

"Well, thank you, Miss Philbin. I'll be at the house this evening, if he wants to reach me."

The Follies girl or a newer diversion? Flavin hung up, angered at having made the calls. The street lamps switched on as she stepped from the booth.

"No luck?" Stephen asked.

"We'll let him find us." The pinks and blues in the sky were darkening. "If by any chance you are thinking, as I am, of dinner," Flavin said, "we might try Pierre's on White Plains Road."

"You bet, I'm starved."

They walked back to the parking lot for the car and drove the mile or so to Pierre's. The restaurant was in a white Colonial house with black shutters and window boxes of geraniums, set back on a lawn from the street. At six o'clock, Flavin and· Stephen were the evening's first customers and given their choice of tables. They bypassed the three small dining rooms, in favor of the lantern-strung garden at the back and a snowy-clothed table under a chestnut tree.

The waiter held a match to the candle and furnished menus, from which they ordered a vinaigrette salad and coq au vin. The French bread was crusty and delicious, spread with sweet butter and sopped in the sauce of the chicken.

Despite her smile and chatter, Flavin seemed to tire during the course of the dinner. Fatigue was catching up, Stephen said. On the go, nonstop, since the ship had docked that morning, it was not to be wondered at.

"We oughtn't to hate for the day to end," she laughed, "with only a few hours to wait for tomorrow."

"I didn't much believe in tomorrows." Stephen's jaw tightened in the familiar grim line. "Takes getting used to, doesn't it?"

"I'm not sure that I want to grow used to it." Flavin looked around her at the tables in the garden, crowded by then with patrons, and at the multicolored lanterns strung across the indigo sky. "I'd rather stay as I am tonight, astonished by happiness and never accustomed to it." She clasped her lover's hand across the table. "If I'm tired, it's only from happiness."

Stephen's voice choked with the emotions that swept over him. "I'll remember this day for the rest of my life," he said. "I'll never forget how it was, not a single moment of it."

"It seems enough for a lifetime ... well, almost."

They lingered over dessert and coffee, the talk veering from the wedding to school, music, painting, but always back to the wedding. The candle was long since gutted in the glass and the tables all but empty again, stripped of cloths, when they left the garden at Pierre's.

Flavin took the wheel for the drive back to Peekskill, since she was to drop off Stephen at the rooming house on Brown Street. A veiled moon floated above the post road and crickets set up a chorus of chirping in the drowsy silence that, except for the hum of the motor, enveloped the yellow sports coupe. A dreamy lassitude overtook the two occupants of the bucket seats, in which talk was not only an exertion but irrelevant. The day had ended sweetly, and tomorrow was a handful of hours away.

The ruffle of the trees in the night breeze was the one sign of animation on Brown Street. Stephen had to rouse himself for the climb from the low-slung car. The steering wheel was a rude obtrusion to the parting with Flavin.

"I'll pick you up in the morning and drive you to school," Flavin suggested.

"Van Pelt's coming for me, but let's meet at school for lunch and we'll tackle Mother Maguire about the chapel."

"Show it to me."

"What?"

"The license."

He produced the precious document, which, after they had examined it in the dashboard light, resulted in a fevered tangle of arms. Stephen reeled from the car to seek composure on the sidewalk.

"See you tomorrow for lunch," he called and went into the house.

Flavin drove up Main Street to the clang of a lone trolley and the whistle toot of the ten-thirty train from the city, bound for the depot. Ten-thirty, eleven-thirty, midnight ... she sped along the country road, clocking the hours till morning.

Not until she had turned into the driveway of Faircrest, did the thought of her father rush at her, together with the ghostly columns on the hill, and send a shiver of apprehension racing through her.

TWENTY-TWO

The house stood faintly illuminated in the glimmer of moon that drifted behind clouds above the hills and river. A light shone from the portico and in the fanlight over the door, but the rows of windows were dark, like those of a house bereft of habitation.

The car's headlights swerved over the white gravel of the drive. Flavin parked a few feet down from the portico. She left the keys in the ignition, ready for the morning. Getting out, she went up the steps and struck the brass griffin door knocker, which was not answered.

She was digging in her purse for her house keys when the door swung back. It registered as a shock, as it had that morning, to find it was not the beloved Jonah who admitted her.

"Good evening, Horace."

Horace's mouth was pulled down in grievance, and his hooded eyes were sparked with resentment. "Kep' me up late, waitin' for you."

Flavin went past him into the great hall. She switched on the sconce lights and laid her purse on the console. "I'm sorry that you were inconvenienced."

The apology failed to mollify the obdurate Horace. "Jetta fix supper, ain't nobody to eat it."

"Supper?" A bath, thought Flavin, and headed for the stairs. "But no one ordered supper."

292

"Yes, dey did."

She started up the stairs. "Aren't you mistaken? I knew this morning that I'd be out tonight, and—"

"Mistuh say to fix it."

"You spoke to my father?" She turned in the curve of the stairs. "He called from the city and ordered supper?"

"Six o'clock . . . he *come* here."

Flavin grasped hold of the banister. "My father is here in the house?"

"Boylan drives him up, an' he send him away an' tell me to fix supper. He go up them stairs, which be the last I seen of him."

She gazed up the stairwell into the shadows that masked the upper landing. "Outside, when I looked at the house, every window was dark."

"It don't mean he not up dere."

She shuddered at what the darkness likely meant, and came down the stairs. "I—thank you, Horace, that will be all."

"Me an' Jetta don' take to late hours."

Flavin was staring at Connolly's portrait, a shadowy presence glinting on the wall. "May I ask a favor, before you retire?"

"What?"

She looked at the stairs with a prickle of fear. "Since Mr. Moore asked for supper, would you take a tray up to him?"

"Like I say, me an' Jetta—"

"Would you do it for me, this one favor?" Never, she thought, would she go up those stairs herself tonight. "Please, would you?"

Some of the urgency of her voice carried to Horace. He begrudged but at the same time took advantage of the request. "Don't get paid for no favors."

It occurred to Flavin that she was in the house with strangers left to their own devices for over a year. "I promise you won't regret anything extra that's asked of you. Please, would you do it for me?"

The hooded eyes weighed the value of her promise. " 'Spect I can."

She watched Horace depart for the kitchen, an ally, however reluctant, that she could not afford to lose. The shadows loomed above the stairs, where almost certainly her father was drinking in his room. She remembered that sometimes Jonah had been able to persuade him to unlock the door. If tonight he were to confuse Horace with Jonah . . .

Flavin went into the drawing room. Switching on lamps, her hand drew dust from the gilt tables and commodes, and she noticed that the display of Fabergé in a cabinet was minus a jeweled snuffbox. The lights in the library, when she turned them on, showed the rare bindings filmed with dust and the absence from the desk of a gold-and-malachite paper cutter. Thieves as well as strangers, she thought, and heard footsteps in the hall.

Horace was going up the stairs, vanishing into the shadows with the tray. She stood at the newel-post, listening, straining to catch the exchange of voices, but all she heard was Horace's gruff rumble.

In a moment, he came back down the stairs, haughty and removed from the situation. "He didn't give no answer, so I leave him de tray."

"Thank you." Flavin knew that further entreaty was useless. Horace disappeared into the passage to the kitchen and left her with the crippling sense of helplessness that had afflicted her childhood.

She crossed the black-and-white squares to the telephone on the hall console. A press of the button would connect her with the garage and bring Boylan or Matt to the house within minutes . . . to save her from what? The car was in the driveway, keys in the ignition . . . to escape from what?

She did not know from what, except that it had been present for years, a nameless dread that her father's attentions had generated in her. She had loved him, obedient and dutiful, but stifled within her was a fear such as . . . *as had possessed her mother?* she asked herself.

Crossing the squares, she moved toward the front door. She would go to Stephen and he would take her to the cottage for the night, safe with him. Ashamed of her cowardice, she rejected the idea. The day had not ended, after all, for night was joined to day and to run from it was the act of a frightened child.

Flavin stood appraising the stairs, telling herself that she must not climb them but instead devise some means of persuading her father to descend.

She went into the music room and switched on the lamp at the Beckstein. She sat at the piano, rifled through the sheet music on the rack, and commanded her fingers to strike the keys . . . Chopin, swift and rushing, but not too softly, loud enough to be heard upstairs.

As she played, she glanced up at the Dutch landscape on the wall where the Sargent had hung, and rather than windmills and canals, she saw her mother's image, the exquisite ice-blue figure seated at the piano. She saw herself stealing down from the nursery to listen to her mother's playing.

> *The pale moon was rising above the green mountain,*
> *The sun was declining beneath the blue sea . . .*

Flavin gasped and pulled her hands from the keys . . . and yet if any melody held the power to draw her father from his room, it was this one. She set her fingers to the keys and resumed, hearing like a whisper the lyrics her mother had sung in her clear soprano.

> *. . . when I strolled with my love to the pure crystal fountain*
> *That lies in the vale of Tralee . . .*

The memories washed over Flavin and her hands on the keys summoned the past that reached out to her in the murmurs and whispers of the house. The image of the portrait whirled in her mind, mixed with her own image seated at the piano, just as her mother had sat on the same bench, lost in her prison . . .

Then the piano keys grew still, and Flavin stared at the empty doorway. She ought to have known that her father would not come, and that finally, inescapably, she must climb the stairs to him. For too long had she been an obedient daughter.

A strange inertia gripped her, which she had to struggle against to get up from the piano bench. It seemed as if it were in some other life and time that she had gone for her marriage license and dined at Pierre's . . . all of it, some other life.

She went through the rooms turning off the lights, one after another. The wall sconces in the hall lit a path to the stairs. She reached for the newel-post and the tiny flash of the diamond ring jolted her into alarm. *The car . . . hurry, hurry to Stephen, it was not too late.*

No, she must not be a coward, Flavin told herself, and grasping the banister, she went up the curve of the stairs into the shadows that beckoned at her from the landing.

She stood in the corridor outside her father's door and raised her hand to knock. Not a sliver of light showed under the door, but he was in there, of course, somewhere in the dark. Why announce herself when he knew of her presence, as she did of his? He would not let go of her, it came to that in the end, and so tonight was inevitable.

She gazed across the corridor at the shadowy alcove that led to her room. The bridal gown had arrived from Callot, and if she were to take it from the box ... no, it belonged to that other life, which was not hers any longer. She hesitated for a moment, and then she walked through the shadows to her mother's door.

The door yielded with a soft click, admitting her to the foyer, and beyond the arch to the lace-swathed bedroom. In the darkness, slits of moonlight, slanting through the blinds across the pale carpet, picked out the vanity and chaise, and the clutter of enamel oil miniatures on the bed table that she had examined with her mother on rainy afternoons. An ivory crucifix glinted above the lacy pillows of the canopied bed. "When you pray, then you are not alone," her mother had told her as a child. Flavin knelt at the bed and a prayer of her mother's sprang to her lips.

"Remember, O, Most Gracious Virgin Mary, never was it known that anyone who sought thy intercession, or fled to thy protection ..."

Flavin's prayer was silenced by the crash of a door in the adjacent dressing room. A light switched on, and in the stream of that light stood Connolly, framed in the doorway. The collar of his shirt was pulled open, the French cuffs rolled above hairy forearms. A belt buckle dangled loose from his trousers. He was barefoot, silver hair a matted tangle above the black peaks of his brows, and he held a whiskey bottle by its neck. Although he'd been drinking since noon, he showed little effect of it—a flush to his face, a slight weave to his motions. His eyes, as he looked toward the bed, were glassy and unfocused.

"On yer knees, prayin', are ye?" he inquired in a slurred brogue that the drinking induced. " 'Tis a help, I give you that," he nodded, pacing back and forth with the slight veering weave. "Sure, 'tis many an hour I've spent in prayer, but then again ... many an hour I've spent with the bottle, which is also a help, I find."

Connolly looked at his kneeling daughter with a mixture of sorrow and pain, love and regret. "Here, take a swig," he said, offering the whiskey. "I stay off it for months, but then the ghosts come back and it helps me to chase them away."

The offer went unaccepted and he raised the bottle to his own thirsting lips. It was empty and he hurled the bottle against the vanity mirror, shattering the glass. "The mercy of forgettin'—it don't last," he cried, and watched the bottle roll under the lace flounces of the bed table.

Lashing out, he swept the oil miniatures to the carpet and kicked over the table in a crashing thud. He shook his head to disavow the violence that had erupted in him and stalked the room as if to flee from it, weaving in and out of the shadows and the slits of moonlight. " 'Tis no forgettin' . . . no use of tryin'."

Flavin knelt at the bed, fixed upon her father in the shadows while he was smashing into tables and chairs in his drunken passage toward the windows. When he had reached them and his back was toward her, she stood up.

At the windows, himself a ghostly shadow among the lace hangings, Connolly was caught in a reverie. He drew from his pocket a white silk scarf, inhaling the scent of it, smothering his face in the silk folds.

Not breathing and grateful for the carpet that muffled her steps, Flavin moved away from the bed.

"I've lost you, Rose . . . in the winter snow." Connolly stared at the crumpled scarf and then swung around from the windows. "Where might you be going?" he asked.

Flavin measured the distance to the door. "I—I'm tired and going to my room."

"How can it be that I, who have everything . . . have nothing?"

She turned to her father, stammering a reply. "It isn't true, y-you're wrong to say it."

Connolly pressed the scarf to his face and gazed at his daughter. "Everything I've loved, I've lost . . . and God with it, I know."

"You mustn't think such a—"

"No, I've lost God for sure." Connolly gazed at his daughter, impaled in the streak of light from the dressing room. "Where did you say you were going?" he asked.

"I—"

"To your room, did you say? Are you that confused in your mind? It's the middle of the night and this is your room," he said.

"*My* room?"

"It was your room the last I heard, when you took to locking me out. Is it the same plea tonight, another one of your sick headaches?"

"Father!"

He angled toward the bed through the slits of moonlight. "Am I such a brute that you lock me out? Is that what I am to you?"

Flavin turned as he circled toward her around the bed. She looked frantically at the door, seized by a violent trembling.

"Am I the offender or are you?" Connolly asked, maneuvering past her, cutting off her access to the door. "What nature of woman are you? A nun? A married virgin? Or is it that you like to be forced?"

"*Father!*"

Connolly caught her by the hair and pulled her against him. Taking the scarf, he wound it around her throat and jerked her closer. "Who is the offender, Rose, the husband with healthy appetites, or the wife who locks her legs and sends him to the whores?"

Flavin screamed and clawed at the scarf. She wrestled free and ran, but he was faster, shutting the door and grabbing her by the wrists. She screamed again and wrenched loose, but a fist lashed out with a savagery that broke her jaw. Blood spurted from her mouth and blackness swept over her. A hand ripped at her bodice, but she was falling, falling down a tunnel and not conscious of it.

Connolly threw her inert form onto the lacy pillows of the bed. He knelt over his daugher, tearing at her skirt, pushing it above her thighs. "Tell me, Rose, who is the offender, the wife who locks her legs, or the . . . ?" Of a sudden, he recoiled, staring in horror at the thought of the brutish act he was capable of, guilty of, and driven again and again to commit.

Horror, nothing but horror and ghosts . . .

Staggering from the bed, Connolly fled from the room and the white scarf that lay torn and violated on the floor.

The slits of dawn light edged across the room and Flavin stirred in the disheveled bed. The zigzags of pain kept her from relapsing into unconsciousness. After some moments she struggled up against the pillows, her eyes traveling over the wreckage of the room.

She lifted a hand to her face. The bruises and swellings made

it feel a stranger's face, unknown to her. Her jaw sent out currents of
pain that triggered a warning. She stared at her skirt, which was
pushed up over her naked thighs, and the terror knotted and told
her not to stay where she was.

Flavin climbed from the bed, steering her feet toward the door.
The cracked mirror of the vanity presented a harrowing reflection
which she paused to examine. To whom did it belong, the lacerated
face, the bloodied mouth and swollen jaw? The dizzying waves of
pain and nausea knocked her to the carpet. Sprawled there, she
stared at the strewn oil miniatures, and a notion came to her of who
she was.

The realization brought her swaying to her feet. Clasping the
bedpost, she looked around the room made familiar by the lace
hangings . . . it was her room, but what had happened in the night
to terrify her?

Was it Connolly?

She stole into the dressing room, careful of the least sound, and
gazed at the connecting door to Connolly's suite. It was against
her marriage vows to leave him, and she must stay for the sake
of the children, but how was she to endure a repetition of last
night?

Flavin tensed, uncertain of whether she had imagined the sound.
She heard it again, a far-off train whistle echoing over the hills. No,
she would not leave Connolly, but was it an offense against him to
spend a day in the city, a few hours with Aunt Bea and Uncle Mike
Nugent?

Surprise trips were the best kind!

Feverish with excitement, she searched the mirrored closets for a
travel costume and selected a dark-blue fitted jacket and skirt, perfect for the train. Quickly, the torn, blood-flecked clothes were left in
a heap on the floor and her hands were frantic with buttons and
hooks. Once she was dressed, the mirror showed a wild, unkempt
creature staring back at her in alarm. Who she was puzzled her
anew, but she hadn't time to think about it, not with a train to
catch.

Hat, she thought as she crossed the foyer to the door. A lady did
not travel without a hat! She spied the white silk scraf on the carpet
and decided it would have to suffice, tying it under her chin.

Flavin crept down the stairs in the wash of morning light. Were the servants awake, or was it still too early? The waves of pain swept over her, but the banister kept her from pitching forward. Let Jonah sleep; she would not bother him or the groom about a carriage. She would enjoy the walk to the station in the peace of early morning.

She went out the front door onto the portico and was confronted by the sight of the yellow sports car parked below on the driveway. At first it completely mystified her, but then it struck a faint, tenuous chord of remembrance.

Unconscious of her bare feet on the gravel or of her bizarre state of dress, Flavin approached the shiny yellow car, and pieces of memory danced a Maypole dance around her.

Stephen and a wedding ... but who was Stephen ... and what had the wedding to do with him or with her?

She stood looking at the car, aware that somehow it was known to her. The canvas top rolled, if you wished it, and the keys in the ignition, when turned on ... *what?* The pieces of memory were as elusive as the air to grasp, and it frightened her that she could not fit them together. Was she two different persons, split apart, shattered like the vanity mirror into fragments of herself?

She got into the car as if it held some clue as to who she really was, but the train whistle tooted again and her fragmented mind focused on the objective of catching the train to the city.

Surprise trips were the best!

She found that she handled the car with practiced ease, switching on the motor and swinging the wheel to go shooting down the driveway and out the wrought-iron gates. She laughed in exhilaration at the thrill of her foot pressed on the accelerator, obliterating the waves of pain.

When she made the turnoff onto Main Street, the speedometer needle flicked to seventy. At the foot of the plunging street, the shingled roof of the depot was silhouetted against the wide curve of the river, molten silver in the morning sun. She pinned her gaze on the depot, listening for the train, and went swerving around a trolley, careening ahead. To the few tradesmen and early risers who were abroad at six in the morning, she was a ghastly apparition at the wheel of the car, but to the traffic officer at the intersection of Division and Main, the hurtling car was a menace, and he shrilled his whistle for it to stop.

Flavin mistook it for the train whistle and pressed the accelerator to the floor. Soon, very soon, she would be with Aunt Bea and Uncle Mike, delivered for a time from fear and loneliness and suffering. Soon, in an hour or two . . .

She whispered a last prayer for her deliverance and careened into the station parking lot. Too late, she pulled at the brake, and the car went hurtling over the train tracks toward the river.

VII
THE HILL OF CALVARY

TWENTY-THREE

The tinted light from the stained-glass windows in the chapel fell in a halo on the throne chair on the altar. The symbol of office that Louise had rejected at Montpellier had been presented anew to her yesterday, a gift of the nuns and therefore not to be refused.

Henceforth, it would be expected of her to occupy the chair at Mass, as she did this morning, on ceremonial occasions such as the Clothing of the postulants, and at Council meetings. The high-backed chair, intricately carved of teak with a purple cushion suggestive of a bishop's throne, was placed at the epistle side of the altar, below the tabernacle steps. It endowed the Mother General with an aura of power and majesty as she followed the rubrics of the Mass.

Louise's expression was as remote and fixed as was her chair from the stalls of the nuns ranged before her. The cameo face, a model of composure, gave no indication of what she was thinking or feeling. Uppermost in her emotions was a surge of relief, like a wave breaking over rocks, at yesterday's reunion of Flavin Moore and Stephen Jarvic. The fears, the alarm, if not groundless, had not been substantiated. The wedding would take place on Saturday in the chapel, and Louise was confident that Connolly would learn to accept it.

Although she regarded the throne chair as a penance to be endured, it had a practical advantage. While paying strict attention to the Mass, Louise at the same time was able to keep watch over the stalls and pews of the chapel. She was gratified to observe that the nuns were all properly intent on the liturgy and yet poised, as it were, for the challenges the day might present. Louise admired this sense of alert readiness in the nuns, the willingness to take up the cudgels, which for so long had governed her days. It reminded her of the appointments that she soon must make ... what of Tracy for headmistress and Friel, perhaps, as Vice-General?

As the six-thirty Mass progressed to the Consecration, Louise felt the misgivings of yesterday, so acute and distressful, depart from her. She was the Mother General, there was no turning back, and so she must forge ahead. With the convent and novitiate built and out of the way, what next on the agenda? A delicate problem, to transfer the ownership of the vineyards to America, but certain of her future plans were dependent on it ...

At the Communion, in keeping with her office, Louise received the Host before the community filed up to the altar rail. She watched the line of black veils in the manner of a general reviewing the troops, approving their order and discipline. If a jarring note was struck, it was in the figure of Sister Bridget, the last in the black line to approach the rail. *"The last shall be first and the first last,"* thought Louise, apprehensively. The realization dawned belatedly that during the trip to Ireland she had not taken a minute's time to inquire into the whereabouts in Dublin of Agnes O'Shea and her child. Well, how could it be helped, given the press of her schedule, with a ship to catch at the end of it?

The white-veiled novices at the altar rail restored Louise's perspective. She counted sixteen of them, the largest number yet for the novitiate, and the band of students who followed the novices to the rail were similar emblems of the future. It was an established truism that from those students who made a daily practice of Mass came the aspirants for the novitiate, the troops multiplying in the benevolent working of providence.

Louise listened at the conclusion of Mass to the chime of the chapel bells ringing out over the campus, carrying the joyous message of a new day to spend on behalf of Rosemoore. Eager for its challenges, she stepped from Blanchard Hall into the fresh sparkle of the morning and the peaceful quiet of the enfolding hills.

The nuns were left behind her, hurrying to breakfast in the dining hall of Blanchard, a hasty meal from which duties would call them before coffee was half finished. For Louise, as usual, breakfast was to consist of a tray at her desk to allow for an early start on her mail and correspondence. As she reached the driveway, it seemed most obliging of the mail truck to appear at that very instant, and she paused to wish the driver good morning.

"What is it?" she inquired when he braked to a stop, which was not his custom. "What is wrong?" she asked, seeing the horror in his eyes.

"It's awful, ma'am—I'll never forget the sight of it, dredgin' the body from the river when I drove past the depot."

"A drowning?" Louise crossed herself, and a vision of Jenny Rocket fished from the lake of Ballymar leaped out of the past. "God save the poor soul, whoever it was."

"That's just it, ma'am." The driver stared at her from the wheel. "I heard 'em say it was . . ."

"*Who?* Who was it?"

"One of your girls, crashed her car in the river," the driver answered, and the light went out of the morning for Louise.

By seven-thirty Stephen Jarvic had eaten breakfast at the luncheonette on Main Street, around the corner from his rooming house. Mrs. Van Pelt wasn't to stop by for him until eight, and on the chance that repairs were finished on his car, Stephen ambled over to Buster Kelsey's garage on Water Street, which fronted the river.

Buster was absent from the garage, as was often the case. The tow truck that he operated as a town service was missing from its space at the curb. It explained where Buster had gone—off to some car accident—but not why Donny, the youth who worked for Buster, was hopping around in a state of agitation.

"What's got you fired up?" Stephen asked.

"Your car ain't ready." Donny hopped from the gas pumps to the cubbyhole office to make change for a customer. "Crikes, didn'tcha hear the police sirens before?"

"Bad accident?"

"Pulled out the body, but not the car yet. Crikes, didn'tcha hear about it?"

"Is that where Buster is—pulling out the car?"

In reply, the agitated Donny scooted out to the curb and pointed at the crowd that had collected a few blocks away at the depot. "Crikes, go see for yourself, that'll tell you."

Not since the war had Stephen been disposed to visit the scene of a disaster, but after a moment's reluctance he went to find out for himself what had attracted the crowd.

By the time Cornelia Van Pelt drove up to the rooming house, she had heard the news of the accident on the car radio. She sat at the wheel, debating the next move with Miss Osborne.

"What if he doesn't know yet? Shall we go up to his room and tell him?"

"I'd rather you did, Cornelia. I'm not adept at that sort of thing."

"Very well, I'll go."

Cornelia got out of her trim new Plymouth sedan, the Marmon having expired on an Adirondack road, and went up the porch steps of the rooming house. Death had always seemed to her an event to be obscured as much as possible by the protocol of good manners, but lately her view of it had changed. Death brought sorrow, and sorrow must be shared rather than obscured. Cornelia credited the pageant of Church history for having attracted her to the fold, not unlike the lure of grand opera, but it was the simple memory of the little Sister kneeling at the altar that had sustained and nourished her faith.

She rang the bell, and when the landlady, upon investigation, reported that Stephen was not in his room, Cornelia got back into her car.

"We must go find Stephen and not leave him to bear his grief alone."

"Well, if you can stand it, Corny, so can I."

Cornelia drove the blocks to the depot, parked the car, and with Miss Osborne shouldered through the crowd of onlookers. Buster Kelsey's tow truck was backed out on a wharf across from the depot. The men in the police launch who had dragged the river for the body were grappling with the dangling chains of the truck. The crowd watched avidly as the chains hoisted the dripping yellow coupe from the waters. Cornelia searched the cordoned-off area of the crash for Stephen Jarvic. "We are friends, needed friends," she informed a policeman, ducking under the ropes with Miss Osborne.

An ambulance had arrived on the scene, and Stephen stood over a white-sheeted stretcher, guarding it from the attendants. When Cornelia reached him he turned blank and uncomprehending eyes upon her, so that finally there was nothing she could do other than to murmur her sympathy.

Stephen received this with utter blankness. He turned to the attendants and surrendered the stretcher to them, climbing after it into the ambulance.

A whistle tooted as the ambulance sped away, and a train clacked into the depot in the everyday continuance of life.

Very slowly, Louise hung up the telephone. The world of Rosemoore had crashed around her and a numbing calm encased her like a plaster cast. She looked at Mother Friel, standing in front of the desk, and at Mother Tracy in the doorway.

"From what the chief of police tells me," she said in a flat, toneless voice, "Flavin's car evidently went out of control. It was seen swerving down Main Street, and then it crashed into the river. The body has been taken to the morgue, pending an autopsy. There are a number of questions left unanswered, but it is not for us to speculate."

The questions hounded her like a chisel digging at the plaster of her calm. Where was Flavin going at that early hour, and why? Was there any answer except one to it? "The police are unable to contact Mr. Moore," she went on. "Whether he is in the city or at Faircrest is not known."

Louise folded her hands tightly in her sleeves. What had sent Flavin to the wheel of her car at dawn? What terrible thing had sent her hurling to her death in the river? The police would examine the car, and were no mechanical defect found . . . an inquest would be held.

She shut out the dreadful visions. "Did you keep the students in chapel, as I asked?"

"Yes, but without an explanation."

"A tragedy has occurred and we must deal with its effect on the school." Louise took refuge in plans and action, her invariable response to a crisis. "I will speak to the girls before the rumors start among them."

The morning freshness took on an ominous aspect as she crossed the driveway to Blanchard Hall. The very freshness was a deception that gave the lie to her illusion that all was well merely because she had decreed it. Where was Connolly that the police could not contact him? Someone must notify Monica and Anastasia . . . and Stephen Jarvic, where was he?

She stood at the back of the chapel, listening to the rows of girls recite the litany of the Blessed Virgin. *"House of Gold . . . Tower of Ivory . . . Gate of Heaven . . ."* The beautiful metaphors sounded a reproach to her pride and willfulness, and she moved swiftly up the aisle and genuflected before the altar. She turned to face the hushed pews of girls and the little painted statue at the Lady Altar caught her eye.

"Young ladies, I come to you with news of profound sadness," Louise addressed the pews. "Earlier this morning, in one of those tragic happenings that we cannot foretell . . ." She faltered and looked at the statue as though it were listening to her. "Flavin Moore, whom some of you knew when she taught music here at school . . . was the victim of a tragic accident that struck without warning . . ."

No, the warning had gone unheeded, ignored, dismissed! "This morning, in the crash of her car into the river," Louise went on, "Flavin Moore's life was taken . . ."

At ten-thirty, when there was still no response at Faircrest to his calls, Police Chief Reinecker telephoned the Plaza Hotel in the city. Advised that Connolly Moore had not spent the night at the hotel, Reinecker drove out to the estate.

Although he went there as an investigator, Dutch Reinecker thought of it as a courtesy call on a man who had once been remarkably kind to him. Each year as a young patrolman, Dutch had canvassed the estate area, soliciting contributions for the Peekskill policemen's widows and orphans fund. The check for a thousand dollars was always waiting at Faircrest, delivered by the butler, but one year Connolly himself had come to the door. He'd taken Dutch on a tour of the house, pointing out the antiques and paintings, and had shown a genuine concern for the young officer's circumstances. "Must be a struggle to get by on what the town pays you. Well, I'm no stranger to adversity." The butler had served tea and cakes in the study, and Connolly had accompanied his visitor to the door. "When I was a poor immigrant, it took me a year to buy a decent suit of clothes to go to church on Sunday and not look like a beggar."

"It's hard to think of you in that situation."

"Look, I've slipped some money in your pocket. Use it to wow the girls in the latest in haberdashery."

"But, sir, I can't—"

"I set up a fund to help out young fellows like yourself. You'll let me borrow from it, won't you?"

The recollection of the visit stirred afresh as Chief Reinecker drove through the wrought-iron gates. Today, he thought, was his chance to repay the kindness and not bear down hard on the questioning. The girl's death, was it suicide? If she was to marry in a few days, why would she take her life? The facial contusions, the blood, and the strange costume that she wore ... someone knew the answers to the tragic puzzle.

Chief Reinecker noticed as he steered up the driveway that the approach of the police car failed to sound an alert in the house. No one had come to the door or was looking from the windows, the usual reaction to the arrival of the police.

Reinecker parked the car and went up the portico steps. No one was at the door, but the door was open, and next a frightened voice called out from inside, "Matt, for God's sake, is it you?"

The police chief hurried into the entrance hall. The wall sconces were lit as if they'd burned through the night, and a man whom he recognized as Connolly Moore's chauffeur stood transfixed on the stairs.

"I couldn't wake him at first," Boylan gasped out in panic. "Me and Mattie heard it on the garage radio and kept waitin' for a call from the house. None, there was, so I ran up the hill to—" Boylan gulped back his fright. "The radio didn't get it wrong, she's drowned, is she?"

"Yes, I'm sorry to tell you."

"What the devil happened last night? She come home late, I heard the car, but after that, what?"

"I've come to speak to Mr. Moore about it."

"Then I did right in telling him. The front door was open, y'see, and the niggers nowhere in sight." Boylan shuddered and clutched at the banister. "I figured they'd cleared out, after maybe harmin' the old man, on top a' the thievin'. I ran upstairs to his room. The door was locked, but I pounded on it till he came stumblin' out."

"He didn't know of the accident?"

"I'll wager he was sleepin' off a drunk, 'tis his curse, the whiskey is."

"You told him of his daughter's death?"

"I did, and it killed him, right before my eyes," Boylan gasped. "The breath went out of the man, like the rattle of death, and the look in his eyes—"

Boylan got no further in his account. A revolver shot rang out from the floor above. It reverberated in the silence, immobilizing Boylan, so that Chief Reinecker had to push past him in order to get up the stairs.

"What's tomorrow?" Stephen Jarvic asked, pacing the tower office, his mind reeling in haphazard sequence. "Is it Wednesday or Thursday? The autopsy's tomorrow."

Louise held out a cup of broth. "Here, you must take some nourishment."

Stephen stared at the broth, not seeing it. "Her face was covered with bruises—was it from the crash?" The disjointed sequence zigzagged ahead in his mind. "The bridesmaids' dresses—I'd better cancel the order."

"Monica is on her way to Faircrest. We'll attend to it."

"We wanted the day to last forever, but last night Flavin said she didn't mind it ending, with only a few hours to wait for tomorrow."

Louise rested the broth on the tea table. "You mustn't worry about your classes, Mother Shearin has taken them over, and—"

"The wedding was to be Saturday." Stephen raked at his hair, trying to straighten out the sequence. "The chapel . . . we'll have the funeral in the chapel, if that's all right."

"Yes, of course."

Stephen shut his eyes, summoning back the radiant girl of yesterday but seeing only the bruised face that he'd kissed good-bye at the morgue. "Father Regan was to marry us . . . well, he can say the Requiem."

"He's already offered to."

"Why the blood and the bruises? Was it from the crash?"

Louise was alarmed by his condition. "I'll ask Father Regan to come now, to be with you."

"No, that's okay." Stephen crossed to the door, unable to blot out the horror. "If you'll excuse me, I think I'll go for a walk."

"Mr. Jarvic, let me phone the infirmary for a sedative to help quiet you."

He leaned against the door, entrapped by the horror. "A walk in the quiet of the woods would help, but I'm so awfully tired."

"Then you must try to rest. We've some guest rooms upstairs, now that we're not so overcrowded, and with a sedative to give you sleep . . ."

"It's no use." Stephen stalked away from the door, raking at his hair. "I'm past trying anymore, it's no use."

The telephone rang, but Louise did not answer it. She waited until Mother Friel came in from the switchboard.

"Monica McNally is on the line and said to tell you it's urgent."

"Thank you, Friel." Louise closed the door and turned to Stephen Jarvic. He was at the window, staring toward the woods. "I beg you, Mr. Jarvic . . . please let me have someone take you upstairs."

"I'd like to sleep . . . maybe if I lie down, I can sleep."

When Stephen had left accompanied by Mother Friel, Louise picked up the telephone receiver. "Are you at Faircrest, Monica? How is your father?"

She listened to Monica's news and likened it to a stone thrown in the water creating widening circles. "My poor child," she said. "Is the wound very grave?"

"The police are here with an ambulance. We're taking him to Phelps Hospital in Tarrytown to find out the damage."

"I will come, if you want."

"Would you? Stacey's on the train, en route from Florida, and I'm so alone."

"I'll meet you at the hospital."

It was to be expected, Louise thought, hanging up the telephone. Taking her cloak, she hurried from the office, the circles ever-widening around her.

Lizzie Devlin crept down the dark stairs. Lights-out was at ten, but she'd waited another hour before stealing from bed. Duffy, the janitor, made a nightly check of the campus at ten, beaming his flashlight on the walks, and she didn't want to get caught in the blob of his light.

She misjudged the bottom step in the darkness and went sprawling to the floor. She lay there listening to determine whether the noise had awakened Mother Donlan, the dormitory proctor. When she heard no footsteps, Lizzie picked herself up and crept from Blanchard Hall.

She shivered in her nightgown, though the night was silken with warmth. From the terrace she made a fast reconnaissance for Duffy's flashlight, in case he'd started late on his rounds. Moonlight bathed the campus and showed not a sign of Duffy, which emboldened her to venture farther.

Lizzie hiccuped, the aftermath of her tears, and stole along the driveway to her hiding place. Trees had always made her think of God, and she peered up at the dark, spreading branches as if He were lurking there, a stealthy presence, but then she remembered that she was finished with God.

It wasn't in her tonight to climb the gnarled trunk. She felt gutted and drained, and so she circled her arms around the trunk and rested her head against the rough bark, no longer the Lizzie of yesterday.

She looked at the towered mansion, wondering which window denoted Stephen Jarvic's room. The talk at dinner was that, verging on collapse, he'd been taken to a guest room and given sedation to sleep. What was the good of it? Lizzie asked herself. Nothing would have changed when he awoke, death was death and Flavin was gone. What had S. J. to live for, what reason to wake up to another day?

Lizzie tensed and hugged the tree in a jump of alarm. So far as she knew, Duffy didn't include the hockey field in his rounds, but there the moonlight revealed him, moving like a shadow across the hockey field.

Let him catch her, she railed to herself. Let the nuns hand out demerits and keep her from graduation, it didn't matter. She was finished with Rosemoore, and with God and tears and parted lovers . . . and trees, she amended. Yes, she had finished with trees and hiding out from . . . *growing up*, thought Lizzie in a rush. She didn't want to grow up, it amounted to that, but the stage was a lovelier place to hide than a tree, and from now on . . .

Lizzie gave a startled hiccup at the sudden question that loomed up in her brain.

If that was Duffy on the hockey field, where was the blob of his flashlight?

She turned to look at the windows of Annunciation Hall, and

after a moment's conjecture, Lizzie propelled her flying legs into the night.

She flew across the hockey field toward the woods as if her life or someone else's depended on it. The woods, when she reached them, shut out all but slivers of moonlight. Brambles tore at her nightgown, and more than once in the darkness she collided with a tree, the breath jolted out of her. The low-slung branches struck at her face and the prickly thickets cut her legs, but Lizzie and the frantic thump of her heart were not to be deterred from reaching the clearing.

The lantern of the moon shone upon the cottage and, as she had conjectured, on Stephen Jarvic. He hovered in the doorway and then plunged inside.

Fear and dread rooted Lizzie to the edge of the clearing, but some other force pitched her forward and over to the cottage. From the moonlit doorway she looked at Stephen Jarvic, who was uncoiling a length of rope and estimating the height of the crossbeams above him on the ceiling.

"No, I won't let you," Lizzie cried, wresting the rope from him. "Isn't Flavin to rest in peace, where she's gone? Isn't it meant for the suffering to end?"

All in a moment, when Stephen crumpled to his knees and she went to comfort him, Lizzie Devlin grew up, and in his upraised eyes the duckling caught a glimpse of the swan.

TWENTY-FOUR

Flavin's coffin was brought that Friday to Rosemoore for her Requiem. The coroner's report, issued on Thursday, had listed asphyxiation by drowning as the cause of death. The facial contusions and fractured jawbone were attributed to the crash of the car into the river, impacting the body against the windshield, but the coroner also stated that the injuries could have resulted from *"causes unknown."*

A copy of the report was immediately sent to Police Chief Reinecker. Since the accident had occurred in Peekskill, the investigation was under his jurisdiction rather than the county sheriff's in White Plains. In studying the report, Chief Reinecker found little to support the theory that had been suggested by the other facts of the case.

The relevant facts in Reinecker's opinion were limited to two: A girl had died in a freak accident under peculiar, not to say suspicious, circumstances, and upon learning of it her father had attempted suicide. It appeared incontestable that something had occurred between them, and Chief Reinecker did not lack for a theory that advanced a different explanation for the lacerations and fractured jaw. The master bedroom at Faircrest had reeked of whiskey and the kicked-over tables, and broken glass in the adjacent bedroom pointed to a violent struggle between father and daughter, but of what nature? The coroner's report contained no medical evidence to support Reinecker's theory. Moreover, the girl was dead and her father in a condition beyond the reach of interrogation. The gunshot wound had not penetrated the vital sections of Connolly Moore's brain, but his condition was that of a man who had sustained severe brain damage. Kept under guard at Phelps Hospital to prevent another suicide attempt, he had fitful periods of consciousness, during which he showed no cognizance of who he was or of the event that had landed him in the hospital.

Chief Reinecker's theory was at odds with his remembrance of Connolly Moore's kindness, but then human nature was riddled with contradictions. Dutch knew of a leading Peekskill citizen, admired, respected, whose wife wore dark glasses to cover up the bruises inflicted by her husband's periodic beatings. Still, without corroborative evidence, Reinecker's theory was nothing more than that and no basis for prosecution.

After studying the coroner's report, Chief Reinecker advised the sheriff in White Plains against an inquest, which in effect closed the investigation. He then notified the morgue to release the body to the family.

The hearse from Brady and McCormack, the funeral directors for St. Patrick's Cathedral, entered the school gates at four o'clock that Friday afternoon. The gates were closed, the first such time in the school's history, and a security guard was posted in front. The city newspapers had picked up the story from the Peekskill *Evening Star* and were in full bloodhound cry on the scent of a lurid scandal. MYSTERY DEATH OF GROCERY KING'S DAUGHTER, one tabloid headline blared. Reporters, tipped off to the funeral arrangements, were camped at the school gates, while a second group kept watch outside the hospital in Tarrytown. GRIEVING MILLIONAIRE SHOOTS SELF, one of the afternoon headlines read. The old debutante photos of Flavin were dug from the files and run with the stories.

She was brought to Rosemoore because, in one sense, she had nowhere else to go. Monica and Stacey were adamant in ruling out Faircrest. Where else then, the Plaza Hotel?

The hearse proceeded up the school driveway in mournful contrast to Tuesday's jubilation. It was four o'clock and classes were over for the day. Groups of students watched the dirgelike approach of the gunmetal-gray hearse to the steps of Blanchard Hall. The young faces were stamped sober with a new comprehension of the fatal uncertainty of life and death, from which no one, young or old, rich or poor, was exempt.

Louise stood at the bottom of the steps awaiting the hearse with Stephen Jarvic. He was in control of his grief, but the wire was stretched precariously taut. For Stephen, the happiest chapters of his life were closed ... "enough for a lifetime," Flavin had said. He was leaving after the funeral tomorrow to return to the farm in Wisconsin, with no other thought than to exist in the memory of what he had lost.

For Louise, the terrace steps were the hill of Calvary. The coffin that the attendants lifted from the hearse was the body taken down from the cross, and Louise judged herself to be among those who had nailed it to the cross.

She followed behind the coffin up the terrace steps with Stephen Jarvic to the tolling of the chapel bells. The funeral arrangements, the telephone calls, the list of guests to invite, were hers to carry out. Stacey Moore had arrived from Florida and was at the hospital with Monica, faced with the harrowing enigma of a vacant, staring father who did not recognize them. The sisters were to attend Flavin's wake that evening, and tomorrow the Requiem would bring to the altar ...

The organ pealed at the entrance of the coffin into the chapel. The nuns, who were assembled in their stalls, rose together with the Sisters and novices in the pews to sing the opening stanza of "Veni, Creator." The music struck at Louise like an avenging sword as she followed behind the coffin up the aisle. Tomorrow's Requiem would return Sean Regan to the school he'd walked away from, out of her life, nearly twenty years ago ... and she would confess her sins to him.

Could she have prevented the tragedy?

The men placed the coffin upon the catafalque in the aisle below the altar rail. The sword of sorrow and guilt thrust deeper and, stifling a cry, Louise knelt before the altar with Stephen Jarvic while the singing continued.

That night, in shifts of two, the nuns kept a vigil at the coffin. It was draped in a blanket of white roses sent by Stacey and Monica, and candles burned in tall stanchions at the head and foot.

Monia and Stacey, dressed in black, stood at the side of the chancel with Stephen, waiting to receive the visitors come to offer condolences. The altar was banked with the wreaths and sprays that had been arriving by messenger since afternoon. If nothing else, the newspapers had performed the service of announcing the funeral plans to those many who had known Flavin, and to the scores of business, church, and political associates of Connolly's. The switchboard in the tower office had been swamped with inquiries about the funeral tomorrow, which was by invitation only.

Acquin McNally, Monica's son, a sturdy three-year-old in an Eton suit, who was experiencing his first encounter with death, clung to his father in the front pew. "Papa, do we have to stay here? Can't we go home soon?"

"Don't be frightened," Billy McNally counseled his son. "When someone dies, it means to pass from one life to another." Billy had grown stocky, as befitted his new executive status at IBM and the multiplying size of his family. "It's just a passing to somewhere else, that's all."

Acquin chanced a look at the terrifying coffin. "Is it awful dark in there? How can Aunt Falvin go anywhere, shut up in a box?"

"It's not easy to understand, but . . ." Billy glanced up at his wife, made a stranger by black, her face struggling with grief and bewilderment. He was as mystified by the circumstances of Flavin's death and her father's involvement in it as by the process that had changed him from outcast to family member, with the dividends that went with it. The annual income from Monica's trust still exceeded Billy's salary and his attempts to ignore it had failed. The trust had bought the house in Riverdale that he'd dreamed of providing himself someday. It had given Billy the sense that he'd been bought too, and had minimized his sense of success at IBM. He didn't understand anything about his sister-in-law's death or her father's condition, except that it somehow tallied with the drastic extremes that had marred the family relationships.

"I won't lie to you," Billy said, snuggling his son against him. "No getting around it, death is hard for all of us to understand."

Acquin squirmed on his father's lap. "Are you scared by it, Papa?"

"Yes, but we've got to try not to think of ourselves." Billy watched one of the Brady and McCormack men carry a spray of lilies to the altar. "Look, tell you what, fella." He glanced again at his wife. "Go up to Mama and give her a big kiss. It'll make her feel better."

"I'm scared to go past the coffin."

"Well, that's easy, go out the other side of the pew."

"Okay, I will."

Acquin McNally, the eldest of three siblings, was accustomed to taking on responsibilities. He scrambled out of the pew only to find himself up close to a nun praying in her stall. Nuns were almost as scary as coffins, and so was life, Acquin was finding out, and he ran to his mother in the chancel for a kiss to chase away his fears.

The students were the first visitors to appear in the chapel. At seven o'clock, the dinner hour over, they ventured in awkward groups up the aisle to pray at the catafalque. The less timid of the girls went to express sympathy to Monica, Stacey, and Stephen, while the others hung back and gawked. It was all to be discussed and hashed over, but later, not here in close proximity to death. Few of the girls stayed long, hastening out of the chapel, conscious of the tolling of mortality.

Lizzie Devlin, who belonged to no category of student, went up the aisle with Floss and Eileen. Lizzie belonged to herself, a new and overwhelming experience that she had not yet assimilated. She felt as if graduation was behind her, and all that was left at school was to bid good-bye to F.M. and S.J., which she had come tonight to do.

The Musketeers knelt together in a pew below the catafalque, and Eileen Birnbaum said the *Kaddish* prayer for the dead with a rosary clasped in her hand, a reflection of the clash of beliefs that she was pledged to resolve. College, the neat dovetailing of studies, Hebrew and Christian . . . and what else, what beyond it? A link was missing, thought Eileen as she prayed, but how was she to forge it? The idea struck her that by traveling to the wellspring of both faiths she would link them together, unbroken. Yes, she would journey to Palestine, soon, it must be soon, before time, made so fleeting by death, canceled it.

Time was at the root of the prayers that Florence Giambetti directed at the altar. The offering she wished to present to God for her family's salvation was herself, but what if she never found the courage to make it? One day in the passage of time she would look back at the years and . . . Florence knelt up straight in the pew. She would break her silence and go to the nuns to tell of her offering, and they would give her the courage to attempt it.

That afternoon Lizzie had gone for a last wandering of the fields and woods, to gather the wild flowers that grew in the grass and at the foot of the trees. She had made a bouquet of wild flowers, the stems wrapped in a paper doily and tied with a white ribbon, which now she carried with her to the catafalque and knelt before it in the aisle.

"Good-bye, F.M.," Lizzie whispered to the coffin. "There's peace in heaven," she whispered, not altogether finished with God, and lay the wild flowers at the coffin's foot.

Then, with Eileen and Floss, Lizzie offered her condolences to the bereaved. "I'm sorry for your loss," she said to Monica and Stacey. "I'm sorry," trembled from her lips when she turned to Stephen Jarvic.

"Lizzie, I knew you'd come, never forgetting, as always."

She had not seen him since the night at the cottage. "I—I never will forget," she stammered.

Stephen clasped her hand in his. "I keep thinking of what you said at the cottage."

"Oh, really?"

"If suffering is meant to end, there's a chance for me, so long as I don't give up. I leave tomorrow, you know."

He was alive, thought Lizzie, and that was her reward for loving him. "Yes, I heard."

"When I look back at the happier memories, one of the best will be of you."

"Well," said Lizzie. "I guess it's time to say good-bye."

And saying it, she turned and went out of the chapel.

"What a good boy," Louise said, lifting the sleepy Acquin from his chair at the dining table. "Such a long night, but not a peep of complaint from you."

Nuns were scary, but this nun smelled nice as soap and was offering a Tootsie Roll. "Chewy candy's best," said Acquin, taking it, "on account of it lasts longer."

Chafing dishes of scrambled eggs and kippers were set out on the sideboard in the dining room of Annunciation Hall. Stephen Jarvic had retired to his room, but Monica, Bill, and Anastasia, who were staying overnight, were at the table. Father Anselm, who had led the rosary that concluded the wake, sat with them, attempting to enliven the meal with jokes.

"The police chief gave it to you?" Stacey asked, of the parcel that Monica had deposited on the sideboard. "When?"

"When he came to pay his respects." Monica was in the early stages of her fourth pregnancy and her eyes were puffy with fatigue. "It's the clothes that Flavin was wearing."

"The death costume?" Stacey clenched her fork, the strain of the ordeal evident in her brusqueness. "I'd rather not look, if you don't mind."

Louise broke the tense silence that had settled over the table. "Well, look who's off to the land of Winken, Blinken, and Nod." She smiled at Acquin, asleep in her arms. "Why don't I tuck him into bed? I'll be down in a minute, and we'll go over the seating charts for tomorrow."

She carried her charge up the oak stairs, beset by strange thoughts. The sleeping child whom she laid on the bed in a guest room was the child she had never borne. She undressed him and slipped a nightshirt over his tousled head, and he was all the children she might have borne, if, years ago, she had climbed into the buggy with Sean Regan . . . a fugitive priest and nun, and yet more good might have come of it than any that in her pride and ambition she had accomplished by staying a nun.

She drew the coverlet over Acquin, cautioning herself to beware of the malice and snares of the devil, which were said to appear in the form of doubts and persuasions. She left the bed lamp burning and went from the room, and the devils of guilt, the guilt of omission, were like stones that weighted her steps on the stairs.

What had preceded Flavin's death and could she have prevented it?

She turned pale as she entered the dining room and recoiled from the scene that had erupted in a hysterical outburst from Stacey.

"Why delay it? Why put it off?" Stacey cried, breaking from Father Leo to lunge at the parcel on the sideboard and tear at the brown paper and string. "Oh, my God . . . whose clothes are these?"

Anastasia held up the crumpled, blood-stained blue jacket and skirt of a bygone era. "Monnie, look, aren't these Mama's clothes? Yes, they must be, but why was Flavin wearing them? Was she in Mama's room that night? Where was Father? Was he drunk? Dear God, what did he do to her?"

In the shocked quiet of the room, Stacey turned to Louise in the door. "What did my father do to my sister that made her crash in the river? Tell me your guess, and then I'll tell you mine."

All through the night the vigil was kept at the coffin in hour shifts by the nuns. The chant of litanies filled the chapel while the Sisters readied it with mop and pail for the morning's solemn rites.

Sister Bridget scrubbed her way up the aisle with Sister Josie, her cohort from the Pow-Wow, who was discussing the funeral.

"We're sure to have a big turnout," Josie remarked, with an Irish penchant for the subject. "Himself is such a personage and Flavin one a' the reigning beauties of New York."

"Poor man," said Bridget, wielding her soapy brush. " 'Tis a mercy he's got no memory to grieve him."

"I tell yer." Josie scrubbed in cozy rhythm and comradeship. "Nivver did I see a man as gorjus as Connolly Moore in that papal outfit, and always a friendly smile."

"May it be the kindness of him that people look back on."

"An' was ivver the likes of him on a horse, royal as a king?" Josie gave a fond laugh, then hushed herself and glanced nervously up the aisle at the coffin. "Has it passed yet, do ya think?"

"What?"

"The soul from the body—*hers*, I mean."

Bridget knelt back and appraised the coffin, wanting a sign. "Flavin's with God, it's not *her* soul that I worry about."

"Whose, then?"

Bridget took up her scrub brush and would not reply. It was the soul of Reverend Mother that worried her, and for that she wanted a sign, but she must wait until she was alone in the chapel. It happened only when she was alone, and was far from certain even then.

When they were finished with the scrubbing, Bridget and Josie submitted to the brisk instructions of Mother Friel, who had taken command of the preparations, quite unbidden. Her presumption had been noted by the nuns, but tonight, with all that had to be done, was the wrong time to contest it.

Fetching and carrying, Josie went off with the black Requiem vestments for pressing, and Bridget set up folding chairs on the altar for the priests who were expected to concelebrate the Mass. The flowers on the altar had to be moved to accommodate the number of chairs. Some of the wreaths were banked in the chancel, and Bridget was given the spray of lilies to place on the Lady Altar.

She lingered at her task, her focus turned from the Sienese Madonna to the little painted statue in the bell jar on the table below.

When the chapel was pronounced fit for the morning, the Sisters were dismissed, which left the changing vigil of nuns at the catafalque. Bridget, praying in the shadows at the rear, heard a chorus of birds outside the windows chirping that the night had passed.

It was dawn and she had yet to be alone. She waited her chance and prayed for the Mother General, lost in guilt, she who would not knowingly harm the leaf of a tree or a blade of grass. How little she knew of herself, how poor she was at judging her worth!

Bridget waited for the shift of nuns to depart and the next shift to take their place at the catafalque, and when they did not appear, she was alone in the chapel.

Hurrying up the aisle, she knelt in the flickering candles of the Lady Altar and fastened her gaze upon the little painted statue.

"Remember the crossin' them years ago?" she asked of Sophie's Virgin. "The babe that my mistress saved from chokin', whose mom gave her yer darlin' statue to keep? Remember me, thinkin' to throw myself into the sea? She saved me from it and give me the joy of livin' for God . . . but now 'tis her that's in need of savin'."

A sparrow in a black veil, Bridget prayed before the statue in behalf of the Mother General. "Oh, she'd want to save the whole world, like the job was up to her, but she couldn't save Flavin from death, not with all that went before. 'Tis eatin' at her soul, destroyin' her, and I ask for a sign, my Lady, that you'll help her out of despair . . . a sign, I ask for a sign . . ."

Bridget's head was flung back, a queer shine in her eyes, and in that shine she saw the statue in the bell jar move and reach out to her.

TWENTY-FIVE

She caught sight of him from the tower window, striding up the driveway from the parking lot. The spring to his step, the shoulders that strained the seams of the black cleric's suit, evoked for Louise the young priest of the *Kronprinz* so vividly that it seemed as if the years had not passed.

She turned away, as disconcerted as then, and listened for the ring of the chimes in the hall below. She trod the carpet, back and forth, hands clenched, knuckles white, and then was stopped motionless by the thought of the Requiem an hour away.

"Is that you, or a monument?" Sean Regan inquired from the doorway. "A monument, I think, entitled 'The Guilty.' "

"Really, you know, I never did appreciate your—" she closed the door upon Mother Friel in the outer office, "your levity, always at the most inappropriate times."

Father Regan scaled the fedora that he never wore onto the coat-tree. "Guilty of what, swiping nickels from the newsstand? Sneaking rides on the El?"

"I . . ." The sudden impact of his nearness registered on her. Up close, the evidence of the years was graphically defined. The thinning hair was touched with gray and his face was cut with lines that ran from nostrils to jaw, deep as furrows. Was there a day that she had not missed him? And he, was it the same for him?

"Thank you for coming," she said. "We have need of you."

"Big commotion at the gates, swarm of reporters and the guard couldn't find my name on the list."

"It was on the list." First on it, but she didn't tell him that.

"Sheer charm got me in, that or the Roman collar." A warmth gleamed in Regan's eyes as he looked at her, but then he glanced away and tugged at the stiff collar. "Stephen was over to see me last night—did he get back all right?"

"He was at breakfast, so he must have—it seemed better that he stay with us."

"And you? What about you?"

"Me?"

The wry glint of humor lit the furrowed face. "I've been a priest long enough to recognize the dyspeptic look of someone aching for the confessional."

Louise fell to her knees. "I'm desperately serious—without it, I can't go on, I tell you."

"Are we a nun and a priest in a movie?" Regan asked, mocking her impassioned attitude. "You, abject on your knees, while I quote from Holy Scripture?"

"Sean, you don't understand what I bear on my soul." She stared up in confusion, at her use of his given name. "I must confess my sins, that much at least."

"Look here." He reached out and drew her up from the carpet. "I've heard the confessions of men who couldn't kneel because their legs were blown off. Some of the guys at the house hobble around on crutches and can't kneel either, so let's skip the formalities."

He led her to the wing chair at the desk and pulled a chair alongside. Taking a purple stole from his coat pocket, he kissed it and draped it over his broad shoulders, after which he cupped his chin in his hand and listened for her to speak.

"If you're going to confess that you're human and not a plaster saint, we'll skip it entirely."

Louise clasped her hands in her sleeves. "Ambition is a sin, when it is given priority to the extent that I . . ."

"What extent?"

She shuddered and closed her eyes. "I contributed to Flavin's death and Connolly's shooting himself by what I didn't do."

"That's a large order of guilt," Regan said. "What convinces you of it?"

"The idea of losing Flavin obsessed Connolly, and one day here at school I saw that ..." Louise got up from the chair, unable to remain in it. "It was after Christmas and we'd had a blizzard the night before."

"And?" Regan prodded.

"I was to give a dinner party the following night, to raise funds for the convent I wanted to build, but there we were, snowbound." She paced back and forth, clenching and unclenching her hands. "The driveway was impassable and some of the roads not plowed. I had no choice but to cancel the dinner, but then I heard the jingle of bells and ran downstairs. In that way he had of disposing of obstacles, Connolly whirled up in a horse-drawn sleigh, to rescue the dinner party, he said ... and I wanted it so badly that I ignored the warning signs."

"What signs?"

"He spoke of Flavin that day and I saw that ..." Louise stood at the window, pulled there by compulsion. "Commencement is in two weeks," she said, looking down at the lush green of the campus, immersed in the Saturday quiet. "We do rather nicely with it, I must say. The exercises, barring rain, are held on the south lawn under the trees, a lovely setting for the girls in their white organdy dresses, each wearing a coronet of—" She gasped and pressed a hand to her lips. "Flavin was rich and not poor, like Jenny Rocket, but the same thing happened to her," she cried. "I might have saved her, if I'd heeded the signs."

"*What* signs?" Regan persisted. "Heeded what signs?"

She moved away from the window, her hand pressed to her lips. "Connolly wasn't himself that day—the erratic mood swings, the veering from one subject to another—he was like someone on the edge of a breakdown, but my concern was for the dinner party, and when he'd arranged for the driveway to be cleared ..."

"What then?"

"He spoke of Flavin, and it was not the normal feeling of a father for a daughter."

Regan stood up, tensed for what he knew was to come. "You found it abnormal?"

"Yes, that! Unnatural, beyond the natural bond of a father's love." Louise gripped the mantel as if for support and stared at the sparkling Bristol glass. "There it is, my everlasting guilt. I *knew*, and yet I did nothing to intervene."

"Such as what?"

"The point is, I did nothing to help her."

"You could not have stopped it, though in fact she wasn't raped."

Louise turned from the mantel, uncomprehending. "But why . . . ?"

"I worried that Stephen might think it, so I went to the coroner yesterday," Regan said. "He showed me the report and it contains no evidence of rape or attempted rape."

"Then what—?"

"It's guesswork, but I'd say that Connolly was drunk that night. Some men turn violent from drink, but if rape was in his mind, he didn't go through with it. Maybe it was some last drunken effort at honor and all the things he wanted to be but wasn't."

Louise moved slowly across the room. "Is it honor that he's tried to buy all these years? The sadness in Connolly . . . I sensed it always, but not the source of it, unless it was his wife's death."

"For that, we'd have to go back to when he was born. Money can buy honors galore and a whole lot else, but usually not love."

"He talked of letting go of those he loved. Did he think that no one loved him in return?"

"If you think it, why not show him that he's wrong?"

"How, in his condition? If you were to visit him in the hospital, those blank, staring eyes . . ."

"Sounds like a victim of shell shock, and I've seen men recover from it, given time."

"Oh, if I believed it were possible!"

"Since when did you give up believing?" Sean Regan demanded. "As I remember the *Kronprinz,* you refused to take no for an answer, from me or anybody else. How ready you were to take on the world single-handed, in the name of God."

Louise shook her head and tears welled up, unbidden. "I'm not that person anymore." She sat at the desk and looked numbly at Regan. "You and I, we've traded places," she said. "The poor and helpless are your province, not mine, as I'd wanted."

"But I didn't want it," Regan protested, and strode the carpet, rubbing his jaw, the careworn lines of his face etched deep. "After I left New York I kept on the run for years, until I got caught in the war, and then I couldn't run, not from those shattered men in the field hospitals. Someone had to look after them, and it turned out to be me. Listen, I can't count the times I've wanted to chuck it all for a grass shack and a dusky maiden in the South Seas, but something always stops me, and every once in a while . . ."

"Yes?" Louise folded her hands on the desk blotter. "Tell me, what?"

"Well, that ramshackle house in Yonkers is half falling down, the roof leaks, and I get fed up with the men and their problems, but every once in a blue moon I'm filled with joy at who and what I am, and I thank God for letting me be a priest, despite myself."

Sean Regan looked across the room at Louise, the purple stole hanging crookedly on his shoulders. "I'm always broke, of course, but every month, amazingly, some anonymous donor sends a money order to keep us going . . . now, who on earth can it be?"

"Who, indeed?" echoed Louise, her hands tightly folded. "Someone who cares about you, I'd guess."

"And the poor and helpless too." Regan's hand went to the stole, straightening it. "You're such a bossy dame, Louise. Ambitious? Yes, but it's inherent in you, and is it wrong of itself? By now, if you'd gone to Wyoming, you'd have founded a dozen missions. I remember that I called you M.G., for Mother General, and so you are today, not to my least surprise."

"I am not a quitter," Louise said with a certain squaring of jaw. "I trust that I'm not a quitter."

"Who would dare accuse you of it?" Sean Regan grinned, and while his tone was jocular, his message was not. "Listen to me," he exhorted her. "Flavin is dead and nothing can change it. Grieve for what you might have done, but go on from it, and hope and pray to do better."

Louise rose from the desk, knelt before him, and crossed herself. "I repent of my sins, Father, and I—I ask for your pardon."

Regan lifted his hand in the sign of the cross and intoned the Latin words of absolution. Solemnity was not his suit of clothes, cleric's black was, shiny with wear, and he laughed as he assisted the penitent to her feet. "Well, where are they?"

"Where are what?"

"When I was a boy and went to confession, I expected to sprout angel's wings on the spot."

"Levity, as usual!" Louise turned and hurried to the window, as if the day were in jeopardy without her supervision. Monica and Stacey were pacing the driveway with Stephen Jarvic, the three of them engrossed in conversation. Out on the south lawn, Billy McNally tossed a gleeful Acquin high in the air, catching him with a jubilant shout. A large number of students had signed out for the weekend, fleeing from sadness, and few were to be seen on the walks. The men from Brady and McCormack were waiting in cutaways on the terrace of Blanchard Hall.

"It is getting time." Louise searched her desk for the seating chart. "The cars will arrive at any minute, Governor and Mrs. Smith, and the Cardinal is sending a bishop."

"He's already here."

She glanced up from her papers, and with some embarrassment Regan indicated the jeweled ring that in her distress she had failed to notice.

"It goes with the new job," he explained by way of apology. "Hayes is shipping me to Washington, to head up the military vicariate. He's assigned another priest to the Yonkers house, or I wouldn't have accepted."

"*When?*"

"My investiture? Last week, but it's not to be announced until—"

Louise clenched the papers in her hand. "When do you leave for Washington? For how long?"

"Years, perhaps, but will I be any farther away from you?" Regan slipped the purple stole from his shoulders and regarded it quizzically. "For a tough pragmatist, I've got a romantic streak a mile wide."

"Oh?"

"I'm not sure about trading places, but you and I . . . we're closer than we'd ever have been if you'd climbed into that buggy with me."

Louise watched him fold the stole into his pocket and start for the door. "Wait," she called, hurrying to the coat-tree. "You forgot your miter," she said, handing the bishop his hat, "and I've exactly the chair for you on the altar."

Then together they went from the tower office and across the driveway to the chapel.

The cars rolled up the driveway, one after another, admitted by the guard at the gates.

The arrival of Governor Al Smith and Mrs. Smith brought the reporters and cameras surging forward. The flash bulbs popped, as they did a few minutes later for James J. Walker, the candidate for mayor in the upcoming November election. The city's favorite son, "Jimmy" to bootblack and tycoon alike, Walker could trace his friendship with Connolly Moore back to his days as a Tin Pan Alley song peddler and the convivial gatherings at Billy Lafitte's saloon, spinning tales and warbling Irish songs at the piano.

The men whose cars deposited them at the terrace steps were of the same cut and breed. Thomas Fortune Ryan, the utilities magnate, Tim Mara, owner of the New York Giants, George Olvany, grand sachem of Tammany, William Kenny, the millionaire contractor, James Farley, of the state Democratic committee, Tom Gavin, the front-page trial lawyer—all were Irish and self-made, risen to prominence in a city that had been in league against them. With Connolly, they formed a select fraternity among themselves, men hardened by the cruel realities of the city, the betrayals and deceits, yet quick with Irish sentiment for the downtrodden, unashamed of the tear wiped from the eye, and fiercely loyal to their comrades.

It explained this morning's large turnout. The daughter of a comrade had died, and the men had come, together with delegates from the Friendly Sons of St. Patrick and the Ancient Order of Hibernians, to mourn her passing, and to receive consolation in the age-old rites of their Church.

The mourners went up the steps and into the vestibule of the chapel, where Stacey and Monica greeted them. Many of the men had known the sisters as children, just as they had been guests at Flavin's debut. Cheer prevailed over gloom in the memories evoked of parties and outings, campaigns and election nights, and the governor's ball. Connolly's absence was remarked upon, as though nothing untoward was related to it. The men, whatever their private speculations, esteemed him as one of their own, a fallen comrade whose tragedy in one guise or another could befall any of them.

Organ music played as the Brady and McCormack ushers conducted the mourners to their pews. As at a wedding, the gray-gloved ushers escorted the young women who had been Flavin's classmates up the aisle. The students slipped quietly into the rear pews and the nuns knelt in their stalls, the Sisters and novices grouped at the front. The world of Rosemoore was convened in the stained-glass light that streamed upon them and upon the coffin that waited for deliverance at the head of the aisle.

Onto the flower-massed altar filed priests of the archdiocese and the various orders, Jesuit, Christian Brothers, Salesian, Dominican, Paulist, that were the beneficiaries over the years of Connolly's generosity. The seating of Flavin's family in the front pew was a cue, as at a wedding, for the ritual to start. Bishop Regan, in black vestments but lacking a miter, knelt for the opening prayers at the foot of the altar steps.

"Introibo ad altare Dei . . . ad Deum qui laetificat juventutem meam . . ."

The liturgy moved swiftly in majestic cadences, a Mass for the dead and for the living as well. As Louise spoke the responses in unison with the pew of worshipers, it carried her back to a world far removed from Rosemoore, but a world from which it had sprung, and was, in essence, the same.

"Dominus vobiscum."

"Et cum spiritu tuo."

She was carried back to the rough stone church of Columkill on the windswept hill above Ballymar, and to the worshipers among whom she had knelt at Mass . . . the black-clad figures who had traveled the dawn roads of the countryside by trap and buggy and foot to reach Columkill . . . the faithful, whose voices at Mass were a river of faith, beyond perishing, beyond extinction.

"Kyrie eleison."

"Christe eleison."

They knelt this morning in the chapel of Rosemoore, the heirs of the faithful, bound together in a belief that was their very sustenance, the bread of life, as promised by Christ.

Louise believed again with the rapture of the young girl who had left the white stucco house to give her life in service to God. There was time yet, and she was not a quitter. If she had failed, someone else had not, who was the savior of the world.

"Credo in unum Deum, Patrem omnipotentum . . ."

She recited the credo, and the doubts and torment of the last days receded. The story was not finished, not for Connolly, not for Rosemoore, and she would make a difference.

Louise took from her prayer book the memorial card that was printed with Flavin's name. Below it were the words spoken to Mary, the sister of Lazarus, who lay in death in the tomb.

"I am the resurrection and the life: he that believeth in Me, though he be dead, shall live."

EPILOGUE

In her brisk manner and rushing stride that seemed to take her everywhere at once, Louise was unchanged. The days rushed along in pace with her stride. Final exams occupied the students the week after the funeral, and commencement was to be held the following weekend. This year, unexpectedly, changes were made in certain of the procedures.

The results of the exams showed the usual quota of failing grades by the students. The policy was to give makeup exams, which more or less assured a passing grade, until Louise called a faculty meeting to question it.

"I propose, as of now," she addressed the nuns gathered in the tower office, "that a student who fails a makeup exam must repeat the subject in summer school. She must earn a B or the equivalent in it, or we will not accept her for the fall semester."

"Isn't that rather severe?" queried Mother Tracy who had been appointed the new headmistress and was tender of heart. "Some girls are less capable than others, and to—"

"Or they are lazier and given to frivolous pursuits."

"But our girls are . . ." Mother Tracy was about to remark that the typical Rosemoore girl was not accustomed to severities, but Louise said it for her, succinctly.

"It is time we were known as something other than a school for rich girls. Of this year's graduates, how many are going on to college?"

"Thirteen, of a class of twenty-four."

335

"We have not encouraged it sufficiently. Well, let's post a notice on all bulletin boards outlining the new policy on makeups, and see whether the girls get cracking."

The meeting was adjourned and the nuns prepared to leave. Mother Tracy hesitated and turned back in the doorway.

"Speaking of the graduates, one of them came to me yesterday in an awful turmoil, but I couldn't get her to talk about it."

"Ah, that would be Florence Giambetti," Mother Friel interjected with a benign smile. "She actually had the temerity to request an interview with Mother General, but I—"

"You sent her away?" Louise took the flustered silence for a reply, and checked her calendar. "Tell the young lady that I will see her tomorrow afternoon at four o'clock."

The next afternoon, seated across from Louise's desk, Florence Giambetti twisted her hands, rolled her eyes, and gulped vainly for speech.

"Are you not Lizzie Devlin's roommate?" Louise asked to put her at ease. "Quite the most enchanting donkey ever to appear in a Nativity pageant."

"Lizzie is a perfect wonder." The dark, timid eyes lit up. "She's just learned that she's to act at the Falmouth Playhouse this summer, the youngest member of the company. Oh, we're bound to hear about Lizzie."

"And you, my dear child? What are your plans for after graduation?"

"I—" Florence gulped for breath and seized the courage stored beneath her timidity. "I want to be a nun, but there are problems with it."

Louise studied the intense young girl poised between alarm and exultation on the edge of her chair. "By that, do you mean your parents?"

"I can't even tell them." The disclosure for Florence was the height of audacity, steeped as she was in a code that denied her a voice in her own existence. "My family would never permit it, if they knew."

"Parents often need to adjust to the idea of a daughter as a nun. Confide in yours, discuss it with them, and—"

"No, I can't, because . . ." Florence struggled for speech. "My family—it's not like any girl's at school." She caught her breath and told of growing up ignorant of her family's business involvements but sensing the furtiveness that cloaked them and cast an aura of menace over the house in Mineola. "The women, we're just expected to stay in the background and pretend we don't notice, but that isn't for me. You see, I've felt for a long time that if I . . ."

"Yes, Florence?"

"If I were to serve God . . . well, then my family would too, since I'm a part of them."

Louise shifted the letter opener on her desk, composing her thoughts. "Wanting to be a nun is a stage that many girls go through," she said. "A new dress or a young man at a dance soon diverts them from it, but I don't think that's the case with you."

Florence looked down at her twitching hands, her voice scarcely audible. "It's all I want . . . and even if my family prevents me from it, I'll go on wanting it, till I die."

"Well, let's not talk of dying." Louise smiled across the desk. "If God wants this for you, we'll find a way, somehow."

The sallow face brightened with hope. "If there's a way, will you help me to find it?"

Louise's response was her commitment. "Yes, I will, and you mustn't let graduation make you a stranger," she said. "Come back as often as you like, and we'll see to the future, do you hear?"

"Oh, thank you, Reverend Mother."

It seemed to Florence Giambetti, as she went across the campus, that she floated on air, and to herself she sang, "I hear! I hear."

In June, Connolly Moore was transferred by ambulance to New York Hospital. The month of quiet and rest had improved his physical condition, but not his mental state, and the doctors had prescribed a series of neurological tests in an effort to reach a prognosis.

Louise made frequent trips to the city, primarily to visit Connolly, though he showed not a flicker of recognition of her. Moreover, he grew agitated if any visitor stayed too long, and so she was limited to ten or fifteen minutes with him.

She drove the school car herself to the city, in much the same spirit that had prompted her to banish the throne chair to the storage basement. "It will come in handy for Shakespeare, with all those kings," she had said, "and we'll haul it out as a joke on Bishop Regan when he turns up again. Pomp and circumstance are not his cup of tea."

The hoard of mementos in the biscuit tin was augmented by the newspaper clippings of Regan's new office. The wide press coverage accorded it was an indication of his emergence as a major spokesman for the men and veterans of the armed forces. Louise had not known until she read of them of the houses for disabled veterans, modeled on the Yonkers house, that had been opened in Boston and Philadelphia. Certainly, Regan had not referred to it.

She sat on the narrow bed in her room and added the new clippings to the cherished hoard. As vicar of chaplains, Regan was currently embarked on a tour of army and navy bases that would keep him in transit for months, and she wondered when next their paths would cross.

"You and I . . . are closer than we'd ever have been, if you'd . . ."

She believed it, with every fiber and nerve and tissue of herself. The quandary of loving Regan was behind her, and when she looked at the faded photograph of the two of them on the steerage deck of the *Kronprinz,* Louise felt proud of the choice she had made, and sanctified by it.

Nor did she mourn for the children that she would never bear.

On her trips to the city, Louise was chauffeur for carloads of nuns who were off to summer seminars at Fordham and Columbia in the drawn-out process of earning baccalaureates. The car, as it sped along Route 9, was always lively with chatter from which Louise would otherwise have been distanced. She had not realized the gulf that the last few years—the meals on trays, the late hours at her desk—had created, isolating her from the nuns as a community of women and their trials and aspirations.

The talk that she heard in the car was a revelation in that it illustrated the range and diversity of the nuns' interests, which were left unfulfilled. Architecture, law, theater, medicine, anthropology—how enriched would they be as teachers, given the opportunity of graduate school and perhaps foreign study? The nuns' educational fund was inadequate for such an undertaking, but that was seldom a deterrent for Louise. Very well, she would devise a means of increasing the fund.

It became her practice that summer to leave her desk in time for dinner at the convent, and to join in the hour of recreation that followed the meal. She threw aside the *General* of her title and put to good use its other attribute. The gaiety of the nuns at recreation was audible clear to the driveway, and Louise was mother of it.

Mourn for her children, when in actuality she was surrounded by them?

The visits to Connolly were less subject to reward. By July, the results of the neurological tests had not revealed any brain damage or disorder. He had suffered a trauma that, two months later, was as fixed and immutable as when it had incapacitated him.

Connolly existed in a perpetual twilight, his memory as vacant as that of an amnesia victim, or the victim of a stroke. The nurses, always two in attendance around the clock, bathed him each morning, and the hospital barber lathered and shaved him. Each week the barber trimmed the silver hair, brushed back over the scar at the temple. After breakfast the nurses exercised Connolly, dressed in an inexhaustible supply of Sulka robes and pajamas, up and down the hospital corridor for an hour. Visitors were permitted in the afternoon, when he was installed in a leather club chair at the window. It framed a sweeping vista of the East River, but it might have been a blank wall that Connolly turned from staring at.

Louise's theory was that the river view reminded him of Faircrest and was painful to endure. Memory, she suspected, was at the root of the agitation that gripped him whenever a visitor stayed too long. It stirred up all that he had retreated from, into a void of dazed blankness.

He greeted Louise on each of her visits in a faltering mumble and frantic eyes that failed to identify not only her but his own daughters.

"Do you think it's permanent?" Stacey Moore asked Louise one July afternoon. "The doctors hedge like crazy, but I haven't seen an iota of improvement."

Stacey was, to everyone's surprise, constant in her visits, appearing day after day to sit with her father and joke and banter in typical fashion with the nurses. She was staying at the Plaza and had shown no inclination to return to Palm Beach.

"Seems my feller up and went back to the wifey," she confided to Louise with a casual shrug. "I hooked up with him partly to infuriate Father, but he's past that now, and so am I ... and he's never needed me before."

"You and Monica, as never before."

"If his condition is permanent, we'll have to decide about the financial side of the picture."

For two months Connolly's business affairs had been held in abeyance, awaiting his recovery. Miss Philbin, a daily visitor to the hospital, continued to manage his real estate properties, but that represented only one segment of Connolly's wealth. The bank accounts, the trusts, the investments and stock portfolios, amounted to several millions of dollars, and required decisions that could not be postponed indefinitely.

"It's a huge joke," Stacey laughed. "Father used to rail that his daughters' only concept of money was how to spend it, and it winds up with the two worst dummies having to take over."

On Louise's next visit, Stacey intercepted her in the corridor. "Guess who was here yesterday, with the swellest little proposition for me? You'd have to know Jack Geoghegan to really appreciate it."

"But I do know him." Louise's recollection of Connolly's attorney had not dimmed with the years. "I tend to be wary of someone who offers to cut off his arm out of sheer devotion."

"It's Father he wants to cut off, by taking him to court to have him declared incompetent. Don't worry, I turned the weasel down flat, and then I phoned our trust officer to start proceedings to fire him."

"In the long run, it ought to be Billy who looks after the money, as one of the family."

Stacey gave a bantering laugh that didn't quite come off. "Flavin always wanted us to stay together as a family, but she had to die for it to happen."

"The effect of her death has been profound on so many of us."

"We're closing Faircrest—recover or not, Father won't want to go back there. I'm not sure what it means in terms of my life, but I haven't forgotten the day we drove you to Hightower and the words you tried to get me to say."

"You still remember?"

"It's not easy to forget very much about you, Mother Maguire."

"And the words?"

Stacey looked at the nun for a moment. "Maybe I didn't think there was any good in me . . . but if it's there, I'll say 'I will' to it."

That afternoon, Louise sat with Connolly at the window, alone with him for the last allotted minutes of her visit. As she talked of school, the fall semester and the new roof for the gym that was under construction, his vacant eyes grew agitated. She took this as a signal to leave, but as she got up from the chair, a quavering hand restrained her, and Connolly leaned forward in a futile attempt to speak.

"Agggghh . . . urghhhh . . ."

The gutteral sounds were as much as he was capable of, and Louise did not press him to go on, but she was certain that for a fleeting instant he had sought to convey that he knew who she was, and the school that she had talked of.

The doctors had not, of course, consulted her, nor had Louise volunteered an opinion as to their patient's condition or prognosis. She held a belief, however, and belief is stronger than opinion and less susceptible to medical charts.

Connolly had inflicted on himself a graver damage than the wound of the revolver shot. He had passed a harsher sentence upon himself than any jury would have rendered. He had judged that he was beyond forgiveness, beyond redemption, and had fired the revolver in verdict of it.

And Louise believed that when and if, through the labyrinth of memory, he found the path to forgiveness, then would Connolly reach the threshold of recovery.

That September, Rosemoore opened for the fall semester of its eighteenth academic year on a warm and summery morning, yet with a tinge of autumn in the air.

Mother Tracy, the new headmistress, stood below the oak stairs in Annunciation Hall to receive the freshman class. It was tradition that they enter here, as the first students had done, and then be served get-acquainted milk and cookies in the drawing room.

Each girl curtsied to Mother Tracy, who extended a hand in welcome and steadied the wobblers with ease, as if she'd been at it for years. The class of thirty-six, divided evenly between boarders and day students, was the largest in the school's history.

"Well, I shan't have to ask your name," said Mother Tracy to one pig-tailed girl with freckles. "You are the image of your mother at that age. She married Helen Driscoll's brother, Ned, the summer after graduation, as I remember."

"She said you'd remember—and to say hello for her."

Five of the freshmen were daughters of alumnae, the second generation at Rosemoore, reflecting the mellowed look of age that had settled like a mantle over the campus.

While the freshmen curtsied to Mother Tracy and sampled the cookies and milk, the brick walks were thronged with upperclassmen shouting hellos and trading the scuttlebutt that concerned the new school uniform. According to rumor, the smart cardigan jacket and tattersall skirt had been designed, only God knew how, by Coco Chanel of Paris, France.

"Fabulous," cried Connie Smiles, a junior from Buffalo, New York. "Too bad we can't splash ourselves with Number Five to go with it."

"Yeah, well, all I know," gloomed Marybeth D'Arcy of Shaker Heights, Ohio, "is that I spent practically the entire summer tutoring in the Latin I flunked in the makeups."

"Well, at least you passed it," said Ruth Mulvaney of Winnetka, Illinois. "Otherwise, you wouldn't be allowed back."

The 8:55 bell rang, which sent the girls scurrying for Blanchard Hall, sobered by the scholastic merit that was now expected of them, but reassured by the familiarity of routine. Classes were not until tomorrow, but they were to report to their homerooms for schedules, assembly was at ten, then lunch, followed by a busy afternoon of dashing hither and yon to obtain mailbox and locker keys, library cards and book lists, capped by a malt or a Coke in the Pow-Wow.

The royal-blue school bus trundled up the driveway, delivering the day students from various Westchester towns. Duffy, smoking his pipe, wheeled out ash cans from the basement of Blanchard Hall. In the gym, Miss Osborne sorted through a tangled assortment of locker keys, while Mrs. Van Pelt dropped by the chapel to consult Sophie's Virgin as to the wisdom of augmenting her opera course with the incendiary passions of *Cav* and *Pag*. Mother Friel was in the library, to which she was newly assigned. She reviewed the books on the shelves, selecting ones for censorship, and masked with a benign smile the cold fury she felt at her reduced status. Still, Claire Friel was not a person to surrender her objectives, but rather to exercise patience in achieving them. She plucked the offending volumes from the shelves as she would like to have done with the students who had met her disfavor.

The nuns greeted students in the classrooms and chalked schedules on the blackboards. The Sisters set the tables for lunch in the dining hall in a clatter of plates and cups, and the eighteenth academic year got off to a start, but with the absence of the woman whose galvinizing presence was so essential to it.

Actually, it was learned in August that the Mother General was likely to be absent for the opening day. The convent grapevine had buzzed with rumors, which Louise had subsequently confirmed at a special meeting of the Council.

"Cardinal Mundelein of Chicago has made us a splendid proposal," she had announced. "He is ready to offer the deed to an excellent property on Lake Shore Drive, and the financial backing of a group of leading Catholics, if we will agree to open a branch of Rosemoore in the Windy City. I must say, it is an attractive proposition, and while it is not without problems as to staff and faculty . . ."

The Council had voted unanimously in favor of the Cardinal's offer, and Louise had made train reservations for Chicago to inspect the property, but she had not boarded the train.

The reason for her absence from the opening day of the eighteenth academic year was Bridget O'Shea, and long before her, Jenny Rocket, who had drowned in the lake at Ballymar.

Although Louise was scrupulous about dinner with the nuns, she was still addicted to trays at her desk. One morning late in August, Sister Josie had appeared with the breakfast tray in lieu of Bridget.

"But where is she?" Louise had asked.

"Poor soul, caught in that downpour yesterday, and tossin' an' feverish in bed as a consequence."

"Ought we to call Doctor Gavin?"

"Sure, 'tis jist a common cold and Bridie's not one for makin' a fuss."

"Quite so . . . well, thank you, Josie."

The morning was punctuated with appointments and the telephone seldom stopped ringing, but Louise could not rid herself of the memory of the stowaway who had leaped onto the rail of the *Kronprinz* to fling herself into the harbor waters. Finally, she had left her desk and gone downstairs to the kitchen.

"I'm perfectly capable of boiling water," she had advised the startled Sisters. "Those little brown earthenware pots, where do you keep them? A rosebud for the tray would be nice, I think."

When she had brewed the tea in the earthenware pot and set it on the tray with the Spode china and the bud vase, Louise bore the tray up the winding back stairs to the attic and the tiny whitewashed rooms still occupied by Bridget and the Sisters, where once for a few weeks she had lived.

"Lord A'mighty—yer Rev'rince!" Bridget had gasped, springing up from the cot, red-nosed and convulsed by a sneeze.

"I've brought you some tea, piping hot, and you are to lie still and let me help you get it down."

Oblivious to protests, Louise had set the tray on the pine chest, poured a steaming cupful, pulled up a straw-seat chair, and held the cup while Bridget sipped from it between sneezes and nose blowings.

"Every last drop now, and I think a mustard plaster would benefit you."

"Sure, the tea's warmin' me up grand, and 'tis me own fault for larkin' in the rain."

Louise had glanced musingly around the tiny, bare room, stripped of adornment, and at the dormer window that held a sparrow's view of the campus.

"It's a sign of age, I imagine, when all of the past turns into yesterday, but doesn't it seem that, Bridget?"

"What, mum?"

"When you and I climbed to this dusty, foresaken attic laden with mops and pails."

" 'Twas yesterday, for sure, what with the years flyin' by in the blessings of the Lord."

Louise had hesitated, reluctant to speak of the person who, like Connolly's ghosts, had come to haunt her. "I've meant so often to ask whether you hear from Agnes . . . still in Dublin, is she, with her child?"

Bridget lay back on her pillow. "The last I heard was from a priest in Dublin . . . at the charity hospital where Ag goes when the asthma turns bad."

"Who looks after the child for her?"

"Little Kathleen?" Bridget lay stoically on the iron cot. "Well, knowin' how Ag takes up with men, she must leave Kathleen with the one that's around at the moment."

"Men off the streets?"

"The streets, I expect, ma'am."

Louise had carried the teacup back to the pine chest. "What did the priest write to you?"

"It's wore her out, the asthma has, and this last time Ag got afraid of dyin' . . . and she asked the priest to write me farewell."

"Poor Agnes and her troubles, but what's to become of her child?" Louise had poured more tea for Bridget, thinking of her train reservations and the opening of school, and then she said, "If you've kept the priest's letter, Bridget, I wonder if I might look at it."

The day of the opening of Rosemoore for the eighteenth academic year, Louise was halfway across the Atlantic, on a ship eastbound for the port of Cobh. She stood at the rail of the ship, the wind playing havoc with her veil, and fixed her gaze on the horizon. What would happen to Agnes O'Shea and her child was not hers to foretell, but she would be there with them, she had not turned away. The trip to Chicago must await her return and school would get along quite well without her.

She grasped the rail, looking out at the sea and the blue pencil line of the horizon. The cabin on D deck was no bigger than a shoe box, and the pitching last night had been fierce, but in the howl of the wind Louise had heard the cry of the steerage immigrants calling to her, as if it were yesterday and she had only begun.